Also by Erin Cornia

The Chicago Series

If It Can't Be Us
The Most Perfect Wrong
A Love That Broke Us (Duet Book 1)
Duet Book 2 – Coming November 2025

Author's Note

Thank you for picking up The Most Perfect Wrong. As an author, my goal is to create a story that stays with you, but I also recognize that my writing style may not be for everyone. This book is written in dual POV, first-person present tense—so if you hate that, well… you've been warned.

Your mental health matters. The Most Perfect Wrong explores deep emotions and themes of emotional and psychological abuse. While at its core, this is a love story, it does not shy away from the complexities of trauma, toxic relationships, and the lasting effects they can have. If you are sensitive to these topics, please read with care.

Additionally, this book includes themes of infidelity—both emotional and physical. While every reader defines cheating differently, there are moments where lines are crossed before a relationship has fully ended. If this is a deal-breaker for you, please keep that in mind before diving in.

This book also contains strong language, on-page alcohol and THC use, explicit sexual content, and graphic descriptions. I don't write to fit a certain mold—every story and character is different. The characters tell their own story, and the language they use reflects their reality. So, if the occasional (okay, frequent) use of words like fuck or pussy offends you, this might not be the book for you. No hard feelings.

But if you're here for an angsty, tension-filled, steamy-as-hell ride, buckle up—I think you're gonna like this one.

Content Warning:

This book contains strong language, mature content and explicit romance scenes that may not be suitable for all readers. It is not intended for public schools or individuals under the age of 18. It also explores themes of emotional and psychological abuse, as well as infidelity.

Reader discretion is advised.

For the ones too afraid to leave, may you find your strength.
For the ones who left, may you always honor your courage.
And for anyone still in the in-between—know this:
you are worth it,
always.

The Most Perfect Wrong Playlist

Music played a huge role in bringing The Most Perfect Wrong to life. These songs helped me tap into the emotions of the story and truly feel my characters while writing. Each one captures a moment, a feeling, or a shift that shaped the journey of Cooper and Ryan.

Of all the tracks, "Stargazing" by Myles Smith stands out as the theme song for this book. It encompasses Cooper and Ryan's story as a whole—their struggles, their growth, and the undeniable pull between them.

I've included specific chapters where I feel certain songs fit best—so if you want to experience a scene with the track playing, it might just heighten the emotions and pull you even deeper into their story.

I hope you enjoy the music as much as I do.

<u>*Playlist:*</u>

"Hide Away"–Daya–*Chapter 1*
"Sound Of Silence"–Disturbed–*Chapter 12*
"Iris"–The Goo Goo Dolls–*Chapter 16*
"Haven't You Ever Been In Love Before"–Lewis Capaldi–*Chapter 18*
"Friend"–Benson Boone–Chapter 19
"Wanted"–One Republic–*Chapter 21*
"Control"–Zoe Wees–*Chapter 24*
"Stargazing"–Myles Smith–*Chapter 25*
"Favorite Song"–Toosii–*Chapter 28*
"Lights Down Low" –MAX–*Chapter 30*
"My Tears Ricochet"–Taylor Swift–*Chapter 31*
"Be Alright"–Dean Lewis–*Chapter 32*
"Champagne Problems"–Taylor Swift–*Chapter 34*
"Lifetime"–Justin Bieber–*Chapter 39*
"Don't Give Up On Me"–Andy Grammer–*Epilogue*

VIII

The Most Perfect Wrong

A Novel

Erin Cornia

Prologue

COOPER

March 11

The Morning After

Fuck.

My head is pounding, eyes heavy. I work to pry them open, one by one.

Where the hell am I, and what is digging into my back?

My vision's blurry as I look around what appears to be a hotel room.

A heavy breath startles me. *Oh, yeah—the hot guy from the bar... Ryan.* I turn to look at the mistake from last night. Though at the time, it felt like anything but a mistake.

Last night was fun.

His head is on my pillow, lips slightly parted, dark tousled hair falling over his forehead. *Damn, he's cute.* I take a moment to admire him while he's peacefully sleeping. His scruff is short, and I can almost feel it again—the way it scratched lightly against my skin as he kissed me. Goosebumps prickle my arms just thinking about it. The warmth of those lips, paired with his smile—*God, he's a great kisser.*

My gaze drifts lower, taking in his sculpted chest, defined biceps, and those six-pack abs. Images of last night flood my mind, and I can't help but smile. That body… hovering over mine, his mouth everywhere, the dirty words he whispered.

Heat pulses through me at the memory and I bite my lip, resisting the urge to reach out and touch him—to wake him up with a kiss and let him fuck me again. Our chemistry was insane. The way he moved with me, like he'd studied every inch of my body—knowing exactly what I needed. Fireworks with every kiss—easily the best sex I've ever had. No question. I mean, look at him. He's perfect.

And… if my memory serves me right, he's also packing the most phenomenal penis. I glance down, lifting the sheet to confirm, peeking at the morning wood that's been digging into my back. A grin spreads across my face. Yep, just as I remember—big, thick, and glorious.

I rake my eyes up and down his body. *Damn, good job with this one, God.*

My phone vibrates, interrupting my thoughts. I grimace and reach for it behind me, pleading for it not to wake him.

Sliding out of bed as quietly as possible, I pick my clothes up off the floor and tiptoe to the bathroom. The lights blind me as I flip them on.

I lean against the counter, my head pounding harder as I try to get a grip on my hangover. I had one too many margaritas last night, that's for damn sure. Splashing cold water on my face, I swallow back the nausea rising in my throat.

I dry my hands and grab my phone, scowling at the screen as a flash of anxiety settles in my chest. My heart begins to race when I see another text from Brad. *God, what does he want now?*

My fingers tremble slightly as I swipe up.

Brad: Baby, I know I've made mistakes, too many to count. But I'm lost without you. I love you. Please, come home.

I sigh, guilt twisting in my chest. But it's not for what I did—it's for how I don't care enough anymore to feel guilty. I'm too numb, and that scares me.

I guess this makes us even… or at least it should, but it doesn't feel that way—not even close.

I get dressed and walk back into the room, looking for my shoes and purse. I find one shoe by the bed and the other flung under the TV. I slip my shoes on and pick my purse up off the dresser below the television. Ryan's wallet sits next to it. Curious, I pick it up, feeling the weight of it in my hand while I contemplate opening it up to snoop. Why does it feel wrong? It's not like I'm stealing from him. I simply want to know more about him. *Oh, for hell's sake, his dick was inside me last night—more than once.* I think that warrants me a tiny peek into the man's life.

Pushing the *'give a fuck'* from my mind, I open it. *Who are you, Ryan?* I rummage through, finding the usual credit cards, cash, a few business cards that aren't his. I find his driver's license and pull it out, glancing his way as I do—paranoid he'll wake. *Who looks this good in their driver's license photo?* I'd do him based solely on this photo…

Oh wait, I already did.

Ryan Brooks—lives in Scottsdale, Arizona.

Damn. I almost let myself hope it would say Chicago.

I slip it back into his wallet, setting it gently on the table. Well, that's it then. A pang of longing tugs at my heart knowing I'll never see him again—the kissing, the touching, our conversations. God, he actually wanted to get to know me—a breath of fresh fucking air.

I sigh, maybe in another life. Because if I could pick the perfect guy for me in my next life, I imagine he'd be something like Ryan.

I take one last look at the hottie from the bar, committing him to memory. Then I tiptoe out of the room.

Maybe I'll remember him in twenty years, like a good dream—vivid in feeling, hazy in detail. But for now, it's goodbye forever to the most incredible one-night stand. He's already fading—just like everything else I ever thought I wanted.

Chapter 1

COOPER

March 10 — Newport Beach, CA

The Day Before

I swear to God, if I have to hear his pathetic apology one more time, I'm going to lose it.

"Come on, baby, pick up. Please pick up. Talk to me. You know I love you, Coop. I never meant to hurt you… I fucked up. It'll never happen again, I promise. Please… just come home."

There's a long pause. Then, his voice, softer, almost desperate. "Okay, well… I guess you're not going to talk to me. I love you."

The voicemail ends, and I delete it without a second thought—like a reflex I've developed after too many of these messages. *Ugh!* I'm tempted to chuck my phone into the ocean. I close my eyes and count to ten, just like my college therapist taught me, taking deep breaths to calm the simmering storm inside.

I stare at my feet as the waves wash over them. The cold water sinks my toes deeper into the sand, and the pull of the tide makes it feel like I'm surfing without moving at all—one of those small joys that never gets old.

I wiggle my toes, the sensation both invigorating and calming as I look up into the morning sky. A cool breeze brushes against my cheeks, and I can't help feeling better—I almost smile. For a moment, the world is quiet.

This is just what I needed to clear my head—to feel something other than the shitstorm that is my life. In the jumble of confusion, one thing's for certain—Newport Beach never gets old. I turn back toward my dad's place, a two-story beach house with a patio that meets the sand.

God, I love it here.

I arrived a few days ago, taking a much-needed break from my boyfriend and all the shit I'm avoiding at home. Well, ex-boyfriend, technically. I broke up with him before I left. But he's not getting the hint. His calls and texts keep pouring in, begging me to come home so we can "talk things out." I've ignored every single one of them.

Back inside, I switch to autopilot—making a cup of coffee and adding my usual splash of creamer. Mug in hand, I head out to the patio where I'll inevitably spend the next hour trying to relax while my thoughts have their way with me. At least I have a great view: the ocean, the sand, the runners—some of whom are *very* good-looking. I know I've only been "single" for a few days, but a girl can still appreciate the scenery.

Am I single?

I don't even know the answer to that question—how pathetic.

I tuck myself into the corner of the outdoor sectional. Crossing my legs and turning toward the beach, I soak in the crisp morning air. I toss a blanket over my lap and, with coffee in one hand and my phone in the other, prepare to do absolutely nothing. Instagram beckons, but my attention shifts to the glaring notifications on my messages. Four unread texts. I scowl as I open them, already knowing they're all from Brad.

Brad: Baby please, don't do this.

Brad: Come on, you know me—I never meant to hurt you.

Brad: This is all a misunderstanding.

Brad: Cooper, if you don't answer, I'm going to have to come to you. Don't make me bring up things I know you don't want to talk about.

The hell he will…

That last text has me typing back so fast, I don't even think.

Cooper: Brad, stop calling and texting me. I'll talk to you when I get back. You know we live together, so it's not like you won't see me. I just need space and time to think. Please respect that.

I stare at the screen, willing him to listen this time. But deep down, I know better. Brad always finds a way to get what he wants. I drop my phone face down beside me with a frustrated sigh. Wrapping both hands around my coffee mug, I stare blankly into the distance, letting the sound of the waves calm my anxiety. Minutes pass as I meditate—eyes open, breathing in and out, soaking in the stillness and the quiet.

Hell yes, here he comes.

A small smile tugs at my lips as the dark-haired hottie I've been eyeing the past few days jogs closer. This is the third morning in a row I've seen him. He's shirtless—six-pack abs, tanned chest, the whole damn package. I try to play it cool, but I'm gawking, silently praying I don't start drooling.

He looks my way and notices me—noticing him.

Smiling, he lifts a hand in a wave just as he's about to pass. I try to act casual, raising my hand in return and doing some awkward finger flutter—quickly opening and closing all five fingers in some kind of idiotic attempt of a wave. His smile deepens before he turns his head back and runs past me.

Jesus, that's a specimen.

I follow him with my eyes until he disappears down the beach. Now the real question is—do I stick around for his return lap?

The first time I saw him, he didn't notice me. Yesterday, he smiled but kept running. Today, he smiled *and* waved.

Hey, it's the little things right now. When you find out your boyfriend has been cheating… again—it's these small moments you cling to. The hot guy running past your house, throwing you a wave—just a little spark of brightness in an otherwise dark, dreary hell.

Damn, it's almost scary how happy that wave just made me. I'm not sure if I ever feel that kind of excitement with Brad anymore. And what's worse is that I *know* I'll go back to him. I always do. It's a pattern I've fallen into. We fight, I run away for a week, then I come back. It's like my body's automatic response. He apologizes profusely, and I cave—not wanting to find a new place to live or risk him making things even harder for me. I know it's unhealthy—none of my relationships have ever been normal. But the thought of leaving? I know how it goes. He twists things, making me question everything—my choices, my worth, my ability to leave. And maybe he's right. I can't fathom starting over, being alone, or finding out this really is as good as it gets. It terrifies me. So I stay, and eventually, we settle back into 'normal.'

I used to be so in love with Brad—I'm not so sure anymore. There are definitely things I still love about him. He's charming when he wants to be. We have fun playing pickleball or golfing on the weekends, and we still have incredible sex—it's not all bad. He's great at making me laugh when he's not being an asshole, and we've built a life together. God, four and a half years—that's gotta mean something. But lately, it's harder to ignore the weight of this relationship pressing down on me.

I also work for Brad's brother. He's great, but that just makes everything more complicated. Ending things with Brad would mean changing every single aspect of my life. So, when Brad's dick wanders and lands in another girl's vagina, I let it slide—literally. Maybe it's because I'm too weak, too lazy, or a combination of both, to do anything about it. Each time it happens, though, it's like a tiny piece of me chips away. I tell myself I'm fine, that we're fine, but deep down I wonder how many pieces of me remain before there's nothing left to hold on to.

The first time Brad cheated, I cried—a lot. I lost my shit. I came out to Newport Beach to stay with my dad, intending to move here. I almost had the guts to pack up my life and leave. That was two years ago. But I went back to him. Then, four months later, it happened again. I cried that time too, but not as hard. He talked me back within four days.

It's strange—the more it happens, the less I recognize myself. I didn't even cry this time. I was pissed… but no tears. I told him to go to hell and that we were finished, then angrily packed a bag and walked out. But I know myself better—and unfortunately, so does Brad.

My dad interrupts my self-loathing thoughts. "Hey love-bug, how's your morning?" He takes a seat across from me, coffee in hand.

"It's good, Dad. Feels great out here. I miss the ocean."

He doesn't know about me and Brad. I'd never tell my parents that he cheated on me. It's embarrassing enough without them trying to micromanage how I handle it. Knowing my parents, my mom would tell me to leave, and my dad would probably give Brad a high-five—two peas in a pod. But then so are me and my mom. And I hate that I'm like her.

"Well, you know I'd never talk you out of moving here to be closer to me and your sister," he says with a wink.

"I know, Dad. Wish I could."

He smiles. "I know. You'd never leave your mom alone in Chicago. You're a good daughter. Are you and Casey still going out tonight?"

"Yeah, she's meeting me at Tipsy for drinks."

Casey's my older sister, and best friend. We've always been close, and she's the only one who knows the whole story with Brad. I tell her everything. After graduating from college, she moved here to be close to Dad and the ocean. Now she lives in Huntington Beach with her husband, Greg, and my adorable two-year-old nephew, Mason.

"I'm glad you girls are going to get some time together," Dad says, taking a sip of his coffee. "Well, I'm off to work. Have fun tonight, kiddo. Tell Brad I say hi." He walks over, bends down to kiss my forehead, and heads toward the door.

"Okay. Bye, Dad. Have a good day."

The door slides shut behind him, and I turn back to my people-watching, scanning the beach for some more eye candy.

* * * * * * * * * *

"Maybe you can all be a throuple," Casey says, taking a sip of her spicy margarita. "Who is this broad anyway? Do you even know her?"

"No clue. I don't even know what she looks like. And a throuple? Hard pass. I don't see how bringing another woman into the bedroom benefits me." I raise my brows. "But… if Brad wanted to throuple with that hottie runner guy I was telling you about, now *that's* something I could get on board with." I laugh, sipping heavily on the last of my margarita, swirling my straw to get every last drop. "Damn, mine's all gone. You down for another?"

Casey and I are sitting against the edge of the patio at Tipsy, a rooftop bar on top of a fancy hotel in Newport Beach. String lights hang above, casting a warm glow over the sleek seating areas and fire pits.

"I better not. I'm already pushing the limit. Mason's been waking up at the butt-crack of dawn lately, and I'm exhausted." My sister tucks a piece of hair behind her ear as she digs in her purse, pulling out some lip gloss. She applies a coat and hands it to me. "Want some?"

"Sure." I'm wearing a black long-sleeved shirt with a deep V-neck, tucked into flowy white pants, so the little pop of pink will look great. I take it and press it to my lips, careful not to let the coastal breeze blow my long blonde hair into it.

"Hi, ladies, sorry to interrupt, but these are from the gentleman at the bar." The cocktail server sets down two more spicy margaritas, and I grin from ear to ear.

"Ha! Now you have to stay and drink it. It'd be rude not to," I snark, grabbing my margarita and glancing at the bar, grateful for guys dumb enough to think buying a woman a drink is a ticket to getting laid.

"Fine, I'll have one more," Casey says, as I lock eyes with the predator.

"Oh my *God*!" I blurt out, whipping my head back to Casey. "It's him," I squeak.

"It's who? What are you talking about?"

"The guy at the bar. It's the hottie runner." Casey starts to turn, but I grab her arm. "No, don't look! God, that's so obvious."

"Oh my hell, calm down. I can be sly," she says, practically shifting her whole body toward the bar. "Which guy is it?"

"The one that's fucking hot!" I snap, completely losing my cool.

"I don't see a hot guy, Coop. Your standards must be getting low after being with Brad for so long."

Casey's never been subtle about her disapproval of Brad.

"What?" I glance back at the bar, but he's gone. "What the hell? Where did he go?" I scan the rooftop anxiously until I spot him in a lounge chair, sitting around a rectangular fireplace with a group of people. "There!" I motion with my head toward him. "The one on the end, facing us, in the white shirt and black jacket."

My heart pounds as I lock eyes with him, a jolt of adrenaline shooting through me. He's staring right at me with a smoldering smirk. *Damn, he's sexy.*

"Oh wow. Yeah, he's a hottie for sure," Casey says as she waves at him.

"Oh my… What? Why are you waving at him?"

"Because he saw me looking at him! I panicked and didn't know what else to do."

"Jeeeesus, Casey." I sink back into my chair, crossing one arm across my stomach and using my other hand to cup the side of my face, blocking my view as if it can somehow shield me from the humiliation.

I casually glance in his direction, and he's still staring, arms crossed, with a confident smile. He gives a subtle nod, cool and collected, before turning his attention back to his group.

"Shit, it's hot out here," I mutter, shifting uncomfortably in my chair. "Is it hot out here?" I grab my drink and take three too many swallows.

Casey giggles. "Calm down, you're fine. Just hot and bothered is all." She mouths something to him and gestures toward me with her head.

"What are you doing?" I hiss in a panic.

He starts to stand.

He begins to walk in our direction.

"Oh, would you look at that?" Casey says, grabbing her phone. "Greg just texted me. I have to go—he needs help with Mason." She rushes to stand.

"What are you… what the fuck, Casey? Don't leave me here!"

She's already halfway up before she leans in close, whispering, "You should fuck him, Coop. Get back at Brad."

"You're dead to me!" I whisper-yell as she whisks away, practically running into Hot Guy.

"Oh, sorry. Excuse me," she says to him. "I have to leave. She's all yours," she adds, waving her hand in my direction.

I. Am. Dead. Seriously, someone kill me now. My foot taps a million beats per minute and my stomach feels like it's in my throat.

I force an awkward smile as he approaches. "Hi… I'm sorry," I stammer. "That's my sister. She clearly doesn't get out much."

He chuckles. "Can I sit?"

I gesture toward the now open chair. "Be my guest."

Hot guy settles into the chair across from me. "I'm Ryan. Ryan Brooks," he says, extending his hand confidently across the small bistro table.

"Cooper Bradley," I reply, taking his offered hand and giving it a firm shake.

A smile tugs at his lips. "It's nice to finally meet you, Cooper."

Finally meet me. Ahh—so he's been checking me out too. "Nice to meet you, too." He lets go of my hand, and suddenly, I'm a mess of nerves. *Calm down, he's just a guy. I've done this a hundred times—it's just... been a while.*

Before I know it, my mouth betrays me. "I wasn't named after Bradley Cooper, by the way. I was born before he was famous."

What am I doing?

"My parents love his movies, but yeah... not named after him. I get that a lot..." I say as I clear my throat. "That, and people are always surprised I'm a girl, when they meet me."

Oh my God. Stop talking.

"Not in person," I quickly add. "Only when they know my name first, and then meet me. They always think I'm going to be a dude."

Yep, still going, sinking the ship faster than it can flood.

"My sister has the same problem."

He doesn't care about your sister or your goddamn name.

"Her name is Casey." I nod, as if that will fix this. "Casey and Cooper Bradley—two sisters who look like brothers on paper."

Holy Jesus fuck.

I reach for my margarita like it's a lifejacket on this sinking ship, sucking down half the glass in one desperate gulp. All the while, he's watching me unravel like some girl who's never spoken... to anyone. *Great. Just great.*

He chuckles, takes a sip of his beer, and licks his lips. "Well, I'm not named after anyone famous, either." His eyes lock onto mine, amusement dancing in them, like he's trying not to laugh at how nervous I am. They're a beautiful light green, and the mix of humor and intensity in his gaze sends a flutter straight to my stomach. "You know," he says, leaning in a bit, a teasing smile playing at his lips, "I didn't expect someone as gorgeous as you to be so…"—he pauses, searching for the right word—"nervous." His smile widens. "But it's nice. Most people try so hard to act cool, but you're just… you know, you."

I laugh. "Oh, so you don't think I'm cool?" I ask, raising an eyebrow, my nerves settling slightly.

He laughs. "No, that's not what I mean. You're definitely cool. It's just…" He pauses, his expression softening, like he's realizing something. He grips the back of his neck, looking a little sheepish. "God, I'm sorry. I suck at this. I'm rusty as hell. Please don't take offense at my terrible attempt to flirt with you."

"Oh, that was flirting?" I ask, teasing. I'm actually stunned. *He's flirting with me? Did he just hear everything I said?* No sane person could witness that disaster and stick around for more. So his only goal here must be to get laid. And I am *not* going home with a rando from the bar, no matter how hot he is.

"Like I said… out of practice."

"Did you just get out of a relationship or something?" I secretly hope I'm not the only one here in uncharted waters.

"Something like that," he says, his eyes drifting down my body a little too obviously. "You know, I half-expected you to tell me to go to hell when I came over here. You're way better looking than I am."

All I can do is laugh. This guy's clearly never looked in the mirror because he's a ten out of ten. "Is it too late to tell you to go to hell?" I ask, jokingly.

He grins. "Never. Is that what you want?"

I contemplate, looking him over. *My God, he is so hot.* And I know what's under that shirt. His body… I stop myself. *We are NOT sleeping with this guy.*

I shake my head. "No. I don't think so…" There's a beat of silence as we assess each other. "Honestly, I'm surprised you haven't jumped ship yet. That introduction of mine was *bru-tal.*"

He chuckles. "I don't know if it was worse than what I just said."

I stare at him until we're both laughing. "Wow, Ryan. You're bad at flirting *and* lying."

"Hey, I thought it was cute. Just shows you're human, and there's nothing sexier than that."

"Well, if you thought that was sexy, let's just hope you're not around long enough to see me bake. You'll be on your knees proposing, turned on from all my *humanness.*"

His smile reaches his eyes, and it's pathetic how fast my heart is beating. The way he looks at me feels different from the usual way men gawk at me—almost like he actually sees me. Like he genuinely wants to talk to me. Or maybe it's because I'm just desperate to feel wanted right now. Even if it's temporary.

My sister's words echo in my head: "*You should fuck him, get back at Brad.*" Suddenly, it doesn't seem like such a terrible idea. An image of Brad with some other woman, one I've built up in my mind to look like a twenty-seven-year-old Gisele Bündchen, flashes before me. They're all over each other, lips locked, clothes hitting the floor, Brad whispering in her ear about how sexy she is. My fists clench at the thought. *Ugh. Fuck him.* Maybe he needs to feel what it's like. I shift in my chair. *Why the hell not?* And let's face it—there are *worse* guys I could use to get back at him.

If I'm doing this, I've got to bring my A-game. It can't be easy to close a guy like Ryan. He could literally pick any girl here to take back home with him, and they'd all feel like the goddamn chosen one.

Sure, I'm a little out of practice, but I can do this. I *need* this. I'm tired of feeling like shit. Tired of Brad. Tired of everything. This isn't about love or connection. I gave up on that a long time ago. I just want to feel good—get out of my head, lose myself in something… someone. Sex is one thing I know I'm good at—it's easy—it's all I have to give right now. And Ryan's already interested—he came to me.

His gaze moves down, lingering just a second too long on my chest. My pulse quickens. *Yep, that's all me, buddy.* A smirk tugs at my lips as I see him subtly readjust himself. He obviously likes what he sees. My stomach flutters, a mix of nerves and excitement swirling inside me. This could be really fun. It's not even about getting back at Brad, not entirely. It's about proving to myself that I still have control over something—that I'm still desirable, even if just for one night. I get to choose the narrative. For once, I decide how my story goes.

Chapter 2

RYAN

She's hot *and* funny. It doesn't get better than that.

I shake my head, chuckling. "Cooper, you just get cuter every fucking minute."

She buries her face in her hands. "Oh my God! Nothing about this is cute. Between the two of us, we should probably do this bar a favor and just leave." She grins, laughing, and points a finger back and forth between us. "I mean, this—this is so bad. If you think any of it's cute, there's something seriously wrong with you."

"Oh, something's wrong with me?" I cock a brow, pointing to myself. "You're the one referencing Bradley Cooper."

She crumples up a napkin, tossing it at me. "And if you were *normal,* you would've bailed the second I mentioned him." She folds her arms, eyeing me down. "And because you didn't, that means you, my friend, are one of three things." She stares at me, her dark brown eyes playful.

"Oh, yeah? And what are those?" I take a sip of my drink, amused.

"You're either crazy," she says, holding up one finger. "Drunk," she adds, raising a second. "Or you haven't gotten laid in a *very* long time." She lifts a third finger, eyebrows raised with a smug, knowing look.

My eyes narrow, hoping she can't see right through me because, *God,* I *haven't* been laid in such a long time. And, yeah, I'd love to, but that wasn't the reason I came over. I start to say something, but instead, I take another sip, buying myself a few extra seconds to figure out how to play this. I grab my chair and swing it around to the side of the table, bringing me closer—our knees almost touching. "Can't a guy just wanna talk to a beautiful girl without an ulterior motive?"

She looks at me and scoffs. "I knew it," she says confidently. "You're trying to get laid." She nudges my knee with hers.

I smother a laugh, biting my lip to keep it in. "Oh yeah? And what brings you to that conclusion?"

"It's like a reverse psychology thing. If you were crazy or drunk, you'd say something to convince me otherwise. But you went with the typical '*I'm not trying to get laid*' answer." She shakes her head, rolling her eyes, but her smile doesn't falter. "You men are *all* the same."

Damn, she's quick-witted, too.

I noticed her on my morning runs—of course I did, she's hot as hell. But now? Being here, talking to her, she's not just a hot girl I saw on the beach. She's a hot girl with a great personality, and I'm having way too much fun. It's been so damn long since I've felt this kind of pull toward someone. It's like my mind is finally giving my heart the green light to consider… something. Whatever that "something" is.

But fuck, I'm dusty—like an old book that's been sitting on the shelf for years. This whole thing—the flirting, the chemistry—is waking up a side of me that's been buried for so damn long. I'm not sure what to even do with it.

I grin. "And what are *all us men* like, exactly?"

"Predictable," she says matter-of-factly. "A little attention, a nice smile, buy us a drink, and you think you've got it made."

I raise an eyebrow, chuckling at her boldness. "And you think I'm like that?"

She tilts her head, a playful challenge in her gaze. "I think you're like the rest. Charming, confident, and a little too sure of yourself."

"Sure of myself? Pretty sure I already confessed that I suck at this, remember?"

She raises her brows. "I think you're better than you realize."

Her words catch me off guard, and I find myself inching even closer, our knees touching now.

"You single?" I ask, wondering why I didn't lead with that. I'm in way too deep for her to tell me otherwise.

She shifts in her seat, throwing me a teasing smile. "Are you?"

I hesitate, my thumb rubbing over the empty spot on my ring finger—a habit that's hard to break. "Yeah," I say, though the answer feels more complicated than it sounds. Not wanting her to press me further, I steer the conversation in a different direction. "Are you from here?"

"Sort of," she says. "My dad lives here, so I spent most of my summers and holidays around Newport growing up. I visit a couple of times a year… What about you? Do you live here?"

"Nah. I'm here for work. Had a conference earlier in the week, but now I'm just enjoying the weekend. How long are you here for?"

"I'm not sure yet. I'll probably stay a few more days and work remotely."

"Oh? What do you do for work?"

"I'm an assistant project manager for a software development company. My job isn't that exciting to talk about, but I enjoy it. It's chill and laid-back." She finishes the rest of her drink. "Are those people you work with?" She gestures toward the group I was sitting with earlier.

I nod in their direction, catching a few of them glancing our way. "Yeah, those are my coworkers. Most of them headed home today, but a few of us decided to stick around for the weekend."

"Are you staying here?" she nods toward the hotel.

"Yep."

"And what do you do?"

I take a sip of my beer. "I'm a Vice President of business development for a tech company. Isn't that exciting?" I say sarcastically. "My job isn't exactly thrilling to talk about either, but the work's interesting, and I'm lucky to work with cool people." We lock eyes for what feels like minutes, and before I can stop myself, the words spill out. "Jesus… you're gorgeous. I'm surprised you haven't been bombarded by guys all night."

Damn. Did I actually just say that out loud? I've always been confident, but right now, I feel like I'm second-guessing every word. It's been over a decade since I've looked at a woman like this, let alone said things like that out loud.

She grins. "Well, the night is still young. And, if you remember, I wasn't here alone. I was with my sister… and then this hot guy scared her off." She leans forward, almost whispering. "Who's gonna hit on me with you around?"

I grin back. Maybe I suck at flirting, but I think she's into it.

"Are you upset about that?"

"I was…" She pauses, letting the anticipation build between us. "I'm not anymore."

"That's good." I let my eyes drift down her body—because, *Jesus, she has a body*. And yes, I'm undressing her in my mind. I can't help it; I feel like a coyote on the hunt—starved and losing control. But then my eyes meet hers again, and something steadies in me, and it's weird—how she makes me feel wild and steady at the same time.

"What are you doing tomorrow night?" I ask. "I'd love to take you to dinner… if you're interested." I have no idea what I'm doing, but I know I need more time with her before I leave.

She takes a breath and sits back casually in her chair, taking her sweet-ass time with her answer. "Look, I appreciate the offer," she says carefully, "but I'm not really in a place to date." She hesitates, her eyes traveling slowly down my body, a hint of a smile playing on her lips, stirring a slow burn of desire deep in my gut.

Her eyes eventually land back on mine, and she adds, "But if you're looking for something with no strings attached… I might be game for that."

My eyes widen. Does she mean a one-night stand? That's not something I'd normally do—or would I? I used to be up for that. Coming over here, I wasn't sure what I wanted or what to expect, but I guess for a guy from out of town, the best possible outcome would be this—sex with the hot girl, no strings attached. *Damn, I'm hard just thinking about it.* I definitely want her… even if I'm still figuring out exactly what that means.

But now that it's on the table, I'm not sure that I want it to go down like that.

She's completely caught me off guard.

"No strings attached? Tonight?" I pause, unsure. *Jesus, is this what it's like dating in your thirties? Women throwing themselves at you with no pretense?* Shit, I can't believe I'm even asking this, but I have to be sure. "You mean… sex, right?"

She laughs. "Let's call a spade a spade, Ryan. You didn't buy me a drink and come over here because you were curious about my job or my relationship status."

That's exactly why I came over here.

She leans in closer, a smirk on her lips. "And yeah, I mean sex." She pauses, letting that sink in. "So, I'll make you a deal: whenever you're ready to leave," her voice lowers to a whisper. "Just say the word."

Holy shit.

My dick stiffens all the way, a full-on boner pressing against my jeans, and I'm stuck between pure need and contemplation, weighing the consequences. My eyes zero in on her boobs. *Jesus, they're big. And I'm so goddamn horny.* When I finally tear my eyes away from them, I meet her gaze, and everything else fades. God, this is a different kind of hunger, one I haven't felt in… forever. It's raw and consuming. My pulse races as she holds my stare confidently. There's an electric charge between us—a chemistry so palpable it's hard to ignore. Is that it? Or am I just so damn horny I'd feel this with anything that had tits and looked at me this way?

I lean back in my chair, crossing my arms, trying to play it cool. "Really?" I ask.

"Really," she whispers, placing her hands on the edge of the chair, squeezing her tits together. She's wearing a very low-cut shirt, but I force my eyes to stay on her face. My gaze slides to her lips instead—full, inviting, and I'm already imagining them on mine. Suddenly, my good intentions go out the window. I want to touch her, feel her skin, taste every inch of her.

"Okay…" I say with hesitation, because what do I say to that? I take a breath. *Focus, man.* Every part of me wants to make a move, but I also don't want to be a dick. I want this to be more than just… that.

I clear my throat, leaning back a little, buying myself a second. "But let's get to know each other a bit first—see where the night takes us."

She cocks a brow, unamused.

I continue. "So… if you're only here visiting your dad, where are you from?" I try to play it casual, but my brain's on overdrive just looking at her.

Her lips curl into a teasing smile. "Are you really trying to make small talk right now?"

"I mean…" I fumble for words, heat creeping up my neck. "Yeah, I just thought—"

"Ryan… I'm not interested in small talk tonight." Her hand slides over my knee, her touch electrifying. Her fingers caress the fabric, pulling my concentration away from the thoughts in my head to the pulsing in my dick. "Look, I'm really attracted to you, but… we're both from out of town. You seem like a great guy, but there's no point in getting to know each other when nothing can come from it. I'm not interested in a long-distance get-to-know-you type of thing." Her thumb circles my inner thigh, branding the skin beneath my pants.

I swallow, struggling to form words. She makes a valid point. There's really no purpose in getting to know each other, or me taking her out—not when I leave in two days regardless.

She pulls her hand back, running it through her hair. "So… do you want to get out of here?"

I stare at her for a moment. "Yeah," I say, the words slipping out as my cock runs the show. "Yeah, let's get out of here."

Jesus Christ. Did I just commit to having sex with her? I'm so hard I can't think straight, let alone be rational. This isn't what I came over here for, but now all I can think about is her—a *naked her*. She's the kind of beautiful that's hard to ignore—intimidating, even. I didn't expect this, but fuck it. I'd be an idiot to say no.

* * * * * * * * * *

The elevator dings and opens. I step inside, and before the doors can close, Cooper's on me. Her arms wrap around my neck, and her lips crash against mine, hungry and urgent. My back hits the wall, and I fumble for the button, her lips never letting up. I recover quickly, gripping her waist and kissing her back just as fiercely. The button for the seventh floor lights up, but I'm already lost in her.

Her lips are plump and incredibly soft. Her tongue toys with mine. The warmth of her lips mixed with the lingering taste of tequila is intoxicating. I pull her closer until there's no space left between us. The elevator hums in the background. Her hands find my hair, tugging just hard enough to make me groan against her mouth. I don't think; I just react. I press her back against the elevator wall, feeling her body arch into mine, her moan vibrating against my lips. *God, she feels incredible.*

My dick presses against the inseam of my pants, hard and throbbing, ready to go—having been neglected for the past few months, with only the occasional jerk-off by yours truly. Cooper's hand travels down, finding its way to my boner. She rubs it and gives it a squeeze through my pants, and I groan loudly.

The elevator stops at thirteen, dinging, the doors opening. I pull away from her, trying to play it cool as an elderly couple steps in. *Jesus, we're a mess.* I glance at her, and she busts up laughing, which makes me laugh too. I try to smother it, knowing we should be respectful. Cooper buries her face in the crook of my arm, shaking with suppressed laughter. I stroke her back. "Shh," I say softly, but I'm still grinning like an idiot. I haven't had this kind of fun in a long time—almost forgot what it feels like to lose myself in the moment. It feels good.

The seventh floor cannot come soon enough. It feels like we're moving in slow motion, every second dragging. Finally, the doors open to my floor. I grab her hand and lead her down the hallway to my hotel room. Our pace quickens. She's urgent, and I'm right there with her, my pulse hammering in my ears.

We reach my door and I fumble with my key card, adrenaline coursing through me. My hands shake a little—nerves, excitement; I'm not even sure. She's pressed up against my side, her fingers running up and down my arm, driving me crazy. I finally get the door open, and we stumble inside, the door slamming shut behind us.

There's no pause, no hesitation. She's on me again, her mouth finding mine in a rush of urgency and need. She's a great kisser, but a thought cuts through the haze. *Is she too drunk for this?* I don't want to be the asshole who takes advantage. I pull back slightly, meeting her eyes, needing to make sure she's fully aware of what's happening.

"Hey," I say between kisses. "How drunk are you?" It feels stupid asking, but I have to know.

She pulls back, scowling. "What?"

"I just… You've been drinking. I don't want to take advantage of you."

Her hand finds my cock again, and I suck in a breath.

"Does it look like you're taking advantage of me?" she asks.

"Maybe we should just slow down a bit… talk for a while," I say between shallow breaths, barely able to think straight. "Let the alcohol wear off a little." *Jesus, I'm being my own cockblocker here. What am I doing?*

"Talk? You wanna talk?" She sighs, exasperated. "There's a reason people do this when they've been drinking, Ryan. A reason you pounded that last beer. I'm not here to talk… I know what I'm doing."

She steps back, her eyes locked on mine, then slowly crosses her arms and grabs the hem of her shirt, pulling it over her head. Tossing it aside, she undoes her pants and slides them down to her ankles, stepping out of them smoothly. She stands there in just a bra and panties, her eyes never leaving mine. Dark, inviting. She bites her bottom lip, watching me closely. "Do I need to keep going, Ryan, or are you going to man up and do the rest?"

My throat goes dry as I take her in. I'm speechless. *Goddamn, her body.* It's better than I imagined. Her skin is fair, but lightly tanned. Her tits are spilling out of her bra, and Jesus Christ, it's hard to look away. Curvy as hell—tiny waist, round ass, everything that makes a guy lose his mind. I can't differentiate between the aching throb of my dick and my heart pounding in my chest. *Fuck.* I want to run my hands and mouth over every part of her. My breath quickens, my whole body taut with anticipation.

She interrupts my thoughts. "Your turn, Ryan." She gives me a pointed look. "Take your shirt off. Let's see that six-pack," she says in a quiet, seductive voice.

I do as I'm told, pulling my shirt over my head and tossing it aside.

She smiles. "Damn," she says softly. "Pants too." Her eyes rake over me, and a shiver runs down my spine—her demands making me harder.

Get it together. She's not here to fuck a guy who needs directions. I lock eyes with her, confidence flooding back. I slowly step toward her, the intensity between us building with every breath. My fingers find the button of my pants, popping it open, drawing her eyes lower. My hand wraps around hers, guiding it to my zipper.

Our eyes lock as her fingers slide down, teasing the zipper open. "You want this?" I ask, my voice low and rough, already knowing the answer—the tension between us thick as mud.

She doesn't answer with words. Instead, her hand brushes over me, igniting the fire that's been simmering since the moment I saw her. I press her hard against the wall, my cock already begging for more.

My lips meet hers with a desperation. And it feels too damn good to stop—too good to be touched, wanted, and lusted after.

Her hands glide up my chest, the heat of her touch searing through me, and I instinctively grip her ass, firm and soft beneath my palms, and press my throbbing cock against her—right where she wants it. She gasps, and my pulse kicks into overdrive. One of her hands grips the back of my neck while the other toys with the waistband of my boxer briefs, dipping her fingers in just enough to drive me mad.

I graze my hand up her side, hesitating just below her chest. I'm about to touch another woman's tits. For a second, I'm nervous—hell, I even feel a little guilty—but I shove it down and keep going. My hand moves over one of her boobs, giving it a gentle squeeze, my thumb brushing against the soft skin. She moans into my mouth, and I'm a fucking goner. They're incredible. Large, soft—a perfect handful, maybe more. Any lingering doubts fly out the window as she arches into me with pure need.

Inhibitions gone, I grip her hips hard, taking control. Tonight, she'll learn exactly how good a night with Ryan Brooks can be. No holding back. I'm going to make her beg, scream my name, and come so hard she'll remember this night for years… and so will I. You never forget the first night with someone new—someone who's not her.

Chapter 3

RYAN

My head sinks into the pillow, a grin stretching across my face that I can't hold back. *Damn.* That was… there are no words.

Cooper slips out of bed to use the bathroom, and I take a moment to catch my breath. When she returns, she leans down, reaching for her shirt.

"Uh-uh." My voice comes out rough, lower than I intended. "Come back to bed. Don't leave yet." I try not to sound needy, but fuck, I'm not ready for this to end.

She hesitates, casting me a look, one eyebrow raised as if she's considering her options. "Fine… just for a little longer. Do you have something comfy I can wear?"

"Yeah." I stand to grab a T-shirt from my suitcase, wondering why she'd need one when I've already seen every inch of her. Tossing it her way, I watch as she slips it on, the edge skimming just past her thighs. I take my turn in the bathroom. When I return, the room's dim, lit only by the faint glow of the TV. Cooper's curled up under the light sheet, eyes following me as I slide in beside her. She shifts closer, draping a leg over mine, her hand tracing a slow path up my chest. Her face tilts up, and our lips meet.

She tugs gently on my bottom lip, teeth grazing. I groan. "God, when you do that…" My voice trails off as a sultry smile spreads across her face. My hand finds her thigh, fingers trailing the skin beneath the shirt. A rush hits me as I realize—she didn't put anything else on. She shifts, her bare skin brushing against my hip, and that's all it takes—I'm hard again, desire flaring even stronger than before.

She presses her lips to mine again, and I respond instantly, gripping her ass and pulling her body flush against mine.

She breaks the kiss, biting back a grin. "So… Ryan," she murmurs, dragging a fingertip down my chest and abdomen. "Do you do this kind of thing often?"

I chuckle, shaking my head. "Not even close." I pause, choosing my words carefully. "I was in a relationship for a while. Still adjusting to single life." My thumb strokes her hip. "What about you? How often does a guy get lucky enough to have a night like this with you?"

A smile spreads across her lips. "Not often." Her voice is quiet.

I raise an eyebrow. "Hard to believe."

"Why is that?"

I shrug, my gaze drifting over her. "You're gorgeous, confident, and, well… you did make the first move."

She laughs, shaking her head. "That doesn't mean I do this all the time." Her fingers drift lower, tracing the line of my hip, close to where my cock aches with need. Every touch feels new, as if we didn't just spend the last hour tangled up in each other.

A sharp breath escapes me as her fingers graze the inside of my thigh. Her eyes flick up, a smirk following. She's in control, and I'm not sure I want that to end.

I move my hand down the curve of her ass, brushing lightly along her skin. She closes her eyes as my fingers glide over the sensitive spot at her core. "God," she whispers, her lips finding mine. We melt together, losing ourselves again—hands exploring, breaths mingling. I slip a finger inside her, and her hand wraps around my length, her grip tightening, sparking a fresh surge of need between us. Our kiss deepens, urgent and almost desperate.

After a few intense moments, I pull back, catching my breath, my gaze locked on hers. "Cooper," I murmur. "Where do you live? Because, fuck… I could do this again. As many times as you'll let me."

She laughs, but her expression's unreadable. She rolls onto her back, and I'm afraid I just ruined the moment.

But then she turns to face me. "Ryan, don't take this personally, okay? I'm just here for a good time—which I am definitely having, by the way. You've been amazing, but that's all this is. I don't want to answer personal questions because that's how feelings get involved. And I don't want any feelings, except the physical ones that feel good. So, ask me something else. Anything that doesn't cross that line."

I grin, unable to hide my admiration. "Damn. I've never met a woman like you." It's the truth. "So, what counts as a non-personal question?" I roll onto my side, scooching closer until our faces are only inches apart.

"I don't know. Random questions that aren't personal." She laughs softly.

"Like?"

"Hmm. Like… what's your favorite city in the world?" Her hand finds mine, fingers weaving between my own.

I grin, glad she's willing to play along—at least a little. "Rome."

"Why?" she asks. "In one sentence."

I raise a brow. "One sentence? That's tough—there are too many great things about—"

She cuts me off, pressing a finger to my lips. "Shh. One. Sentence."

There's a heat in her eyes as I take her finger into my mouth, sucking it slowly, savoring the taste of her skin.

She grins. "That was hot… Now, convince me to go to Rome… in one sentence."

"Fucking impossible."

She laughs, and it's the cutest damn thing I've ever heard. "Just try. I've never been."

"Alright… You should go to Rome because in one ten-minute walk, you'll see ancient ruins, incredible art, sip espresso, and eat the best damn food of your life."

"Sounds amazing… What about the sex?" she asks with a grin.

I chuckle. "Depends on who you go with, I guess. Whoever goes with you is having some of the best sex of their life, but I can't guarantee the same for you… unless you were there with me, of course."

She bites her lip, nudging my shoulder. "Are you saying you want to take me to Rome? God, get to know me first, Ryan. You don't even know where I live." She laughs at her own joke, and I join in.

"What about you?" I ask. "Got a favorite city?"

She pauses, her expression thoughtful. "I don't know if I have one favorite. Every time I go somewhere new, it feels like the best until I visit the next place. I love each city for something different." Her eyes light up. "But my favorite trip would have to be a humanitarian trip I took to Africa when I was twenty."

"That sounds cool. Tell me more about it… and feel free to use more than one sentence."

"Alright. I went with three friends from college. We volunteered at an orphanage in South Africa, and it was… life-changing. It made me see just how much excess we live with, and it brought everything into focus—what really matters." Her voice softens, almost wistful. "I wish I could carry that clarity with me every day, but you know… we come back and get swept up in the American way. It's so easy to forget."

As she speaks, I feel a surge of awe. And I know it's crazy because I barely know her—I *don't* know her—but there's something here.

An unexpected ache of longing hits me. It's like this irrational fear that I'll never have the chance to fully know her before she slips away. I want to ask every personal question in the book. But I don't. I reel it in, respecting her wishes.

"Sounds like I need to go to South Africa one day."

"You definitely should."

Silence stretches between us, thick with tension as my gaze travels over her face, committing every detail to memory. The freckle at the corner of her right eye, the bow in her lips, the rich, chocolate brown of her eyes. My thumb glides along her jaw, tracing up her cheek to tuck a piece of hair behind her ear, my hand finally resting at her neck. I pull her to me, my lips claiming hers, drinking in the sweet taste of her. She meets me with equal intensity, her fingers digging into my back.

My hand slides beneath my shirt she's wearing, her warm skin soft against my touch. My hand finds its way to her tits, and she gasps as I pinch her nipple between my fingers.

She arches into me, her voice a breathless whisper, but demanding in my ear, "Fuck me, Ryan."

I chuckle against her mouth. "Anything you want, gorgeous."

* * * * *　　* * * * *

My alarm startles me awake. I reach for my phone to hit snooze, but then remember Cooper, and I silence it instead. I place my phone back on the nightstand and turn to make sure I didn't wake her.

The bed is empty.

I sit up slowly, blinking into the early morning light, running a hand through my hair, still groggy. My chest tightens as I scan the empty bed. *Where the hell did she go?*

I get up and open the curtains, letting the light trickle in. My eyes scan the room for her belongings, hoping maybe she just ran to grab coffee or use the bathroom, but everything's gone. Purse, clothes—gone. She left. *Seriously? Not even a goodbye?* A weird mix of disappointment and confusion settles in. What the hell did I expect?

"Dammit," I mutter under my breath. She's gone, and the message is loud and clear: it was a one-night stand, and that's all it was.

I step into the shower, the hot water pounding against my skin, waking me up—but it does nothing to wash away the thoughts at the back of my mind. *Did I fuck up somehow? Was she not into it?* No, she was definitely into it. That was some of the best sex I've ever had. It wasn't just about that, though. I had fun—she had fun. I know she did. We talked, we laughed, we played… Dammit, I guess it was exactly what it was supposed to be. No strings.

As I towel off and get dressed, the confusion turns to frustration. I sit on the edge of the bed, ready to dive into some work emails to distract myself, but my phone rings. It's Beth.

Shit. I send it to voicemail and toss the phone aside, the weight of it sitting heavy on my chest. My throat tightens, and I can't quite shake the gnawing guilt creeping in. Why the hell would I feel guilty?

Images of last night flood my mind: Cooper's lips on mine, her naked body pressed against me, and those sounds she made—*fuck*. But then Beth's voice creeps in. Her laughter, her smile, all the moments we've shared over the past ten years. Last night with Cooper was intoxicating, but Beth's presence feels like home. She knows me better than anyone.

I rub my forehead, trying to push it all down. Whatever I felt for Cooper no longer matters. She's gone.

My phone dings with a voicemail. Beth again. *Jesus.* I play it, just to get rid of the notification.

"Hey… it's me. Um…" There's a long pause, followed by a sniffle. "Ryan…" her voice breaks. "I need to talk to you." Her voice quivers. "It's important. Call me back."

Chapter 4

COOPER

September — Chicago, IL

Six Months Later

"Hey, do you remember Genevieve from my sorority?"

"Yeah… vaguely." Brad leans against the kitchen countertop, folding his arms. He's shirtless, and while he's always been lean and in decent shape, he's been getting up early to hit the gym before work, and it's starting to show. His abs are more defined, his pecs are filling out, and his shirts have begun to hug his arms a little tighter. He looks good—really good. I can't help but admire his physique, the way his muscles move subtly with each breath.

"Well, she reached out last week about a job opportunity. She's a talent acquisition and development manager for a large tech company. They own a smaller company that's growing fast, and they're looking for a Project Manager. It sounded like a great opportunity, so I met her for coffee yesterday to hear more about it." I pause, feeling a flutter of excitement. "And, Brad, it really is a great opportunity. It seems almost too good to be true. I can't stop thinking about it."

"Okay… but what about my brother? You wouldn't leave him high and dry, right?" Brad looks at me skeptically. "You don't need to stress about making more money or moving up the ladder, baby. I'm on track to make partner in the next year or two, and you won't even have to work a single day when we have kids." He shrugs. "Why would you want to put yourself through the hassle of learning a new job when you just don't need to?"

"It's not about the money, babe. And I would never leave Mike high and dry if I got the job. I'd give him plenty of notice and help find a replacement." I keep my voice steady, but there's a slight edge to it now. "The pay is really good. I know we don't need it, but it would make a big difference." *We* don't need the pay, but *I* do.

Brad sighs, rubbing a hand over his face. "I just don't see why you have to go and complicate shit. Things are really good right now. You get a new job, and all of a sudden you're working more, trying to prove yourself at a new company. The stress will pile on, and pretty soon we'll never see each other. Not to mention, it'll be awkward as hell with Mike."

Well, I *was* turned on by Brad being shirtless—until he opened his mouth. Why does he always make me feel like I'm being ridiculous? I know his concern for Mike is valid. Mike's been supportive and has provided me with great opportunities over the past few years, but people move on all the time in the workforce. He might stress about me leaving, but he'll be fine—he'll get over it.

God, for a moment, I thought I could be excited about something. But sitting here, watching him dismiss my ambition like it's a passing phase, I feel the excitement draining away. I glance down at the engagement ring on my finger. It's pretty—a beautiful ring. I couldn't have picked out a better one myself. Brad knows me well, and I know he loves me—at least in his own way.

Brad proposed three months ago. It was perfect, of course. Everything Brad does is well-thought-out and executed flawlessly. From the morning bike ride to the rooftop champagne, every detail was meticulously planned. We'd been in a pretty good place then. We tend to have our moments of good and bad, just like every couple. But lately, there's been a little more friction, which is making our engagement feel more like a distant memory than the life I'm actually living.

"Why are you just assuming the worst here? This isn't about you or Mike; this is about me. I have a degree, aspirations… goals. I like working. What else would I do all day? And you're gone anyway, so who cares if I decide to work more?"

"Oh, great, now you're going to turn this back on me about how I'm not a good enough boyfriend."

"No, that's not what I'm doing," I reply, my voice tight with frustration. "I think you're a great boyfriend, and I love you. I know making partner is important to you, and I've tried to be really supportive of that." *God, here we go.* Somehow, he always manages to twist things around—make it about him.

He rolls his eyes, turning away as he starts rummaging through the kitchen cabinets for his protein shake powder. "So, what did you tell her?" he asks, his voice clipped.

I hesitate. *Do I just lie?* "I told her I was interested, and she asked me to come by tomorrow for an interview. The place sounds really cool. It's one of those workplaces where they rent out space, and it's all open concept. The building is called Elemental WorkHub. You can work in shared spaces, on a couch, or in the café. There's a gym, a wellness area, a coffee shop—and it's all included for anyone who works there. It seems really chill. No dress code, flexible hours, as long as you get your work done. It doesn't sound like it'd be stressful… maybe just at the beginning, while I'm learning the ropes."

"Sounds like you've already made up your mind. Do what you want—you don't care what I think anyway."

Fucking dick.

I blink back tears of disappointment. What did I expect?

He puts his hands on the counter, leaning against them, his arm muscles rippling up to his chest. He's sexy, I guess, but it doesn't do much for me anymore. For some reason, the sight of Brad flexing his muscles sends a flash of Ryan into my mind. Now there's a man who could do something for me—the way his body had moved against mine, how his touch burned into my skin. I shift in my seat, trying to focus, but my body remembers too well. *God, Ryan.* It was hot—he was hot. And Jesus, the way he made me feel… it nearly scared the hell out of me. It still does. The things I felt with a stranger are things I hardly ever feel with Brad.

I'd wanted to stay in his bed that night, to wake up with him, share coffee, talk about anything, everything. But it was pointless—a fleeting distraction. What would've been the point of chasing something with a guy

I'd never see again? Besides, Brad was waiting when I got back. He apologized like he always does, saying and doing all the right things. And I eat it up because it's easier than dealing with the consequences and *what-ifs* of leaving.

I never told Brad about my night with Ryan. The thought of him finding out sends a chill down my spine. I know exactly how he'd spin it—*yeah, no thanks*.

I can feel his eyes boring into me, bringing me back to my current dilemma. "That's not fair," I say quietly. Then, because pursuing this conversation further is pointless, I look him in the eyes with a slight smile. "I'll think about what you said."

A job like this could be my escape route. I'd have the pay raise to finally afford my own place downtown. It might not be as nice as this apartment, but it would be mine. I swallow, feeling the weight of that thought settling in. I need the power to stand on my own—I need options. Just in case.

Brad leaves the kitchen to get dressed, and I follow suit, changing into my running clothes.

I pass Brad in the living room on my way out for my walk. He's in a suit, looking every bit the handsome successful lawyer that he is. I press a hand against his chest, trying to smooth things over. "Hey," I say apologetically. "I don't want you to leave for work upset with me. I love you. Let's have a date this weekend."

I kiss him, letting my lips linger longer than usual. The kiss is meant to be an apology, but it feels like a band-aid over a wound that keeps reopening. I pull away, forcing a smile. "Have a good day."

He wraps his free arm around my waist, pulling me closer. "I love you too," he murmurs. "I don't want to fight, baby."

I pull back and pat his chest. "I don't either. You look handsome. Go kill it."

He grins. "You too." He gives me one last peck and a playful smack on the ass as I head out.

I turn right instead of left like I normally do, deciding to walk past the building where I might be working if I get the job. I want to get a feel for it, familiarize myself with the area—check out the vibes.

The address Genevieve gave me is one-point-two miles away. I sprint the last quarter mile, slowing to a walk as I catch my breath, taking in the surroundings. It's close to the financial district, not far from Brad's office. I usually only come to this area when I'm seeing him at work or meeting him for lunch. Occasionally, I'll bring him dinner when he's working late.

I pull up my maps, checking for restaurants and coffee shops near the office building. A few good ones pop up, and I feel a rush of excitement—though I know I'm getting ahead of myself. Still, it's a great location, just a few blocks from Millennium Park.

The building is cool—modern and chic. I can already picture myself walking through those glass doors. I'm looking forward to finally seeing the inside tomorrow for my interview.

On my way home, I redirect, plugging a nearby coffee shop into my phone. A few minutes later, I'm sitting inside *Roasted Perks,* sipping on my latte and people-watching by the window. The steady hum of conversation and clinking coffee cups fills the air. My attention shifts to two men on the other side of the street, coffees in hand. One of them catches my eye. He's hot. I can't help but fix my gaze on him as he draws nearer. Chicago definitely has its fair share of good-looking, successful men.

I watch the guy walk down the street, wondering if he's single. *God, what's wrong with me?* I toy with my engagement ring. *Ugh*. I'm a terrible fiancée. I'm not any better than Brad—though I'm not acting on my feelings… except for that one time, with Ryan.

I let out a quiet sigh, Brad's earlier words lingering in my mind. I hate how easily he can brush off something so important to me. I guess I could try harder.

I pull out my phone and stare at the blank message screen, mustering up something fun to say.

> **Cooper:** Hey babe. I keep thinking about how good you looked this morning. Do you think you could get home early enough to spend some time together? Take a test drive out on those new abs you're rocking?

I add a winky emoji and stare at the screen for a second, wondering if the message feels as forced as it does in my head.

I grab what's left of my coffee and head out.

By the time I get home, I only have thirty minutes before I have to leave. My phone buzzes with a text from Brad.

> **Brad:** I won't be home for dinner… but I'll try my best to be home before you're in bed. Nothing I'd love more than to do things to your naked body that make you moan tonight.

I smile at his message. This *almost* makes up for him being a dick earlier.

* * * * *  * * * * *

It's ten thirty, and I've all but given up on seeing Brad tonight. I just wish he'd text me when he knows he won't make it before I fall asleep. I hate the hoping, the waiting. I was actually looking forward to connecting with him physically tonight. Sometimes I feel like that's the only healthy part of our relationship—the one thing that still works. We've always clicked in the bedroom. I stand in front of the mirror, brushing my teeth, glancing at my reflection. I even put on a sexy little pajama set for him—a lace cami with matching cheeky shorts. Brad's a sucker for a tank and short pajama set. He says it's better than lingerie because of the element of surprise— sexy without trying too hard.

I hear the apartment door open. I spit out the toothpaste just as Brad walks into the bathroom.

"Hey, you," I say, eyeing him through the mirror.

He comes up behind me, wrapping his arms around my waist and pulling me close. His lips nuzzle against my neck, soft kisses trailing down. "Hey, baby. You look super sexy," he murmurs. His hand glides up from my stomach, cupping my breast, and I already feel myself getting turned on. "God, it's been a long day. I just want to forget about work for a while and get lost in these boobs of yours."

I laugh, turning to face him with a kiss.

He pulls me in close, kissing me fiercely.

What the hell?

There's alcohol on his breath.

I pull back. "Brad," I say as he keeps kissing me. "Brad, stop."

He finally stops and meets my gaze.

"Have you been drinking?" I ask, trying to keep my voice light.

"Yeah," he says casually. "A few of us went out for drinks after we closed a deal today. It was a stressful but rewarding day."

"Well, that's great that you closed a deal babe. I just…" I scowl. "So when I asked if you could come home early to be with me, you finished work and then decided to go get drinks with your coworkers instead? And not tell me?"

"God, Cooper…" He lets out an exasperated sigh. "Can you not start?" His grip on my waist softens. "Look, I'm home. I came home in time to be with you. And I want to be with you. There's nothing I want more right now than to kiss this beautiful mouth of yours." He leans in, kissing me slowly, brushing my cheek with his thumb. His lips find my ear. "And touch your sexy body," he whispers, his voice low and deep, as his hand slides down to my ass, caressing it.

He kisses my neck tenderly. "Come on, baby," he murmurs, pressing kisses along my shoulder blade. "Let's destress together." His hand slips into the back of my shorts, gripping my cheeks. "Don't be mad at me." He pulls his hand back slightly, then runs his fingers along the waistband of my shorts to the front, teasing me.

Goddammit. I want to push back, to tell him how much it bothers me that he keeps doing this—showing up late, putting me second to his job. But the way he looks at me, the way his hands move over my skin… it's easier to just give in. Plus, I'm horny, and this always feels good. So I do. I cave. That warm tingle spreading through my insides—it gets me every time. And he did get home before I went to bed.

I sigh. "Okay. Let's destress together." I search his eyes, wanting to connect with him.

I glide my fingers up his chest, feeling the firm muscle beneath, and cup the back of his neck.

He kisses me and lifts me effortlessly, my legs wrapping around him as he carries me into our bedroom. He lays me down on the bed, crawling over me, his body hovering above mine. We make out for several minutes, hands exploring—playing. He's so good at knowing exactly what I need. I relish in these moments because it reminds me how good we can be when we work together—when we're a team. When we're like this, it's easy to forget about the fights. It helps me feel close to him.

We strip each other's clothes off, and Brad pauses, hovering over me, his gaze fixed on mine. "Coop. You're so beautiful." His thumb brushes over my bottom lip.

I smile, feeling the warmth of his words.

"You know I love you, right?"

"Of course," I whisper softly. "I love you too." Brad's fingers find their way to the aching need between my legs, and he knows exactly how to release the pressure building inside me. I cry out in pleasure as waves of euphoria rush through my body, leaving me breathless.

When we're finished we both head to the bathroom to clean up. When I come back to bed, Brad's back is already turned, lights off, ready for sleep, and this is when I feel that familiar ache—the one that comes after. The one that tells me this isn't enough, that it hasn't been enough for a while. But I push it down, like always, and remind myself that this is what we're good at. It's better than being in a sexless relationship. My fingers trace circles on the soft sheets. It's strange how I can feel so close to him, in my most vulnerable state, but as soon as it's over, I'm left feeling more alone than before.

Chapter 5

COOPER

"Well, I think you'd be a fantastic fit for Nexlytic, Cooper. Not to mention, I'd love working with you. And you'll love the workspace." Genevieve closes her laptop, flashing me a bright smile.

"Thanks, Genevieve. I truly appreciate the offer. Would it be alright if I take a few days to think it over? Talk to Brad?"

"Of course! Take your time." She leans back in her chair. "Would you like a tour of Elemental before you go?"

"Oh, I'd love one!" I say, standing up from the booth near the café, which is connected to a cozy coffee shop.

We begin walking toward the elevator. "So… floors two through eight are all office space," Genevieve explains. "Each floor has a slightly different design element. Some are dedicated to meeting and conference rooms, while others have private offices and more common areas. Floors six through eight are full-floor offices. We're on the sixth floor, which Nexlytic shares with its parent company, VantageSphere."

We step off the elevator onto the sixth floor and into a sleek, open common area. "This is super cool," I say, looking around.

"I know, right? It's a really fun concept," Genevieve says as we walk into the common space. "We call this the lounge." She moves through the middle, and I follow. "Everything to the left is VantageSphere—private offices and meeting rooms." The walls are mostly glass, giving the entire space an open, expansive feel.

We turn down a hallway. "My office is the first one on the right." She gestures toward it with a quick wave. "And this larger corner office belongs to our Vice President. Let's see if he's around—I'd love for you to meet him."

We reach the corner office, but it's empty. "Ah, shoot." She glances at her watch. "He's probably out grabbing lunch."

Genevieve continues the tour, showing me the rest of the floor. Nexlytic occupies the right side of the common area, sharing the space with VantageSphere. Since VantageSphere is the larger company, they have the majority of the private offices, but both companies share the meeting and conference rooms, as well as the booths, open desk areas, and lounge.

"Each floor also has a fully stocked kitchen," Genevieve adds as we pass one. "Free beverages, plus a fridge and microwave for everyone to use."

"Now for the fun part," Genevieve says as we walk toward the elevator.

We step inside, and she presses the button for the ninth floor. When the doors open, I'm greeted by a full-blown gym—not some cheap hotel fitness center, but a massive space with everything you could ever need.

"This floor has the gym, sauna, a meditation and wellness room, and even pickleball courts," she explains.

"Are you serious? I love pickleball."

Genevieve grins. "Yep, and anyone who works at Elemental has full access to all the facilities."

"You're convincing me to take this job with each passing minute," I say.

She finishes showing me around the ninth floor and then takes me up to the tenth—the top floor.

"This floor houses our wet bar, and rooftop patio, as well as the cocktail lounge, which is open from 5:00 PM to 11:00 PM on weekdays, and stays open until 1:00 AM on the weekends," Genevieve explains. "It can also be rented out for private parties and events. The owner of Elemental, Leo Weston, usually hosts holiday parties and regular events up here—anywhere from weekly to monthly—for the companies that rent space in the building. He's really cool. And between you and me… he's a total looker." Her eyes go wide as she smiles, and I laugh.

"You'll have a chance to meet him if you decide to take the job," she adds with a playful grin. Then, she turns to me with mock seriousness. "Oh, and I forgot to mention, our VP is also very good-looking. But this is all hush-hush, okay? I wouldn't be spilling workplace secrets if I didn't know you. So let's just pretend we didn't talk about the hotties."

I laugh again, shaking my head. "Got it. Your secret's safe with me. Geez, you're making it hard to say no. All these amenities and perks— plus, they come with a side of eye candy? Who wouldn't want to work here?"

"I'm doing my best to convince you," Genevieve says with a smile. "I know you're engaged, but hey, no one said you couldn't look."

"True," I say, grinning. "Are you still with Collin?"

"Yeah, we live together now. He actually works on the fourth floor at a software engineering company. After VantageSphere moved to this building about a year ago, Collin came to visit me at work and couldn't believe how great it was. He pitched the idea to his boss, and five months later, when their lease was up, they moved here too." She laughs. "I love teasing him about all the hot nerds I work with. He hates it."

I could never joke about working with hot guys. Brad would get so jealous.

She laughs and leads me around to the other side, where there's an entrance to a cocktail lounge roped off, called *Viv's Cocktail Lounge.* "Leo's girlfriend is Vivian," Genevieve explains. "She's really great— gorgeous too. You'll get to know her. She's pretty involved, and helps Leo out with the business."

"Gosh, this all seems amazing," I say. "I'll talk to Brad about every-thing tonight and get back to you by Monday. Does that work?"

"Absolutely, Coop," she says, smiling. "Like I said, you'd be a valu-able asset to Nexlytic and the team."

We ride the elevator down to the first floor, and Genevieve gives me a hug before I leave, filling me with an overwhelming sense of belonging. I want this so much, but the thought of talking to Brad about it makes me nauseous.

I just want him to be happy for me—it's really not a lot to ask for.

On the walk home, I go over every scenario in my head, trying to figure out the best way to bring it up. I'll for sure do it naked. Make him dinner, have sex, and then slip it into the conversation. That always works with him. Feed him, tell him he's amazing, stroke his ego, please him in bed—then ask for what I want. Hell, it's worked my whole life with men. I call it the P.O.P.—power of the pussy.

* * * * * * * * * *

"God, that was great!" I sigh, rolling my sweaty self next to Brad and resting my head on his chest, my leg wrapping around him, determined to keep him pinned here for a while longer. I trail my fingertips lightly across his pecs and down his abs.

Brad lets out a long exhale. "Yeah, it was. I love watching you suck my cock—the way I can push you deeper, and you take it like you're made for me."

His comment grates a little, but I'm used to it. I shove my irritation down. No point in derailing things now. I gave him really great head, then finished him off in reverse cowgirl. Now, it's time to make my play.

"I'm glad you got home a little earlier tonight so we could spend some time together," I say, splaying my hand flat on his chest. My fingers glide over the hard lines of his muscles. "Those gym hours are paying off." I look up at him, flashing a playful smile. "You look real sexy… You need to come home early more often."

He caresses my back with his fingers, his touch light and casual. "Thanks, baby. You know I always think you're sexy. I'll try harder to get home sooner more often… especially when you make it so damn worth it."

We lay there in comfortable silence for a minute, his fingers tracing lazy patterns on my skin, while I try to gather the courage to bring up the job. The words are sitting on the tip of my tongue, but I hesitate. I know I can take the job, it's not like he won't let me. I'm just afraid he'll suck the joy out of my excitement.

"How was that interview?" Brad asks suddenly, breaking the silence, catching me off guard.

I turn, propping myself up on my elbow. My long hair spills over my shoulders and gathers on the bed, my breasts peeking through. "It was so great." I kiss him on the mouth, lingering for a moment before pulling away slowly. "She offered me the job, and it's a really great offer. The workspace is amazing, and I'm really excited about it." I can't help grinning as wide as my cheeks will allow. "I want the job—it just feels right, you know?"

I kiss him again, this time softer, trying to gauge where his head is. I press gentle kisses along his cheek and neck, searching for any sign of how he's feeling. My stomach knots. I hate that this has always been my go-to move to get what I want—it feels gross. "What do you think about that?" I ask, threading my fingers through his hair.

He grunts low and deep, his expression thoughtful. "Hmm. I think… it's a good thing your tits are in my face because I don't love the idea of it." He pauses, a teasing smile tugs on his lip. "But… I can see that you're happy about it, and I want you to be happy, so if that's what you want to do, I support it."

"Really?" I kiss him hard, excitement bubbling up inside me.

He chuckles. "Yes, really."

"Ah! Thank you!" I grin, kissing him again. "I'd much rather take the job with your support than without it."

"Right. Just please tell Mike right away, and promise you'll stay until he finds a replacement. He values you a lot at the company."

"I know. I will, I promise." I'm completely elated. I straddle him, pressing my lips to his, playfully. His strong arms wrap around my back, pulling me closer. "You're a smart man, Brad Sterling," I whisper in his ear, teasingly. "You know exactly how to play your cards to get what you want in bed."

He chuckles, his grip tightening around me. "And I'd say you played your hand just as well, Coop—getting what you want."

I pull back, grinning at him, biting my bottom lip. Just when I'm ready to give up, Brad surprises me with a response like that. Maybe we'll be okay for a while. But deep down, I can't shake the feeling that his 'support' has strings attached—it always does.

Chapter 6

RYAN

October

"Right. We want this to be mutually beneficial, so let's adjust the percentage to give both sides some room to breathe as we integrate. I'll send over the revised terms, and we can aim to finalize everything by Friday."

As I finish speaking, I notice Genevieve peering through my office windows, mouthing something to me. I give her a quick wave, inviting her in. She steps in quietly, waiting for me to wrap up the call.

"Yep. Appreciate the conversation, Paul. Looking forward to wrapping this up. Let's reconnect later this week. Talk to you soon." I disconnect the call and remove my earbuds.

"Hey, Genevieve, what's up?"

"Hey, Ryan. I have a new employee I'd love for you to meet when you have a minute."

"Great. I'll be right out."

"Okay, we'll be in the lounge."

I jot down a few notes from my call with Paul and fire off a quick email, my to-do list growing longer by the second. Grabbing my water jug to refill while I'm in the lounge, I head out to meet Genevieve.

I spot Genevieve as I turn the corner, her back to me, standing next to a blonde. I hate to be that guy, but I can't help checking out this woman's ass. Her long hair falls past the middle of her back, and her pants show off her body in all the right ways. I do what any guy would do—I look.

"Genevieve," I call out.

Both she and the blonde turn around, and my heart stops dead in my chest.

"Hey, Ryan. I wanted you to meet our new Project Manager, Cooper Bradley," Genevieve says professionally.

I freeze for a moment. Cooper and I lock eyes, and I can tell she's just as surprised as I am. Before the awkwardness sinks in, I grin and extend my hand. "Cooper. It's been a while."

She hesitates, then takes my hand, smiling. "Yeah, it has. Nice to see you again, Ryan."

"Wait… You two know each other?" Genevieve's surprise is nothing compared to the shock that I'm feeling.

"Yeah…" Cooper speaks slowly. "Ryan and I met in Newport back in…" She turns to me. "Oh, when was that? March?"

"Yeah, I think so, about mid-March," I say grinning. She grins back, and God, her smile.

"What a small world." Genevieve turns to Cooper. "Ryan's the VP of VantageSphere. His team works across this floor, so you'll probably run into each other a lot. Since you'll be collaborating on a few projects, I thought it'd be good for you two to connect early."

Holy shit, this is insane. What are the chances that, six months later, she'd end up working not only in the same building, but on the same floor as me? I have no idea what to make of it.

I find myself staring at her because fuck, how can I not? She looks incredible—just as gorgeous as I remember. She rubs her lips together. God, her lips—her body, her smell. *Jesus, what am I doing?*

She glances up, catching me staring, and I quickly look away, pretending to focus on Genevieve's words. I nod and respond when necessary, but I'm not really listening. My thoughts are completely consumed by that night we spent together in Newport.

I've replayed it over and over—the way we clicked, the morning after—wondering why she didn't stick around.

We had a great time together—I'm sure she felt it too.

I sense her eyes on me and shift my focus just enough to catch a faint smile. My pulse quickens. *Hell yeah, she's still attracted to me.*

"So, if you have any questions about that, you can always ask Ryan." Genevieve looks at me expectantly, and I realize I have no idea what she's talking about.

"Right," I say, nodding like I'm totally in the loop. "My office is always open." I smile and extend my hand again. "Well, Cooper, it was great seeing you again. I look forward to catching up and working together."

Cooper takes my hand. "Yeah, me too. It's great seeing you."

"Thanks, Ryan. I've got to get Cooper over to Jason so she can start training for the day," Genevieve says, ushering Cooper down the hall toward one of the smaller conference rooms.

I slip back into my office and slump into my chair, swiveling back and forth as my mind races. Cooper Bradley. What are the odds? What the hell does this mean? I tap the end of my pen against my chin, deep in thought.

I left Newport without answers, and now she's here, right in front of me. But everything is different now. My life's a goddamn mess. I feel a mix of nerves and excitement, but reality hits me like a club to the head. *Newsflash, Ryan: she's your coworker now.*

Hell, I couldn't sleep with her again even if I wanted to.

I stare at my computer screen, the endless list of to-dos piling up, taunting me. No distractions, I tell myself. But my thoughts drift back to her—her smile, the way she flirted with me, and her fucking adorable laugh.

Jesus. Who am I kidding? I'm already distracted.

* * * * * * * * * *

"Beth?" I call out as I walk into our four-bedroom townhouse in Lakeview—about a twenty-minute drive from downtown, assuming the traffic isn't horrendous. I fight the urge to toss my things onto the couch and instead stop to hang my jacket in the closet, setting my backpack at the bottom of the stairs to take up later.

"I'm in here," she calls from the kitchen.

I make my way through the living and dining room to the kitchen. Beth's at the stove, cooking.

"Hey," she says, glancing over her shoulder. "How was your day? You hungry?"

"Yeah, I'm starved. My day was fine. How about yours?"

"It was fine… Had lunch with my mom—you know how that goes."

I chuckle, making my way over to her. She stops what she's doing to embrace me. I hug her tightly, kissing the top of her head. "How are you feeling today?"

"Oh you know, I'm just tired." She goes back to the stove while I sort through the pile of mail at the end of the counter.

My mind drifts back to the day—back to Cooper. I still can't believe it. It's been hours, and I can't shake the way seeing her made me feel.

"Hey," Beth says loudly.

I look up. I can tell from the look she's giving me that she either said or asked me something that I didn't hear. "Sorry, what?"

She shakes her head. "Never mind. You seem distracted. What's going on?"

I furrow my brows. "Oh, it's nothing. Just a bit of a weird day." I'm not about to tell her the woman I slept with six months ago now works in my office.

She narrows her eyes, searching my face. "Weird how?"

"Just work stuff," I say, brushing it off. "What are you making? It smells good."

"Fajitas."

"That sounds great… You know you don't have to cook for me, right?"

She gives me a soft smile. "It's no problem, Ryan. I'm cooking any-way, and I'm happy to cook for you. I *like* cooking for you."

"Well, thanks. I know you're probably not up for it, but I appreciate it."

* * * * * * * * * *

Later that night, I half-watch a football game, a beer in one hand and the other tucked into my joggers. My thoughts drift to Cooper. An escape. A way out of the swirling clusterfuck my life has become. But the more I think about her, the more conflicted I feel.

I scowl at the TV. *Why can't I stop thinking about her?* Because I'm horny as hell. That night with her is all I've been able to think about for months. I've jerked off to the memory of her more times than I care to admit—and now I'm going to be seeing her every day. *Great.*

"Hey," Beth's voice interrupts my thoughts. "I'm going to bed… goodnight."

"Night." My attention shifts back to the television as I hear her ascend the stairs. I let out a long sigh, running a hand through my hair. My life has done a complete one-eighty over the past year—and not in a good way.

* * * * *   * * * * *

My eyes keep drifting to Cooper as Jason speaks. She's wearing a tight dress, and I can't stop fidgeting with the pen in my hand. My mind slips into an alternate universe where I've got her alone in my office. She's undressing for me, just like she did in Newport. I'm about to bend her over my desk when I realize she's scowling at me.

Oh, shit. I've been caught.

Her lips press together, fighting back a smile. She quickly shifts her attention back to Jason, but I keep mine mostly on her.

Our early morning meetings bring both companies and their department heads together. It's Cooper's third day here. I barely saw her yesterday, and it was probably for the best. I've got so many meetings, the busyness keeps me from thinking about her too much. But right now? With her sitting right in front of me? She's all I can think about.

Jason turns the rest of the meeting over to me, and as I wrap things up, I scramble for any reason to talk to Cooper. My mind comes up blank. There's nothing pressing we need to discuss, and she's still glued to Jason most of the day with her training.

"Alright everyone, great work here. Let's have a productive day."

As the others gather their things, I'm about to head out when Cooper approaches me.

"Hey, Ryan," she says.

"Hey," I reply, surprised. *Okay... she came to me. This is good.* "I've been meaning to come find you, but I've been slammed with meetings. How are you liking your first week?"

She shrugs with a playful smile. "It's been good so far... a little surprising," her eyes glance over me. "But good." She bites her bottom lip, and something in her tone feels very flirty.

I can't help but smirk. "Anything in particular surprising you?"

"Mostly just you... And it's been the change I didn't know I needed."

"That's great. I'm glad you're enjoying it. And yeah, seeing you here on Monday was... well, unexpected, to say the least."

Her eyes light up. "How long have you worked here? I thought you lived in Arizona."

I cock a brow, amused. "I don't remember us talking about where we lived. How'd you know that?"

She shrugs, grinning. "I took a peek at your driver's license before I snuck out. Okay, maybe a little creepy," she adds, laughing. "But I honestly didn't think I'd ever see you again, so I figured... why not?"

I chuckle. "You did a little research, huh? I'm flattered." I lean in slightly, teasing her. "I thought you didn't want to know anything personal about me."

She smiles. "I didn't... until I did."

Her eyes meet mine, and it's as if no time has passed at all. I'm right back there, in that bed with her. The bow of her lips, the freckle by her eye—still sexy as hell. I swallow. "You know, you could've just asked me before disappearing like a ghost."

Her cheeks flush. "Yeah, well, that wasn't exactly part of the plan."

"So, what was the plan?" I ask, raising a brow. "Why did you leave?"

She hesitates, fidgeting slightly. Her fingers twist a strand of her hair, and that's when I notice the giant ring on her finger, catching the light like a punch to the gut. My stomach knots. *How did I miss that?*

I force a casual tone. "That's... a nice ring."

My mind races with questions.

The tension between us shifts, something heavier settling in. I can't believe I didn't see it before—probably didn't want to. I scoff, feeling like a fool. "So, what? You're married?" The words slip out before I can stop them.

She shakes her head. "No," she says a little reluctantly. "I'm engaged." She clasps her right hand over her left, as if she can hide the fact that she's engaged—that she slept with me and was just now flirting with me.

Engaged. My mind races. It doesn't add up. Six months isn't long enough to meet someone new and get engaged… unless she wasn't single back then.

I smile softly, trying to mask the ache of disappointment. "Right. Well, you should probably get back to Jason. I've got a meeting."

I head toward the door.

"Ryan, wait," I hear her call out, but I don't stop. I go straight to my office and close the door.

I drop into my chair. *What the fuck?* The walls feel like they're closing in on me, and I scold myself for getting my hopes up. She's not available. God, no wonder she snuck out while I was sleeping. *Did she cheat on him?* The thought makes me cringe. I've been cheated on before—I know how that shit feels, and I never thought I'd be the guy to play any part in it.

I can't help feeling slightly disappointed. We had great chemistry. But dammit, it wasn't just the sex. There was something about the way we clicked, the conversation, the flirting—the teasing.

And now, seeing her every day is going to mess with my head.

Chapter 7

COOPER

It's Friday, and after today, I will have officially completed my second week of training at Nexlytic. There's a lot to learn, which is a bit overwhelming, but I think the work will be interesting. I'll be busy enough for the days to fly by, but the environment and the people are so laid-back that it makes the parts that would normally stress me out feel surprisingly manageable. So far, I'm liking it, but this thing with Ryan hovers over me every day—a stormy raincloud that's gloomy as fuck.

I haven't run into Ryan all week. I've caught glimpses of him from a distance, just enough to know he's around, but it seems like we're both purposely steering clear of any real encounter. I'm almost positive he thinks I cheated on Brad, and I don't blame him. But I didn't—did I? I don't know why I haven't had the nerve to just go talk to him, explain everything. Part of me feels justified in my actions, but that other part... well, it feels guilty.

I'm sitting in the conference room, waiting for Jason while my thoughts have their way with me. How did this even happen? Seriously. What are the odds? It feels like I'd have a better chance of being struck by lightning than meeting a stranger across the country, sleeping with him, and then—six months later—not only living in the same city, but working in the same space. It's surreal. I can't help but wonder why—what it all means. I'm not usually one to read into these kinds of things. I don't believe in fate or that things happen for a reason.

But *this*—this feels like the universe perfectly aligned just to fuck with me. I can't believe I didn't think about my ring. And he noticed it while I was flirting with him—great timing. *Good job me.*

Still, part of me wants so badly to talk to him—to really get to know him on a deeper level. I think about that night way more than I should—especially for someone who's engaged. But the other part of me? That part says I'd be perfectly fine avoiding him forever. Except… I think that part of me is lying.

Jason pops his head into the room, pulling me from my thoughts. "Hey, Cooper, I've got a situation I'm dealing with. Can you meet me back here in thirty? Feel free to take a coffee break."

"Okay."

He's out the door before I can say more. *Feel free to take a coffee break?* Now *that's* what I'm talking about. This place has such a European vibe—no stress, take time for yourself, sip your coffee, maybe even lie down, get comfy while you work. Whoever came up with this concept deserves a medal.

I take his suggestion and head for coffee. As I walk into the café, I spot Ryan standing in line. My instinct is to turn around and make a quick escape before he notices me, but before I can, Rebecca—a young twenty-something from my team—passes by with a smile.

"Hey, Cooper!" she calls out, her voice ringing through the café.

Shit. Ryan turns at the sound of my name, raising his brows and giving me a pointed look. I wince. My heart skips a beat as I lock eyes with him. Dammit. There's no backing out now. Looks like I'm getting in line.

I reluctantly step behind him, feeling his eyes on me. "Hey," I mutter, keeping my gaze fixed forward.

"Hey." Ryan turns around, but after ten seconds, he turns back, his expression shifting slightly, like something's bothering him. "So… do you and your *fiancé* have any fun plans this weekend?" he asks, folding his arms across his chest.

I take a deep breath. "Yeah, actually, we do." I glance at the barista before meeting Ryan's eyes again. "We're trying out a new restaurant tomorrow night."

He scoffs. "And do you two actually date each other, or is it more of an open relationship where you sleep with other people? You know, like back in *Newport*?"

I glare at him as we inch forward in line. *The audacity*. "I wasn't engaged in Newport, Ryan. Not that it's any of your business."

"Not my business?" he murmurs. "I'd say it's definitely someone's business to know if the person they're about to sleep with is in a relationship. Engaged or not, you never said you were involved with someone. Would've been nice to know before I decided to sleep with you."

"Why are you so hung up on this, Ryan? It's not like you were complaining when you were in between my legs." The words are out before I can stop myself, and I feel a jolt of satisfaction with a tinge of regret.

"Jesus Christ, you're something," he mutters, turning to the barista just in time for his order. "Can I get a sixteen-ounce latte?" Then, before scanning his phone over the reader, he turns back to me. "What are you getting?" he asks, his voice deceptively casual, like he didn't just call me out a moment ago.

"You're not buying my drink."

"Why not? You didn't have a problem with it in Newport." He turns back to the barista and pays for his drink. Without another word, he steps aside, waiting for me to place my order.

I feel my face flush with irritation. "Can I get a twelve-ounce latte?" I ask, hyper-aware of his gaze on me. I pay and follow him to the other side of the counter to wait for my drink. "I didn't ask for you to buy me drinks in Newport. It's not my fault you were so desperate to get laid."

"Oh, *God*. That's rich. Because I distinctly remember asking you on a date. You, however, couldn't get your clothes off fast enough. Does your fiancé know about our little rendezvous?"

I stare him down. "Again… I wasn't engaged."

His eyes narrow. "Oh. Sorry. So, your boyfriend was cool with you hooking up with random guys?"

My jaw clenches, a hint of nausea rising to my throat. But I keep my voice steady. "I wasn't sleeping around. It was a one-time thing."

"Sure it was."

I can feel my composure starting to crack. My blood is boiling—a cocktail of anger, frustration, and the maddening fact that, despite everything, I still find him attractive.

Both of us have our arms crossed.

"You can judge me all you want. You don't know me." My voice is laced with irritation.

"Oh, I know enough."

"You know I could report you to HR for this, right? This conversation is completely inappropriate for work. And honestly, I'm feeling a little harassed."

Ryan scoffs, shaking his head, his tone edged with bitterness. "Yeah, I guess you could. But then what? You'd have to explain why you slept with me when you were in a relationship. And I'm pretty sure you don't want that out there." He takes a step back, his eyes flicking away for a moment. "Look, I'm not here to make your life hell. But damn, Cooper, you could've been honest. It's not like I would've pushed for anything if I knew you were involved. *You* were the one who pushed for it."

We glare at each other. What was once pure sexual tension is now layered with sheer hostility, and I'm not backing down.

He grabs his latte, his voice softening just a touch. "I get it—you probably have your reasons. But I'm not the bad guy here. I never was." With that, he turns to leave, pausing only to add, "See you around."

He walks past me, and exits the café, leaving me standing there, flustered and furious, heat rising in my chest with every breath. My hands tremble as I grab my coffee cup.

The nerve. *Fuck him.* He must think pretty highly of himself to treat people like that—especially at work.

Any attraction I once had is completely gone. He's not *that* good-looking. *Jesus, who am I kidding?* No matter how much of a smug ass he is, the way he affects me is unnerving. I hate that I even care what he thinks, but I do. Maybe it's because he saw me at my most vulnerable, or because I had more fun that night than I have in a long time. Or perhaps it's because a part of me knows that what he's accusing me of is partially true. I'd broken up with Brad—but had I really?

I take a deep breath and, with coffee in hand, I head back to the conference room to meet Jason. He's planning to have me go over some tasks on the company software before we prep for a meeting that I'm helping lead.

I'll just have to steer clear of Ryan. That's not impossible, is it?

* * * * *   * * * * *

"What the hell is his problem? Such a dick, right?" I say to Casey. I'm FaceTiming her, having just finished venting about my encounter with Ryan yesterday. I'm out on the balcony, keeping my voice low. I don't want Brad to hear—he's inside, working.

"Yeah, that's pretty dick of him. It's one thing to ask you about it, but accusing you? And at work?" Casey shakes her head.

"I know. It's so awkward… Let's just hope I don't ever have to work too closely with him. I'm able to avoid him most of the time right now." I press my forehead into the palm of my hand. "Ugh. Why did this have to happen? I love this new job, and he's ruining it for me."

"I'm so sorry, Coop. That really sucks," Casey says sympathetically.

"Want to know the worst part?"

"Yeah, what is it?"

"It's that when I first saw him in the office, I was actually excited. It felt like the universe had aligned. Like, my heart skipped a beat." I cringe admitting it out loud.

"Well, that makes sense. I mean, I remember you saying the sex was mind-blowing. 'Mind-blowing' was the phrase you used. And yeah, he's hot as hell, right? You also had a great time and thought he was really nice… but that was back then."

I let out a frustrated sigh. "Yeah, he was all those things. I was so nervous after you left me with him, but he was sweet and made jokes. We laughed a lot, and… I was just so comfortable with him." I lower my voice to a near whisper. "The chemistry was insane, Case. I've never had that kind of instant connection with someone." I glance around, making sure Brad can't hear.

"Really? Even in college? What about that one guy you hooked up with right before you started dating Brad? What was his name? The foreign exchange student?" Suddenly, she shouts. "No, Mason! Don't touch that!"

Her screen shifts, showing the ceiling. "Sorry, Coop. My face will be right back—keep talking, I'm listening."

"Oh my God, how could I forget about Marco? He was ridiculously hot—the accent, the body, all of it. That was the best sex of my life… until Ryan."

"Okay, okay, so Ryan was even better than Marco?" Casey presses, clearly intrigued.

"God, yes. But let's be honest—while it was great with Marco, we were only twenty-two. Not exactly a fair comparison."

"Well, you've only been with Brad and Ryan since then, right?" she asks as her face comes back into view, slightly breathless from chasing Mason around.

"Yeah."

"Well, what about Brad?" Casey asks, her tone shifting slightly.

"What do you mean—what about him?"

"How's your relationship… in the bedroom?"

I don't hesitate. "Well, that's where our relationship is the best," I say confidently. It's the truth. "It's always been great with Brad in that area. Sure, the excitement has worn off a little, but I'm easily turned on by Brad, and he always makes a point to get me off first. It's the one part of our relationship where he's very selfless." I pause for a second, my thoughts lingering. "That's normal, though, right? The excitement wearing off after this many years?"

"Yeah, I guess," Casey replies thoughtfully. "I don't know if it's the excitement that wears off, or maybe just that anticipation of something new. You know, those butterflies you get when you first start seeing someone? Those definitely fade, but I still look forward to having sex with Greg."

"Yeah, that's a better way of explaining it," I agree. "I still look forward to having sex with Brad. Last night was amazing. He went down on me for so long. It was glorious."

Casey laughs. "Ah, that's the best. How are things with you guys otherwise?"

I pause for a moment, wanting to be honest. "It's actually been good lately. Brad's been super supportive with the new job, and we've got a date planned for tonight. He's been really attentive and present when he's home. And when he gets home late, he makes a point to connect with me physically. Things have actually been better than they've been in a long time." I stop to think about the last time I could say that truthfully—it's been a while.

"That's great. That makes me really happy..." Casey's voice trails off.

"What?" I ask, immediately sensing there's more she's not saying.

"It's nothing. I don't want to put a damper on your happiness right now."

"Well, now you have to say it," I reply, concern creeping into my voice.

"It's just that... you know, most of the other times you've said things were going well with Brad... he was cheating on you. He'd always get extra nice and attentive at home, like he was trying to cover up his guilt."

I'm stunned into silence. This is what she thinks? My best friend, my sister, my greatest confidant in the world believes that Brad being nice to me must mean he's cheating? I don't even know how to respond—don't know what to think. Is she right? Is this a pattern I've been ignoring?

A flutter of panic tightens in my chest, that constricted feeling you get when you're scared of something.

"So, you think Brad's cheating on me?" I finally ask, hoping she'll tell me I'm wrong, that I'm just overreacting.

"I'm sure that's not the case, Coop. I'm sorry I said that. I shouldn't have. Brad's been great... and he proposed. You two are getting married, and I'm really happy for you."

"Do you not like Brad... like, at all?" I ask, needing some kind of validation.

She lets out a long sigh. "It's not that I don't like him... it's just that he's been the source of some of the greatest pain in your life. It's hard for me to forgive him for that, and even harder to look past it. I don't know him like you do, but I do know and love you… I just want you to be truly happy, you know?"

Her words settle like shards of glass in an open wound. She's right—he's hurt me, over and over. No matter how good things seem now or how supportive he's been lately, the doubts creep in like shadows. I hate that she's planted them there.

"Um, okay…" I pinch the bridge of my nose, squeezing my eyes shut, trying not to cry. "God, I don't know what to do with that, Case. Your opinion means more to me than anyone's. Brad's going to be your brother-in-law someday—my *husband*—and you don't like him. You think he's still cheating?" But even as I say the words *brother-in-law* and *husband*, a knot tightens in my stomach. The words feel hollow, like I'm repeating a mantra. It's like deep down, I know it's never going to happen. And worse, I don't know if it's something I even want anymore.

Suddenly, Mason starts crying in the background. "Oh, shit! Shoot." Casey cries out as she drops the phone, and my screen shifts to show a blur of carpet. "I've got to go, Coop. Mason just bumped his head on the table. I'll call you tomorrow."

She's gone before I can even say goodbye. *Great. This is just fucking fantastic.* What am I supposed to do with that conversation? My mind immediately spirals. Is he cheating on me again? How would I even know?

No. I shake my head, forcing myself to stop. I'm not going to go there. If I suspect something, then I'll deal with it. But right now, I have no reason to believe Brad is cheating. We've been getting along, connecting… I'm not going to assume it's just him covering up guilt. I refuse to believe that.

I head to the kitchen to grab a snack before leaving for tennis. I play in a women's league on Saturday afternoons—something I've done my whole adult life, and I love it.

"Hey, Coop?" Brad calls from the office.

I cross the living room and pop my head into his office. "Hey, what's up?"

"Who were you on the phone with?"

"Casey," I reply casually.

"Oh. And how is she?" he asks, glancing up from his computer.

"She's good. Had to cut the call short—Mason bumped his head and was screaming in the background. But she's fine."

"That's good. Have you had lunch?" he asks.

"No, I was just about to grab a small snack before heading out for tennis. Want me to bring you something?"

"That'd be great, if you don't mind." He looks up at me with a soft smile. "Come here," he says, his tone soft.

I walk over to him, and he spins his office chair to face me, pulling me between his legs. His arms wrap around my waist, drawing me closer as he presses his head into my chest, his hands gripping my ass. "You're so sexy," he murmurs, lifting his head to meet my gaze. I lean down to kiss him.

"Mmm," he grunts softly. "Do you have time for a little fun?"

I smile, playing along. "Hmm. Let me think…" I tease him, letting the moment linger, kissing him slowly. "I guess I could spare a few minutes," I finally say with a grin.

Without hesitation, he knocks my knees out from under me as he stands, scooping me up in the process. He carries me into our bedroom, lays me down gently on the bed, and pulls his shirt off.

His mouth meets mine, and the kiss is so good that I melt into it, losing myself as his hands roam over me, touching me in all the ways I crave. I push away the lingering echo of Casey's voice in the back of my mind. *This is real.* We're good. There's no way he's cheating on me again. Not when we're this good together.

Chapter 8

RYAN

"Ten, seven, one. Game point," Leo calls out, his tone easy but competitive. He nails the serve, driving it deep into the court. We rally a few times, each hit getting faster and more precise. When the ball comes to me, I step forward for the return, aiming low and landing it just inside the sideline, barely brushing the edge of the kitchen. Michael darts after it, stretching out, but he misses by a hair. The ball bounces out, and just like that, Leo and I win the game.

We try to play pickleball every other Sunday, while Michael and Leo's wives are at their girls brunch. Leo technically isn't married, but he might as well be. He's in a serious relationship with his girlfriend, and they've got a baby together. We all call her his wife.

When the weather's nice we play outside, but it's early November in Chicago. This morning was brutally cold for this time of year, so we're at Elemental Hub.

We tap paddles over the net, offering the usual "good game" before grabbing our water bottles and towels. Sweat drips down my face as I wipe it away, my arms feeling heavy. Five games in, and I'm spent.

"How long is brunch today?" I ask Leo and Michael.

"Hell if I know." Leo chuckles, shaking his head. "It's different every week. Sometimes brunch is two hours, sometimes it's six. You know how women are—they get to talking, and next thing you know, it's dinnertime. All I care about is that Viv comes home happy and tipsy after a few drinks.

That's when the fun starts, mate." He slaps me on the back, as if I've got the same setup waiting for me at home. I don't.

"God, when is Vivian going to get sick of your ass?" Michael snarks. "I swear you two have more sex than couples who just got together. It's like you're permanently stuck in the honeymoon phase."

"Ah, I do remember the honeymoon phase," I say, a little nostalgia creeping into my voice. "Those were the good ol' days."

"Right? Stella never wants to have sex anymore. I'm lucky if I get it once every ten days," Michael says, shaking his head. "It sucks."

"Hey, at least your forearm's getting stronger for pickleball," Adam quips, earning a round of laughter from all of us.

"Well, she *is* pregnant, mate," Leo adds with a knowing look. "That's pretty normal for a lot of women. Although, it wasn't with Vivian. She was even hornier when she was pregnant."

"Of course she was," Michael scoffs. "Vivian apparently has the libido of a teenage boy. I don't know how you managed to land someone like that." He turns to the group. "Bet Ryan doesn't even know Leo never wanted to be tied down, but somehow, the guy ends up with a girl whose sex drive matches his."

Leo grins, folding his arms across his chest, looking smug as ever.

I glance at Adam as he chimes in. "Wish I had something interesting to add to this conversation, but I've got nothing. Did hook up with a really hot girl last week, though, so that was cool." He turns to me. "Oh, and in case you didn't know, Ryan, Leo's probably slept with half the women in Chicago."

Leo shoves Adam, laughing. "Oh, so now you fuckers are ganging up on me because I get laid more than the lot of you?" He grins. "Same old story. But seriously, Adam, tell us more about this girl. Was it a date or just a one-time shag?"

"Well, it *was* a date. Didn't plan on it being a one-time thing, but now she won't return my texts. I hit her up three times, then just gave up," Adam says, shrugging. "She was hot, though."

"So you slept with her, and now she's ghosting you?" Michael grimaces. "You worried she wasn't satisfied?"

Adam scowls. "No! Trust me, she was satisfied."

"She could've been faking it," Michael shoots back.

"You're such a dick, man. You're just pissed you can't get your own wife to sleep with you."

Michael laughs. "You got me there, Adam. I'm jealous. Jealous of all you guys and your fantastic sex lives."

"Hey, I don't have a fantastic sex life. I don't even have a sex life right now," I say. "Don't be jealous of me. I'd give my left nut for sex every ten days right now." I laugh, but admitting it out loud stings more than I expected.

"That's rough, mate," Leo says, shooting me a sympathetic look. "Any prospects?"

I'm the newer guy in the group. I moved to Chicago about fifteen months ago and met Leo because he owns Elemental. He's originally from London, and we hit it off right away. After our first meeting, he invited me to poker night and got me into pickleball with the guys.

Leo's extremely wealthy. He's built an empire—real estate, businesses, investments. But he's also a psychologist and therapist, so when things got complicated in my life, he was there for me. Never pushed advice or judged—just listened. And when I did ask, he'd offer new ways to see things, new perspectives.

Since moving here, I've grown closest to Leo, though he's got a lot of friends. Michael and Adam are great too, and I've enjoyed getting to know them. Outside of pickleball, we've only hung out a handful of times— poker nights or whenever Leo hosts something.

I've been spending more time with the guys lately, especially since things with Beth have been… complicated. I told them about Cooper when I got back from Newport, but I haven't mentioned that she's now working with me.

"Unfortunately, no prospects," I admit. "But I'm not really out there dating or actively looking. Things with Beth are difficult right now, and I'm trying to be respectful of the situation."

I hesitate, debating whether to bring up Cooper. "Do you guys remember that super hot chick I hooked up with in Newport Beach?"

"Yeah, I remember. Didn't you say she was great in the sack?" Leo says, and the others nod, remembering.

"Yeah. Well… she's the new project manager for Nexlytic." I can't help but laugh at their shocked faces. "Riddle me that, right?"

"Hold on," Leo interrupts. "Nexlytic, as in the company that works with yours at Elemental?"

"Yup," I say, folding my arms.

Adam jumps in, eyebrows raised. "Okay, but that's great, right? You gonna hook up with her again?"

"Hold on a second," Leo interjects, narrowing his eyes. "Things are a lot more complicated now that she works with him."

"Yeah," I scoff. "That, and the fact that she's apparently engaged. I think she may have cheated on him when we hooked up." I still don't know if I feel guilty or just pissed that I got involved—or maybe it's that I spent seven months thinking about her, only to find out she's not who I thought she was. Either way, it's not sitting right with me.

"Holy shit," Michael blurts, eyes wide.

"Did you ask her about it?" Leo asks.

"Yeah, I confronted her." I shift my weight from one foot to the other. "And I'll admit, it wasn't exactly my most mature moment… and I definitely crossed a line in terms of professionalism."

Leo winces. "Shit, mate. That's not good. What did you say?"

"I was a total prick. Made some asshole remarks about her fiancé and whether they were in an open relationship." Michael and Adam's shocked laughter bounces off the court walls.

"What'd she say?" Michael asks, still chuckling.

"Told me it wasn't my business, and then threw out something about reporting me to HR. I don't know… I fucked up. If she reports me, I could lose my job."

Michael whistles low, shaking his head. "Man, that's a mess."

"What do I do?" I ask.

"Just keep it professional. Stay cordial. That's all you can do," Adam says. "Do you work with her directly?"

"Not right now, but there's a big project coming up. I'll be working with her boss, and she'll probably be involved. We'll have some one-on-one interactions." I sigh, running a hand through my hair. "Worst part? I'm still so damn attracted to her."

Michael and Adam exchange glances, then burst out laughing.

I scowl. "What's so funny?"

Adam grins. "Dude, you're screwed. Just admit it—you wanna fuck her."

"Yeah, I definitely do," I admit. "But with her being a coworker, and everything with Beth… it just feels wrong. And now that she's engaged, it doesn't even matter anyway."

"Tread lightly, mate. You don't want to make this more complicated than it already is. Just keep it professional," Leo says.

"If she's engaged, there's really nothing you can do." Michael adds. "The past is the past—just leave it there. What's her name?"

"Cooper."

"Okay, so focus on your work and leave Cooper at the office. But, seriously, man, you might want to get laid—just to get her out of your head, for your sanity." Michael waves his hand like he's solved all my problems.

Adam glances at Michael and chuckles. "You might want to consider getting laid yourself… you know, for your sanity." He slaps Michael on the back, and we all crack up.

"Shut up," Michael mutters, rolling his eyes.

Leo checks his phone and grins. "Well, gentlemen, duty calls," he says, holding up his phone to show us the text from Vivian—an eggplant emoji followed by water drops.

"God, I hate you," Michael says, pulling out his phone. "I'm texting the same thing to Stella. Any bets?"

"'Fuck off'?" Adam suggests, laughing. "Or maybe she'll send back a pencil. You don't exactly give off eggplant vibes, bro."

We all crack up as we head toward the elevator.

"Oh, and Leo does?" Michael shoots back.

"Leo's proven he can pull off the eggplant emoji," Adam replies with a grin.

Michael's phone buzzes, and he bursts out laughing, holding it up for us to see—a middle finger emoji from Stella. Leo tries to smother his laugh but fails.

The elevator doors open, and Leo, still grinning, pats Michael on the back before stepping out. "See you later, guys."

"See you," I say as we all head our separate ways.

The guys are right. I just need to focus on work and forget it. She's engaged now—end of story.

Chapter 9

COOPER

November

Ryan scans the room before speaking. "Next on the agenda is the planned expansion into new markets. Jason, you've been leading this—care to give us an update?"

Seated at the head of the conference table, Ryan shifts his attention to Jason.

"Sure thing, Ryan. We've been exploring several potential markets, and I've gathered some preliminary research. But here's the thing... my plate's pretty full with the merger. This expansion is too crucial to split my focus, so I've decided to delegate this project to Cooper."

What? I hope my surprise isn't as obvious as everyone else's. I knew I'd be helping with this project, but being handed the reins is a complete shock. Jason could've at least given me a heads-up. I've only been here a month—I'm not sure if I'm ready for this.

Ryan raises an eyebrow, clearly caught off guard. It's obvious this decision wasn't run by him first. "Cooper? Are you sure about that? This is a high-priority project." His skepticism is anything but encouraging.

Jason shifts his gaze between Ryan and me, his tone steady. "Absolutely. She's proven more than capable. Cooper will be taking the lead on this project. You'll both run point on the execution and make key decisions together. I'll still sign off on anything major, but I trust her to manage the overall direction."

I swallow my anxiety, forcing a confident front—if only to shove it in Ryan's face. He clearly doubts me. "Thank you, Jason. I'm ready to step up and take on the challenge." I smile and turn to Ryan, locking eyes with him in a pointed stare.

Genevieve claps her hands together, beaming. "I think this is a great idea. Cooper's proven she's adaptable and handles pressure well. With your oversight, Ryan, I'm confident you two will do a great job."

Ryan nods, his eyes still sizing me up, doubt lingering. "Alright then. Cooper, let's set some time aside today to go over the initial plans. We'll need to hit the ground running." He clears his throat, shifting gears. "Okay, with that settled, let's move on to the budget and financials for this expansion. Melissa, I believe you've put together a preliminary budget overview?"

Melissa, the finance director of VantageSphere, stands to speak. "Yes, I have. Based on the initial market analysis…" She goes on about the budget for the project, and I know I should be paying closer attention, maybe even taking notes, but my mind is racing, and I can feel Ryan's eyes on me. I force myself to stare at Melissa, nodding at the right moments, but my thoughts are divided—half with the meeting, half with the idea of working so closely with Ryan.

For the past few weeks, we've mostly managed to stay out of each other's way. I avoid him as much as possible. Aside from morning meetings and the rare question, we barely interact. And when we do—it hasn't been pretty. But this project will change all that. We'll have to spend time together—every day, and I know he doesn't like me. Whether it's because he thinks I cheated on Brad, or something else entirely, his resentment is palpable.

I've caught him staring at me more than once. I never know if it's out of spite or if he still finds me attractive. He always brushes it off, quickly focusing his attention elsewhere, but the unspoken tension between us is impossible to ignore. And the thought of working with him one-on-one— it makes my stomach twist.

After Melissa wraps up, Jason finishes the meeting by covering a few key details about the expansion, and this time, I make sure to pay close attention.

"Alright, if no one has anything else, that's it from me. Let's have a productive day, and I'll see you all tomorrow morning at nine." Ryan's gaze lands directly on me. "Cooper, can you meet me in my office to go over our schedules for the next week?"

"Sure," I reply with a nod. "Can you give me ten minutes?"

He glances at his watch. "Yeah, but I have a meeting in thirty, so if you could swing by sooner, that'd be great." With a quick turn, he strides out the door, his irritation hanging in the air. *Great. This will be fun.*

I roll my eyes as soon as his back is turned. I had planned to grab a coffee, but instead, I trail after him to his office.

"I thought you needed ten minutes," Ryan says, his tone clipped.

"Yeah, well, I made it work now," I shoot back, the sharpness in my tone surprising even me. I remind myself that, no matter how much we both hate being stuck working together, Ryan is my superior. I soften my voice. "I know you're busy. Can I sit?" I gesture to the seat across from him.

He waves dismissively toward the chair as he sits, his focus already back on his computer, clicking away.

"Look, Ryan, I know you don't think I'm capable of managing this project, but I promise I am. I'll need some guidance… I'm new, after all. But with your oversight, and Jason's, I'll be teachable and adaptable."

His eyes shift from the screen to me, a pause stretching between us before he finally speaks. "I never said you weren't capable."

"Then what is it? Are you just upset that you have to work with me? I know it's not ideal, but—"

He cuts me off. "I never said I don't want to work with you, Cooper. It's fine, really. I was just surprised."

"Trust me, I'm as surprised as you are."

He turns his screen toward me. "We need an hour today to put together a project plan and schedule. There'll be daily check-ins and longer weekly meetings. I'm slammed with meetings today, though. Can you stay later tonight? We could meet in my office at five-thirty."

"I can do that. But can we meet in the lounge instead? Maybe one of the booths?" I suggest, not wanting to be stuck in this stifling office with him.

"Why the lounge? Afraid your fiancé might find out you're spending time alone with me? Or worried he'll hear about what happened last time we were alone?"

I roll my eyes. "You're unbelievable, you know that? This isn't about him. I just prefer the open space."

Ryan leans back in his chair, a smirk tugging at his lips. "Right, because last time we were alone, you couldn't wait to leave the open space to get me into a more… confined room with you."

There's that smirk again. Is he pissed, or just trying to get under my skin? Probably both.

"But hey, don't worry. I'll keep my shirt on this time. Wouldn't want to tempt you with my six-pack… again."

"God, you're arrogant," I mutter, exasperated. I take a breath, meeting his gaze, and my tone evens out. "Listen, if we're going to work together, we need to be on the same page. So if you've got any lingering comments about Newport, now's your chance. I don't want to start dreading my workdays because of this kind of bullshit. After today, if you cross that line, I'm taking it to HR. So if you've got something to say…" I exhale sharply. "You better say it now, because I'm done with it. I'm not putting up with this—even if you are my superior."

I cross my arms and stare him down. *Damn.* I'm proud of myself. I never stand up for myself like this with Brad. *Never.*

He holds my gaze, almost daring me to keep going. He's such an asshole. I can't believe I slept with him.

After what feels like minutes, Ryan breaks the silence. "Okay." He turns back to his computer, clicking his mouse like nothing happened.

Okay? That's all he's going to say?

"You don't have anything to add? No comments? No questions?"

Ryan's expression shifts, and he leans back in his chair, his composure annoyingly calm. "I guess I have a couple of questions."

I gesture for him to go on.

"Were you and your fiancé together when we slept together?"

"No," I say firmly. "We were broken up. I swear."

"Okay. How long were you broken up?"

I hesitate. "Why does that matter?"

"It matters," he says, matter-of-factly.

I sigh. "A week." *Well shit—this doesn't make me look great.* Especially because it was more like four days.

"A week?" Ryan scoffs. "You don't waste any time, do you?" He shakes his head as if I've somehow let him down. "Does he know you slept with me?"

"No. And I'd like to keep it that way." I hate how desperate I sound, almost pleading.

He pauses, his eyes narrowing thoughtfully. He's doing something with his mouth—maybe sucking on his cheek—and I hate that I find it sexy.

His voice softens. "Why didn't you tell him?"

"Because…" I fumble, my gaze dropping to my hands, my thumb nervously spinning the ring on my finger. "Why tell someone something that'll only hurt them?"

He arches a brow. "Is this really about protecting him, or are you protecting yourself?"

I glare back. "Okay, I think that's enough." The sting of tears threatens, and the last thing I want is for Ryan to see he's gotten to me.

He glances at his screen again. "I'll meet you at five-thirty…" He pauses, looking up. "In the lounge." Then, back to his computer. "Have a good day, Cooper," he says, a half-smile tugging at the corner of his lips. I hate how it makes my knees weak.

I don't even say goodbye. I just book it out of his office—his smoldering arrogance somehow pissing me off and turning me on at the same time.

I am *dreading* five-thirty tonight.

I wait for Ryan in one of the booths that line the lounge wall. Most people have gone home by now. Since the space is designed for remote work, the majority leave around four, knowing they can finish up at home or in the café downstairs. A few hit the gym upstairs or grab dinner before coming back later.

At five-forty, Ryan finally slides into the seat across from me, his laptop landing on the table.

"Hey," he says.

"Hey." I attempt a small smile. "How's your day been?" I pep talked myself all afternoon for this moment, determined to smooth things over with Ryan. I need him to like me—if we're going to be working together, we can't be at each other's throats.

"Very busy." He's clearly distracted, his gaze flicking to his phone as he types something quickly.

"Oh." *Okay…* I scramble for something to break the tension. We have to get past—whatever this is, or working together will be unbearable.

"Shit," Ryan mutters, still looking at his phone.

"Everything all right?" I ask.

He stares blankly at his phone for a moment longer. "Yeah," he finally says, putting it down. "Sorry, I just realized I double-booked myself for tomorrow morning. It's fine, I'll figure it out. Should we get started?"

He finally meets my eyes, his focus shifting.

"Did Jason get you caught up on what he had for the expansion today?" he asks.

"Yes," I say, trying to sound confident. "I feel good about it. I'm prepared."

He offers a slight smile. "Good. Do you want to take notes for us?"

I nod. "Sure."

"Let's start by outlining our objectives and reviewing the budget Melissa gave us," he suggests. "Then we can brainstorm potential cities that align with the company's goals. Did Jason already have some in mind?"

"Yeah, he sent me a list. Let me pull it up." As I search for the document Jason sent, I can feel Ryan's eyes on me, making my heart race. "Here it is." I turn my laptop so he can see.

"Okay, let's see. San Francisco, Austin, Boston…" He looks over the rest of the list. "This is a good start. We'll need to delegate research on these locations. We're on a tight deadline with the holidays coming up, so I'd like to condense what would usually take six weeks into four. That way, we can start traveling to whichever city we choose by mid-December and avoid the holiday travel chaos."

"Wait, we're traveling? As in, you and I?" My eyes widen. I didn't realize this was part of the expansion project. I guess it makes sense— we'll need to find a building and establish a presence—but I hadn't expected to be part of that.

"Yeah. Is that going to be a problem?" Ryan asks, his tone cautious.

"No," I reply quickly. "I just didn't know I'd be traveling. I'm just… surprised." *Oh my hell, I'm going to be traveling alone with Ryan?*

We go over our timeline, delegating tasks and setting deadlines, creating a schedule for when we'll meet to review progress and work together.

"Shit, I'm sorry. I have so many damn meetings every day. It's going to be hard to fit this into normal work hours. I hate to make you stay late, but we'll probably be having some long nights over the next few weeks," Ryan says, sounding apologetic.

"That's okay. I don't have much going on in the evenings. I'd rather stay busy. I can stay late tonight, too, if you think it'll help."

"Yeah, that'd be great. Why don't you start by creating a project plan that outlines our timeline and projected goals—something we can update as we go," he suggests. "Meanwhile, I'll outline a budget projection based on Melissa's numbers and look into potential real estate partners in each city. Then we can compare notes and decide on the best approach."

I nod, opening my laptop again. "Sounds good."

After a few minutes of silence, Ryan glances at me. "Don't you want to spend time with your fiancé?" He raises his hands in mock innocence. "I'm asking, genuinely."

I pause, unsure how much I want to share. I guess a little chit-chat won't hurt. "He's a lawyer, so he works a lot. He's on track to make partner. He rarely gets home before I'm in bed."

"Oh. That's got to be tough," he says, sounding sincere.

I shrug. "Yeah, it can be. But we make it work." I smile softly, appreciating the shift in his tone. "What about you? Anyone special in your life? Dating anyone?"

"Nah. I mean, I've got special people in my life, but not like that. Not right now."

"So… special people… family and friends?"

"Yeah, mostly," he says, his focus split between me and the computer screen.

"Are they here or in Arizona?"

"Both, I guess."

"Do you have any siblings?" I ask, hoping to get more than a few words out of him.

"Uh, yeah, I do."

Man, this is like pulling teeth. "Seriously?" I glance over, but he's still focused on his computer screen. "Yo, earth to Ryan."

Finally, he looks up. "What?"

I laugh. "I'm trying to get to know you a bit. You know, if we're going to be spending long hours working together it might be nice to know a few things about each other. Could you give me more than two or three words?"

He smiles faintly. "Sorry, I'm not great at listening and multitasking. I've been told it's a guy thing."

"Well, you're the first guy I've ever heard admit it. So, props to you."

He chuckles and closes his laptop. "What do you want to know?"

My heart skips a beat as his eyes lock onto mine, his attention completely on me—almost like the night we met. Heat rushes to my cheeks. God, I can't think. I break eye contact, glancing at my screen. "How many siblings do you have?" I ask as casually as I can manage.

I catch his grin out of the corner of my eye—like he knows exactly the effect he has on me. He's so damn cocky.

"Am I allowed to use more than one sentence?" The look he gives me carries a nostalgia in it that makes my pulse quicken.

I smile softly. "Yes. Look, Ryan, I…" I take a breath, calming my nerves. "I swear my intentions were in the right place… that night. I was trying to move on. Haven't you ever been so heartbroken that you just needed to numb the pain?"

His expression softens as he gives me a nod. "Yeah… I guess I have."

We don't break eye contact, a silent peace offering hanging in the air.

He finally breaks the silence. "I've got two younger sisters: Natalie, who's two years younger, and Erica, four years younger. They both live in Scottsdale with their husbands. Natalie has two girls, and Erica has a one-year-old boy." He grins. "How's that for more than two words?"

He leans back, stretching his arms above his head, and his shirt pulls tight against his muscles, just enough to remind me of what's underneath. Dammit. I drag my eyes back to my laptop, but it's no use. My brain keeps replaying the way his abs felt under my fingertips when he kissed me. *Jesus*. A pulsing starts between my thighs, irritating the hell out of me. How can I still be attracted to him when he's been such an arrogant prick? I force my mind back to the present—to focus on what he just said—because, unlike Ryan, I'm perfectly capable of listening and multitasking.

"Very good, Ryan. You officially know how to engage in a conversation," I tease.

"Your turn," he says.

"Well, you have to ask me a question."

"Tell me about your family. I know your dad lives in Newport, and you have a sister. What else?"

"Well, I'm from Chicago. Grew up in Arlington Heights, north of the city. My parents divorced when I was ten, which was rough, but I always loved visiting my dad in California. It felt cool as a kid—to get on a plane and fly to see my dad who lived on the beach. My friends were jealous, and I kind of relished that. But I was also the only one with divorced parents, so really, I was jealous of them." I furrow my brows. "Ugh, sorry, getting all nostalgic and sappy."

"Anyway, my sister Casey—who's my best friend—lives in Huntington Beach, near my dad. She's married to Greg, and they have my nephew, Mason, who's two. And my mom lives here in Highland Park with her very wealthy husband, Steve. And that's my family in a nutshell. Fascinating, right?" I say, sarcastically.

"Is your dad remarried?" Ryan asks.

I scoff. "Not at the moment. I love my dad, and we have a great relationship, but he's not the monogamous type, if you get my drift. He cheated on my mom, and he's been married five times. And now, when he's seeing someone"—I make air quotes—"'seriously,' it's hard to want to build a relationship with them because I know she's just the flavor of the week, you know? Casey and I were super close to his third wife, Jill. I loved her—we still keep in touch. But it gets old falling in love with someone, only to have them disappear from your life a few years later." I blow out a breath. "Geez. Sorry, I just dumped all that on you."

Ryan laughs. "Hey, I asked."

"But you didn't ask for a monologue."

"I enjoyed it. I'm glad you vomited your entire life story on me," he says, grinning.

We get back to work, but I can't help glancing at him every few minutes. He really is so cute. I honestly don't know how he's single. I keep my eyes on my computer while casually asking, "So… really, no girlfriend?"

I can feel his eyes on me, burning my skin with the intensity. "Nope. No girlfriend."

"Not the relationship type of guy, or what?" I keep my focus on my screen.

"I wouldn't say that… I'm just not dating at the moment. Are we asking more personal questions now?"

I allow myself to look over. "I guess. I mean, isn't that how you get to know someone?"

He grins. "Good, because I've been dying to ask you about your tattoo. You know… the one on your ass."

I purse my lips to prevent myself from smiling. "I don't know if that's an appropriate question to ask at work."

"Why not? You're asking about my relationships. I can't ask about a tattoo? It's not like I asked you to show it to me. I can close my eyes and see it anytime I want to." He grins again, and my God, his smile could melt anyone. He closes his eyes. "Ah, I can see it right now. Those little words… two, I believe, they're definitely on the right cheek."

"Okay. Stop that."

"Stop what?"

"Open your eyes, Ryan."

"No way in hell. Not until you tell me."

I can't help but laugh. "Fine. I'll tell you, but you have to open your eyes first." He opens them with a winning smirk on his face. "It says beach bum. And it was something my sister and I did impulsively when I turned twenty-one and I was staying at my dad's. Satisfied? Now stop picturing my ass. Coworkers aren't supposed to know these things."

He sits back, folding his arms with the most cocky grin on his face. "Oh, I know a lot more than that, Cooper… I've seen you naked, remember?" He leans forward, looking around to make sure no one is close by, even though he knows we're practically the only ones here. His voice drops to a low whisper. "And I've heard those sounds you make when you're about to… you know."

A tingly sensation spreads through my entire body as he locks eyes with me. My body reacts before I can stop it, the tension between us becoming almost unbearable. But he's not the only one who's seen the other naked.

I lean in too, lowering my voice to match his. "You sure remember an awful lot about that night, Ryan…" My lips curve into a playful grin. "You know, I can picture you naked too. And I remember the sounds you made that night as well." I bite my bottom lip for effect, keeping my eyes locked on his.

His smile falters for a split second, and I revel in the brief look of surprise before he regains his composure.

"Really?" he says, his voice still smooth but with a hint of something that feels like a challenge.

I nod slowly. "Mhm. I have a pretty good memory."

His eyes darken, his smirk returning but this time with more edge. "Yeah? You like what you see?"

I freeze for a second, my heart racing at the shift in his tone. His words send a confusing bolt of electricity through my veins, but I don't want to give him the satisfaction of knowing just how much he's getting to me.

He leans in closer, his voice dropping even lower. "Go ahead, Cooper. Close your eyes. Picture it. It doesn't bother me—in fact, I quite enjoy the fact that you picture me naked."

I swallow, my throat dry. He's definitely taking this further than I expected, but there's a thrill in the way he's challenging me. My heart pounds in my chest, and I know I should shut it down, push him away. But we've only just scratched the surface of the sexual tension, and it's too tempting not to explore. I bite the inside of my cheek, refusing to look away.

"Is that what you do?" I ask, my voice quieter, but steady. "Close your eyes and picture me?"

His smile widens. "More often than you think."

Did he just admit to picturing me naked? Has he jerked off thinking about me? God, that turns me on. I stare at his lips, remembering what a great kisser he is—warm, controlled, commanding. *I am engaged. I am engaged.* I repeat it like a mantra. But the part of me that should stop this is nowhere to be found.

Before I can respond, I hear footsteps approaching. I glance over my shoulder just as one of our coworkers walks by, giving us a polite nod before heading into the office kitchen.

I turn back to Ryan, who's watching me intently. "Saved by the bell," he murmurs.

I shake my head, forcing a smile as I turn back to my computer. "You wish."

I don't get home until close to eight, and I'm exhausted. I don't know how Brad does this every day. My brain is fried. All I want to do is veg out in front of the TV. It might be a *Sex and the City* kind of night. I step off the elevator onto the sixteenth floor and walk down the long hallway to our apartment. When I push the door open, I'm hit with the smell of dinner cooking. My mouth waters at the sight of Brad standing shirtless over the stove, Post Malone blasting in the background.

He must not have heard me come in because he doesn't turn around. I texted him earlier to let him know I'd be working late, and he said he would be too. I walk over and wrap my arms around him. "Hi," I say softly. "I thought you were working late too."

"I was… but I managed to sneak away early, to surprise you, make you dinner." He turns to greet me with a proper hug and kiss.

I'm stunned. "Thank you, babe. This is so nice… I'm starving. I'm exhausted too—I don't know how you work these hours every day."

"Well, coming home to you makes it a little easier." He tilts my chin up and kisses me, longer this time.

Brad rarely does this—leave work early—and to cook for me? It's incredibly thoughtful—but also a little out of character. I want my fiancé to be this guy—thoughtful and sweet because he loves me. But the nagging feeling inside me won't go away—that quiet voice in the back of my mind that whispers Casey might be right. That he does this when he needs to make up for something. Maybe this is the new him, though. He's been more considerate since I got this new job.

I wrap my arms tighter around him and sigh.

Chapter 10

RYAN

December

I stare at my screen, my brain's fried. It's Friday night, and Cooper and I are at it again. It's already seven, and I can feel myself tapping out. We've got so much to catch up on. I've been gone all week, traveling for work. The nice thing about traveling is that usually it's to Phoenix, where headquarters are, so it's a free ticket home to see my family and friends. I left for Arizona Tuesday morning and got back late last night. I managed to squeeze in a night with some friends and stopped in to see my parents while I was there.

Cooper and I have been working on this project for almost three weeks now. In a week and a half, we head to Austin, Texas—where we decided to base the new expansion. Austin's a big tech hub, and the numbers made sense. We'll be there for three days, trying to get a feel for the place and hopefully find something that fits. Then, we'll go back in January to finalize everything.

Things have been pretty good with Cooper. Surprisingly good, actually—almost fun. There've been moments of flirtation, which confuse me, considering she's engaged. I know I'm partly to blame for it; I initiated it. And I feel a little bad about it, but it's also innocent… mostly.

It's been fun getting to know her beyond the initial awkwardness. She's smart, quick-witted, and has a sense of humor that matches mine in the best way. She's proven to be a valuable asset—not just to this expansion, but to Nexlytic as a whole. Her ideas are sharp, and her drive is impressive. If I'm being honest, I like her more than I probably should.

I still don't know how I feel about the whole *sleeping with me while she was broken up for a week* thing. It bothers me, but hey, I got to sleep with Cooper Bradley, so no real complaints here. The problem is, every time I look at her, I wish it would happen again. I think about it too much—at work, at home, everywhere. It's becoming a distraction. And if she wasn't engaged, maybe I'd stand a chance.

I close my laptop, too distracted to think. "Want to take a break? Grab a drink at Viv's upstairs?" I ask.

She pauses. "Is that allowed?"

"Sure it is. Honestly, almost anything's allowed as long as we get our work done. I wouldn't recommend drinking before three on a workday, but hey, to each their own. Come on, I need a break. We can bring our work with us."

We gather our things and head to the elevator, riding up to the tenth floor. It's not crowded yet, since it's still early. I assume most of the people here this early work in the building. It usually picks up around ten. Soft bench-style seating lines the far end wall, with round tables spaced between and lounge chairs and stools on the opposite side. We grab a table in the corner, Cooper taking the booth side while I sit across from her in a chair.

The cocktail waitress comes over, and I order a tequila with soda water. Cooper orders a spicy margarita. "Is that all you drink?" I ask, remembering that's what she was drinking in Newport.

"No," she says with a smile. "I usually drink spiked seltzers or darker beer, but at a cocktail lounge, you order a cocktail. And spicy margs are my favorite."

"Is Brad working late tonight?" I ask. I recently found out her fiancé is Brad, though I haven't met him yet. She says he works nearby, and I wonder why he never swings by to say hi, or meet her for lunch. That's what I'd do if I had a fiancée working close by.

"No. He's been in New York all week for work. He comes home early tomorrow morning."

"How often does he travel for work?"

"It varies, but usually three to four times a month, depending on the deal and where it is. Most of the time, it's just short trips—two or three days. But this week, he was trying to finalize a merger and close another big deal, so he extended his trip."

She opens her laptop to start working, and I know I should do the same, but I just need a break. I can't help but watch her as she focuses in, pursing her lips together. *God, her lips.* She's got that whole Scarlett Johansson vibe—full lips, flawless skin, striking features, big boobs—she's curvy. *Shit.* I can't be thinking about her body right now—or ever. We're still at work, and she's engaged. I've got to keep things professional.

Her long hair is down, one side tucked behind her ear, the other falling around her face. We have a pretty chill dress code, but management positions are expected to keep it slightly professional. Cooper always does. She's in a tight white dress that shows off every curve. Her arms are toned, just enough to give them that sexy shape.

We work for a solid thirty minutes, mostly in silence, with only the occasional question or comment. We're on our second drink when she shifts in her seat, bumping my leg under the table—giving it a playful kick. "God, get your long-ass legs out of here," she teases. "You're in my personal space."

I can't help but smirk. "Your personal space? You're the one trying to play footsie."

She kicks me again, more firmly this time. "Footsie? What am I, twenty-one, trying to flirt with my boss? Get them out of here!"

"Ow! Is that a fucking heel?" I laugh, giving her a gentle kick back. "Maybe that's exactly what you're doing, and you just don't know it yet."

Her eyes narrow, then she raises an eyebrow, her tone turning unexpectedly bold. "Trust me, if I was flirting, you'd know."

There's an intensity in her voice I wasn't expecting, and suddenly, the room feels hot. And *damn* if it doesn't do something to me.

I lean back, pretending to be unaffected. "So, this isn't flirting?"

She rolls her eyes, a smile playing at the corner of her lips. "Not even close."

I raise an eyebrow. "So what does flirting with you look like, then?"

She bites her lip, as if considering how to respond, her gaze meeting mine. "I guess you'll never know, huh?"

I chuckle. "Oh, I highly doubt that." I cross my arms confidently, then lean forward on them, resting on the table.

"I wouldn't hold my breath, Ryan… unless you're planning to stay single forever."

I grin. "So you're telling me there's a chance." I say, mimicking Jim Carrey in *Dumb and Dumber.*

She laughs at that. "Well, lucky for you that we spend so much time together." She leans back. "Plenty of time to wait and see, I guess."

"I guess so," I reply, eyes locked on hers.

She scoffs. "You really need to get laid." My heart skips a beat. She lets her eyes roam over me, like she's remembering what it was like to be the one to do that, and it catches me off guard. This is definitely getting interesting. If nothing else, it's making work a lot more fun.

"Who says I'm not getting laid?"

She raises an eyebrow. "Are you?"

"Why? You jealous of all the women I'm sleeping with?"

She snickers. "Please." Her eyes shift from her computer screen back to mine. "You're such a liar." She shakes her head, like she's trying to convince herself I'm bluffing—almost as if she's jealous, and that thought sends a surge of satisfaction through me.

"Think what you want—but I'm more than satisfied with my sex life. It's not that difficult to find someone to sleep with. You remember, right?" I hold her gaze confidently, not giving anything away. She doesn't need to know the truth—that the only other woman I've slept with in the past year is Beth. It's been months since I've had sex, and it's *killing* me.

"Whatever helps you sleep at night." She laughs softly, not looking up.

I turn my attention back to my computer, though my eyes keep drifting to her. It's annoying, how she can take up so much space in my head without even trying. A few minutes later, she scowls at her screen.

"Hey, can you take a look at this property in East Austin? I'm trying to figure out if the zoning would allow us to add another floor if we buy it. Does that seem possible?" She turns her laptop toward me, but I get up and move to her side, leaning in to look at her screen. My arm brushes against hers as I peer at the map.

"Let me see… It looks like it's in a mixed-use area. We might be able to go up another floor, but I'm not sure about the exact limits here." I point to a section on the screen. "Hmm. I could run this by Leo to be sure—he knows all about these kinds of regulations." I click on a link to read more. Cooper's no longer looking at the screen—her eyes are on me, and it makes the blood in my veins run hot. "Yeah, I'm pretty sure it's possible, but I'll check with Leo." I pull away from the screen, turning to meet her gaze.

She smiles. "Okay. Thanks for looking."

For a moment, I'm transported back to Newport, lying across from her, staring at each other. I swear, for a second, her eyes flick to my lips and back. I swallow hard, my pulse racing.

"Cooper," I start, glancing at her mouth, but before I can say another word, she cuts me off.

"I should probably get going," she says. She closes her laptop and starts gathering her things, hurriedly. "It's getting late. I need to call Brad before he goes to bed." She stands with her stuff in hand. "Do you want to walk down with me, or are you going to stay a bit longer?"

Well, that's one way to get out of a situation that's starting to blur lines.

"I'll come with you. I should get going too," I say, glancing at my watch.

"Oh, you got a hot date?" she teases.

I chuckle softly. "Not exactly."

I gather my stuff, and we head to the elevator. She's antsy as we wait for it, checking her watch, like the one-minute wait is too much.

"You in a hurry to get somewhere?" I ask, raising my brows.

She looks over at me. "Sorry, I just didn't realize the time, and it's an hour later in New York. I really want to talk to Brad."

I don't buy it. She felt something at that table. I know she did—because I felt it too. Now, she's running from it, which I can respect. She's doing the right thing. But it doesn't mean she didn't feel it. "Can I drive you home?"

She takes a deep breath. "No, I'm good. I'll call an Uber."

"Cooper, I'm not going to let you take an Uber alone. You've been drinking, and I feel it's my responsibility to see you home safely. Please. As your boss, I'm asking you to let me drive you—for liability reasons."

"You're not my boss… And you've been drinking too."

"Not your direct boss, but close enough. And I can hold my liquor—takes more than a drink to get me buzzed."

She sighs. "Fine. You can drive me. But I have to stop on our floor to get my coat and the rest of my things."

"That's okay. So do I."

We ride down in silence, the air in the elevator growing thicker with each passing second. When the doors finally open, we both rush out, heading in different directions to grab our things.

We meet back at the elevator and head down to the parking garage. Once we settle into my Range Rover, I hand her my phone so she can enter her address. It's only a little over a mile away.

"Are you bringing anyone to the Christmas Party tomorrow night?" Cooper asks.

"Nope."

"Why not?"

I furrow my brows. One thing I've noticed about Cooper over the past few weeks—she's nosy. Never shies away from an uncomfortable or personal question.

"Just don't have anyone I'm interested in bringing," I say, shrugging.

"Well, why not? Do you even try to date? Are you on all the apps?"

"Jesus, Cooper. Can't you just ask normal questions?"

"What? I can't ask why you're not dating?" she presses.

I change my voice, mocking a friendly interview. "Hey, 'What's your favorite movie, Ryan?' My favorite movie? Why, thank you for asking, Cooper. My favorite movie is *Borat*. 'Why?' you ask. Well, because I can't *not* laugh my ass off when I watch it." I turn to her with a grin. "What about you? What's your favorite movie?"

She rolls her eyes, clearly annoyed. "Fine. My favorite movie is *The Devil Wears Prada*. I don't know why, I just like it. And I've never seen *Borat*, but it looks dumb."

"See? Not so hard to ask normal questions. And *Borat* is not dumb. It's hilarious."

"Yeah, that was fun. Thank you for that profound insight," she shoots back. "Now… why don't you date?"

"Why do you care about my love life, anyway?" I ask, forcing a casual tone. The last thing I want to do is explain the fucked-up reality of my life right now.

She leans back, watching me. "I don't *care,* I'm just… curious. You don't strike me as the 'forever single' type."

I let out a short laugh. "What do I strike you as?"

She shrugs. "I don't know… the relationship guy."

"I guess I'm still looking for that special someone. Sometimes life doesn't go according to plan."

Her eyes narrow slightly. "So… what? You just haven't found that special someone? You don't even date. How do you find what you want when you're not even trying?"

"I had what I wanted, it's just…" I look over at her. "Never mind."

"What do you mean, never mind?"

I hesitate. "Nothing… It's complicated."

"Complicated how? Is this about the relationship you mentioned in Newport? Was it serious, or…?" she trails off, maybe sensing she hit a nerve.

My grip tightens on the steering wheel. "Something like that," I mutter.

She turns to look out the window, and I catch her reflection in the glass—her lips pressing together like she wants to say something more but isn't sure she should. "Complicated doesn't mean impossible, you know."

There's something in her voice that makes me glance over. She's still staring out the window, but I can tell she's thinking hard about something.

We drive in silence for a minute. Finally, I break it. "So, Brad's coming to the party tomorrow night?"

"Yeah," she says. "He wasn't going to, but I guess he wants to meet everyone, see what it's all about."

I nod. "Should be interesting." The words come out heavier than I intended. I'm not sure what's worse—the idea of meeting her fiancé or the fact that I'm going to our work Christmas party alone.

We pull up in front of her building, and she starts to unbuckle her seatbelt. Then she pauses, her hand on the door handle, and turns to look at me. "Thanks for the ride, Ryan. And for… you know, not letting me take an Uber."

"No problem," I say, trying to keep my voice even. "And, Cooper?"

She pauses, her brow furrowing slightly. "Yeah?"

I take a breath, choosing my words carefully. "About earlier… I know it's complicated. But if things were different, I think you'd know exactly what I'm looking for…."

A moment of silence fills the car while she just looks at me. And then a slow, almost sad smile forms on her lips. "Goodnight, Ryan."

She steps out of the car, closing the door softly behind her. I watch as she disappears into the building, then lean back in my seat and let out a long breath. Damn, I'm playing with fire.

Chapter 11

COOPER

The ringing of my phone startles me awake. I push my sleeping mask up, wincing as the daylight blinds me. *God, what time is it?* My hand fumbles for my phone on the nightstand, and I squint at the screen—Casey's calling, and it's almost 11:00 AM. I swipe to answer, my voice groggy. "Holy shit, sis. I'm just waking up."

Casey laughs. "Oh my God. Isn't it like eleven there? Are you hungover or something?"

"No. I had a couple of drinks last night, but only two. Ugh, I hate sleeping this late. Makes me feel tired all day."

"Yeah, I hate that too." Casey pauses. "Hey, did you book your flight out here yet? Or at least figure out the dates? I'm trying to plan some holiday stuff and I don't want to overlap with your visit."

"I haven't booked it yet. I'm still waiting on Brad. But don't plan around me. I'll be there for at least a week, maybe longer. I'll talk to him today and let you know."

"Okay. So, did you go out with girlfriends last night?"

"No, I was working late."

"But you said you had drinks," she says, confused.

"Oh. Um, yeah. I had drinks with Ryan, at work, if you can believe that." I laugh, trying to downplay it. "I actually drank margaritas at work, with my sort of boss, while working. How cool is my job?"

"What? Yeah, your job gets cooler every time I talk to you. But can we go back to you having drinks with Ryan? What's that about?"

I laugh uncomfortably, feeling a weird knot forming in my stomach. "Well, we were working late, and he said he needed a break—asked if I wanted to go upstairs to the cocktail lounge for drinks. He said we could work there. So, we did, and it was productive and fun."

"What do you mean by fun?" she presses, her tone full of curiosity.

I choose my words carefully. "I don't know. We worked, we laughed, it wasn't anything serious. That kind of fun."

"Uh-huh. Sure. Are you slowly falling in love with your boss?"

"Okay, shut up."

She laughs. "Relax. I'm joking. I just find it interesting that Ryan went from one-night stand, to boss, to hating him, to working with him, to now you're having drinks together and enjoying his company. I mean, it's confusing, sis."

I roll my eyes as I get up to make coffee. "Yeah, I guess it is," I mutter.

"Do you like him?"

"Casey, don't ask me that. Why would you ask that when you know I love Brad?" I reach for the coffee grounds, my fingers fumbling as I try to sound casual. "I know you don't like him, but..."

"But," Casey cuts in, her voice dripping with teasing sarcasm, "it's hard not to notice you're having fun with your boss—oh wait, I mean the guy you had the most incredible sex of your life with."

My heart skips a beat. I try to laugh it off, but the comment hits me like a ton of bricks—forcing me to look at it—the truth of it. I open my mouth to respond just as the front door unlocks and swings open. Brad walks in, his keys jangling as he steps inside.

"Oh, hey, Brad just got home. Can I call you back later?"

"Yeah, call me tomorrow. I'll be busy the rest of the day."

"Okay, great. Love you," I say, keeping my voice steady as I glance toward Brad, who's setting his things down on the countertop.

"Love you too, sis," Casey replies.

I end the call, walking over to Brad. "Hey, I didn't think you'd be home for another hour or so."

"The flight landed early." His eyes travel over me. "Did you just wake up?" he asks, chuckling.

I glance down at my oversized T-shirt and bare legs, trying not to laugh. "Yep," I admit. I wrap my arms around his neck and kiss him, trying to shake off the lingering unease from my conversation with Casey. "How was your trip? Did you get everything done that you were hoping for?"

"Yeah. It was a very successful trip. I managed to satisfy our pain-in-the-ass client and close that deal."

"Ah, that's great, babe. Are you hungry? I can make us some brunch." His hand slides under my shirt, his fingers tracing the bare skin of my waist.

"You don't have any shorts on?" he says, raising an eyebrow.

"No, sir, I do not," I reply seductively.

Brad lifts me onto the countertop, his hand sliding up my thigh. "Then I know exactly what I want for brunch," he whispers, his lips brushing mine. I inhale sharply, letting my legs spread to make room for him.

"I missed you," he murmurs against my lips.

"I missed you too," I whisper. His body feels good against mine, familiar. I melt into his kiss, his hands wandering higher, fingers brushing the edge of my underwear. A pulse beats between my thighs as his mouth trails down my neck.

"I want you," I murmur, my hands caressing the back of his neck, desperate to forget my phone call with Casey.

"Patience," he says with a chuckle, slipping his hand beneath the fabric. I gasp, letting go of everything but the way he makes me feel.

We don't make it to the bedroom. We stay right there on the counter, lost in each other. Afterward, I clean up and make us some brunch.

"What time is that party tonight?" Brad asks, as he takes a bite of his burger.

"It starts at seven, so I was thinking we could get there around seven-thirty?" I sip my water. "I know you don't love these things, but I appreciate you going."

"I don't mind going, baby. I'm actually looking forward to seeing where you work."

I smile. "Well, that's good then."

As I get ready for the party, my anxiety starts to get the best of me. I can't stop thinking about last night—Ryan's words echoing in my head: *If things were different, I think you'd know exactly what I'm looking for…*

What did he mean by that?

If things were different… I hate how much I care. It's ridiculous. I just had incredible sex in the kitchen hours ago with my fiancé, the man I love. But somehow, when I'm with Ryan, I miss Brad less. And when I'm not with Ryan, I find myself missing him, too.

I'm nervous about Brad meeting Ryan. Brad's not stupid, and he's always been the jealous type. I haven't been completely honest with him either—he thinks I'm working on this project with a whole team. I told him Ryan, Genevieve, and I are the leads, but I left out the part where it's just been Ryan and me staying late. And I definitely didn't mention that it'll only be the two of us traveling to Austin.

Shit. I suddenly feel like bringing Brad into my work life is a terrible idea. I stare at myself in the mirror, taking a deep breath before slowly blowing it out. *I can do this.*

"*I am strong. I am brave. I am beautiful. I am enough,*" I whisper to my reflection, repeating the mantra I've told myself countless times when I've felt like I couldn't keep going. These words have been whispered into this mirror hundreds of times—sometimes through smiles, but mostly through tears. *I've got this.*

I smooth down the rich burgundy fabric of the dress I bought, the one that hugs my curves perfectly. It fits like a glove, from the sweetheart neckline down to the hem that lands mid-thigh. Thin spaghetti straps leave my shoulders bare, and the corset-style top makes my boobs look incredible. Cinched tightly at the waist, it gives me that perfect hourglass shape.

I turn slightly, peeking at the back. *Damn, it's a pretty dress.* The back laces up in a crisscross of thin straps, giving it just the right amount of playful edge. It feels sexy, the way it shows off so much of my back, but there's something empowering about it, too. The deep color pops against my fair skin, making me feel bold and confident.

I finish putting soft waves in my hair and can't wait to see Brad's reaction when I step out. He's always been a sucker for a sexy dress. But in the back of my mind, I hope Ryan notices me in it, too. And God, the guilt washes over me.

Is it normal to feel something like this when you love someone else? Is this what Brad feels when he cheats on me?

Brad walks in, eyes widening. "Holy shit, baby."

"Agh, you're not supposed to come in yet! I was going to make a dramatic entrance."

He grins, looking me up and down. "I don't need a show. I want you bent over somewhere, in this dress, *now*," he playfully demands.

"Well, you're just going to have to wait."

Brad steps closer, arms reaching for me, lust clear in his eyes.

"No, babe," I say, swatting his hands away and pulling back. "No touchy. Not yet. Let it build."

"Jesus. You're killing me," he groans, shaking his head.

I press a hand to his chest with a smile. "You'll survive. Besides, look at you—you're devilishly handsome tonight." I plant a soft kiss on his lips before stepping back. "Come on, let's go."

* * * * *   * * * * *

We've been here for thirty minutes, and I've somehow managed to avoid bumping into Ryan. I'm postponing that meeting for as long as possible, guzzling my drink like a twenty-one-year-old at their first bar. I've caught Ryan's eye from across the room a couple of times. It felt like he was checking me out, but I can't be sure—there are a lot of people here.

The entire floor is decked out with classy holiday decor, from garlands and bouquets to sparkling centerpieces on every table. The bar area is dimly lit, creating a warm, moody ambiance, while a live piano player in the corner fills the room with soothing renditions of classic Christmas music. Whoever planned this party nailed it—everything feels elegant yet inviting. I've introduced Brad to a few people on my team, but we've spent most of the night chatting with Genevieve.

"So, Genevieve," Brad says, swirling his drink, "Cooper mentioned you're working on this expansion with her?"

Genevieve looks at me, clearly confused. I shoot her a pleading look, silently begging her to cover for me.

"Oh, yeah," she says, smiling smoothly at Brad. "It's been really busy, but exciting. Cooper does most of the heavy lifting, though. She's great at her job."

I mouth a silent thank you to her, and she gives a subtle nod.

Then Genevieve's eyes light up as she spots someone behind me. "Oh hey, there's Leo and Vivian. Have you met them yet, Cooper?"

"No, I haven't had the chance."

"Well, let me introduce you both. They're with Ryan—come on," Genevieve says, leading the way. I hesitate for a split second, but reluctantly follow.

"Ryan?" Brad asks, his curiosity piqued. "Isn't that the guy you and Genevieve are working with on the expansion?"

"Yeah… I'll introduce you." I send a silent prayer up that this stays normal.

"Ryan!" Genevieve calls out. Ryan turns toward us, his gaze landing on me before shifting to Brad, then back to me.

"Hey, Cooper," he says, flashing a smile that feels both too warm and too knowing. Then, turning to Brad, he offers his hand. "Hi, I'm Ryan. You must be Brad. I've heard so much about you."

Brad shakes his hand, but his smile doesn't quite reach his eyes. "Nice to meet you, Ryan. Funny thing—I've heard almost nothing about you," he says, his gaze sliding over to me. "Except that you're on this expansion project with Cooper and Genevieve."

Oh. My. God. I feel my stomach drop.

Ryan gives me a knowing look. "Well, there's not much to tell about me. Just a guy who works a lot—like you, I've been told."

Genevieve jumps in, *thank God.* "Ryan, Cooper hasn't met the Westons yet. I thought you could introduce them since they're your friends."

"Oh, sure." He turns and taps a man on the shoulder, who turns around. And *holy hell—hello Mr. Weston.* Genevieve wasn't exaggerating—Leo is incredibly attractive. He taps the woman next to him on her shoulder, and when she turns, I realize this must be Vivian. She's just as stunning as Leo, a real Hollywood red-carpet-worthy couple.

"Leo, this is Cooper, the new Project Manager for Nexlytic, and her fiancé, Brad. Cooper, this is Leo and Vivian—they own Elemental Hub and are the hosts of tonight's party."

"Nice to meet you, mate," Leo says, shaking Brad's hand first, then extending his hand to me. "Cooper, it's great to finally put a face to the name. I've heard great things about you," he says. There's a brief pause before he adds, "and your work," as if catching himself.

Brad raises an eyebrow. "Leo Weston? As in *the* Leo Weston—big-time real estate investor, Leo Weston?"

Leo gives a small, self-deprecating smile. "I dabble here and there, but yeah, I've done a bit of real estate."

"More than a bit," Brad says, grinning. "You're practically a legend. I've followed some of your projects—you've built quite a portfolio."

Leo nods modestly. "That's kind of you to say. What line of work are you in that has you following my projects?"

Brad leans in, his interest evident. "I'm in mergers and acquisitions. I've handled a few deals involving property development and investment portfolios, so your name comes up quite a bit. It's impressive."

The two of them dive into conversation, leaving me to wonder why Leo Weston would know anything about me. Heard great things about me? Why? My mind spins, and as I glance at Leo and Ryan, now fully engaged in a conversation with Brad, it hits me—they're friends.

And then it dawns on me. Ryan might have told him about me—about Newport.

And that is not ideal.

Vivian gasps. "Cooper, I love your dress. It's gorgeous."

"Thank you. That's so nice of you. I love yours as well," I say.

"Thank you. So, how are you liking it here?" Vivian asks me.

"I'm really liking it… It's been good for me."

"That's great. And you've got such a solid team. I heard you and Ryan are working on a project together?" she asks, glancing over at him.

"Yeah, we are. It's a lot of work, but it's coming together," I reply, trying to keep my tone casual.

"That's good. Well, Ryan's a great guy. I'm sure he's easy to work with."

"Yeah, he is a good guy," I say, though what I really want is to pull Vivian aside and ask all the things Ryan won't tell me.

"Oh! Vivian, I've been meaning to ask," Genevieve says, lowering her voice slightly. "Have you heard anything about Beth recently?"

Vivian shifts, casting a quick glance at the guys. "I have… but I'm not sure if I should be the one to talk about it. You'll have to ask Ryan."

Genevieve sighs, clearly disappointed. "Yeah, okay. That makes sense."

I frown, feeling suddenly out of the loop. "Who's Beth?" I ask, trying to mask the unease rising inside me.

Genevieve turns to me with a quick glance at Vivian before her voice drops to almost a whisper. "Beth is Ryan's wife."

Wife?

I freeze, my heart sinking into my stomach. I can feel my pulse quicken as my mind scrambles to process what she just said.

"Wait, what? Ryan's married?" *What the fuck?*

Genevieve turns to me, eyebrows raised. "Yeah, you don't know about Beth? I figured, with how much time you two spend together, it would've come up."

My mind reels. *Married?* After everything he's said to me about Brad? The anger boils up inside me, a knot of betrayal tightening in my gut.

Vivian looks uncomfortable, her brows knitting together. "I don't think we should talk about Beth here. It's Ryan's life, and I don't feel right discussing it."

I force a smile, my throat tightening. "Will you excuse me?" I say, my voice strained. "I'm going to grab another drink. Do you ladies want anything?" They both tell me they're good, and I'm beelining it to the open bar before I really process their answers.

Ryan's married. I let that fact sink in. The nerve of him—the audacity—to confront me that first week of work, accusing me of being dishonest about my relationship with Brad. *Ugh.* He made me question myself, made me feel like a cheater, like a shitty person. And all along, he had a *wife?*

"Can I get a shot of tequila, please?" I ask the bartender. The glass appears, and I kick it back with ease. I need more than a buzz to numb the thoughts that are spinning in my head.

I turn to find Brad, to drag him out of here, but then I see Ryan approaching the bar. His eyes lock onto mine, and that cocky grin of his surfaces, as if he hasn't been lying to me for months now.

"Can I get a Blue Moon, a Guinness, and a tequila neat?" he asks the bartender before his attention flicks back to me.

He chuckles. "Did you just take a shot by yourself?"

"Yup. Sometimes you just need to take the edge off." I pause, asking myself if being a total bitch is necessary—and yeah, it is. I turn to him. "You ever think you know someone and then"—I smack my hands together, the sound sharp—"bam, surprise, you didn't know shit?" My tone drips with sarcasm as I stare him down.

Ryan's eyes narrow slightly, but he plays it cool. "Alright, subtle. Are you talking about me? If you've got something to say, just say it."

I let out a dry, humorless laugh, shaking my head. "Why would I have something to say to you? It's not like you tell me shit."

His gaze sharpens, but he still doesn't push. Is he confused? Does he know why I'm pissed, or is he just too arrogant to care? Either way, I'm done.

I grab the Blue Moon that I know is for Brad and walk off to find him.

"Hey, babe, I brought you your beer," I say, handing it to him.

Brad takes it, eyeing me. "Thanks. Were you just taking shots with Ryan?" His tone is casual, but the question catches me off guard.

"No. I took one by myself, and then Ryan came over to get drinks for you guys."

Brad raises an eyebrow. "You never take shots. What's up?"

I shrug, playing it cool. "I don't know, just felt like one."

"Is something wrong?"

Great. Now I have Brad up my ass with suspicion. "No. You know I'm just more of an introvert. I'm feeling anxious, I guess."

"Why do you feel anxious?" he asks, his tone cautious, probing but not aggressive.

"Brad, don't quiz me right now, okay? I just wanted to loosen up. I wasn't really feeling my drink, so I took a shot to get a little buzz going quicker." I flash him a flirty smile, rubbing his arm. "Besides, you've never complained about me getting drunk before."

He smiles for a moment but then his expression hardens. "That Ryan guy wants to fuck you."

I laugh it off, shaking my head. "What? No, he doesn't."

Brad's chuckle is humorless, his voice dropping. "You're too trusting. I know when a guy is into someone, and he's definitely into you. I'm not thrilled about you going out of town with him next week."

"God, Brad. That's ridiculous. For one, Ryan's married. And two, I'm with you—I love you and would never cheat on you. This is my job, and I like it. And while I appreciate your concern, your suspicions don't get to dictate whether I go out of town or not for a project I'm leading."

Brad's expression tightens, but his voice is calm. "I'm not trying to control you, baby. But I've got valid concerns here. I don't know this guy, and I don't trust him. And honestly, I'm not sure you do either."

I grab his arm, pulling him farther from the crowd, my heart racing as I glance around to make sure no one's listening. "You don't need to trust him, Brad. You need to trust me."

His jaw clenches, and he gives me a long look. "It's not about you. I trust you. But you're being naive. Guys like Ryan… when they're interested, they find a way. Married or not, they'll push until you're right where they want you to be. I've seen how this goes down. I'm just trying to keep you from making a mistake you'll regret."

I take a step closer, my voice dropping to a near whisper, eyes locked on his. "Oh, speaking from experience, are we? You'd know all about guys who can't keep it in their pants, wouldn't you?"

Brad's face goes cold, the color draining from his cheeks. For a moment, he's speechless, and I relish the silence.

"Don't throw that in my face, Cooper."

"Oh, I'll throw it in your face every time you act like a hypocrite," I snap back, my voice shaking with anger.

What am I doing? Normally, I'd never push back like this—especially not in public. I hate scenes, hate the fallout that comes later. But tonight? Tonight, I can't help myself. Is it because I know there's truth to his accusation—that I want it to be true? *Dammit, I don't know.*

Brad's jaw clenches. "Alright, let's be done here. I'm ready to fucking go."

I take a deep breath. "No, Brad. If you want to go, go. But I'm staying. I'm here with my colleagues, and I'm going to enjoy myself."

Brad takes a breath. I know he's pissed, but I also know he won't make a scene. "Fine. If that's what you want, we'll stay. I'll deal with your problems like I always do."

There it is. He always manages to twist things so I'm the problem, the difficult one. Even when he's the one who cheated, somehow it's still about him—how he's not getting what he needs from me. God, I'm getting so sick of it. I'm exhausted with this whole situation. For a moment, I let myself flirt with Ryan, indulge in the idea of something more—but turns out, Ryan's just like Brad. Hell, just like all men. They want one thing, and that's it. Fine. I'm here for it—I like good sex as much as anyone—but let's not pretend it's anything more.

Chapter 12

COOPER

The car ride home is filled with awkward silence. My arms are crossed as I stare out the window, fuming.

Brad finally breaks the silence. "You can't be mad at me for pointing out the obvious, baby. All I said was the truth."

"The truth? How would you know what that is, Brad? You don't even know Ryan."

He looks over at me, one brow cocked. "And you do?" He scoffs. "Just how well do you know him, Cooper?"

I let out a sigh of disgust. "You just never know when to quit, do you?"

"Well, I'm sorry that I'm not comfortable with my gorgeous girlfriend hanging out every night with a guy who clearly wants to fuck her... let alone going on a trip together."

"Oh my God! We aren't alone. And it doesn't matter, Brad—it's for work. I'm not trying to sleep with Ryan."

"Has he ever made a pass at you?"

"What? No!" I answer too quickly, knowing it's a gray area.

"And have you ever wanted him to?"

"Oh... my God." I shake my head in frustration. "I can't... I can't keep talking about this. It's so fucking stupid."

"Come on, Coop. You don't think there's any validity to my feelings? I mean, God, I worry about you cheating on me all the time. I mean, look at you... What guy wouldn't want to sleep with you?"

I scoff. "I don't know, Brad. Why didn't you ask yourself that same question when you were fucking Jessica?" Dammit, I wish I could take that one back. But it's out now, and I brace myself for Brad's retaliation.

He raises his voice. "There it is. You can't *not* go there, can you? Always throwing the past in my face. And you think I don't have a valid reason to be concerned when you're still this angry with me?"

"What's *that* supposed to mean?"

He shakes his head, his grip tightening on the steering wheel. He takes a breath, steadying himself. "I just mean… I'm sure you'd love to get back at me." He glances at me, his voice softer now. "Do you ever think about that? About getting back at me?"

"Honestly?" I say, my patience wearing thin. "Yes. Yes, I have definitely thought about getting back at you." The silence stretches, so I keep talking just to fill the discomfort. "I did, actually." *Fuck.* I swallow, staring down at my hands. *Why did I just say that?*

He furrows his brows, confused. "What do you mean you did?"

I muster up the strength to look at him. "In Newport… back in March, when you and I broke up. After you…" I can't say it. "Anyway, I slept with someone—a random guy I met at a bar—because I was so mad at you, so hurt…. I was so angry, Brad." I take a shaky breath and exhale slowly, releasing the tension that's been there for months. *God, that's a weight off my chest.*

I watch him, uncertain of what this will look like or where it's going to go. I've never been the one in this seat—the one admitting things, holding back truths, confessing secrets. My heart races. Brad's jaw tightens, his eyes narrow, his grip hardening on the steering wheel.

"You fucking slept with someone nine months ago?" He looks over at me, his tone sharp. "And you're just now telling me? Who the fuck was it?"

I shrug, letting out a defeated sigh. "I don't know, Brad. Just some guy. I don't even remember his name. I'd had some drinks, and I was hurt—wanted to move on, get over you. So yeah, I slept with someone else." I pause, gathering the courage to say what I've wanted to for so long. "Just like you have. And honestly, Brad, I'm willing to bet there were more than just the three women I know about."

He exhales loudly. "That's all there was, Cooper. I swear it… Why are you telling me this now?"

"I don't know. I guess it felt shitty keeping this from you." I shut my eyes, praying the tears that threaten stay contained. "I don't fully trust you, Brad. I haven't for a while now, and apparently you don't trust me… I just feel like we've backed ourselves into a corner, and I don't know where we go from here." I pause, letting it sink in, fixing my gaze on the side of his face. It hurts to be here, admitting all of this out loud. "If we don't have trust… does anything else even matter?"

I don't know where this truth serum came from. I never intended to tell Brad about Newport. Obviously, I'm not going to mention it was Ryan, but at least I'm coming partly clean.

We stop at a red light. He looks at me with sorrow in his eyes, and brings my hand to his lips. "You're right." He takes a deep breath. "I'm sorry, baby." His eyes close for a moment. "God, this fucking stings. I can't believe you slept with someone else." He shakes his head, rubbing his forehead. "Sorry, I'm just… I'm in shock. I don't even know how to process this right now. It's killing me." He glances at me again. "This is all my fault. I know I've been a dick, and I deserve this—I do—but… shit, it hurts."

I'm stunned into silence. Brad has never—and I mean never—taken the blame for anything this big. Ever. The sincerity in his voice tugs at my heartstrings… but only a little. Maybe it's because I know how this goes. He's apologized before, but it's always followed by something worse—a cutting remark, a backhanded compliment, a veiled threat.

I stay quiet, afraid that if I speak, I'll start apologizing, like I always do. And I don't want to apologize. I'm not sorry that I slept with Ryan, that I lied about it, or that I'm still partly lying. *God, what does that say about me?*

Then it hits me: Brad brought this on himself—when he chose to cheat the first time, and the second and third and *God,* I don't even know how many times. *He's* pushed me away. *He's* broken our trust… *He* broke us.

He slams his hand against the steering wheel, teeth clenched. "Fuck," he says, his voice raw. "I can't get the image of you with someone else out of my mind. I need to know who it was, Cooper. I need a name, what he looked like, where you did it, what he did to you. I need to know. This is going to drive me crazy. You've got to give me something," he pleads, his voice trembling.

I sigh. "No, Brad. You don't need to know." I look at him intently as we approach our building. "It was one time. We had broken up. And it hasn't happened again. I know it hurts. Trust me, I know it hurts," I say, biting back tears.

He just shakes his head, letting out a bitter scoff. I turn to look out the window as we pull into the parking garage. I should feel awful seeing him like this, broken, but I don't. Not completely. After all the times he's hurt me, lied to me, how could I?

We don't speak as we ride the elevator, and suddenly, *The Sound of Silence* takes on a whole new meaning. My head fills with the noise of quiet: the hum of the elevator, our breathing, the faint buzz of electricity… my heartbeat. It's like I can hear everything, even though there's nothing to listen to.

We get inside, and I go straight to our room to ready myself for bed, desperate to be alone.

Brad comes into the closet as I'm hanging up my dress. "Did he come inside you? I need to know."

I glare at him. "No. God. He wore a condom." I take a steadying breath. "Don't do this to yourself. I've been down this road, and it's not a fun one. Just let it go. It happened a long time ago… Would you rather have not known?"

"Maybe. I don't like that you kept it from me… but I don't like knowing either."

I give him a tight-lipped smile. "Yeah, well… It sucks to find out the person you love had sex with someone else. It really sucks, doesn't it?" I'm torn between being empathetic and a complete bitch. I don't want to hurt Brad, but part of me savors that I've hit him where it hurts… where he's hit me.

"Did he lick your pussy?"

"God, Brad," I recoil in disgust. "I'm not talking about this anymore. You don't need to know the details."

"Yes. I do, baby. I need to know. I need to know if his mouth was between your legs."

"Stop." I scowl at him, anger bubbling up inside of me.

He steps toward me, grabbing my hands, pleading, almost desperate. "Baby, please. I've been so supportive, I've been trying so hard—you owe me this much. Please. Did he eat you out? Because that… I can't handle that. I can't deal with it."

My patience snaps. I've gone from empathy to fury in a matter of seconds. "Oh, I don't know. Why don't you tell me how many pussies you've eaten out?" I yank my hands from his grip, crossing my arms and raising my voice. "*You* don't get to question me!"

I storm out of the closet, heading to the bathroom to brush my teeth. I just want to go to bed and end this. But he follows me.

"Coop. Don't walk away—I need to know this."

I squeeze toothpaste onto my brush, scrubbing my teeth with a force that can't be healthy for my gums. He steps up behind me, resting his forehead on my shoulder, his hands gripping my hips. "Please, baby," he pleads softly. "Please. Tell me."

I spit and rinse, then glance at him in the mirror. "God, Brad. This is ridiculous." I turn to face him. "You're acting like a crazy person!" The words feel surreal coming out of my mouth because they're the same words Brad's thrown at me too many times to count. Words that have stung more than anything else. I almost laugh. Turns out, crazy isn't a personality flaw—it's what happens when the person you trust the most deceives you.

We stare at each other. Me, fuming, and Brad, completely lost.

He breaks the silence, defeated. "Will you at least tell me where you met him? Where you did it?"

I sigh. He's not going to stop until I give him something. "I was at Tipsy with Casey. She left, this guy came over, and we started talking. One thing led to another, and we ended up in his hotel room." I raise a brow. "Satisfied?"

He scoffs, giving me a hard, pointed stare. "And did you let him go down on you?"

I roll my eyes. "Oh my *GOD!* I'm not doing this anymore." I turn and walk out of the bathroom. "Don't follow me," I say, glancing over my shoulder as he comes after me.

"Come on, Cooper. I'm not going to stop until you tell me. Just tell me. Did he go down on you?"

I've had it. I swing around to face him. "Yes!" I shout. "Yes, he went down on me! And it was *incredible*! There. Are you happy?" But I don't stop—I keep going. I'm so damn angry at him for pushing me, and now all I want to do is drag this out—torture him. "It was the best damn oral I've ever had… and I think about it *all the time*. I came over and over. His tongue…"

Before I can finish, Brad backs me up against the wall, his one hand gripping my waist while the other cups the back of my neck, pulling me into a deep, heated kiss. He bites at my bottom lip, just enough to make it possessive, but not enough to hurt.

"Don't fucking say that, Cooper. You don't mean it."

I shove at his chest. "Yes, I do." I feel the tears threatening, and there's nothing I hate more than to let him see me cry—it's like giving him the winning hand in a poker game.

He shakes his head. "No, you don't, baby." His mouth is on mine again, more tentative this time. He kisses along my jaw and neck, up to my ear, and whispers, "I don't want anyone else touching you… ever." His hand slides down into the front of my shorts, cupping me, and I gasp. "This is mine." He pulls back, meeting my gaze. His fingers stroke me over the fabric. His possessiveness pissing me off more.

I laugh, breathless, shoving at his chest with everything I have. "Fuck you!" My voice cracks, and the tears I've been holding back burst free, unstoppable. His eyes flash with something dark—something I don't recognize—and for a second, I have no idea what he'll do next.

"Fuck me? How about I fuck you, instead?" he snarls. He spins me around, backing me against the opposite wall with a force that's just a little too hard. His hand grips my waist tighter, his fingers digging into my skin while his thumb swipes across my lips, his hand gripping my jaw. It doesn't hurt, but it's jarring enough to make me freeze. Panic rises in my throat—he's strong.

He leans in again, his mouth crushing against mine. I try to shove him away, but he grabs my wrists, pinning them to the wall above my head. For the first time, fear flickers through me—real fear. Brad's never been like this before, never pushed it this far.

And yet… I kiss him back. It's easier. It's safer. This is what we do. We fight, we yell, we make up. And somewhere in the chaos, I convince myself it's okay. And for the first time, I'm scared—scared to push back.

I take his tongue into my mouth, kissing him with everything I have left to give. He releases my wrists as he feels me kissing him back, and I wrap my arms around his neck. His hands slide under my shirt, pulling it over my head. God, the pent-up tension—the frustration, the hurt, and now the confusion from finding out Ryan has a wife—it all churns inside me. This feels like the only way to let the storm out before it tears me apart.

He tugs my shorts down, and I step out of them, reaching for the button on his pants. We push and pull, shove and yank, until we end up on the bed, tangled in a mess of incredibly heated, sweaty sex. It's raw. It's emotional. And right now, it's the only thing that feels somewhat real between us.

But it's not love—far from it. It's almost a hateful vengeance, a desperate grasp for something tangible in this disaster we've built together. Maybe that's why I give in every time—because it's the only thing that grounds me in this relationship. And if I'm going to be stuck with him, I need something in return to make this bearable.

It's fucked.

It's broken—I'm broken.

But right now, it's all I have. It's the only thing that gets me through each day.

Chapter 13

RYAN

It's Wednesday, and we leave for Austin in less than a week. I'm on my way to the lounge to meet Cooper. We were supposed to meet the last two nights, but both days I had meetings and things to catch up on. By the time I got out here, she'd already left. Feels like she left early on purpose—avoiding me. She's been nothing short of hostile since the Christmas party, and I have no idea why.

Maybe someone said something, or maybe it's Brad. He seems like a conceited asshole—the possessive, jealous type. Who knows? But something changed, and now she won't speak to me unless she absolutely has to, and when she does, it's always with an edge in her voice—like she's pissed at me.

I called her into my office yesterday to ask if something was wrong. She just looked at me tight-lipped, and said, "Nope. Can I get back to work now?"

Either way, I need to figure out what's going on, and today's my chance. She's already in our booth, waiting for me. I set my things down across from her, ready to get to work. We have a lot to get through before our trip.

"Do you mind working somewhere else?" she asks, not bothering to look away from her computer.

"I do mind, actually. We need to do this together, so whatever your problem is, you're going to have to bury it for a few hours. We have work to do."

"Fine," she says, snapping her laptop shut. "Then I'll move." She starts gathering her things, standing to leave.

I chuckle despite myself, even though it's not funny. Not even a little. "Cooper, sit down. I don't like pulling rank, but I'm still your superior. We have a project to finish, and that means working together. So, please… sit."

She exhales loudly. "Sure, you don't," she mutters under her breath.

My patience is wearing thin, but I try to keep my voice steady. "You're walking a fine line right now. I don't know what's going on with you, but let's keep work and personal separate, alright? Can you do that?"

"Oh, God, please." She laughs, a harsh, bitter sound. "It's not like we have some kind of personal relationship at stake. I fucked you one time to get back at my boyfriend. Period. Let's not pretend there's something more here." She glares at me. "What do you want to work on first, Mr. Vice President?"

I feel a mix of irritation and something else I can't quite name—a pang of… what? Resentment? Regret? I push it down, trying to regain control. If I don't get a handle on this, we'll never get anything done.

What's even more infuriating is that ever since the Christmas party, I can't help but picture her naked—and often. That dress she wore had me imagining things no one in the workplace should. And since I've seen her naked—felt her body pressed up against mine, those incredible tits in my hands, the way she rode me—it's damn near impossible to get the images out of my head. It bothers me that she has this hold on me—sexual, physical, whatever it is. If I didn't want to push her up against a wall every time I saw her, I'd have a lot less patience for her attitude.

I snap back to the present as she sits down with an annoyed exhale, but at least she's staying. I cut straight to business; there's no time for tiptoeing around whatever's going on with her.

"Alright, we've got a lot to get through," I say, pulling out the project file. "First up, we need to finalize the site visit itinerary for Austin. I don't want to waste any time traveling between properties."

She doesn't look at me, but I notice her eyes narrow slightly as she stares at her screen. "I already sent over a draft itinerary this morning. Did you not see it?"

I didn't, but I'm not about to admit that. "I glanced at it. I think we need to reorder the site visits. Start with the downtown properties before heading to the outskirts. We want to hit the most competitive locations first."

"Fine," she says, her tone clipped. "I'll adjust it. What about the budget breakdown? Have you reviewed the cost comparisons I pulled together?"

She's trying to be all business, and maybe I should be grateful for that. But the way she's ignoring me—like I'm just a voice in the background— is grating.

"Yeah, about that. I noticed some inconsistencies with the construction cost estimates for a couple of the sites. We need to get those nailed down before we go, or we risk looking like idiots in front of the executive team."

Her lips tighten, and I see her back straighten. "There are no inconsistencies. Those are estimates directly from the contractors we're meeting with. If you want different numbers, maybe you should talk to them yourself."

I take a deep breath, trying to reel in my frustration. "Look, Cooper, I'm not questioning your work. I'm saying we need to have all our facts straight. We can't afford to have errors in our presentation."

She finally looks up at me, her eyes cold but focused. "Then why don't you tell me what's wrong so I can fix it?"

"How about we go through it together? Start with the sites that need the most attention."

"Fine."

"Do you want to come sit over here so it's easier to see?"

"No. I can see just fine from here."

Jesus Christ. How can someone so beautiful be such a pain in the ass?

We work for a good ninety minutes with no breaks, going over cost comparisons and each site listing. The tension is thick, but we manage. Now, we're on our itinerary.

"What time is our flight on Tuesday, and when do we land?" She looks to me for the answer.

"I don't know. Didn't you book the flights?" I ask.

"No," she says, irritation clear in her voice. "You were supposed to book the flights. I booked the hotel."

I scowl. "I thought you were booking all travel."

She sighs, her frustration spilling over. "I was going to, but you wanted to book the flights on your card for the extra miles or whatever. You wanted to be reimbursed, remember?"

I press my hand to my forehead. "Fuck," I mutter. I reluctantly make eye contact with her. "You're right. I did say that… I forgot. Let's hurry and do that now."

She glances at her watch, clearly eager to get out of here. "Look, I need to get going soon. Just book the flights, okay? And let me know when it's done."

I watch her for a moment, noticing the tightness in her expression. "What's the rush? Got somewhere more exciting to be?"

She rolls her eyes. "I've got to get home. Brad's not exactly a fan of me spending all this time around you." She shuts her laptop and starts packing up her things.

I lean back, smirking. "Ah, he doesn't trust you with me? Or is it just me he doesn't trust?"

She shoots me a glare, her lips pressing into a thin line. "Does it matter? Either way, it's always the woman who gets the blame. Men can't trust their girlfriends or wives to be alone with other men, and yet it's usually the men who aren't to be trusted." She puts on her coat. "Fuckin' creeps," she mutters, just loud enough for me to hear.

I raise an eyebrow, caught slightly off guard. "You think all men are creeps?"

She shrugs, gathering her things. "If the shoe fits."

I let out a low chuckle. "Someone's bitter."

She slings her bag over her shoulder. "Yeah, well, maybe I'm just tired of all the double standards. I'll see you tomorrow. Text me the flight details when you have them."

I watch her head toward the door. For a moment, I almost want to say something to break the tension—something to make her stay. But then she's gone, leaving me alone with the weight of her words.

I sit back, thinking about my situation—the one I'm always avoiding going home to. I know it's not all black and white, not just one person to blame for how things have turned out. But maybe there's some truth to what Cooper said. Men can be creeps—we don't always think with the right head. *Did I miss something? Was there something more I could have done?*

Hell, maybe there is a double standard. We're quick to call a woman a slut, a whore. But what about the guy? Was I too quick to point fingers? Too hard on her? Maybe I bailed too soon. I didn't exactly take my time getting my dick wet when things went south. My ring was still warm when I met Cooper in Newport.

I don't know, maybe I'm overthinking this. Either way, the truth stings. Man or woman—a cheater's a cheater.

* * * * *　　* * * * *

Mentally exhausted from the workday and all the crap with Cooper, the last thing I want is to face Beth. I just want to drop my shit by the door and crawl into bed.

I stayed at the office as late as I could, arriving home at ten-thirty.

Trying to sneak in, hoping to avoid Beth, I quietly open the door and slip inside. The house is dark, except for a soft light coming from the master bedroom upstairs. I remove my shoes and walk up the stairs. I stop at the bathroom in the hallway, shutting the door behind me softly. After brushing my teeth, I open the door to find Beth standing there waiting for me.

"You're home late."

"Yeah. Sorry if I kept you up," I say, trying to sound apologetic, but I'm just spent.

"You didn't keep me up." She purses her lips, something that she does when she's thinking. "Are you avoiding me? You know, you don't have to stay at work until ten in hopes to not see me, right? I can always go stay with my mom."

I sigh, my shoulders slumping. "God, no, Beth, I told you in the beginning… I'd never make you move out. I always planned to be the one to leave, at least until we sell the house."

"Why shouldn't I be the one to move out, Ryan?"

I steady my breath—my emotions, and the stress from the day, getting the best of me. "Beth…" The words don't come—because I look at her, and I see how different she looks. The stress and guilt of everything weighing on her. She's lost weight, and she looks so goddamn tired. But still, she's the same beautiful Beth that I fell in love with and married. "You've suffered enough. I'll look for a place soon." I take a step toward her and cup her face in my hands. "We'll get through this." I say reassuringly.

She swallows hard, nodding her head as a steady stream of tears starts to fall.

I kiss her forehead. "Come here." I pull her into a hug, and she sobs on my chest.

"I'm so scared."

"I know you are. I am too. But everything's going to be fine… eventually." I rub her back and kiss the top of her head.

She pulls back, wiping her tears with the back of her hand. "Right. Eventually." Her voice is still shaky, but she looks up at me. "You seem tense. What's going on?"

"Agh, just work shit. It's been stressful making sure everything for this trip next week is ready to go. I've already got a lot on my plate during the day, and on top of that, I have a coworker who's being difficult."

"Oh. I'm sorry. Difficult how?"

I grip the back of my neck. "I don't know. She just pushes back on a lot of things. It's starting to piss me off."

"You know you work too much. It's too many hours—too much stress… You need a day off."

"I'm fine. I like the distraction." As soon as I say it she flinches, and I realize how it sounded. "Not from you… just… from everything."

"Come here." She takes my hand and leads me into the bedroom, sitting me on the bed. Standing between my legs she starts to rub my shoulders. "Your shoulders are really tight. Try to relax."

"That's just from my workout. You don't have to do this Beth. I'm fine."

"Stop. I want to." Her fingers knead into the muscles of my shoulders and neck, easing the tension, and God, it feels good. She's in her usual pajamas—a tank top and a pair of shorts. They never match, but that's always been her style, and I never cared. It's so Beth, and it showed just enough skin to keep things interesting. Tonight, it's a gray tank top and red shorts, her breasts right at eye level. She's never had big boobs, but they've always been perfect—perky, with great nipples.

Beth's hands work their way up to my scalp, her fingers threading through my hair. I let my head fall forward, resting against her chest. Her skin is warm, and I breathe in her familiar scent—the same Dior perfume she asks for every year for Christmas. It's comforting in a way I haven't felt in a long time.

I haven't been touched like this in months, and suddenly, every muscle in my body is aching for more, craving her touch. But I'm unsure if it's Beth's touch specifically that I'm longing for, or if it's just the feeling of being touched at all.

Without thinking, my hands slide up her thighs, gripping her hips. I feel myself hardening, my body responding to the simple touch, the closeness. God, I'm tired. Tired of holding everything in, of feeling like shit every day. I press my face into the space between her breasts, breathing her in, feeling that old pull—the one that's both familiar and frustrating.

She feels it too. I can tell. Her fingers still for a moment before she looks down at me. "Ryan," she whispers. Her hands slide down from my hair to my shoulders, her breath shallow.

My fingers press into her skin, needing something—anything. I lift my head, brushing my lips against her chest, then her neck. She shivers, a reaction I haven't seen in a long time.

"Wait," she murmurs, her hands firm on my shoulders, stopping me. "Let me… do this for you," she says softly, already starting to lower herself to her knees in front of me.

I blink, confused. "Beth, you don't have to—"

"No, I want to," she insists. Her eyes meet mine, earnest and a little desperate. "You've done so much for me, and I know things aren't the same between us. But I want to do this... for you."

I hesitate, torn between frustration and the way her fingers graze my thighs, already undoing my belt. She's right; things aren't the same. They never will be. But right now, with her looking up at me, offering something I haven't felt in months—relief, release—I'm too far gone to care.

"Okay," I murmur, my voice thick. "If you're sure."

Beth nods, giving me a small, sad smile. "I am."

I lift a bit as she tugs at my pants and boxer briefs, pulling them off, and I can't help but let out a sigh as her mouth wraps around me. *Fuck.* It feels so good—too good. I close my eyes, leaning back, trying to focus on the sensation and not everything else. Not how she's trying to fix something that's beyond repair. Not how I'm letting her, using her, even though I don't want to be here. *God, I'm a dick.*

The tension from the day—the bullshit with Cooper, the stress of this trip, everything—starts to melt away. But as much as I want to just give in, I can't shake it. The guilt. The frustration. Cooper's voice in my head calling men creeps, and here I am, proving her right. My wife is down there, trying to please me, trying to make things right, and all I can think about is how much I'd rather be doing this with someone else. Someone who doesn't look at me with sad, hopeful eyes... Someone like Cooper.

I'm just like the guys Cooper hates. And maybe she's right to hate them. Maybe she's right to hate me.

Beth's rhythm picks up, and I push those thoughts away, focusing on the sensation, trying to lose myself in it, even if it's just for a moment.

Chapter 14

COOPER

I scowl at Ryan as he takes his sweet-ass time getting ready for our work session tonight. It's been a long goddamn day, and I'm over it. The past nine days following the Christmas party have been hell. A slow, burning, torturous hell. Not only do I loathe Ryan and everything that he's about—or at least that's what I tell myself—I loathe my fiancé at the moment as well—they're one and the same. Men who lie and put their physical needs before the people they claim to love.

To top it all off, I started my period about an hour ago, and I feel like the devil reincarnated. My hormones are raging, I've got cramps, a headache creeping in, and I'm tired. I'm also sick of fighting with Brad. He has not relented with the snarky, suspicious comments about Ryan and me working together. And now, with my admission about Newport, he's got fresh ammo. He's great when he wants sex though—yup, he can magically flip that charm right on, like none of it ever happened.

I'm at the end of my rope, and I'm afraid that when I snap, it's going to be on the wrong person—Ryan. Sure, I have a right to be upset with him, but I've taken it too far. Aside from being a hypocrite, his life shouldn't affect mine this much.

It's Monday, and we leave early tomorrow morning for Austin.

God, any day now, VP. I've started calling him that—only because I can see that it bothers him.

"Alright, let's get right to it. Should we go over what we want to accomplish tonight before we tackle our itinerary?"

I glare at him. Is he being serious? I've already been sitting here, waiting for him, for over an hour. "Great idea, VP. Let's add another meeting to discuss how to make our meetings more efficient. That'll get us out of here quicker."

"Great," he says, rolling his eyes. "The wicked witch of the west is still here."

"Oh, look, and I got stuck with the scarecrow, who doesn't have a brain."

I stare him down, daring him to push me further.

"God, if only sarcasm burned calories—you could be a fitness influencer. Then you could quit, and leave me the hell alone."

That's it—I've hit my breaking point.

"Oh, I bet you'd like that, huh? You'd be creeping on my Instagram page… Do you think about that when you jerk off at night, VP?"

Ryan chuckles. "Not if I wanna come, sweetheart."

His comment catches me off-guard, and I'm torn between wanting to throw something at him and laugh. *God, what is wrong with me?*

I settle on a smirk. "Didn't seem to be an issue for you in Newport, bud."

"Oh, it was all I could do to shut you up, babe. Tell me, do you scream for Brad, too?"

I roll my eyes. "You wish, Ryan. It didn't last long enough for me to even remember your name, let alone scream it."

He leans forward, his voice lowering. "It was long enough to make you come… multiple times."

I lean in too, our faces inches apart. "Ever hear of *faking it*, VP?"

He scoffs. "If that was faking it, you're the best goddamn actress I've ever seen. Didn't think people could make themselves convulse on demand."

"Well, thanks for the compliment. It was my first time ever having to fake it—I'll take that as a win."

We glare at each other, fuming. He's tight-lipped, chewing on the inside of his cheek, giving me that sexy, smoldering look that only pisses me off more. I catch myself staring at his lips, then force my gaze back to his eyes. *God,* I want to punch him—or drag him somewhere private and tear his clothes off.

Ryan rubs his temples and sighs. "Okay, Cooper, I get it. You think I'm a scumbag, and you hate me for reasons I can't even begin to fathom. But we have got to stop this for tonight. Can we please," he pauses, taking a deep breath, "please, just be cordial for an hour or two so we can go home? You can go back to hating me tomorrow."

"Fine," I say sharply. "But just so we're clear, I never stop hating you."

"Fine, whatever," he mutters.

I raise an eyebrow, waiting for him to take control. He's the boss, after all—he's made that perfectly clear. "Well then, lead the way, VP," I say. "Let's see if you're better at this than you are at… other things."

* * * * * * * * * *

I drop my bag on the kitchen counter with a heavy sigh, the sound echoing in the empty apartment. My mind's still racing from the confrontation with Ryan, but at least Brad's out of town until Wednesday. *Thank God.* I can't deal with him tonight. Never knowing which version of him I'm going to get—accusing, condescending Brad, or sweet, loving, horny Brad—it's exhausting either way.

I flop onto the couch, anxiety heavy in my chest. *What is my life?* How did I get here—constantly catering to someone else's needs and emotions while mine slip through the cracks?

I think back to Gavin. God, he really did a number on me. I wish I could go back to my fourteen-year-old self for a redo—learn how to use the word no, for starters. Tears sting my eyes, and I blink them back as I get up to finish packing.

I open my bathroom cupboard to get tampons for my suitcase. *Of course, I start my period at the most inconvenient time. Lucky me.* I grab an unopened box and eye my bin of sex toys. I rummage through it until I find two of my favorite vibrators. Yeah, I'm definitely going to need these this week. If Ryan and I keep going at each other's throats, I'll need some way to decompress.

With Brad, I know the cycle—argue, make up, rinse, repeat. But with Ryan… it feels different. The way we fight leaves me charged. *Why? Why am I so drawn to him?*

I picture Ryan pushing me up against a wall, hands pinned behind my back, telling me what to do—demanding me. Staring at me with that sexy, smoldering look before his lips crush into mine.

Jesus—I might need one of these bad boys right now.

I toss two vibrators into my suitcase and grab another to take to bed with me, its familiar shape already calming my nerves. Yeah, this little guy is going to have to do the heavy lifting tonight—and afterward, I'm going to sleep like a baby.

$$* * * * * \quad * * * * *$$

I exit security and make a beeline for the nearest Starbucks, needing coffee twenty minutes ago. I placed a pickup order while waiting in line. The airport isn't too crowded yet, but it's only six-thirty—a disgustingly early time to be here. I'm not a morning person, and with a heavy flow, no caffeine, and Ryan on my plate, it's not exactly a promising combination.

As Starbucks comes into view, I remind myself: I have to get along with him today. Whatever I'm feeling, I need to bury it—at least a little. I have to try harder.

I find my name in the pile of pickup orders and savor the warmth in my hands. Taking a sip, I close my eyes, letting the hot liquid travel down to my belly. *Okay, one of three problems solved.* I head toward Concourse B to meet Ryan at our gate. We agreed to get here early to go over a few last-minute details so we can hit the ground running.

We spot each other at the same time. He gestures toward the tables I just passed, and I nod, turning back to take a seat at one of the open ones. I push my luggage aside, reminding myself this is work. *Be nice.*

"Good morning," Ryan says cautiously, gauging my mood as he sits down.

"Morning," I reply, keeping my eyes on my coffee. I said I'd be nice, not overly nice.

"Did you sleep well?" he asks, testing the waters.

Really, though, with the small talk? Fine, he wants small talk, I'll give him small talk.

I shrug casually. "Eventually. Needed a little… release first." I glance up, a sly smile tugging at my lips as I catch his reaction.

His eyebrows lift, amusement flickering in his eyes. "Thinking about me naked again? Or is Brad just not cutting it these days?"

I roll my eyes but decide to play along. "Brad's out of town, and let's just say I have a healthy libido. I'm good at taking care of myself."

Ryan chuckles, his gaze lingering a beat too long. "I bet you are." His eyes drop briefly—either to my lips or my cleavage, I'm not sure. "Good to know you're resourceful. Makes for a more productive trip, I suppose," he adds, shifting the conversation back to work.

I give him a sweet, too-innocent smile. "Let's just hope all the time I'm spending with you doesn't make me need my vibrators every night."

Wait. *Crap.* That didn't come out right.

It's too late. He's grinning from ear to ear, fully aware he has the upper hand. "Oh, I'll never complain about being the reason you need to 're-lease,' Cooper. Whether it's for pleasure or frustration." He laughs. "Didn't think that one through, did you?"

I groan. "Ugh. You're so… God, there isn't even a word for what you are."

"Charming, handsome, intelligent?" he suggests, still grinning.

"Try condescending, arrogant, hypocritical."

"And there she is." He leans back, clearly satisfied. "Alright, as fun as this is, let's pocket it. We've got work to do."

"Fine." I exhale, giving in, holding back a smile. "What do you wanna go over first?"

Ryan opens his folder as we go over the details of our day. After twenty minutes of focused work with no bickering, my eyes wander to a couple across from me. The woman hands the guy her bags before heading to the restroom. He's good-looking—and so is she. But the moment she's out of sight, he immediately zeros in on a woman standing a few feet in front of me. She's attractive, sure, but completely overdressed for a flight, like she's headed to a nightclub instead of a plane. It's not subtle, and the guy's expression practically burns with lust as he rakes his eyes over her.

A monster claws at my insides, twisting everything up in knots. *Is this how Brad looks at women the second I'm out of sight?* The thought hurts like hell, a brutal realization I wasn't prepared for. Even if Brad isn't cheating again, he's been that guy. The one who can't resist ogling other women, almost right in front of me.

I automatically scoff in disgust, muttering "asshole" under my breath.

"What's got you so pissed off now?" Ryan asks, bringing my attention back to him.

I shake my head, the irritation simmering. "That guy," I nod toward the man. "His girlfriend or wife is in the restroom, and the second she's out of sight, he's undressing another woman with his eyes. Can't men control themselves?"

"So, what? All men are cheaters now, too?"

I turn to him, eyes narrowing. "Well, aren't they? Seems like every guy I know is either thinking with his dick or cheating with it. Maybe some are just better at hiding it." Our flight gets called for pre-boarding, and I start gathering my things. "Come on, let's go. I assume we're sitting together? We can work on the plane—not that I couldn't use some space from you."

Ryan gives me a smug look. "Well, it's your lucky day. I got upgraded to first class. Diamond status with Delta," he says, his tone dripping with pride.

"Congratulations. You've officially hit peak corporate cliché." I try to hide my disappointment but fail. "Didn't you book our flights together? Whenever Brad gets upgraded, he upgrades me, too."

"I guess I snagged the last seat." He shrugs. "Didn't expect you to miss me so much."

"How insightful of you, VP. I'm at an absolute loss over what to do without you for a few hours. Oh, I know—maybe I'll finally get to enjoy some peace and quiet."

"What was that? Sorry, I can't hear you from *all the way* back there."

"Ugh. You're the worst. Enjoy your fancy little bubble. I'm sure they'll treat you like the king you *think* you are."

I turn on my heel. He follows me toward the gate.

"Oh, I will. Especially if it means taking a break from you and your *charming* company."

"Please," I say. "My company's the most exciting part of your day—right up there with your hand at night."

He laughs. "Jealous of my hand now, are we? I'm sure you remember just how *skilled* I am with it." A fire surges through me, a blend of frustration and something else, as I reluctantly recall just how good he is with his hands. He leans in, his voice dropping lower. "Hope your vibrator's handy in that carry-on of yours. You're gonna need it after that core memory." He clicks his tongue and strides toward the gate.

I start to follow, but he turns back, smirking. "They're not loading the peasants yet. Have a nice flight." With a smile, he scans his phone and disappears down the jetway, leaving me standing there, gaping.

Damn. He definitely won that round. But this isn't over. Not even close. We've got four more days on this trip.

Chapter 15

RYAN

I settle into my comfortable seat in first class, stretching out my legs. If this were an evening flight, I'd be ordering alcohol after my encounter with Cooper. Instead, I open my laptop and prepare to work as people pass by, herded like cattle to the back of the plane. I'm focused when I feel a kick to my foot. I look up to see Cooper smirking at me. She kicked me on purpose. *Is she five years old?*

"How's your throne, VP?"

God, she's so provoking. I smirk back, sticking my foot out just enough to trip her as she takes another step.

She stumbles over my foot, losing her balance. Not wanting to knock into the person in front of her, she leans toward me, bracing one hand against my chest and the other against the seat above my shoulder.

"What the hell, Ryan?"

She's so close I can feel her breath on my forehead. The mix of her perfume and the sight of her tits just inches from my face makes me feel disoriented. She's wearing a low-cut shirt under a denim jacket, and from this angle, all I can see is skin—smooth, tempting, and way too close for comfort. *Fuck.* I keep my gaze on her face, but it takes everything in me. She has no idea what she's doing to me—or maybe she does. I plaster a smile on my face. "Karma's a bitch, sweetheart."

She pushes herself off me with a disgusted exhale and continues on her way to the back of the plane. Part of me wishes she were sitting next to me, if only so I could push her buttons. I don't know why it's so fun, but I'm starting to look forward to her snarky remarks. It keeps things interesting, never knowing what I'm going to get. Sometimes it feels like she hates me, pouring the wrath of hell onto me, and other times it's like immature flirtation—like we're back in high school. I can't figure her out. She went from hostile to friendly, warming up to me before the Christmas party—shit, I would've even called her a friend. But afterward—pure seething hatred. I have no clue what happened at that party.

All I know is that she's hot as hell, great in bed, and I like arguing with her.

The plane starts to taxi. I connect to the Wi-Fi and decide to have a little fun. I shoot her a text.

Ryan: How's your seat back there?

Cooper: Everything I dreamed of, and so much more.

Okay—she didn't shut me down.

Ryan: Did you manage to grab your vibrator before you had to put your luggage away?

I add the smug-faced emoji at the end. I also know that if anyone ever saw these texts, I could possibly lose my job.

It's a dangerous game.

Cooper: You wish. Have you managed to jerk off in the bathroom yet? I saw your eyes wandering. #subtleVP

"Oh, shit," I mutter under my breath, laughing.

Ryan: Can you blame me? Even the guy in the window seat's jealous of the view you gave me.

She sends an eye-rolling emoji.

Cooper: Is he an asshole too?

Annnnd the wicked witch is back.

Ryan: Did you forget to take your medication this morning, PM?

Cooper: PM?

Ryan: Yeah… project manager. That's YOUR new nickname.

Ryan: Or maybe peasant… It's still up for debate.

Cooper: Ha. Ha. Ha. You're so funny.

Ryan: Thanks. I think so.

Cooper: Did you and window seat create a brotherly bond over your "view"? #ASSHOLES

Jesus Christ. She really is something. I hesitate before I type.

Ryan: What do you want me to say, PM… you've got a great rack.

Ryan: But seriously… What did Brad do to make you hate men this much?

I watch the text bubble disappear and reappear on her screen, waiting for her to type something back. She takes longer than usual, then the bubble vanishes again. I start to panic. *Dammit. I went too far.* The bubble finally reappears.

Cooper: Fuck. You.

Cooper: Why don't you worry about your own fucked-up life, VP?

Shit. If she didn't have a reason to report me to HR before—she sure does now. I hit a nerve, and it's not pretty. But if I'm right—if Brad's cheated—I understand her bitterness. I've been in those shoes. But I don't understand why she's taking it out on me.

I scowl at my phone. I feel like a dick. If she and Brad are struggling, and if it's because of infidelity, the last thing she needs is me being a prick. I don't want to give her any more ammo, or prove her right. Not all guys are assholes and cheaters.

Ryan: I didn't mean that, Cooper. I'm sorry if I crossed a line.

She doesn't respond for the rest of the flight, and I'm not going to lie—I'm a little terrified to land. *Why did I do that?* We were in a good spot, flirty banter instead of angry, and then I took a wrong turn.

We land at 2:30 PM, and I immediately call the hotel to see if we can get an early check-in. I'm waiting anxiously in the terminal for Cooper to exit the plane, not knowing what I'm going to be faced with.

She walks toward me, not missing a beat. "Let's go, VP."

Alright, better than expected. We grab our rental car and head to the Fairmont in downtown Austin. The car ride is quiet, aside from the occasional question about today's properties. We've only got time to see two of them today. Travel days always feel like such a waste of time. Cooper texts the realtor and confirms our 4:30 PM appointment.

We check in and head to the elevator.

I glance at my phone for the time. "You want to meet back here in fifteen minutes after you change? Is that enough time for you?"

"Jesus, Ryan, I just have to change my clothes."

I roll my eyes, pressing the button for the fifteenth floor. "I know, but I didn't know if… you know… you had to get ready or something."

She laughs as the door opens. "Don't flatter yourself. It's not like we're going on a date. I'd never need to—" she makes air quotes, "'get ready' for you."

We walk down the hall together, and it takes everything in me not to lose my shit right now. I'm already teetering on the ledge—just waiting to be pushed off the cliff.

"Whatever. Just meet me in the lobby in fifteen minutes."

She doesn't respond, just swipes her key card and disappears inside. I take a deep breath and open the door to my room, already savoring the next ten minutes of peace without her.

Seventeen minutes later, I'm in the lobby, about to text her when she steps off the elevator—and goddamn, she looks incredible. She looks *very* ready. Professional and sexy as hell. She's wearing one of those… I don't know what it's called, but it's all one piece. Whatever—it's black, sleeveless, and shows every curve, especially her tits. She's got a coat draped over her arm, and looks ready to take on the world.

"You ready?" she says coolly.

"This is you *not* getting ready?" I snide.

"I didn't say I wasn't getting ready, VP. I said I wasn't getting ready for *you*."

"Right." Why does it feel like that's *exactly* what she did? I wave my arm out in front of me. "After you."

* * * * * 🕊 * * * * *

The first property was a bust. We're now at the second location with the realtor. I like it, Cooper does not.

"What don't you like about it?" I ask, needing to know she's not just trying to be disagreeable.

"I don't know. It just doesn't feel right, you know?" She turns to the realtor. "The vibe's off."

"The vibe's off?" I repeat, skeptical. "How are we supposed to rationally pick a building when you're just going off *vibes*?"

"That's not all I'm going off. But yeah, I think it's an important detail. It has to *feel* right."

"Right. Because you're such a good judge of character," I mutter under my breath.

"I heard that," she says coldly.

The realtor looks between us. Her name is Kellie, and she's in her mid-thirties. She and Cooper hit it off immediately, chatting like old friends.

"I completely understand, Cooper. It has to *speak* to you," Kellie chimes in.

"Yes! Exactly!" Cooper exclaims, grinning. "Don't mind him. He hasn't been laid in a long time."

They both laugh.

Holy fuck. I'm in hell—a girlfriend's retreat, and I'm their target practice. This is going to be a long week.

They lower their voices to a whisper, probably thinking I can't hear them, but everything echoes in here.

"Well, I could fix that for him. Is he single?" Kellie asks Cooper.

"Yeah, but… he's gay."

Typical. *Add cockblocker to the growing list of names I've got for her.*

"Of course he is. The hot ones always are," Kellie says.

I can't help but laugh to myself.

"You're not wrong there," Cooper agrees.

"Okay, well, if the vibes are off, let's get the hell out of here. I'm starved," I say, my patience running thin.

Cooper shrugs. "I guess we're done for the day."

Kellie walks us out. "I'll see you two bright and early tomorrow morning?"

"Yeah, see you then. Thanks, Kellie," Cooper says, waving.

Once we're in the car, Cooper slides into the passenger seat and immediately turns to me. "Well, you were rude."

"I wasn't rude. I just don't want to waste any time." I grip the steering wheel. "You know, maybe tomorrow we can bring a psychic along. Get some expert opinions on these 'vibes' you keep talking about."

She lets out a sharp laugh. "Oh, I didn't realize you were so into expert opinions, Ryan. Maybe I should call my friend—she's a therapist. She might be able to help you."

"Oh, you're a comedian now too. What hat will you be wearing for the rest of the trip, Cooper? Because I never know which version of you is going to show up."

"Oh, God. You're just such a lonely, middle-aged man who desperately needs to get laid."

I scoff. "Oh, that's original. Maybe I should give Kellie a call. She seemed more than eager to help me out with that. But wait, I forgot. I'm gay."

She bursts into uncontrollable laughter. "Oh my God, you heard that?" She doubles over, struggling to breathe.

I can't help but laugh along with her. That laugh—so unexpectedly cute—brings me back to the first time I heard it, and I feel myself softening toward her despite everything.

She sits up, wiping tears from her cheeks, struggling to contain herself. "Oh, God. That's good stuff."

We ride in silence for a few minutes, Morgan Wallen playing in the background, Bluetoothed from my phone. Cooper grabs my phone, swipes up, and holds it in front of my face for facial recognition.

"What are you doing?" I ask, suspicious.

"What does it look like I'm doing? I'm playing DJ."

"But I like this song."

"Well, I don't," she replies with a scowl. "I'm not exactly a big fan of country."

"Okay… So what are you putting on?"

"Something fun. You'll see." She types into my phone, a grin spreading across her face. "You need to loosen up."

"I'm loose."

She glances at me, unconvinced. "You will be in a minute when I hit you with this banger playlist."

Eminem's "Lose Yourself" starts playing, and she begins bopping to the beat.

"Are you ready for this, VP? Come on, I know you know this song. Everyone your age knows it."

"Oh, I know it," I say.

"But do you know it better than I do? Because we're about to have a rap-off."

I laugh. "I know every word. You're going down."

"I'll believe it when I see it."

We both start in, "His palms are sweaty," neither of us missing a beat. By the chorus, she cranks up the volume, and we're rapping as loud as we can. We make eye contact mid-song and both burst into laughter. She can't rap anymore, too caught up in the moment, but I keep going, nailing every word.

I point at her, letting her know I'm still in the game, finishing the song with a triumphant grin. "Whoo! Damn!" I clap my hands together. "Did I win? I think I won."

She claps in mock admiration. "Damn, Ryan. That was impressive." She cups her hands around her mouth and yells, "Eminem in the house!" She giggles, and it's the cutest damn thing.

I soak it all up—because when Cooper Bradley is laughing with you, you want to be fucking present for every single second.

We pull into the valet and step out of the car. "Do you want to grab something to eat together?" I ask, trying to sound casual but secretly hoping she'll say yes.

She hesitates. "No, I'm good. I'll just order something to my room. I just kind of want to be alone, if that's okay. Thanks, though."

I nod, forcing a smile. "No problem."

She turns and heads inside, and I can't help but think it's a shame—a girl like her spending the night alone, dwelling on… well, whatever it is that's weighing her down. It's like there's always something just out of reach with Cooper, something she's not letting anyone see. And for some reason, that only makes me want to get closer.

* * * * *  * * * * *

I'm up early the next morning, about to grab a coffee and head to the lobby to get some work done, when I hear Cooper through the wall. Her voice is raised, and she sounds upset.

"God, it's not like that," she says, her frustration clear. "I told you already, there's a whole group of us." There's a pause. "I'm staying with Genevieve; we're sharing a room." Another pause. "He has his own room. Do you bunk up with coworkers when you travel?" Another pause. "I don't know what floor he's on, but he's not on mine."

Holy shit. They're fighting about me. And she's lying through her teeth about it. I feel uncomfortable listening, but my curiosity gets the best of me, so I stay.

"Ugh, you're so paranoid, Brad. It doesn't matter if you like him or trust him. I work with him." There's a longer pause. "This has nothing to do with you." She starts crying, and it pisses me off that this asshole has pushed her to tears. "I've never done anything to make you question my integrity. I've been so loyal to you…" This next pause is even longer. "Oh, but you can fuck whoever you want?"

I take a deep breath. Time to go. It was wrong of me to listen. I grab my shoes.

"You bet I am… If you're going to accuse me of things I've never done, I'm sure as shit going to bring it up."

I open the door quietly and slip out, my heart pounding in my chest. Jesus, the unhealthiness of her relationship. I don't even know what to think, but I know one thing—I don't want to be in the middle of it. Yet, somehow, from what I overheard—I already am. Brad must really be threatened.

* * * * *　　* * * * *

Ten minutes later, with coffee in hand, I decide to text Cooper.

Ryan: Hey, I'm in the lobby. Want to meet me for coffee and go over a few things?

Cooper: I thought we were meeting at 9 for a quick review before heading out?

Ryan: That works too. Just figured I'd ask since I'm down here already. If it works out, great. If not, I'll see you at 9.

Cooper: Give me twenty minutes. Can you order me a latte, please?

Ryan: Yeah, sure.

I brace myself for whatever mood Cooper's in. After the morning she's had, I doubt she'll be easy to get along with today. But I'm determined to give her a break and take the high road.

Twenty minutes later, she sits across from me in a short black dress. A really short dress. She's wearing sheer black nylons, but still—I can't even think straight. Great. How the hell am I supposed to focus on work when I'm fighting back a chub all day? She has this way of making sexy-as-hell clothes look professional, or maybe it's professional clothes that look sexy as hell. Either way, I'm in a real spot here.

"Why are you staring at me?" she asks, raising an eyebrow. "Do I have something in my teeth?"

I snap out of my trance. "No," I shake it off. "Sorry, I was lost in my thoughts."

"Oh. Okay. Well, thanks for the coffee."

"You're welcome." I study her for a moment. No signs of distress or sadness. She's really good at hiding her feelings. You'd never know she had a fight with her fiancé this morning. "You look… really pretty," I say, unable to help myself.

A small, sad smile crosses her lips. "Thanks, Ryan."

* * * * * * * * * *

Today was different. Instead of Cooper's snarky, sharp attitude, she's been soft, quiet, and reserved. It's depressing as hell. It's like she couldn't care less whether I'm here or not. As much as the hostility gets under my skin, at least it's interesting, fun even. But this? I don't even know what to call it.

I've had time to think, and I'm starting to believe Cooper actually likes having me around—maybe even likes me, at least a little. All the time we spent working together before the Christmas party, when things were good, has to count for something. I don't think she's mad at me; I think she's mad at Brad—hurt and upset.

I just wish she'd talk to me. She's barely said three words all day.

We did find a place we like—a spot similar to Elemental. It's called Austin Work Space, right downtown. Cooper said the vibes are good, and I couldn't agree more. We spent most of the day touring buildings with the realtor before meeting the leasing manager at Austin Work Space. I'm relieved. It's going to be so much easier to sign a lease at a place like this instead of building out from scratch. All we'll have to do is hire a team and move in.

"Let's get some food," I say as I pull up to the valet.

"I'm not very hungry."

"Come on, Cooper. You haven't eaten all day, and your mood is depressing as hell."

We walk into the lobby. "I was actually planning to go to the pool. You can come if you want," she says, rushing to the elevator. I follow her.

"The pool?"

"Yeah… I just want to zone out and relax." She presses the button for the fifteenth floor.

I think about it. The pool does sound tempting. It's a rooftop pool, heated, and the idea of being alone with Cooper in a swimsuit suddenly makes me forget I'm hungry. Besides, blowing off some stress would be nice.

We step off the elevator and head toward our rooms.

"You coming or not? I don't have the patience to wait for you," she says, turning to her door.

"Yeah, I'll come."

She blows out a breath. "Alright. I'll meet you down there in ten."

I dress quickly, tossing my clothes on the bed like she just invited me to something more than a swim. I almost didn't pack a swimsuit, but after reading about how great the pool and hot tub were, I figured I'd better. With how freezing Chicago has been, I'm definitely not passing this up.

At the pool, I find a lounger and drop my stuff. It's not crowded—only a handful of people. It's getting dark, and the lights are on in the pool. I guess this would be what Cooper calls a *good vibe.* It's chilly by Texas standards, but warm compared to home. I glance up as Cooper walks in, wearing one of those coverups with holes in it. Never understood the purpose, but if it's to get a man's attention, it's working.

She drops her things next to mine and pulls off her coverup, her movements bringing me right back to that night in Newport. *Jesus, she looks incredible.* The swimsuit leaves her practically naked—a shimmering little thing with ties in all the right places. I could just pull one string and she'd be bare. I smirk, caught up in the memory. "Not the first time I've seen you do that," I say without thinking.

Without missing a beat, she shoves her hand in my face, turning my head. "Don't be a creep."

I chuckle inwardly. *Yes. She's back.* Does this mean I can play back? I hesitate, knowing she had a rough morning, but maybe teasing her a bit will keep her from dwelling on it—help her loosen up so she can enjoy herself tonight. "So I'm back to being a creep?"

"You've never not been one, Ryan."

"Did you bring any snacks? We might be here for a while. I'd hate for you to get hangry and overshadow that charming personality of yours."

She grins, digging into her bag. "Oh, I've got something better than snacks." She pulls out a small tin. "Got some edibles. You want one? Or do you enjoy being a stiff asshole?"

I raise my eyebrows, leaning back on the lounger. "You brought edibles?"

"What? Are *you,* of all people, judging me?"

I furrow my brows. "What's *that* supposed to mean?"

She rolls her eyes. "Please. You know exactly what it means."

I sit up. "Jesus. If it'll make you less of a pain in my ass, I'm in."

She rolls her eyes, popping one into her mouth. "Why do you think I brought them in the first place? I knew I'd need to get high after spending so much time with you." She ruffles my hair. "Desperate times, Ryan. Go on, take one. Maybe it'll help you remember how to have fun."

I chuckle, grabbing an edible. "Alright, but if I end up high and have to listen to you rant about how all men are assholes, I'm throwing you in the pool."

She narrows her eyes, but there's a hint of a smile. "Oh, trust me, if you throw me in, I'm dragging you in with me." Her gaze flicks down before meeting mine again. "Maybe the water will help you get that boner in check."

I laugh. "Touché. May the best man win."

Without hesitation, I scoop her up and hoist her over my shoulder, walking toward the pool.

"Ryan, don't! I swear to God, if you throw me in, there will be hell to pay."

"Oh, I'm already in hell with you, babe." I toss her in, knowing she'll make me pay—and I'm looking forward to it.

Chapter 16

COOPER

I break the water's surface, zeroing in on him with a glare that could cut glass. "Oh, you're going down!" My voice echoes across the pool. I know I'm not strong enough to physically drag him in, but I don't need to. I'll get him back in the way I know best—by toying with him, turning him on, and leaving him hanging.

Because, let's face it, Ryan's just like every other man in my life. A liar, a hypocrite. He made me feel guilty as hell about Newport, but he never said a word about his wife. How's that for double standards?

The worst part? Even with all of that, there's still something about him that gets to me. I hate that I like him. But I do. I have from the start. So maybe that's why I'm here, in this pool, ready to flirt and see just how far I can push him. Deep down, maybe I want him to break. Maybe I want him to finally admit what he's been hiding. Or maybe I just want to punish him for making me feel like shit.

It's messy. I'm messy—but so is this whole thing. I just have to keep my head straight. But with the edible I just took, that's going to be a hell of a lot harder in about an hour because damn, the temptation is there, right in front of me. And Ryan is one *hell* of a temptation.

Ryan stands on the side of the pool, arms crossed, grinning. I splash a wave of water at him.

He just laughs, dipping his foot in before kicking some back at me. I retaliate, splashing more water his way, thankful the few people here are off in the hot tub. As he dips his foot in to splash me again, I seize the moment, diving under the water and swimming fast toward him. I pop up by the edge, grabbing his foot.

"Oh, shit!" he laughs, stumbling. "Stop!"

"No way in hell." I tug harder, knowing he'll either have to jump in or risk falling on the cement. He curses under his breath, and then, finally, he gives in, diving in with a splash.

When he surfaces, he shoots me a playful glare. "You're so dead." He tries to push me under, but I beat him to it, ducking beneath the surface and filling my mouth with water. Gross, I know. But as soon as I come up, I spit it right in his face.

"Ew. I haven't seen anyone over the age of four do that."

I laugh. "Clearly, you don't hang out with fun people."

Before I know it, he scoops me up and hurls me into the deep end. I resurface, swimming back toward him, fully expecting to be tossed again, but then something shifts. My pulse quickens, a flutter stirring in my stomach. *Do I actually want Ryan to throw me again?*

I glance at him from across the pool. *Why am I so attracted to him?* His stupid six-pack hovers above the waterline. *Why does he have to be such a dick—and so great at the same time?*

He grins at me, eyes glinting with mischief. "You coming back for more?"

Yeah.

I think I am.

"Do you know what's really weird?" I ask, leaning against the side of the pool, facing Ryan.

"What?"

"Pubic hair."

Ryan bursts out laughing. "What?"

"It's weird, right?"

"What the fuck?" he manages through his laughter, which only makes me laugh harder.

"I'm serious! Don't you think it's weird that we just naturally have this big ball of hair down there?"

Ryan cups his forehead, still chuckling. "Oh my God."

"Who the fuck designed that? Nobody wants that. I mean, sure, it made sense once upon a time, but seriously, can we get a new model?"

Ryan tries to contain his laughter. "You've lost it."

"And why are we laying the carpet so wide? Can I get a hell yeah for a landing strip?"

Ryan looks away, laughing even harder.

"I'm serious…" I can barely get it out, my stomach hurts from laughing. "It's weird."

Ryan tries to look at me but can't. He's laughing so hard his shoulders are shaking. "I'm crying," he manages between breaths. "I'm crying."

I think the edibles have kicked in.

We laugh for what feels like minutes before it finally fades. I lose my balance and grab Ryan's shoulder to steady myself. His hand grips my waist, and the warmth floods through my body. I space out, falling into what I call 'the deep hole of thoughts', envisioning an entire night of sex with Ryan in what's probably seconds but feels like hours. When I snap out of it, his hand is gone, and he's leaning back against the side of the pool.

I startle. "How long have we been in here?"

"I don't know, but it feels like hours." Ryan looks at me, and he doesn't look away.

I focus in on him. The heated electricity between us practically sizzles in my ears. My heart beats in my throat, and my head is buzzing. Every sense heightened. What was I thinking, taking an edible with Ryan? Everything's more intense on these… Sex is incredible on these. And right now, I cannot be thinking about that—but it's all I can think about. *Sex with Ryan.*

I lean an arm on the cement, propping my head up as I face Ryan. "You know, you're almost bearable when you're not acting like a VP with a stick up his ass."

He chuckles. "And you're pretty fun when you're not being Satan."

"Ahhh… nice one." I nudge his shoulder playfully. "Maybe you're not as bad as I make you out to be," I say, more seriously this time. *But seriously—maybe he's not.*

"You know," he pauses, a smirk tugging at his lips. *God, those lips.* "For someone who thinks I'm such an asshole, you sure don't seem to mind spending all this time with me."

I lean forward, patting his chest. "Sometimes you just have to settle." *Oh Lord, his chest. These muscles. His warm skin. Shit.*

He inches closer. "And here I thought you were actually starting to like me." And then he moves another inch.

I want to laugh, make a joke, but I can't. I'm frozen as his eyes lock on me. I force a sarcastic laugh. "In your dreams, Ryan."

He moves even closer, and my breath catches. *No! I am not turned on… I'm mad at Ryan. He's a liar and a cheater—but is he?* Dammit! This is what I wanted—to play with him, make him want me, and then pull back. But I can't seem to pull back. Everything feels so good right now— so perfect. No matter how much I want to hate him, I want him. I want him so badly—even if he is married. *God, NO! That is so wrong.* I inch forward anyway, we're almost touching now. His eyes burn into mine. I want him to touch me, hold me—make everything in my life better.

He chuckles, low and deep, and I fixate on the sound. *Damn.* I can feel that too. He leans forward, his chest pressing against mine, and whispers in my ear, "You want to know about my dreams? Newport was PG compared to my dreams about you."

Oh.

My…

He grips my hips, pivoting us until my back is pressed against the wall of the pool. My breathing becomes shallow as his gaze fixes on my mouth. I can't look away. My stomach flutters in anticipation as I feel the ache between my legs starting to drum, a heavy pulsing that's desperate for friction. Everything is so confusing.

His thumb starts caressing my hip, and it takes everything in me to not arch into him. Here's the test. Will he make a move? Will he go too far? I silently plead that he will. It's selfish and wrong—I know—but it would feel so good right now. And I want him. I really do. He slips his thumb beneath the edge of my swimsuit, hooking it around and giving it a slight tug. I gasp, surprising myself, and without thinking, I wrap my arms around his waist, pulling him closer.

He closes his eyes and takes a deep breath. "Cooper." He rubs his lips together. "We should probably get out of the pool."

Wait. What? No.

I let my hands trail slowly up his chest, wrapping them around his neck, hoping to push him just far enough that he won't say no.

Come on, Ryan. Make your move. Kiss me. I can't tell if I want him to kiss me so I can call him out or if I just need to feel his lips on mine.

His eyes lock with mine, and I see a storm of lust mixed with something that looks like disappointment. His hand hovers near my hips, indecisive. Before I can stop myself, I press my lips to his. For a moment, he doesn't pull away, he kisses me back. His hands tighten on my waist. I can feel my body coiling up, begging for release.

He pulls back suddenly, taking my hands in his and gently lowering them into the water, as if breaking the moment is the hardest thing he's ever done. "You're engaged, Cooper. Don't be that person," he murmurs, his voice strained, his breath hot against my lips.

What? He's pulling that card on me? Acting like I'm the bad guy? The cheater?

I step closer, our lips almost touching. "Oh yeah? And what about you?"

He scowls, confused. "What do you mean?"

"Your wife, Ryan… or did you forget about her?"

With a disgusted sigh, I dip under the water and push myself toward the stairs.

"Cooper," he calls after me.

I don't look back as I climb out of the pool.

"Cooper!" Ryan shouts from the pool. I gather my things, my movements jerky and rushed, as I see him push himself up on the edge, ready to hop out. I spin on my heel, storming off as fast as possible.

"Cooper!"

I walk faster, almost running. I'm dripping wet, and the second I get inside, I stab the elevator button repeatedly. "Come on, come on, come on," I plead, my voice rising with panic. The elevator to my right dings open just as Ryan reaches for the handle of the glass door.

I hammer the close doors button in the elevator. "Come on, come on," I mutter loudly, teeth clenched. The doors start to close as Ryan lunges forward. They shut just in time, my eyes locking with his, my glare cold as dry ice, burning to the touch.

I release a breath I didn't know I was holding. My heart is pounding like a drum in my chest, my hands trembling. I will them to steady as the elevator climbs to the fifteenth floor. I know he's going to follow me, and I'm realizing I haven't thought this through. As soon as the doors open, I rush down the hallway, slipping inside my room just as I hear him call my name.

What am I even doing? What am I going to do now—just hole up in my room like a child? *Shit. What have I done?* Why didn't I just ask him about his wife? Did I really just create all this drama because I can't decide if I want a reason to hate Ryan or to fuck him? Maybe I just want to feel something—anything—different from what I have with Brad.

Maybe I want to feel what I felt in Newport.

God, I'm so fucked up.

That's when the tears come.

And the pounding on the door.

"Cooper! Open the door."

I squeeze my eyes shut and slide my back down the wall, letting my head hang heavy in my hands, elbows resting on my knees.

"Cooper. Open the goddamn door. Let me explain."

I don't say anything. I just silently sob.

I silently hate myself.

What kind of person does this?

The kind that feels trapped.

Chapter 17

COOPER

I cried myself to sleep after the pool, a mix of emotional exhaustion and the edible catching up with me. I woke up at 11:00 PM and I've tried to fall back to sleep, but now I'm too restless. My mind is going a million different directions. Sitting up, I reach for the remote. Some mindless television might help. But a few minutes later, I find myself in bed with the lamp on, staring at the TV, without actually watching it. My thoughts are all over the place. I think about Brad, Ryan, hell, even my mom and dad. How did I end up in a relationship like theirs? Is cheating like abuse—one of those cycles that's hard to break? Is it a pattern that gets passed down?

I wonder what it is about me that makes me stay with Brad—what's different about me and Casey. Are we different, or did she just find one of the good ones?

Do I really believe Ryan's an asshole? Is Brad actually a good guy? How can I love my dad so much when he betrayed my mom too many times to count? And why do I blame her for everything, even when she was the one who was hurt the most? Is this a me problem or a them problem—or are we just humans that sometimes lose ourselves when it all goes to hell?

I groan in frustration. The real question I should be asking myself is: *What am I going to do about this mess I've created?* I'm at a loss. Ever since the Christmas party, I've been so in my head. Brad and I haven't stopped fighting, and Casey's words about him being so nice because he's cheating again echo in my mind every single day. The worst part is, if I just looked, I'm sure I could find evidence. But I'm scared to look—scared for it to be true. What would I even do if I found it? Try to break it off again? I know how that goes—how he goes. *God, I don't think I can do this anymore.*

I grab my phone.

"Shit."

Three missed calls and multiple texts from Brad. I stare at them, too drained to even read what he's said. *I'm so tired of fighting with him.* There's also a text from Ryan. My pulse quickens as I tap his name, holding my breath. There are two texts, the first one sent about thirty minutes after he stopped knocking on the door.

> **Ryan:** Tomorrow, we need to check the terms of the lease before the next property meeting. I'll handle it if you still want to visit the co-working spaces in the afternoon.

> **Ryan:** I wish you'd at least let me explain. Then you could decide if you really hated me.

I sigh. Things are going to be so awkward tomorrow. I suddenly feel as if I'm being suffocated, the air too thick to breathe. I need to get out—*now.* I throw on some leggings and a tank top, and grab my book. Maybe the lobby has a vibey place with a fireplace that I can cozy up to and read for a bit. That usually helps clear my mind.

* * * * * * * * * *

I step onto the shiny marble floor from the elevator. The lobby's still buzzing with noise, music and people, even though it's close to midnight. I decide to take a lap around the main floor, scope out a spot for my reading. I walk toward the main bar—it has a vibe, but too loud for reading. It's not overly crowded, being a weeknight, but there are still a handful of people scattered throughout.

One of them… is Ryan.

I freeze. He's sitting alone at the bar, hands cupped around a glass, his eyes glassy and distant. He looks miserable.

But damn, he also looks hot as hell. He's wearing a T-shirt with his hair a little messy on top, like he's run his hand through it a few times. The fabric of his shirt stretches against his biceps, and for a second, I forget why I'm even mad.

Ryan picks up his glass and takes a sip, his eyes finding mine as he sets it down. His expression stays neutral, unreadable. And now I have a choice to make. I could turn around and deal with this tomorrow, push it off for another day, or I could face the mess I've created—let him explain. *God, when did I become such a chickenshit?*

I take a deep breath and exhale slowly, steeling myself as I walk toward him. His eyes follow me every step of the way.

"Is this seat taken?" I ask softly.

"Why don't you tell me? You seem to know everything." His tone is flat, and it's clear from his glassy eyes and the way he holds his drink that he's had more than a few.

"I didn't come over here to fight with you, Ryan." I slide into the chair next to him, even though it's obvious I'm not exactly welcome.

He scoffs. "Sure you didn't." He takes another sip.

The bartender comes over, and I order a shot of tequila. Because holy shit, I need one right now. He pours it, and I throw it back, biting into the lime as the burn slides down my throat.

I slam the glass down, trying not to cringe. "Can I get another one?" I'm going to need a buzz to get through this.

Ryan raises an eyebrow, his voice edged with bitterness. "Am I *that* hard to be around?"

"You have no idea," I say, tipping the second shot back, then meeting his gaze. "But not in the way you think."

He laughs, low and bitter. "So… what are you here for then?"

"I didn't know you'd be down here. I came to read… but then I saw you."

"Couldn't sleep?" he asks, finally turning his head to look at me.

I shake my head. "Nope. You?"

"Same." He turns back to his drink.

I watch as Ryan stares down at his glass, swirling it like he's searching for answers in the amber liquid. He looks… tired. Not the kind of tired you get from work, but something deeper.

He leans back, his eyes leaving the glass long enough to meet mine. "So, why'd you come over here if you were just going to read? Did you come to torture me some more?"

I scowl. "No… I don't want to torture you."

His gaze drops to my chest, his expression unreadable. "Sure, you don't." He grips his glass tighter, taking another sip. "You're good, I'll give you that."

"I don't know what you're talking about. You're just drunk, talking nonsense," I say, my defenses rising.

He chuckles softly, shaking his head. "Maybe. But earlier… at the pool. Your whole seductive show. The touching, the teasing—turning me on. If that's what you were trying to do… well, congrats, it worked." His voice is rough. He kicks back the rest of his drink, as if he's trying to drown the thought. "Made me want to fuck you right then and there. Isn't that what you wanted?" He shakes his head, looking away for a moment before meeting my gaze again. "Because I sure as hell don't know what you want from me, Cooper. I'm tired of guessing."

I blink, caught off guard. I don't know what to say. But *damn, he wanted to fuck me?* My stomach tightens, fire surging through my veins, heat flashing under my skin. I lift my glass and take a sip of water, hoping to steady the chaos raging inside of me.

"Is it to prove I'm an asshole? That I'd cheat on my wife if you pushed hard enough?" His eyes lock onto mine, the hurt and frustration clear. "Is that it?"

"Ryan… I—"

He cuts me off, his tone sharper. "And then when I stop it… because *you*, Cooper, are engaged—you still call me out. You still think *I'm* the asshole. Even though I would *never* sleep with you knowing you're with someone else, out of respect for Brad, even though I *don't* respect him… and even though I'd love nothing more than to take you back to my hotel room right now."

His words hang in the air between us. My face heats up, and every breath becomes a struggle. His eyes burn into mine with such an intensity, I can't tell if it's pure hatred or desire. But *God,* I hope it's the latter because hearing him say that… it makes me feel alive.

I take a deep inhale, trying to string together one rational sentence—anything that might make sense. "Is that what you think this is? Some game to see if I could get under your skin?" I know, on some level, that's exactly what it was, but I never considered what it would do to him—to Ryan. I was so sure he was just another cheater, and it felt justified. But, if I'm being honest with myself, I think I also just needed to know if he still wanted me—if he still found me desirable.

He gives a half-shrug, but there's an edge of defeat in his voice. "Isn't it? Seemed like a pretty damn good way to keep hating me. Or at least make me feel guiltier than I already do." He slams his glass down onto the counter. "I'm tired. I'll see you tomorrow."

He starts to stand, and I reflexively grab his arm.

"No, Ryan. Stay. Look, I didn't come down here to keep this war going. I came to fix it. I want to understand—about your wife, about… everything."

He lets out a bitter chuckle. "Oh, so now you want to understand? Could've fooled me with the whole 'drag me to hell' routine."

"Okay, fair. I deserve that. I've been a total bitch, okay? I admit it. Just… sit down. Please."

He hesitates, but reluctantly sits.

"Look, when I found out that you had a wife… I was shocked… and… I was so mad at you. You judged me so harshly when you found out I was engaged, made me feel so guilty about Newport." I press a hand to my chest. "Something I've never wanted to feel bad about because…"

I stop myself. *Did I really just almost admit to Ryan Brooks how incredible he is in bed?*

A knowing smirk tugs at Ryan's lips. "I knew it." He chuckles. "Go on, say it."

I can't stop the smile sneaking onto my face. He knows, but my pride won't let me say it. "Never." I bring my water to my lips, hiding behind the glass as the cool liquid hits my tongue, my eyes never leaving his.

He relents. "Fine. I'll say it." He leans in closer. "That night was un-believable. God. That was the best damn sex of my entire life. *You* were unforgettable." His eyes drift over me, smoldering. "I've thought about it more times than I'd care to admit."

Jesus. If words could make a girl come…

I smother the grin that threatens to spread across my face. I guess flirting is still in the bounds of his integrity. "Really? The best you ever had?"

"The best," he says, unapologetically.

"Fine. You weren't bad yourself."

He scoffs, shaking his head. "Right." He knows I'm lying.

I smile and take a deep breath. "Let's try not to get sidetracked. Since we're on the topic of Newport… Tell me about your marriage. Did you make me the other woman? Because I had broken up with Brad. I know it was only for a few days, but I wanted to be done, wanted to move on." I pause, my voice softening. "I don't want to hate you, Ryan. But I need to know."

He furrows his brows. "No. I would never cheat… on anyone."

"But you had a wife, and you still have a wife. So, how the hell could you have not cheated? If you're married, it's called cheating. If you're…"

"Cooper," he interrupts, his tone firm. "Just let me explain, please. Let me get it all out before you say anything, alright?"

I exhale loudly, rolling my eyes. "Fine," I mutter.

"My wife and I moved to Chicago a year and a half ago. We both started working immediately. She took on an executive admin position, and within three months of being here, I found out she was having an affair with her boss."

Whoa. Okay, this is not at all what I expected. I blink, momentarily caught off guard.

"I guess I'm not one of those people who can stay with someone who cheats." He shrugs. "And maybe that makes me a shitty person. But I checked out immediately—physically and emotionally. I moved into the guest bedroom, cut off all physical touch… told her I wanted a divorce. Mentally, I was a fucking mess." He pauses, bringing his hand to the back of his neck, gripping the skin. His eyes close, wincing, as if he's reliving the pain. He brings his arms down to the counter, leaning on them for support. "She threw away ten years of marriage for a guy she barely knew."

"Oh my God. Ten years?" I ask automatically.

He nods. "By the time I was in Newport, it had been six months, I'd moved out, and was living in an Airbnb, looking for a permanent place. I'd filed for divorce. She'd already been served the papers." He looks at me. "Then I met you."

I swallow hard, trying to process what he's just said.

"The morning after you and I… slept together, I woke up to you being gone, and a voicemail from Beth. They'd found a lump in her breast, and she was scared—asked if I'd go with her to the appointment." He pauses for a drink of water, his throat noticeably scratchy. "Anyway, long story short—she has breast cancer. She was on my insurance, and the coverage her company offered wasn't great. Plus, she needed the emotional support. So, we stayed married on paper, and I moved back into the guest bedroom to help her through the radiation…" He chokes up. "To be there for her."

He looks at me, smiling softly. "I still love Beth. She was my best friend for twelve years. We had a good marriage…" He does the sexy cheek-sucking thing. "I thought we did anyway." He takes a deep breath, and presses his forehead against his fingers, rubbing the skin. "I still feel like shit every day when I look at her—because she's in hell, and I can't be that man for her. The one that forgives—gives her another chance… And then there's you." He pauses, his gaze fixed on me. "I told her I slept with you when I moved back in. She was hurt, but she understood. We were over. There was nothing for her to be angry about."

I meet his gaze, my own emotions threatening. There's something so broken in his tone. I didn't think I'd ever see him like this—unguarded, bruised, and a bit lost. Maybe I'm not the only one trapped in a mess I don't know how to fix. And *damn*, Ryan's actually a really good person.

I reach for his arm, resting my hand on it. "I'm so sorry, Ryan. Truly."

He nods, his expression softening for just a moment before he continues. "Do you want to know one of the hardest parts about all this?"

"What is it?" I ask sincerely.

"Not only am I constantly worried about Beth… but I'm racked with guilt. She wants to work things out—go to couples therapy. And here I am, leaving my wife while she's fighting cancer… all while thinking about this she-devil who knows exactly how to push my buttons."

He chuckles bitterly, shaking his head. "She teases and tempts me—drives me fucking insane." His gaze flicks to mine, and there's a moment of raw vulnerability in his eyes. "And the worst part? She's in a relationship where she doesn't even seem happy."

His eyes lock onto mine, piercing, unflinching. "So, tell me, Cooper. Why do you stay with Brad?"

His words hit me like a freight train. *Am I that transparent?*

Does he know about Brad? About the cheating? God, Ryan was with his wife for twelve years. She had one affair, and he was done. Does that make me weak for staying? Or stronger for trying? I don't know anymore. I just know I'm too embarrassed to admit I've been in the same boat—and I keep choosing to stay.

Is it even a choice, though? It feels more complicated than that. Because every time Brad and I come to a head, every time he twists that knife, planting those doubts and pleading his case, it makes it that much harder to leave the next time.

I wish I had Ryan's courage.

I wish I could just fucking leave.

But life's not that simple for me.

Chapter 18

RYAN

I watch her as she processes everything I just said. Maybe I've had one too many drinks—I definitely said too much. I've been too honest, too blunt, too bold. But I'm too tired to care anymore. While I love the flirtatious banter, I'm over this up-and-down bullshit that she keeps dishing out.

I'm crazy about Cooper. I think about her constantly. Fuck, even when Beth's mouth was around my cock, I thought of Cooper. And maybe that makes me a complete asshole, but I can't help it. I want her. And I want her to break up with her douchebag fiancé.

I lost my head tonight in the pool. She was testing me, pushing my limits—I could see that. But part of it was real. The fun, carefree Cooper who laughed and played in the pool with me like we were teenagers—that side of her was real.

She's now scowling at me. "What makes you think I'm not happy in my relationship?"

Ah, so she's going to avoid everything I said about her and go straight to defending Brad.

I shrug. "Mostly comments you've made… A few things, actually. The way you roll your eyes or sigh when he texts or calls. The way you were on edge at the Christmas Party, and then I saw you two arguing—the fact that you're still fighting ten days later. And, honestly, the fact that you just kissed me in the pool." I hesitate, unsure if I should say more, but I do. "I heard you two this morning… arguing." I grimace. "Was that about me?"

I wait for some snappy response about my huge ego.

She sighs heavily. "God, this is so embarrassing." She leans back, folding her arms. "Brad's always been a little insecure when it comes to me. He's very much the jealous type." She pauses, like she's debating how much to tell me. "He thinks you want to fuck me. That's what we were fighting about at the Christmas party… and again this morning. And ever since then, it feels like we fight about every little thing. It's been… really shitty."

"I'm sorry," I say, and I mean it. I never wanted to be the cause of contention between them, but Brad's not wrong. He sees it clearly—because it's true. I do want that. I want her. I want all of her. And maybe that makes me selfish, but I can't pretend otherwise.

"I keep reassuring him that you're married, and that you're not interested." Her eyes find mine, biting her lip, hesitant. "Even though I know that he's right," she whispers.

I smile, laughing softly. "Yeah. I think we've established that." She laughs with me. "Are you happy?" I ask.

She pauses, her eyes going misty before she shakes her head. "No. Not really… I used to be, but I haven't been for a while now." She scoffs. "Lately, it seems like the only thing keeping us together is sex. That's it. And even that's become toxic most of the time."

"Why do you stay then?"

She lets out a sharp, hollow laugh. "I ask myself that question all the time." She shakes her head, taking a deep breath before exhaling slowly. "I don't know… Somewhere along the way, I just completely lost myself—my courage, my confidence." She shrugs, avoiding my eyes. "It's embarrassing, really. And now… I don't know how to leave. Or maybe I've just convinced myself I can't." Her gaze finally meets mine. "And every time I try, I just end up back where I started."

"What do you mean you don't know how to leave? You just pack up your things and go."

"It's not that easy, Ryan. I love Brad, or at least I used to. He just… Ugh! He's good at playing the victim, you know? Sometimes I feel like a puppet, and it drives me crazy, but it's easier to keep the peace than to disturb it."

Fuck. Brad sounds like a controlling asshole. Everything she's saying screams manipulation.

"I don't know what to say," I finally admit. "But you deserve more than a guy who makes you feel like a puppet, Cooper."

She shrugs. "Maybe… Maybe not."

Shit, hearing this pisses me the fuck off. If there's one thing I know about Cooper, it's that she's feisty as hell. I'd never guess she wasn't the one calling the shots in her relationship, and the fact that she's not says a lot about Brad. If she were mine, she'd have me wrapped around her tiny little finger. I place my hand on her back. "You ever think about what it'd be like if you left?"

She laugh-cries, wiping at her eyes. "All the fucking time."

A heavy silence stretches between us. I should probably back off, give her space. But I don't. "Then leave. Why stay with a guy who doesn't see you? Who doesn't deserve you?"

She bites her lip, and for a second, I think she might actually tell me. But then she shakes her head. "You wouldn't understand."

"Try me."

She squeezes her eyes shut, her voice barely a whisper. "I don't really want to talk about it."

"Hey," I say softly, rubbing her back. She leans forward, cupping her forehead, hiding her eyes. "Hey." I feel her take a breath, and after a moment, she sits up, dabbing at her eyes with a cocktail napkin.

"Has he ever hurt you?" I have to ask it.

"No. God, no. He would never." She shakes her head, folding her arms tightly. "I promise. He's not like that, he's just… I don't know. Selfish. And he can be mean—not physically, but with his words, you know?"

She looks away, taking a shaky breath. "I'm starting to wonder if maybe I'm one of those women. Stuck in this cycle, making excuses for him, brushing things off. Is he a narcissist? Am I just brainwashed? I don't know. But I keep letting him pull me back in, and it's like… God, I don't even know who I am anymore."

I want more than anything to fix this for her, but the words sit there, lodged in my throat, useless. What the hell am I supposed to say? I've heard about situations like this, but I've never had someone I care about stuck in one.

She's strong as hell, though—more than she knows.

She musters a small, shaky smile, her eyes glassy. "But what about you? What are you going to do about Beth?"

I take the shift in conversation as a sign that she's done talking about it and force myself to follow her lead.

I shrug. "What is there to do? I just have to be patient. Pray for her next follow-up to go well, and try to move on with my life."

"You really don't want to work things out? You can't forgive her?"

"It's not about forgiveness. Sure, I can forgive her, but I can't just forget what happened. I thought everything was great, you know? I'd never be able to fully trust her again." I pick up my glass, swirling the ice inside. "It wouldn't be fair to either of us." I take a long drink of the cold water. "If you don't have trust in a relationship, you don't have anything."

From the look on her face, you'd think someone just knocked the wind out of her.

"Did you ever ask her why she cheated?" she asks. "It's just… you said you thought things were going well. So, I wonder… did you ask her *why* she did it?"

I raise a brow. "Would it matter?" I ask. Of course, I asked Beth why. That was one of the first things I wanted to know. But now I'm curious where Cooper is heading with this.

"I think it does. Usually, when a man cheats, it's physical—something about sex or opportunity. But when a woman cheats, it's often emotional. A need isn't being met, and someone else starts filling that role. So, I don't know… maybe you were working too much, and she felt disconnected—maybe she didn't mean for it to happen… Maybe it just did."

"I think it's a lot more nuanced than that." I scowl. "You're being awfully sympathetic to my wife who had an affair, when earlier you were ready to cast stones because you thought I was a cheater. Why the double standard?"

"Because it's different. Wanting to fuck someone isn't the same as wanting someone because they make you feel something."

"I would've rather she just fucked some guy. That would've hurt a hell of a lot less than developing feelings for someone."

"I don't think it's better. Especially when the other person is at home, willing and waiting for them."

"Are we talking about you or me now?" After hearing her argument with Brad this morning, it's pretty clear he's cheated on her.

"You," she says quickly. "I just can't imagine Beth went looking for someone else just for sex. It's not like you weren't home ready to be with her. And let's be honest, you're not ugly—something was off. But if it were reversed, if *you* had the affair… it'd probably be all about the physical desire, about the sex."

I lean in, my eyes laser focused. "Why do you want me to forgive my wife so much? Why are you so convinced she's innocent in all this?"

"I don't think she's innocent. I just…" She glances down at her hands, and then back to me. She exhales. "Because if I slept with you, I don't think I'd feel bad about it."

My pulse skips a beat. My eyes drop to her mouth, and I force them back to hers. I can't go there. It's not even on the table. She looks at me with a longing that breaks my heart. There's nothing I'd love more than to make her last sentence a reality. But it's not right. I sigh. "You're really that checked out?"

She nods, swallowing hard. "I think I've been checked out for a while. I just haven't wanted to admit it."

I reach over, brushing my hand against hers. "Look… if you need help with anything—somewhere to stay, or even just someone to talk to—I'm here. I'm a friend, Cooper."

"Thanks, Ryan." She smiles softly, her voice lighter than before. "So… apparently you're not an asshole."

I chuckle softly. "If only you'd asked me about Beth weeks ago."

"I know… I'm sorry that I didn't."

"It's okay."

"Why didn't you ever tell me about her? I mean, cancer, Ryan. *God*, that's heavy. I thought we were friends… before the Christmas party anyway." A smile tugs at one corner of her lips.

"I don't know," I say honestly. "I guess you were a bit of an escape." I let out a soft laugh. "You have a way of making me forget about all the shit—the cancer, the affair—Beth."

She licks her lips, her expression serious but unreadable.

"You know, if you do ever break up with Brad… I'd love to take you out—on a real date." I clear my throat, suddenly nervous even though I've confessed worse. "I've wanted that since the moment I laid eyes on you. Come on, Cooper. There's something here—don't tell me I'm the only one who feels it."

Her smile's soft, and her gaze drops briefly before meeting mine again. "Maybe you're right."

I lean closer. "I bet we'd discover a hell of a lot more in that pool without the boundaries. No bullshit. Just us."

Her lips twitch, mischief dancing in her eyes. She tilts her head, her voice dipping into a sultry tease. "So… you're saying it'd be all about the orgasms, then?"

Just hearing her say the word orgasm gets me hard.

"Well, if I remember correctly, you had a lot of those in Newport." I smirk, cocking a brow. "And I know you weren't faking it."

She smacks her lips together, shaking her head, trying to hold out, but finally she relents. "Fine. You win." She holds up her hand, mouthing 'five' as she grins.

"Five?" I ask, my eyes widening. "You had five orgasms?"

"Mm hmm." She pats my arms. "But I'll still never admit it was good."

"Oh!" I say laughing. "You just confessed to five orgasms. I think that speaks for itself."

"Well, I've always orgasmed easily, so don't let it go to your head."

"Still… five?" I shake my head in disbelief.

I watch her for a moment longer, not wanting the night to end, but knowing we have a long day ahead of us tomorrow. We've settled into something comfortable, and part of me wants to stay right here, keep talking. But we both know where this is headed if we keep it up, and it's probably not the best idea.

"We should probably head upstairs," I say reluctantly. "Looks like they're closing up, plus we have a busy day tomorrow."

"You're probably right." She slides out of the stool, turning to wait for me as I close our tab.

We walk back to our rooms in a comfortable silence, side by side. And for the first time since the Christmas party, it doesn't feel like we're at war.

When we get to her door, she turns to me. "Thanks for talking to me, Ryan."

I don't bother hiding the seriousness in my voice. "Anytime. Just… think about what you want. And if you need to talk, you know where to find me."

She swallows, her eyes flicking to my lips for a split second. I could kiss her right now, pull her into my room—pick up where we left off at the pool. But I don't. Instead, I pull her in for a hug. She wraps her arms tightly around my waist, and I grin. We've broken past the angry barriers she put up. We're friends again—though I want so much more. I want her so badly it hurts.

When she steps back, she lingers, staring at my mouth. "Good night, Ryan." She slips into her room without another word.

Chapter 19

COOPER

"Are you going home for the holidays?" I ask, kicking back the last drop of wine from my plastic cup.

"Yeah, but not until Christmas Eve," Ryan replies. "What about you? You spending Christmas with your dad or your mom?"

"My dad. I spent last Christmas with my mom, so I'm going to Newport this year." I smile. "I'm excited to spend time with my sister. I haven't seen her since…" I pause, looking at him. "Well, since… you know, the last time I was in Newport."

The plane hits turbulence, and I instinctively grip Ryan's thigh, my whole body tensing as I squeeze my eyes shut. "Shit," I whisper.

Realizing my hand's on him, I start to pull back, but his hand covers mine, weaving our fingers together. His thumb brushes gently along my skin, each stroke sending a fire through my veins, igniting something deep within my core.

"You okay?" Ryan's eyes meet mine with a tenderness that makes me melt.

I take a deep breath, trying to focus. "Yeah, I'm okay." I say, forcing a small smile. "I just… hate flying. Turbulence freaks me out."

He gives my hand a squeeze before letting go. "Well, I'm right here if you need me."

"Thanks… Are you spending time with your sisters while you're in Arizona?" I ask, eager to keep the conversation going.

"Yeah, for the holiday stuff. The whole family will be at my parents' place on Christmas Day—my sisters, their families… and me, alone, for the first time in eleven years."

It's me that reaches for his hand this time. I place mine on top of his, resting on his leg. "I'm so sorry, Ryan." I furrow my brows. "I can't imagine what you're going through." And I mean it. Ryan's leaving someone he actually gets along with, someone he's loved for so long. Plus, I know he's worried sick about Beth.

"Thanks. I appreciate that." His gaze holds mine, and for a moment, I forget that I'm engaged—that my fiancé is waiting for me at home. It's just me and Ryan, like we're a team. He breaks the moment, clearing his throat. "Is your dad bringing anyone new this year?"

I laugh. "God, I hope not. Not that I know of, but a lot can happen in a week with my dad."

"And what about Brad? Where does he fit into your holiday plans? Is he going to Newport with you?"

The discomfort of his question lingers between us, and I break our gaze, looking down at my hands. "Yeah. Brad's coming to Newport. He has a work trip right before Christmas, so he won't come until Christmas Eve. But we'll do Christmas morning with my dad. Casey and her family will come over for brunch and presents around noon." I can feel his eyes on me, daring me to look at him, so I do. "It should be fun." I add, forcing a smile.

"That's great," he says, though his sincerity falls flat.

I sigh loudly. "Look, Ryan, I know I said things last night—things I probably shouldn't have. But I had that edible, and those shots… I was feeling vulnerable and on edge from my argument with Brad… and my day with you."

He interrupts me. "Why shouldn't you have said things? Was it the truth?" He looks at me with a challenge in his eyes, and I know he sees right through me. "That was the most honest I've ever seen you. There's no reason to feel bad about that."

"Of course I feel bad. I took almost five years of my relationship and discredited it in thirty seconds. I still care for Brad. He has a lot of great qualities, and I made him out to be some asshole just because things are rocky right now. We've had our moments, you know? Times when it felt… good, sometimes even great."

"Okay. You don't have to justify anything to me, Cooper. This is your life, not mine. If you say things are good, then all I can do is hope that they are."

God, he doesn't believe me.

I don't know if I even believe myself.

"Okay. Can we please just talk about something else?" I ask.

"Sure. What do you want to talk about?"

"I don't know. Anything but this. Do you like rom-coms?"

"Random… But yeah, I enjoy a rom-com, as long as it's not too girly."

"What's your favorite rom-com?"

He grins. "*Wedding Crashers.*"

I laugh. "Is that just the universal favorite for all men?"

"Don't you like it?" he asks.

"Of course I like it. Who doesn't like that movie?"

"So what's your favorite rom-com then?"

"*When Harry Met Sally,*" I say, unable to keep from smiling. "I just love the whole friends-falling-in-love thing. They just have each other's backs, you know? They support each other… and there's this deep trust. It's just a beautiful story. The kind of relationship where, when they're old and gray, Harry can't get it up, and Sally's too tired, it won't matter." I glance at Ryan, and he's smiling. "They've built this solid friendship underneath it all. They'll still have things to talk about, or just enjoy sitting in silence. That's a rare find." I shrug. "I don't know. I guess that's something I hope for one day."

Ryan stares at me, like he's seeing straight through to my soul. "It is a rare thing. And I hope you find it someday," he says softly.

* * * * * * * * * *

Ryan and I walk through the terminal together in comfortable silence, having already talked plenty on the flight back. Today went well. It was our last day in Austin, and it was productive. We visited a few more co-working spaces, reviewed lease agreements, and ultimately chose Austin Work Space, securing corporate approval. It's a relief to have that stress lifted.

Things have been easy between us today, though after the kiss in the pool, our late-night confessions, and the almost-kiss last night, the tension between us is high—an undeniable chemistry, simmering just below the surface.

Ryan and I reach the point where we part ways—him heading to parking and me to passenger pick up, where Brad's waiting for me.

He stops, turning to me with a small smile. "Well, I'll see you Monday. Interesting trip…" He chuckles. "But productive, at least."

"It was definitely interesting," I say, managing a smile.

He pulls me into a hug, and I can't help myself—I melt into it. When I pull back, Ryan's eyes meet mine. "Be strong, alright? Don't be a puppet."

I nod. "See you, Ryan." I turn to head toward Brad, unsure of what awaits me—or what I'm leaving behind.

$* * * * *$ $* * * * *$

Brad pulls up and hops out to grab my bag. "Hey, baby." He pulls me in for a kiss, and I reluctantly kiss him back, though my instinct is to resist.

I settle into the passenger seat, my guard up, ready for battle. As Brad pulls onto the road, I turn up the music, hoping to avoid conversation.

After a few minutes, Brad reaches over, lowering the volume. He gives me a sidelong glance. "Are you just planning to not speak to me, Cooper?"

I shrug. "I really don't know what to say."

"Baby." He takes my hand in his. "I don't want to fight anymore. Can we just let this whole work trip thing go? Start tonight with a clean slate?"

I furrow my brows, pursing my lips. "That's not really how things work, babe. You didn't just accuse Ryan of using this trip to get close to me—you insinuated I went on this trip because I wanted to sleep with him to get back at you."

"Well, do you?"

"I'm not even answering that. It's pointless. You don't listen anyway."

His eyes narrow. "It's not like it'd be the first time. I mean, Jesus, Cooper. How am I supposed to trust you now that I know about your little affair in Newport? What am I supposed to think?"

Hot tears sting my eyes as my breath comes sharper and sharper, nostrils flaring with each exhalation. Anger tightens in my chest and I clench my fists, my voice brittle with emotion. "God, Brad." My voice cracks, adrenaline slicing through me. "I can't do this anymore." I hold back the tears, refusing to let him see me break. "I'm done. I'm just fucking done."

He scoffs. "I knew it."

I let out a defeated sigh. "You knew what?"

"You fucked him." He glances at me. "You fucked him, didn't you?" He turns back to the road, and all I can do is stare.

My gaze burns into the side of his face as I choke back the emotion, the hurt—the pain. I shake my head slowly, too defeated to even defend myself. I can't win. I never could with him. "Whatever, Brad." My voice is quiet, all the fight in me—gone.

"Baby, I need to know. Did you?"

I stare out the window.

"Coop." He grabs my hand, squeezing it.

I keep my eyes on the passing cars. "Why do you even ask when you don't believe me anyway?"

"Coop, come on, look at me."

Reluctantly, I meet his gaze.

"Did you sleep with Ryan?"

I shake my head, my voice barely a whisper. "No."

He sighs, pressing my hand to his lips. "Baby, I'm sorry. I'm sorry for being possessive and jealous—for accusing you. I worry all the time that you're going to leave me. And honestly, I wouldn't blame you after what I've put you through." He takes a deep breath, and I just stare, trying to decide if he's being sincere or feeding me a load of crap. "And then I meet this Ryan guy… he's good-looking, and he obviously has a thing for you. You're around him all the time at work, and now with these trips? I've been a mess, Coop—stuck in my head, thinking the worst. Almost preparing myself for the day you come home and tell me you slept with him… or that you're calling off the engagement."

I feel trapped between my feelings, the lies, and Brad. "Nothing happened. We worked. We looked at properties, had meetings, ate meals. That's it. You don't need to worry. We're still engaged." I give him a reassuring smile as he glances at me.

"Coop, I really don't know what I'd do if I lost you. I can't lose you. God, I love you so much." He chokes up. Brad doesn't ever cry. My heart lurches. I feel for him—I remember the paranoia and constant fighting after I first caught him cheating. But I also can't keep going in these circles.

"I'm so sorry if I've been absent, or an ass, or both. You're my number one priority for now on. Let's pick a date, baby. Let's pick a date and start planning our wedding." He squeezes my hand.

The walls of the car seem to close in on me, crushing my airway—I can't think. "Okay. Yeah, let's pick a date," I say automatically, as if I'm a robot that's been programmed to just agree.

Brad starts talking about a fall wedding for next year, but I'm only half-listening. My mind races. *What the hell is wrong with me?* I was ready to leave a few minutes ago, and now I'm nodding along to wedding plans. I think about how I'm assertive in every other part of my life, but with Brad, I become this passive, wimpy person I barely recognize—and I don't like her.

When we get home, I head straight to my closet to unpack, hoping Brad leaves me to the silence of my own thoughts—even though they're torturous right now. I hang up the clothes I didn't wear, replaying the week in my mind: the time spent with Ryan, the laughter in the car, us playing in the pool, the vulnerable moments, our confessions. God, I wish I could stop thinking, just for one second.

Exhausted, I crawl into bed and turn off my lamp, praying Brad doesn't want sex. *Who am I kidding?* If there's one thing I know about Brad, it's that he'll definitely want to have sex.

I feel him sink into the bed beside me. He scoots behind me, and sure enough, his arm slides around my waist as he kisses my shoulder. His hand wanders down lower toward my shorts. I turn to him, meeting his lips in a quick kiss. "I'm exhausted, babe. Can this wait until tomorrow, when I have more energy?"

Brad sighs, disappointed. "Sure. I just missed you… it's been a week."

Guilt tugs at me. "You're right," I say softly. "Maybe I can be on bottom tonight?"

"God, never mind. If you don't want to have sex just say so."

I thought I just did.

"I do want to… I'm just tired, so I'd like to be on the bottom. Feel that strong body over mine," I add, coaxing him. Brad may know how to pull my strings, but I've learned a few tricks myself. I turn toward him, my hands gliding over his chest and stomach.

"Are you sure?" he murmurs, a bit softer now. "You know I don't want it unless you're into it. I want to make sure you feel good. That turns me on."

"Yeah, I'm sure," I say, grinding against him, playing up my desire.

A few minutes in, he rolls me on top of him, and I'm beyond annoyed. I play along, half-heartedly, then finally shift to my back, reaching for him in ways that'll keep him happy so I can lie here and zone out. Brad pushes into me, but my thoughts drift to Ryan again and our conversation at the bar. He really listened—heard me, saw me. Brad doesn't see me, and he sure as shit doesn't hear me.

My eyes fix on the ceiling fan, and I count each click as it spins around and around, anything to distract me from Brad's rhythm, which feels more like a drill than passion.

"Baby," Brads voice snaps me to the present. "Where are you? I feel like I'm fucking a starfish."

If I tell him I spaced out, he'll be offended—I might as well tell him I fell asleep.

"I'm here, babe," I say, trying to sound convincing. "Just focused… I'm almost there. Don't stop, or I'll lose it."

That satisfies him. He keeps going, and I make all the sounds he wants to hear, gasping and moaning as if I'm caught up in the moment. "Oh God," I cry, "I'm going to come." But I'm not. I tip my head back, pretending to orgasm—something I've never done—until now.

Ryan's words echo in my mind: *Don't be a puppet.* The irony isn't lost on me—I feel like a marionette, with Brad pulling every string, performing a part I didn't audition for. I act like this is everything I want, that he's everything I need. But every day, I'm realizing more and more that he's not. This isn't what I want—I'm not happy.

Later, I lie in bed, my mind racing as silent tears fall down my cheeks. And for the second time this week, I cry myself to sleep.

Chapter 20

RYAN

"No, no, no, no! Hold on to the damn ball!" I shout at the TV, while Leo groans in frustration beside me. "What was that?" I ask, shooting him a look.

"They're playing like shit," Leo mutters.

It's Sunday night football—Bears vs. Rams—and the Bears are getting their asses kicked. It's halftime, and we can only hope for a better second half.

Vivian comes down after putting their daughter, Isla, to bed. "Who's winning?" she asks, standing behind the couch. She tips Leo's head back to give him a kiss.

"The Rams," I answer with a sigh.

"Mmm," Leo responds to her kiss. "How'd she go down, babe?"

"Pretty easily tonight. Had to read *Guess How Much I Love You* three times, though. She's obsessed." Vivian's hands move to Leo's shoulders, kneading them gently.

"That's my girl. She knows what she wants and doesn't take no for an answer—just like her mum. Come sit, babe." Leo pats the seat next to him.

"I can't. I've got some work to look over before tomorrow. But you two enjoy the game. Ryan, can I get you anything? I stocked the bathrooms with everything I could think of, but if I missed something, just let me know."

"I will, Vivian. Thank you, again," I reply.

She leans down, whispering something in Leo's ear that makes him grin.

"Oh, I won't, babe."

She kisses his cheek before heading up the stairs.

I watch her go, a pang of sadness gripping my chest, as I remember how Beth and I used to be like them. I look over at Leo. "You two seem really happy."

He glances at me, nodding. "We are, mate. Happiest I've ever been." He pauses, his expression thoughtful. "I'm sorry about you and Beth. How are you feeling about your decision?"

"I mean, it's real shitty. But I know it was the right thing to do for me. And Beth's going to be okay. She's always been strong and independent."

I officially moved out tonight. I only packed a suitcase for now—I figure I can always go back for more. It was a sudden decision, one I made after coming home from the work trip with Cooper. I didn't make the decision because of Cooper, but I know my feelings for her influenced it. Leo offered up his place temporarily while I look for something permanent. I mentioned wanting to move out after we played pickleball, and he insisted I stay with them. I hate feeling like I'm intruding, but they have the space, and their townhouse is perfectly located—right off the river. I have an entire floor to myself, and I can walk to work.

"And she has a follow-up tomorrow?" Leo asks.

"Yeah. She's been on hormone therapy for a few months now. Things are looking as good as they can. We just hope she continues to move in the right direction."

"How did she take the news about you moving out?"

I sigh. "She was disappointed… obviously. She's been holding out hope that I'd come back around… But I don't think she was surprised." I run a hand through my hair. "She took it well, all things considered."

She really did. I know she's devastated, that her heart is broken. But she was understanding, and for a moment, it made me second-guess why I'd leave someone like her.

"And what's the deal with Cooper?"

"Fuck, man, I don't know. Her fiancé's a real prick. Controlling, jealous, manipulative… She doesn't seem happy with him." I take a sip of my beer. "Hopefully, she'll break up with him soon."

"C'mon, c'mon, go, go, go! YES! Touchdown!" Leo shouts, and I whoop at the TV.

As we settle down, the score getting tighter, Leo glances at me sideways. "He's controlling?" He raises a brow in question.

"I think so… She made a comment about him being selfish, saying she turns into a puppet around him." I shrug. "Says she feels like she lost herself a long time ago."

Leo lets out a slow breath. "Fucking wanker. I've worked with my share of couples in that kind of relationship." He shakes his head. "That's a shame. I hope she gets out of it."

We both leap up, shouting as the Bears score another touchdown. "YES!" I pump my fist in the air, and Leo whoops, clapping his hands loudly.

"That's what I'm talking about, baby!" Leo exclaims.

"Babe?" Vivian calls softly from the bottom of the stairs.

"Hold on, babe," he replies, holding up a finger.

"Hey, I just need you to keep it down a little, so you don't wake Isla."

"Alright," he says, glancing her way. "We'll keep it down." But his focus snaps right back to the TV as the Bears kicker lines up for the extra point.

He makes it, and we whisper-shout, high-fiving each other as the game ties up. We sit back down, still amped from the excitement.

Leo looks over at me. "So, did anything happen in Austin?"

"No. I mean, she's engaged. Nothing can really happen."

"You know what I mean."

"Yeah," I smirk, laughing. "A lot happened in Austin. She spent the first day giving me hell."

Leo gives me a look, clearly waiting for me to explain.

"She's got this way of flirting with me—witty, mean, funny as hell. And I dish it right back. It's different, but I like it. It's fun, and I don't know, kind of a turn-on."

Leo chuckles. "Fuckin' women."

"Then one night, she invites me to the pool." Leo raises a brow, intrigued. "I get down there, and she's in this swimsuit that's… I mean, she's practically naked, man. Her tits are—" I let out a puff of air. "She looks so damn good. Then she pulls out edibles and offers me one."

"Oh my God," Leo laughs, shaking his head. "You didn't stand a chance."

"No, I didn't. We take them, and then we're flirting and playing in the pool like a couple of kids for over an hour. The edibles kick in, and we're laughing so much—just having fun. Then we get to this spot where I've got her backed against the wall, hands on her waist, ready to go in for a kiss. But she's in a relationship. So, what do I do? I do the right thing. I tell her we need to get out of the pool."

"That's some fucking self-control, mate."

"Yeah, well, then she kisses me." Leo lets out a low whistle. "God, she's just taunting me—testing me, seeing how far I'll go." I pause, and Leo nods, encouraging me to continue. "I back off, tell her we need to stop—that she's engaged." I scoff. "Then she gets upset, throws something about me being married in my face, and storms off."

Leo grimaces. "Ouch."

I chuckle softly. "Anyway, I ended up getting drunk at the hotel bar. She came down later, and we talked. She told me how unhappy she was, said she thinks about leaving him… *Brud,* every day." I lean back, crossing my arms. "The chemistry between us is insane. When I walked her back to her room, we almost kissed again." I press my face into my hands and groan. "I wanted to pull her into my room. But it's wrong. I *won't* be that guy—but it's so damn hard."

"Well, that alone makes you a good man. Not many would've done the same."

"But if she had kissed me…" I shake my head. "I don't know if I'd have had the self-control to stop again." I pause. "It's more than just being attracted to her. I *like* her. I like her a lot. She's different from any other girl I've ever met. She makes me laugh all the time. She just loves to have fun, you know?" I sigh. "And I don't know if I've ever been around someone who turns me on so easily. I can't stop thinking about her. It's driving me crazy."

Leo chuckles, shaking his head. "I've been there, mate. I thought I'd lose my damn mind before Vivian and I got together. When it comes to feelings and women—it's a mindfuck. Just mental gymnastics all day, every day."

I look at him, a part of me jealous of what he has. "So, what did you do?"

"Well, our situation was different. But I ultimately had to step up and be the man she needed me to be… I almost lost her." He looks at me intently. "I think all you can do is be the man she wants and needs, without crossing lines, of course. You know… be a good friend. Hopefully, in time, she'll be brave enough to leave and give you two the chance. She obviously likes you."

I exhale loudly. "Yeah. I know she does… You're probably right… Fuck," I groan. "Why can't she just be single?"

Leo shrugs, giving me a sympathetic smile. "Timing can be a bitch sometimes. Just be patient. She'll figure it out. And in the meantime, it wouldn't hurt to explore other options—maybe see what else is out there for you. Sometimes, stepping back can give both of you clarity. It's strange, but when people sense they're not the center of someone's world, they often realize what they truly want. You never know—just being less available might lead to some bold moves on her end. It's the strangest fucking thing, but… happens all the time."

Before I can respond, the TV erupts with cheers as the Bears make a game-winning play, and we're pulled back into the game, celebrating as quietly as possible.

"Yeah… you're probably right. It might be good to get my mind off Cooper for a minute." I pause, letting that thought settle. "Hey, thanks again for letting me crash here for a bit."

"No problem—stay as long as you like. Seriously."

I nod in appreciation. "Well, you better get up to that hot wife of yours… from the way she whispered in your ear, seems like you might be getting lucky tonight."

Leo chuckles, shaking his head. "Wife," he repeats, amused. "Let's just say I have a very attentive girlfriend, and I'm a lucky bastard." He grins and I can't help but laugh.

"Damn, you're a good friend. If I had someone like that waiting up-stairs for me? I would have left my sorry ass an hour ago."

He waves a hand like it's no big deal. "She wants to try out a new toy. Trust me, mate. She'll wait for me."

"God, what I'd give to be in your shoes right now. If I don't have sex soon, my dick's gonna fall off." I groan. "It's been way too long." I stand. "Alright, I'll let you get to it. Night, man. Thanks again."

"Night."

I head up the stairs while Leo turns off the lights and locks up.

Lucky bastard.

I sit on the edge of my bed, phone in hand, scrolling to find Cooper's name.

I read the last text she sent and laugh to myself.

Cooper: The guy next to me smells horrendous.

She'd sent it on the plane. She had the middle seat, me—the aisle, and the guy next to her at the window. I shake my head. *God, she's so much fun.*

Before I even think, I'm texting her.

Ryan: How's your weekend been?

Shit. I know I shouldn't be texting her unless it's work related, but I can't help it. If I don't talk to her, I'll just sit here and go insane. I settle into bed and turn the TV on. Ten minutes later, she responds.

Cooper: Couldn't wait ten more hours to talk to me, VP?

She sends a winky face emoji with its tongue sticking out.

Damn, is flirting off the table? If I knew she was in a solid relationship with a good guy and happy, I wouldn't even go there. But knowing she's not? It makes it a hell of a lot harder to leave her alone.

Ryan: Obviously not. Just thinking about you… our conversations. Wanted to see how you were doing?

Cooper: Thinking about me, huh?

God, that's so Cooper—deflecting, avoiding the tough questions, and *always* fucking with me.

Ryan: Get your dirty mind out of the gutter, haha. I'm just being a friend here.

Cooper: Riiiiigggghhhtttt. A friend. Okay—my weekend has been fine. How was yours? You working that right hand?

Cooper: God, sorry. I don't know what's wrong with me.

Cooper: How's Beth?

I shake my head, laughing. She just can't help herself.

Ryan: She's pretty good.

Cooper: That's good… Why did you text me, Ryan?

Ryan: I don't know. Do you not want me to text you unless it's for work? Because I won't… if that's what you want.

Cooper: I don't want that.

Dammit, what is this? We both want more, but there's a goddamn Mount Everest between us named Brad.

Ryan: Okay… What's your favorite color?

Might as well use this time to get to know her a little more.

Cooper: My favorite color? Wow, you know how to get into a girl's pants. It's blue. But a very specific blue—not quite true blue, and not quite navy, but something in between. What's your favorite color?

I grin.

Ryan: I'm not trying to get into your pants. That's Brad's job. Mine is green.

Cooper: That's so hot. I bet if you told me what your favorite food was, that'd be even hotter.

She's evil in the best way.

Ryan: I love smoked tri-tip… and pizza. Does that turn you on?

Cooper: Oh, you have NO idea. Lol. Who's your best friend?

Ryan: In Chicago, Leo. In Arizona, my childhood friend, Jeremy. We played soccer together our whole lives. Who's yours?

Cooper: My sister, Casey. And my tennis friends. We don't do much together outside of tennis, though.

Ryan: I didn't know you played tennis.

Cooper: There's a lot you don't know about me.

Ryan: But I know the things that matter.

Cooper: Ha. Yeah, right. Like what?

Ryan: I know you love sleeping in. You love lattes—hot, extra foam and whole milk. When you're feeling really wild, you'll add a dash of honey and cinnamon. You love bowls or salads for lunch. You have a tattoo on your ass that says 'beach bum.' You have a sick talent for rapping, and don't like country music. You have a small scar on your ribcage—right above your tattoo—the small bouquet of flowers. You smile when a song comes on at work that you like. You think scare pranks on Instagram are hilarious.

Ryan: You hate the wind. You think pubic hair is weird. You look phenomenal in a swimsuit...

Ryan: And naked...

Ryan: You love the show Pretty Little Liars. Should I keep going?

Jesus, what am I doing? This is too much. But dammit, she needs to know there are better men out there.

Cooper: Oh

Cooper: My

Cooper: God.

Cooper: Wow.

Cooper: I don't even know what to say. How do you know all that?

Ryan: I pay attention to the things I'm interested in.

She doesn't respond for a few minutes, and I'm about to give up and go to sleep.

Cooper: Now that actually turns me on.

I grin, pulse quickening. *And I can't do a damn thing about it.*

Ryan: Well then, I'd better say goodnight. See you tomorrow.

I turn my phone on silent, set it on the charger, and roll over to sleep.

Chapter 21

COOPER

Ryan's not in his office, and I can't find him anywhere. He led our morning meeting, but after that, he just disappeared. I knock on Genevieve's office door, and she gestures for me to come in. I lean in, keeping my tone casual. "Hey, do you know where Ryan is?"

She shakes her head. "He's not here. Took the afternoon off. We're both scheduled to conference into a meeting with the executive team at four. I assume he'll be back by then."

"Okay. Thanks," I say, nodding.

She raises an eyebrow. "Anything I can help you with?"

"No. I needed to talk to him about the expansion." It's true, but it's hardly urgent. I don't really have a reason to be looking for him—other than the fact that I want to see him. I want to hear his voice, see his smile. After his text last night, I can't stop thinking about him. Spending the entire weekend at home with Brad left me feeling claustrophobic. I need a reason to stay late tonight, to work, to not be at my house—to be around Ryan.

Back in the lounge, I sprawl across the sofa, pulling out my phone.

Cooper: Hey VP, where are you? Was hoping we could discuss our next steps with the new property in Austin tonight.

I place my phone face-up next to me, laptop open, and force myself to work. But I'm glancing at my phone every few minutes, driving myself crazy, waiting for a response. Nothing.

Is he mad at me? Did I come off too strong last night? Maybe I shouldn't have sent that last text—the one about his text turning me on. But my God, that shook me in the best way.

Two hours later, he still hasn't texted back. I'm going to go insane. I force myself to take a lunch break.

By the time I get back, he still hasn't responded, and my mind is spiraling into ridiculous scenarios. Maybe I shouldn't have kissed him in the pool. Or maybe I should have kissed him again in the hallway. What if he got back together with his wife? Shit. He's probably with her right now. I can't even be upset about that—if anything, I feel bad for both of them. Meanwhile, I'm stuck in hell at home—arguing with Brad, faking orgasms, and clinging to the one thing we have left: sex. But even that's taken a turn for the worse.

Jesus, I'm a mess.

The rest of the day flies by, and by five, I'm walking toward Ryan's office again, butterflies in my stomach. I know this feeling all too well—that buildup before something good… or bad happens. I round the corner and practically bump right into him.

"Oh, hey!" I say. "I was looking for you."

"Hey. I was just coming to find you to talk about tonight. Sorry, I didn't text back."

"That's okay. Where'd you go?"

He gestures to his office. "Let's go in my office."

I follow him inside, and he shuts the door. God, he looks like pure sin in that crisp white shirt—sleeves rolled up just enough to show off his strong, tanned forearms. The way his blue pants hug his thighs, leaving just enough to the imagination, but not really—I know exactly what he's working with, and it's enough to make my knees weak. Damn, he looks good.

My mind spirals with dirty thoughts of him stepping behind me, pushing me up against his desk, and taking exactly what he wants. I wish these walls weren't glass. *Jesus.* Last night, I had a good-looking naked man on top of me, and I felt nothing. But now, just seeing Ryan—fully clothed in his office—I'm ready to rip his clothes off. It's not just the physical with him, though. There's this raw pull I feel in my chest, a breathlessness when he's near. I want him to pull me close. To look at me. To listen. I want to be intimate with him in every way. *God, what is happening to me?*

He takes a seat, and I settle in across from him.

"What's going on? Everything okay?" I ask, desperate to distract myself.

"Yeah, everything's good. I was just at a follow-up appointment with Beth."

"Oh, you were? How did it go?" I swallow, steadying myself, shutting down the dirty thoughts running rogue in my mind. We're talking about Beth—cancer. It's not the time.

"On the outside, things are looking good. We won't get her scan results for a few days, but… we're hopeful things are still on the up and up."

"Well, that's great. I'll send good vibes," I say, a smile playing on my lips.

He chuckles. "Everything should work out then if you're sending those good vibes."

"Good vibes usually work… So, what will you do if all the scans come back… you know, with good news?"

"I'll serve Beth papers," he says, his voice flat.

I glance down at my fidgeting fingers. "And what if it's…" I look up, making eye contact. "What if it's bad news?"

He holds my eyes, unwavering. "Then I'll serve Beth papers."

The intensity of his gaze makes my breath hitch. "Oh," I manage, my voice unsteady. "What about the insurance?"

"Beth got a new job a few months ago. She wanted to simplify things… especially after she had an affair with her boss." He lets out a frustrated sigh, and his hand brushing over his jaw. "I know she was hoping I'd stay, but…" He trails off. "Anyway, once the new year starts, she'll switch to her insurance."

The way he says it—matter-of-fact, not bitter—makes my chest ache. How is he this good? This strong? If I were him, I'd be wrecked—I am wrecked. He's nothing like Brad. Beth was so damn lucky, and she threw it all away. She threw *him* away. And me? I'm just… weak.

"Look, I wanted to tell you…"

A rush of nerves tighten in my stomach, and tears threaten—tears I can't even place. If I don't get out of here, I'm going to lose it. "Shit," I blurt, glancing at my watch. "I totally forgot—I told Jason I'd meet him before he heads out. Are you staying after to discuss Austin?"

"Yeah, does that work for you? If you want to get home to Brad, I understand."

He's probing, trying to gauge where things stand with Brad. "Brad won't be home until late. I'm good to stay."

"Alright. I should be done by five-thirty. We need to plan our next trip out for interviews. Genevieve's vetting candidates over the next few weeks."

I nod, emotion sitting in the back of my throat. "I'll see you in a bit," I manage to choke out, reaching for the door. I don't dare look back as I make my exit, shutting the door before he can respond as a tear slips down my cheek.

* * * * * * * * * *

We've been working for over an hour at Viv's. I nurse my second cocktail, a strong buzz setting in. Ryan's on his second beer, looking more relaxed than I've seen him all week. I've always been attracted to him, but since the pool, our come-to-Jesus at the hotel bar, and that text message the other night, I'm a mess of nerves and raw need around him.

It's been a long damn week, and he's been on my mind constantly—whether I'm at work, finding excuses to be near him, or lying in bed re-playing every word he's said.

When I'm alone at night, the thoughts become something else entirely. His hands on me, his voice, the way he looks at me—it's all-consuming. I've lost count of how many times I've given in to the ache, imagining it's him instead of my own hands—or Brad's.

We laugh, we banter, and I can't help but flirt with him—it's just too much fun. I feel good when I'm around him, better than I've felt in a long time. And as much as I hate to admit it, he's become a good friend—one of my closest friends.

I've only ever confided in Casey, but I find myself sharing more and more with Ryan. It's nice. I haven't had anyone else in years. Brad doesn't like me spending time with other people—he always has some excuse, some way to make it feel like I'm doing something wrong. And when I did try to open up to my old friends, they were relentless, constantly pointing out all the things I couldn't bring myself to see.

Eventually, I stopped trying. It was easier to let the friendships fade than to keep defending something I wasn't sure I believed in myself. That's why it's easy to have my tennis friends. We just play tennis—no deep talking, no uncomfortable questions. They usually go to lunch after, but I head home, avoiding the awkward conversation.

I've started looking for apartments—just to see what's out there. If moving in with my mom becomes my only option, I know I'll never break things off with Brad. She and I do not get along. We've been butting heads for as long as I can remember, screaming at each other almost daily in high school. Between me blaming her and my rebellious nature, we never stood a chance. I have to find something else.

Brad left for New York this morning, and tomorrow I leave for California for Christmas. The past three nights with him have sucked the life out of me. He's been more possessive, more jealous, more paranoid than ever. And when he gets like that, he needs more sex. Three nights of constant arguing, yelling, throwing things, and meaningless sex—ending with me crying myself to sleep. It's hitting me now, harder than ever, just how unhealthy this has become.

I want out. I *need* out. No matter how terrified I am, I'm determined to find a way. But leaving Brad wouldn't be clean—it never could be. He wouldn't let me walk away unscathed, happy, or free. And the thought of what that might cost—my job, Ryan, everything—I shove it down before it can consume me.

I know Ryan won't cross the line. It's one of the things I admire most about him. He's honorable; he does the right thing. But me? God, between my trust issues and my constant need to justify my actions, that line between right and wrong feels fuzzier every day.

I watch Ryan, his focus shifting from me to his laptop, then back to me, frustration evident. I lean back in my chair, nudging his foot under the table—lightly, almost absently—while I stretch. "You look so serious," I tease, grinning as I catch his eye.

He lets out a deep exhale. "Sorry, I'm distracted."

"What's going on?"

He checks his watch. "Um… it's nothing. Sorry."

I scowl at him. "Don't say it's nothing when it's clearly something. I know you better than that."

He hesitates, meeting my gaze. He's acting weird. "Fine. It's just… I have a date tonight. And… I'm nervous, I guess." I try to hide my surprise and disappointment as he continues. "It's been a while since I've taken someone new on a date."

Well, shit. My stomach twists, the grin frozen on my face as I try to process his words. Of course he's trying to move on. What did I expect—that he'd sit around and wait for me while I can't even decide what it is that I want? Or when I don't have the balls to do the same? But still… it stings. More than I want to admit.

He glances at me, a look of resignation on his face. "Sorry… I wasn't going to tell you about it."

I attempt to play it cool. "Why weren't you going to tell me?"

He shrugs, looking almost guilty. "I don't know. I didn't want things to be… weird between us."

"Weird? Why would I care if you're dating someone?" I flash a smile, ignoring the knot twisting tighter in my stomach. "I mean, I'm happy for you. Really."

His eyes narrow slightly, searching my expression. "Yeah?"

"Of course. I just hope she's not boring." I give him a teasing grin, raising an eyebrow. "I doubt she's as much fun as I am."

He raises an eyebrow, a smirk tugging at his lips. "Oh, you think you're hard to beat?"

I lean in a little closer. "I mean… I'd be surprised if she could match the kind of fun we had in the pool… And don't even get me started on Newport. But hey, maybe you'll get lucky."

He lets out a soft chuckle. "Oh, I think she could surprise you," he replies, a bit more smugly than before. "She looks pretty hot. A gymnast too—flexible." He waggles his brows.

I smother a laugh, but as his words sink in, my confidence wavers. Okay, I guess this is how I handle jealousy—turn it into a game, throw in some jokes, and hope he doesn't notice how much it's killing me inside. God, I hate how much I want him to only want me.

"Aren't you worried she might be catfishing you?" I quip, keeping my voice light.

"Nah. She's got a lot of pics on her profile, and she's consistently good-looking in all of them. Body looks phenomenal. I bet she's great in bed." He smacks his lips together, biting back a grin and raising his brows. He's trying his best to get under my skin. And it's working, but I can play this game too.

"Well, good for you, Ryan. You might finally get your dick wet. If you're lucky, she might give you a night that's… almost memorable." I add a small laugh, but my pulse is racing—praying she doesn't give him so much as a kiss. "I hope you don't end up lying there wishing it was me." I flash him a grin as I sit back in my chair, crossing my arms.

He chuckles wickedly. "Oh, I already know you'll be under your covers tonight with your vibrator, jealous, thinking of me while Brad's out of town."

He's not wrong, but this time, I'm not afraid to own it. I raise my brows. "Wouldn't be the first time this week. Last night I had a wild little fantasy—three words, Ryan: office, desk, you." I say in a sultry voice, feeling smug as hell.

"Jesus Christ." He glances down, clearing his throat. "Are you ever going to break up with Brad?" he says seriously, a smile tugging at his lips, his gaze locking on mine.

The way he asks it, with a longing in his eyes and desire in his voice—it catches me off guard. "I don't know. I want to." I shift uncomfortably. "Did you leave your wife yet?"

"Yeah… I did."

His answer knocks the wind out of me. "Really?" I ask softly.

He nods. "I moved out on Sunday. Beth and I are done. There's no point in dragging it out anymore. I tried to tell you the other day, but you rushed out." He pauses. "I'm staying with Leo and Vivian while I look for a new place. It sucks, but I know it's the right thing to do for me… and for Beth."

He hesitates, then adds quietly, "I just… couldn't keep living in limbo." He glances down at the table, then back up at me. "I guess I just realized how unhappy I've been… how badly I want to be with someone who really wants to be with me."

Oh, shit. Does he mean me? I feel my heart rate spike.

Ryan takes a deep breath. "I guess what I'm saying is… I'm ready to move forward. And…" He hesitates, his sexy smolder taking over as he chews on the inside of his cheek, something he does when he's nervous or deep in thought. "I don't know… Maybe you deserve that too, Cooper."

The implication of his words sends a tingly sensation through my body, but it also makes my chest feel tight.

"Ryan, I…" I start, then stop, uncertain. Do we have to talk about this right now? Can't we just sneak off somewhere and do it—see if this is real or if we just need to get this sexual tension out of our systems? I look at him, taking a breath. "Did you leave Beth for me?" My voice is small, uncertain.

He ponders this for a moment. "No," he says, his voice steady. "I didn't leave for you. I would have left Beth anyway, that's been the plan all along. I left for all the right reasons; I know that. But…" He looks away for a second before locking eyes with me again, a small, self-deprecating smile on his lips. "I can't help but hope you'll decide to leave Brad."

My breath catches. Holy shit. Ryan wants me to break up with Brad so he can be with me? My brain can barely process it. *God, I don't deserve someone like him.* Ryan's moral compass is rock-solid, and mine has been cracked for a long time now.

"I don't know what to say," I murmur, searching his face for answers he doesn't have. "I'm scared." I admit, exhaling slowly. "I can't leave right now, not before the holidays. Brad's meeting me in Newport next week, and it's just not the time to be alone or find a new place." I lean back, as if convincing myself. "But I will… soon."

Ryan holds my gaze, a flicker of doubt in his eyes as if he can already see through my excuses. He swallows, his voice gentle. "Okay… It's your life. I just want you to be happy. You deserve that. You know that, right?"

I scoff, barely meeting his eyes. "Yeah, I guess."

Ryan shakes his head, looking almost defeated, as if I just crushed his last hope. "Everyone deserves to be happy, Cooper." He swallows, pausing. "We have work to do. Let's get back to it."

We work in silence for about ten minutes, but my mind won't stop racing. He wants to be with me. And he's taking another woman out on a date? Finally, I can't hold back. "Where are you taking your date?" I ask, curious—and obviously envious as hell.

"I'm just meeting her for a drink at a bar Leo recommended. Apparently, it's best to keep things casual at first, feel out the chemistry before committing to a full-blown dinner."

I smile, though it aches a bit. "That sounds nice. I'm sure she'll have a great time—it'd be hard not to with you. I hope you have fun." And I do mean it, even though I wish it were me.

Ryan raises a brow. "Wow. Thank you. I know that couldn't have been easy to say."

"Why would that be hard for me to say?" I spit out defensively. "I'm not a total asshole. I care about you—I want you to be happy."

He grins. "Even if you're jealous, wishing it were you on the date?"

"I'm not jealous." I scowl. "Besides, like you said, I'll have my vibrator. I'll be perfectly content."

"Content?" His grin widens. "Then you must not be fantasizing about me. If you were…" He leans closer, voice dropping. "You'd be more than content."

"You're awfully confident in your ability to get someone off without being present. Trust me, I'll be more than content." I bite my lip, debating how far to take this. "Like I said, it wouldn't be the first time you've made an appearance in my fantasies. You're getting good at knowing what I like."

"Don't lie. You're just fucking with me."

"Am I?" I lean in. "Some days, you look so good at work, I can't wait to get home and be alone."

"Fuck," he mutters, shaking his head. "Are you serious? Do you have any idea what that does to me, Cooper?" He exhales. "You shouldn't be telling me this."

I raise a brow, feigning innocence. "Why? Does it turn you on?"

His eyes darken, and I can see his control slipping. "You thinking about me when you touch yourself?" He leans in closer, his voice a low murmur. "Of course it turns me on… You've gotta stop messing with me like this because I'm going to lose my goddamn mind."

I hold his gaze, letting the heat between us simmer. "So… you don't want me thinking about you when I touch myself?" I'm laughing inwardly at the torment I'm putting him through—it's so fun, and he's so close to breaking.

He groans softly, and so obviously rearranges his dick that I have to bite back a laugh. "We shouldn't be talking about this, Cooper." He drags a hand over his face. "We're at work. This could blow up in both our faces."

As if that's ever stopped us.

I keep my tone light and easy. "We're just talking, Ryan. You asked a question, and I answered."

"You are such a fucking tease."

I smirk. "Good thing you have that date tonight. It might help you get rid of all this… pent-up tension." I slip off my shoe, dragging my foot slowly up his calf. "I've got plans for mine."

He jerks his foot away, and I can't tell if he's pissed or so turned on he's barely holding it together. "Jesus, Cooper. I can't have you tempting me like this unless you've broken it off with Brad." His voice is low, restrained. "I'm not that guy. But I only have so much willpower… Don't start games you can't finish."

I trail my fingers to the top button of my blouse, watching his jaw tighten as I test his limits. I pop the button open slowly. "Who said I don't plan to finish?" *God, this is too easy.*

"You live with another man," he says sternly. "And if I'm doing this, I'm all in. I'm not sharing you—not only because it's wrong, but because I want all of you. No games. Period. It's him or me. Your choice."

He turns back to his laptop while his words soak into me like a drug hitting my bloodstream. *All of me?* My stomach flips, a mix of excitement and fear. This isn't the playful Ryan I'm used to—this is him being real. He's serious. He wants me to leave Brad… for him. But what if the second

I walk away, he loses interest? What if this is all about getting me into bed, and once he does, it's over? Just like everyone else.

Except Ryan's not like everyone else. At least, I don't think so.

God, it'd be so much easier if I could just have him on the side. No complications. No heartbreak. Just Ryan when I need him. But that's not how life works. He's not a goddamn bandaid—he's a person. A really great person.

I swallow hard, my heart pounding. "Do you really mean that?"

His eyes lock on mine, intense, serious. "What do *you* think?"

It's strange how comfortable I feel staring into his eyes, holding his gaze. But as my pulse races and a twinge of panic builds, I find myself deflecting. Before I even realize it, I'm making a joke, trying to break the tension because I don't know how to handle it.

"You sure you don't want to cancel your date? The bathrooms would be perfect for a quickie." I tease, leaning forward, my blouse dipping just enough to give him a good look. "You really going to wind me up like this and send me home to my vibrator?"

He scoffs, clearly unimpressed. "You're unbelievable. So what, I either fuck you, or you'll keep torturing me and go home to your fiancé?"

I cross my legs deliberately, letting a playful smile spread. "If that's how you want to put it… then yes, that's exactly how it's going to be."

He lets out a low chuckle, his gaze darting briefly to my chest before meeting my eyes again. "Fine," he murmurs. "You wanna play games? Let's play games."

His voice drops, his tone darker now. "Then I hope you think about all the dirty things I'd do to you while Brad's on top of you. Like bending you over my desk, taking you from behind. Or how a girl in college once told me I was so good at eating pussy, I ruined her for life."

Oh, sweet Jesus. What is he doing?

"But you remember, don't you? You came… how many times was it again? Five?" He leans back, a smirk pulling at his lips. "I lost track, honestly. I was too busy memorizing the sweet sounds of you coming in my ear." He straightens, snapping his laptop shut with purpose. "Seems like I might actually enjoy this little game you're playing. I'm free now, Cooper, nothing holding me back. Got a date with Liz tonight." He glances at his watch. "In fact, it's time for me to go meet her. If I managed to get some-one as stunning as you into bed on the first try, I'm sure that Liz won't be hard to convince. Meanwhile, you get to go home to your vibrator... or worse, Brad."

My body reacts instantly: a steady thrum builds between my thighs, my pulse races, and my breaths become shallow.

Fuck.

As he stands, he leans in close, his breath warm against my ear. "Hope he makes you come as much as I do." He pulls back, flashing that teasing grin. "You're right; this will be fun. I've gotta go. Maybe I'll fuck Liz so well, it'll push you out of my goddamned mind."

I quickly shove my things into my bag and follow him, catching up at the elevator. I grab his arm, my gaze locked on his. "You won't, though," I say, trying to keep my tone confident. "You'll end up going home to jerk off."

The elevator doors slide open, and Ryan stabs the button for the lobby as we enter.

Damn. What if he clicks with this girl?

"Won't I?" he says confidently.

I take a breath, steadying myself. "No, you won't." I force a small smile, as if I'm sure of it—even if a part of me isn't. He wants me. He's made that clear. But now, there's competition.

With a surge of boldness, I shove him against the elevator wall as the doors close. Wrapping my arms around his neck, I press my body flush against his. "You'll be too busy wishing it was me on this date, and when you get home, you'll jerk off to thoughts of me... my mouth on your cock, sucking you so deep you wouldn't last a minute. I bet that's all you'll think about tonight—the way I'd take you, the sounds I'd make, and how I'd swallow every drop when you come." I pause, leaning into his ear, and whisper, "You remember how good I am too, don't you, Ryan?"

He swallows, hard.

The elevator dings, and I step back, patting his chest like I've already won. "Good luck getting Liz to take me off your mind tonight. I'll be wait-ing to hear all about it tomorrow," I say, biting my lip to hold back a grin, my voice dripping with seduction.

I turn to leave, but before I can take a step, he grabs my arm and pulls me back, slamming the "close door" button with his fist. The doors shut, and in an instant, he's pressing me against the wall, one hand pinning my wrist above my head, the other gripping my waist. His breathing is ragged, mirroring mine, his eyes wild and dark, blazing with an intensity that sends a shiver down my spine. Our lips hover close—if either of us moved even an inch, they'd meet.

Time seems to stand still. My head spins, and I can't bear the anticipation. My free hand glides along his bicep as I tilt my head up, letting my lips brush against his as I murmur, "Ryan…"

His eyes squeeze shut, a low growl escaping as he pulls back just enough to mutter, "What the fuck are you doing, Cooper?" His voice is tight, raw with frustration. "You can't keep fucking with me like this."

His hand slides down my arm, his fingertips skimming my collarbone, grazing over the curve of my throat. My pulse hammers against his touch, and I can't catch my breath. This is pure, agonizing torture in the best way. His finger trails lower, just skimming the edge of my bra, lighting fire under my skin. Instinctively, I arch toward him, my chest brushing his hand as his hard-on presses against me. Every inch of me is screaming for more of his touch—of him.

But just as quickly, he pulls back—just far enough that I can't reach him. He's taunting me, leading this push and pull like it's a game he's determined to win. His hand slides to the back of my neck, his thumb brushing along my jaw. He leans in, whispering against my lips. "God, you turn me on." And then, in one swift motion, his lips crash into mine, rough and demanding. He doesn't just kiss me—he claims me, seizing control. It's possessive. It's fierce. It's sexy as hell.

I forget to breathe.

His tongue sweeps across mine, his mouth crushing against me, deeper, hungrier. His hand finds my waist, pulling me roughly to him— his cock pressing perfectly into me, sending a surge of desire low in my stomach. I push into him, and he groans, a sound that sends shivers racing down my spine. His hand slides lower, fingers brushing my upper thigh, his thumb grazing that sensitive spot between my leg and the pulsing ache.

My breath catches, my body arching instinctively, desperate for more.

He obliges—barely. His fingers skim over the sensitive center, light as a feather, tracing the inseam of my pants with maddening slowness, teasing me to the point of trembling, nearly undoing me. I'm shaking, aching for him to go further, to let this spiral into exactly what we both want. A whimper slips from my lips, unbidden. "Ryan."

But then he stops, his eyes meeting mine, dark and intense, his chest rising and falling as if he's as affected as I am.

"Unless you've broken up with Brad…" His voice is low, dangerous, trembling with restraint. "Don't. Fuck. With me, Cooper."

He slams the "open door" button, and before I can say a word, he storms out, leaving me up against the elevator wall, breathless, stunned, and completely shaken. His scent lingers, and my heart races. Every nerve in my body feels wired—restless, unsatisfied, and craving more.

"Holy shit," I whisper shakily. "Holy fucking shit." I take a deep breath, exhaling slowly as I grip the elevator wall, my heart still pounding. The doors close, and I don't even care where I'm going as the elevator rises. *What the hell was that?* I'm delirious, dizzy, still turned on. *Jesus,* I'm heading into my holiday break with that mindfuck? I'm so totally screwed.

Chapter 22

RYAN

I'm still reeling when I pull into the parking garage, with no memory of the drive back. The entire way, my mind replayed every second with Cooper, layering it with a hundred what ifs. Walking away just now was one of the hardest things I've ever done. My body's a mess—cock raging, mind spinning, desire coursing through me like fire. I had to pry myself off her.

I sit gripping the steering wheel, trying to shake off the charge she left me with. What the hell is she doing? She just tore through every professional line without looking back. When she brushed her lips against mine—I was gone. If she wants me this much, why won't she break up with Brad? Does she really plan to leave him? The not knowing... it's going to kill me.

And now I'm supposed to go meet some random woman for drinks? That's the last thing I want. After my talk with Leo on Sunday, I decided it was time to move on. Part of me hoped the date would make her jealous, and it seems like it did. Shit. I can't believe I kissed her. I crossed the damn line. I'm only barely better than Beth's boss. I'm practically having an emotional affair with Cooper. And I don't know if that's any better than the physical act.

Fuck.

When I finally step out of the car, the cold air hits me, grounding me for a second, but it's not enough to keep my mind free from her. No. She's a virus that's planted herself in my brain, one that'll slowly take me over through the holiday break. Not seeing her, but having that last encounter seared into my memory? I shake my head, muttering another "fuck" as I open the door to Leo's.

* * * * * * * * * *

I follow Leo through the bar to our reserved seating, his hand resting on the small of Vivian's back, a silent claim daring any man to make a pass at her. Leo's one of the nicest, most generous men I know, but he strikes me as someone you wouldn't want to get on the wrong side of—though I doubt anyone's ever needed to find out. He exudes wealth and seems to be both liked and respected everywhere we go.

We're at a members-only club, *Tapped Out*, where the dress code is strictly cocktail attire. Leo and Vivian reserved a larger space tonight for some close friends for a holiday get-together. Michael and his wife Stella will be here, along with Adam, Leo's good friend Meredith, and her partner, Piper, who I've met a handful of times. We're led to a corner with a large, rounded booth with a plush sofa. It's dim, and in every corner there are dancers—not strippers but acrobatic performers who blend into the club's upscale ambiance.

I have yet to see a cocktail waitress who isn't attractive. They're all wearing short, sexy black dresses that push their tits up. This place is classy—movie kind of classy. Average guys wouldn't even know it exists, but for guys like Leo? Of course, he's a member. I'm sure it comes with a hefty price, too. It's a far cry from my usual scene, but I'm ready to take it all in.

Most of our employees have been out this week, and Cooper left yesterday. I fly back to Arizona tomorrow for the holidays, but tonight, I'm excited to unwind here with friends.

Leo lights a cigar, passing one to me, and Michael and Adam take one too. We order another round, and about an hour in, I'm on my third drink, feeling the buzz settle in, ready to kick off the holiday break officially.

"Ryan, that cocktail waitress keeps checking you out, and she's gorgeous," Vivian says with a subtle gesture toward a stunning brunette by the bar. The waitress catches me looking and arches a brow, a smile playing on her lips.

I grin, shaking my head. "You're right, Viv. She's gorgeous, but that's just not the type of girl I'm looking for."

"What? You're crazy, man. That girl is hot," Adam cuts in, eyebrows raised. "If she were looking at me like that, I'd be all over it."

"Yeah, well, that's just not what I'm here for." I shrug, not really in the mood to get into it.

Leo gives me a steady look. "You know, you don't have to hold back on our account. Our house is your house."

Vivian rolls her eyes with a playful smile. "Don't encourage him, babe. Not everyone wants to sleep with anything that moves."

"Ohhhh!" Adam and Michael hoot, grinning. "Nice one, Viv," Michael says, laughing.

She laughs, giving a playful shrug. "Gotta joke about it when I can."

"Oh, come on, guys. I wasn't *that* bad," Leo says, trying to defend himself.

Vivian gives him a pointed look. "Babe, it's a good thing you're cute. Denial doesn't look good on you."

Meredith raises her glass, grinning. "She's right. The only thing worse than a man-whore is a man-whore in denial. Thank God, those days are over."

"I'll drink to that," Leo says, lifting his glass. We all join, bringing our glasses to the center.

"To great friends," he toasts, looking to Vivian with an intense focus. "And to the love of my life. I don't know where I'd be without you."

As we clink glasses, Michael calls out, "Probably on top of one of these girls, brother."

We all burst out laughing, and Stella playfully smacks Michael's arm. "Way to ruin the moment."

Leo kisses Vivian, and she pulls back with a smirk, looking around the room. "Alright, which one would've caught your eye tonight?" She locks eyes with him, teasing. "Blonde? Brunette? Maybe a redhead?"

Leo chuckles, shaking his head.

"He likes them all, Viv, but he's always leaned toward brunettes," Meredith says, grinning.

Vivian scans the room. "So… that one over there? Would she do it for you? She's a hottie."

Leo's gaze meets hers. "I only have eyes for you, babe."

I watch as they eye-fuck each other in utter amusement. Most women would feel threatened by a partner's past conquests, but she's so confident in herself and their relationship that she just gives him shit—and Leo takes it like a champ. Honestly, it could get old quickly, especially since Adam and Michael love bringing it up, but Leo just laughs it off.

Damn, I admire them. I thought Beth and I had something like this once, and maybe we did. But somewhere along the way, we lost it. I hope Leo and Vivian never do. I hope they realize how special what they have is, and always put in the time and effort it takes to keep their relationship alive.

My thoughts drift to Cooper. That woman's a straight-up pain in my ass. I haven't heard from her since I stormed out of the elevator, and I can't wait to see what's in store after the holiday break. Will we be friends? Enemies? Is she going to flirt with me or act like I don't exist? I never know what I'm going to get with her, and maybe that's what makes her so damn interesting—why I can't seem to shake her.

My thoughts are interrupted by the beautiful brunette. She's flirting with someone—or maybe someone's flirting with her. But it's not the flirting that catches my attention; it's the guy. It's fucking Brad. Even from here, he exudes that trademark douchebag arrogance. His hand slides to her waist, but she steps back, clearly not wanting him to touch her. He eventually gives up, and I watch him walk over to another table, where he wraps his arm around a different girl's shoulder. She leans into him, and he kisses her. They start making out right there in the booth, shameless, for several minutes.

My jaw tightens, fists clenching. What an asshole. I pull out my phone and snap a picture of him, locking lips with this girl. I don't even know why. It's not like I'd ever show Cooper. I can't tell her—not directly. The person being cheated on never forgives the messenger, and the last person I want hating me is Cooper.

But the sight of Brad here, doing this… My blood is boiling. I'd love nothing more than to beat the shit out of him right now. He might look like he's in decent shape, but not like I am. And Leo? He's in even better shape than me and practically a martial arts expert. With Leo backing me, I'd be able to give Brad exactly what he deserves.

Leo notices the shift in my demeanor. "Hey, mate," he says quietly, catching on. "Something wrong?"

"You remember Cooper's boyfriend, Brad?" I ask, my jaw tight.

"The arrogant lawyer?" he says, eyebrows raising.

I nod, jerking my head toward Brad's table. "He's here. Making out with some chick."

"No fucking way. Where?" Leo leans in, his eyes scanning the room.

I subtly point him out. "Over there."

"What a bastard," Leo mutters, shaking his head.

Cooper's in Newport, waiting for her doting fiancé, and he's here with his tongue down some other woman's throat. I'm sure he'll go home with her and do so much more, while Cooper innocently believes he's on a work trip.

It's guys like Brad that give men a bad rap—make girls like Cooper believe that all men are cheaters. My mind races, replaying things she's said, how she always assumes the worst, that every man she knows cheats.

That son of a bitch. He's been doing this the whole time. Hell, he's probably cheated the entire relationship, but Cooper only knows about bits and pieces. *Jesus Christ.*

Brad's gaze suddenly meets mine across the room. I don't look away. I glare at him with every ounce of disgust I can muster. Good. Let him know that I see him. Let him panic, knowing his girlfriend spends every day with me. And he knows she's attracted to me. Good. *Fuck him.*

But then a dark thought hits me—will he take this out on her somehow? She says he doesn't hurt her, but how do I know that's true? I don't know this guy. He shows one face to the world and another behind closed doors. Even if he's not hurting her physically, he's clearly some manipulative asshole who's got a grip on her.

"Fuck," I mutter under my breath.

Leo glances at Brad. "Shit, mate. He knows you saw him."

Brad strolls over, straightening his jacket, the cocky grin now replaced with something more calculated—smooth, like he thinks he can charm his way out of this. He nods at me and Leo, keeping his cool, acting like he didn't just get caught red-handed.

"Leo, Ryan," Brad greets us, his voice annoyingly steady. "Mind if I join you?" But he's already lowering himself into a chair. "Great spot you've got here. This place is something else, isn't it?"

"It sure is…" Leo pauses, feigning uncertainty. "Brad, is it?"

I stifle a laugh, staying quiet as Brad redirects his attention entirely to Leo, the real target.

"Leo, I didn't realize you were a member here."

Leo raises a brow, casually leaning back. "I'm not just a member, I'm a silent partner at this club, Brad."

I actually didn't know that—damn, Leo has a hand in everything.

"Are you, really?" Brad recovers quickly, forcing a charming smile. "I've been considering a membership myself. I'm here with a friend who's a member… Listen, I've heard about the Midtown deal you're working on. It's a big one, right? You're the kind of guy who leaves nothing to chance. I'd be more than happy to help keep things running smoothly. I've handled similar deals; I could make sure everything stays on track. We should talk—see how I can add value."

Brad's charm is dialed up, playing the polished, successful lawyer.

Leo takes a slow sip of his drink, his eyes never leaving Brad. The silence is perfectly measured, long enough for the tension to settle, but not so long that Brad could think he's won any ground.

"Appreciate the offer," Leo says smoothly, his voice calm, unwavering. "But I already have a lawyer I trust. Loyalty's a big deal to me—in business and in life. I've found how a person handles themselves personally tends to reflect how they conduct business. So seeing how your loyalty wavers…" Leo's eyes flick briefly to the booth where Brad was caught. "Well, that's a red flag. Sorry, mate."

Leo lets the words hang in the air, pointed but not aggressive, just a calm observation.

Brad's smile tightens for a second, but he doesn't lose his composure. "I hear you, Leo. Loyalty's everything, I completely agree. But I want to make one thing clear—I'd never be disloyal when it comes to business. I've built my career on trust and respect. I mean, come on, I wouldn't be where I am if I wasn't someone people could rely on. Personal life, sure—sometimes things get a little messy. I'm sure you've been there a time or two… But business? I'm rock solid."

Leo doesn't blink, his expression calm but unmoved. "Problem is, Brad, I need people I can trust in all aspects of life—and no, I've never been there. I don't let my life get messy where the people I care about are involved."

Brad opens his mouth to respond but shifts his attention to me instead, his tone turning casual, as if he's appealing to some kind of 'guy's guy' understanding.

"Ryan, we're cool, right? Look, this is just a one-time thing. A fun night—nothing serious. No need for Cooper to get dragged into this, you know? She doesn't need to get hurt. Why ruin something good over one night? I love Cooper." It's almost impressive how Brad's able to justify cheating like it's just a casual night out with the boys.

I feel his eyes on me, waiting for me to back up his bullshit, but I'm not giving him an inch. I scoff. "You have an odd way of showing love, man. Look, it's not my business to tell Cooper. She's my coworker," I say, my voice even, letting it hang for a second. "But it is *yours*." I pause, watching his expression shift. "You've got a month to do it, Brad. After that? Hard to tell what will happen." I take a steady sip of my drink, keeping my eyes on him.

Brad's grin falters again, but this time he knows he's not getting what he wants from either of us. He chuckles, but it's hollow now. "Right. Sure. Anyway, think about what I said, Leo. I'm always around if you change your mind."

With that, he gives a quick nod and walks off, his usual swagger a bit more forced. I glance at Leo, who's watching Brad go with a look of disappointment, though he doesn't seem surprised.

Leo shakes his head, watching Brad walk away. "Some people just don't know when to quit, do they?"

I raise my glass to my lips. "You've got that right."

Leo turns to me, his tone sharpening. "Listen, mate, she needs someone who actually respects her, not some prick like him who treats her like an afterthought." He gives me a pointed look. "This isn't about you, Ryan. And it sure as hell isn't about sex. Sometimes people get stuck in these situations—they don't know how to leave. Maybe it's time you stopped playing it safe. She deserves a man who doesn't just want her around, but actually wants her. Be that push she needs. Show her the difference—maybe blur the line a little…"

Leo pauses, his lips pressing together, then exhales. "But not too much. You're better than that. Help her see what she's missing—what she deserves—but don't lose yourself in the process."

"I think you're right," I murmur, nodding, feeling a new determination settle over me. Leo's absolutely right—it's time I stop playing it safe and make it damn clear what Cooper could have with me compared to what she's been stuck with. This isn't about breaking the rules or revenge. It's about waking her up to what she deserves.

I'm done holding back, done letting Brad think he's got her wrapped around his finger. Over the next month? I'm turning up the heat. Every look, every text, every laugh—I'll make her feel it. She'll know I'm here, wanting her in every way that Brad clearly isn't.

I've already crossed the line—more than once. The pool, the elevator. And I feel guilty as hell for it. But seeing the way Brad treats her? It's clear: he never had a line to begin with. Still, I can't let myself slip again. No physical boundaries crossed—not even a kiss—until she leaves him.

Everything else? The green light's on.

Chapter 23

COOPER

"Has Brad landed yet?" Casey asks, taking a sip of her hot chocolate.

I check my phone again. "Not yet," I say, as I wrap my blanket a little tighter around myself. It's late, dark out. The heat lamps on my dad's patio are turned up, and we're both dressed for the cooler temperature. The Christmas lights wrapping around the patio railing are on, and it's pitch black as we stare into the abyss. Only the sounds of the ocean and the waves crashing against the sand proves that there's a big body of water out there. "He should be landing any minute."

It's almost eight. This is Casey's and my Christmas Eve tradition when we're at my dad's house. We eat dinner with my dad on the patio and watch the sunset, then me and Casey sit here with our hot chocolate until she leaves. We used to stay here until we were falling asleep, but now that she has Mason, she leaves a little earlier to get him to bed.

She checks her watch. "I've got to get going in a few minutes."

My phone lights up. "That must be Brad." I pick it up, and my heart stops. It's not Brad—it's Ryan. I haven't seen or heard from him for four days—since the elevator incident.

I instinctively suck in a sharp breath, my hand flying to my mouth in shock.

"What?" Casey asks.

"It's Ryan."

Casey's eyes go wide. "Well, what does it say?"

I shouldn't want to look at it as much as I do. Brad's on his way, and it's Christmas—my favorite holiday. I usually love spending this time with him, but this year, I have mixed feelings about it.

I open my messages, letting out my breath in disappointment.

"What does it say?" Casey presses, more urgently this time.

I hesitate. "It says '*Hey…*'" I don't know why I feel let down. What was I expecting? *Hey, Cooper, can't stop thinking about you. Want to sneak off and bone?*

I laugh to myself, tipping my chin toward the sky.

"Okay…" Casey says slowly. "A little anti-climatic, but hey—he's thinking of you."

"Right," I say. "And why is that something that makes me happy?"

Casey shrugs. "Because you like him." She smiles softly, and I appreciate her honesty. But sometimes, I wish she'd just smack some sense into me, tell me what to do. I know she's never liked Brad, and part of me wants her to outright say, 'Leave him.' But she won't. That's not her style. She doesn't believe in telling me how to live my life, even when I wish she would. Even when I'm desperate for someone to pull me out.

"Well text him back," Casey urges.

Instead, she just encourages me to flirt with Ryan. To pretend Brad doesn't exist. To be dishonest. Just like she did that night in Newport. And for some reason, I take Casey's advice as gospel, even when I know it's wrong. It makes it easier to justify because part of me already feels this way—like if two of us think it, it can't be entirely wrong.

"What do I even say? Just… *Hey?*"

"Yeah. Or you could just skip to the chase and send him a nudie." She laughs, and I join her.

"Oh, he'd love that."

"Who wouldn't? You're a hot piece of ass, Coop. Any man *should* feel like the luckiest man alive to be with you."

I catch the emphasis on *should*. "Subtle," I say. "Brad knows he's lucky."

"Does he?" she asks, a sad expression on her face.

"Yes, he does. You'll see—he's missed me all week. He may even surprise you… Maybe you'll finally warm up to him."

God, why did I just defend him?

"I'm not holding my breath. Are you texting him back or what?"

I hesitate. "Yeah. I'll text him back."

Cooper: Hey back.

"You really went with 'hey back?' Come on Coop. Turn up the heat!"

"Chill. I'm feeling it out. I've got to see where he's going with this. Our last encounter wasn't exactly… normal." Just thinking about it gives me butterflies—the elevator, his kiss, how he left. Good Lord.

I get another text.

"Oh. It's Brad." Disappointment slips into my voice, and Casey gives me a pointed look.

Brad: Hey baby, just landed. Grabbing an Uber. Can't wait to see you.

I force a smile. It's not that I don't want Brad here, or that I'm not happy to see him—it's just that Ryan seems to overshadow everything lately. But does that feeling disappear once you cross the line? That's where I hesitate. Is this all fun and games because I'm not supposed to want Ryan? Because I'm going to text him back? Because I don't want Brad to know?

Casey grabs my phone and starts typing.

"What are you doing?" I ask, panic rising in my throat.

"What you should be doing." She gives me a bold look—daring me to stop her.

I know it's pointless to try to take it back—plus, part of me doesn't want to. "Casey, don't. Just don't make me look desperate or… embarrass me."

She chucks it back.

"I didn't. Just sent enough to get the conversation going."

"Glad you texted. I've been thinking about you. Really? Way to give him the upper hand, Case. Now he thinks I've been sitting here obsessing over him for days."

"Two things: One, you *have* been sitting here obsessing over him. And two, it never hurts to stroke a guy's ego now and then. Sometimes, you just have to make the first move."

"You're giving me a lecture on initiating? That's how we ended up in that elevator mess in the first place. I initiated… hardcore. I don't know if I want to keep playing that game."

"Of course you do. You just need to break it off with Brad first… I've gotta get going. Say hi to Brad for me—or don't. Whatever."

"You're such a jerk." I stick my tongue out at her.

She laughs, standing. "Enjoy your conversation with Ryan," she says teasingly. "Don't let Brad see those messages."

"I won't. I'll delete them… and I'm done texting him."

"Sure you are." Casey winks, and I stand to give her a hug goodbye. "Love you, sis. See you in the morning."

"Love you back. See you."

As she walks inside, my phone buzzes again. I settle back, bracing for some fun.

Ryan: Ah, you're still thinking about that kiss in the elevator? Just a taste of what could be…

Ryan: If you were single.

A grin spreads across my face, heart racing a little faster.

Cooper: And you're still full of yourself…

As soon as I hit send, I wish I'd gone with flirty instead of snarky. I scramble to redeem myself.

Cooper: Of course I think about it. Every. Damn. Day.

Ryan: Too bad that's all we'll ever have to think about… well, that and Newport.

Cooper: What do you mean? Trust me, I think about way more than that.

Ryan: Yeah, but those are just fantasies. Too bad we can't make them come true…

Cooper: Why not?

Ryan: You know why. Starts with B, ends with d.

Cooper: An affair could be exciting, tho. Sneaking around, hooking up in random places, trying not to get caught. Admit it—that's hot. (winky face emoji)

Ryan: Yeah, I've been on the other side of that, and trust me… not so hot. Also, never worth it.

Cooper: Relax. I'm joking.

Ryan: Brad there with you?

And… just like that, he killed the vibe.

Cooper: Almost. In an Uber.

Ryan: Well, enjoy your time with him. He's a keeper, that one. You're a lucky girl. Just… try not to think about me while he's touching you tonight. Not fair to Brad.

Cooper: Nice try, Ryan. #eyeroll

Ryan: Lol. Night, Cooper.

And that's it. I sit in the silence for a while, listening to the ocean until I hear Brad's Uber pull up. I head inside, trying to muster up some excitement.

I force a smile as Brad steps through the door, willing myself to look excited.

"Hey, babe!" I greet him with a hug and quick kiss. "How was the flight?"

"Hey, baby. It was good." He holds on to me a bit longer than usual, his arms tightening around me.

My dad comes to the door. "Hey, Brad. Good to see you." They go in for a man hug, slapping each other's backs. My dad's always liked Brad. Maybe they share some unspoken connection—cheaters' instincts, or something. I hate that they share the thing I dislike most about them.

"Hey, how's my favorite father-in-law?"

"I'm good, really good." They pull apart from their bonding hug, and my dad turns to Brad with a grin. "So, when's the big wedding? I can't get her to give me any details," he adds, glancing at me with a raised eyebrow.

"We don't know yet, Dad," I say just as Brad answers, "Hopefully soon." We exchange a look that says it all—proof we're on entirely different pages.

"I keep trying to nail down a date," Brad says, pulling me closer.

Without meaning to, I pull back slightly. "There's no rush, though…" I say gently, catching Brad's frown and my dad's puzzled look. "I just want things to be perfect. No need to rush into anything," I add, hoping it'll satisfy them both.

"Right," Brad says as he looks at my dad. "We were talking about the fall a few weeks ago." He looks back at me. "That should give Cooper all the time she needs to plan and make everything perfect."

I smile. "Yep. Fall would be pretty."

"Well, I wouldn't stall much longer," my dad chimes in. "Trust me, after a few weddings, I know venues book up fast." I roll my eyes, which doesn't go unnoticed by my dad. He pauses. "I don't know about Chicago, but you'd have a hard time finding a venue in Newport even a year out."

"It'll be fine, Dad. Worst case, we can always get married right here." But even as I say all the right things, I know it's never going to happen. Just hearing about the wedding makes me feel like I'm suffocating. I fake a yawn. "Think I'll head to bed. You coming?" I glance over at Brad.

"Yeah, I'll be right there."

I head up the stairs and crawl into bed. I skip my nighttime routine, hoping Brad will stay downstairs talking to my dad long enough for me to fall asleep first. Pulling out my phone, unable to help myself, I open the text thread with Ryan. I read and re-read his words, the glow from the screen lighting up my fingers and blankets. I hover over the keyboard, wanting him to know he's on my mind, but I'm not sure what to say. Before I can second-guess myself, my thumbs move quickly, and I hit send.

Cooper: Sweet dreams, Ryan. I know mine will be.

I silence notifications and set my phone to sleep mode—just in case he texts back. The last thing I need is a blaring message from Ryan on my screen when Brad comes to bed.

* * * * * * * * * *

I slip out of bed early on Christmas morning, unable to sleep. It's barely five. Bundling up, I grab my phone and head outside for a walk, hoping to clear my head. I have a message from Ryan that was sent late last night. My pulse quickens as I swipe up to read it.

Ryan: Any dream with you in it would make me more than happy.

I smile as I read it. I text him back, hoping I don't wake him.

Cooper: So, turns out I had a super weird dream. You were in it, but it was like an episode of *The Office*. We were at work, and I kept asking if anyone had seen my vibrator. #awkward

Thirty minutes later, as I round the corner to my dad's street, my phone buzzes with another text from Ryan.

Ryan: Why are you up so early? Excited for Santa? Also, I hope I was Jim and you were Pam—you know, cuz they end up doing it.

I shake my head, laughing. *God, he's such a nerd.*

Cooper: Couldn't sleep. And… DOING IT? Are you thirteen? Lol.

Ryan: What do you have against doing it? Did you and Brad do it last night?

Cooper: God, you really are thirteen… Let me guess, you jerked off into a sock last night and left it under the bed for your mom to find later? Merry Christmas, Mom! Here's a crusty gift from your 30-something son. (How old are you, anyway?)

I head out to the back patio and sink onto the sofa, grinning from ear to ear. Why is this so much fun?

Ryan: Hey, a man's gotta make do with what he's got. But what do you expect when all I can think about is your beautiful body pressed against me in that elevator? That cute laugh… those lips? Fuck. Don't even get me started. #sorrymom #cumsocks—oh, and I'm 34 btw. How old are you?

I laugh out loud.

Cooper: That actually made me laugh out loud. I know you're joking, but also… that was hot… I'm 27.

Ryan: What are you doing?

Cooper: Sitting on the patio, watching the waves…

Ryan: Ah… waiting for me to run by. Hate to disappoint, but no sexy men will be by today.

Ryan: Are you alone?

Cooper: Yes. Why?

Ryan: What are you wearing?

I roll my eyes, already knowing where this is going. "Oh God," I say out loud, shaking my head. So typical.

Cooper: Is this where I'm supposed to text back "nothing"?

Ryan: Come on. Just play along.

Cooper: I'm in sweats—big, comfy joggers and an oversized Chicago Bears sweatshirt. UGG slippers, too, with a big blanket wrapped around me. It's practically lingerie.

Ryan: Sexy to me. Joggers, huh? Easy access… kinda does it for me.

Cooper: Shut up! No, it does not.

Ryan: Do you have any idea how good you'd feel against me in your sweats?

Wait, what?

Ryan: I'm picturing it right now. What it would be like to be there with you.

Okay... where is he going with this?

Cooper: Tell me more about that... what would it be like?

Ryan: I'm thinking how I'd love to be sitting on the couch with you. Wrapped up in that blanket together. You'd be on my lap, my arms wrapped around your waist. Maybe a hand finds its way under your sweatshirt.

Is he... sexting me? What the hell is happening? I decide to play along, because—why not? I want to.

Cooper: Consider me intrigued.

Ryan: I'd run my hands down your body, fingers tracing over your skin... teasing you. Making you want more.

Ryan: You'd like that wouldn't you?

Cooper: Maybe... not totally convinced yet.

Ryan: Oh, you would. And then I'd lean in, kiss your neck—just soft enough to keep you wanting more... You'd press back against me with that beautiful ass of yours—moaning, driving me insane.

A tightening knot forms low in my stomach, heat spreading through me like wildfire. Okay. He's doing things for me... I'm all kinds of turned on, right now.

Cooper: Jesus, Ryan.

Ryan: You like that, don't you? Just picturing me touching you... slowly, deliberately... really feeling every inch. It's driving you crazy, isn't it?

Cooper: Maybe a little... but don't let it go to your head.

Ryan: Just a little? I'll have to do better then. I want you so turned on you can barely stand it—I want you desperate.

Jesus Christ. I'm there—practically desperate already.

Cooper: Oh yeah? And how exactly are you going to do that from Arizona?

Ryan: Picture this—I'm there with you—I've laid you down on the sofa on the patio. I've removed your sweatshirt because we don't need that. I'll keep you warm. I'm hovering over you as I whisper in your ear everything I'm about to do to you. My hand slides down, inch by inch, until it's right where you need me most... but I stop, just to hear you beg for it.

Cooper: Right. Except I'd never beg for "it".

Ryan: Not yet. But you will.

Cooper: Prove it.

Ryan: You asked for it. I'd kiss you, long and deep, then work my way down—your neck, your shoulders, taking those sweet tits into my mouth. You'll love it, of course. You'll press into me, wanting more. I'd drag my tongue down to your stomach. God, I can practically hear your moans right now.

Cooper: Still not begging.

But holy hell. Inside, I'm practically begging.

Ryan: Now imagine my hand slipping into your pants, my fingers teasing you, just enough to get you worked up. You can feel how close you are, but I make you wait for it. So, tell me, Coop… are you getting turned on?

Holy shit. Yes. I'm so turned on, it's ridiculous. I sink down into the couch, getting comfortable. I might have to grab my vibrator soon, but I'm way too into this to move.

Cooper: Fine… yeah.

Ryan: Good. Let me take it a little further.

The text bubble pops up, then disappears.

Cooper: I'm waiting…

Such a jackass. He knows exactly what he's doing to me.

Ryan: When I finally touch you, you'll be so wet that my fingers will slide right in. But I won't give it to you—not right away. I'll keep you close, almost there… until you can't take it anymore.

Sweet Jesus. This man.

Ryan: I want you to touch yourself, Coop—pretend it's me. Imagine my hands on you, feeling every inch of you. Every second is about you—making you feel so fucking good. Those are my fingers on your pussy, taking my time. Even from here, I want you to feel how good it would be if I were there, with nothing in the way.

Oh. My. God. Is he serious? I glance around and check my watch—it's only six. No one else should be up for at least an hour, and the beach is empty. For now.

Cooper: Seriously, what are you doing? You're killing me here.

Ryan: I know. Trust me, you'll love it. So… is your hand in your joggers?

I hesitate. Am I really going to do this? Or am I just going to tell him I am? It's hard to text one-handed—especially with my left. But I'm so turned on, I'd kill for a release right now… and I'd love for it to be with

Ryan in my head. I slide my hand into my pants and switch to voice-to-text.

Cooper: Yes.

Ryan: Slide your hand lower. Start slow. Imagine it's me. Soft, teasing touches... just enough to make you lose it.

I run my fingers along my clit. *My God—I'm so wet, it's insane.* The pulsing between my legs is so strong, I'm already close.

Cooper: Ryan, I swear... if you tell anyone about this, I'll strangle you with my bare hands.

Ryan: Feel how wet you are. You're soaked, aren't you?

Cooper: Yes.

Ryan: Good girl. That's because of me.

Damn. I've been seeing this side of Ryan more and more—demanding, teasing, always leaving me wanting more. And it just makes him that much harder to resist.

Ryan: Now keep going. Move your fingers just a little faster. You're close, aren't you, Coop?

Cooper: Almost there.

Ryan: You wanna cum, don't you? But you're not ready yet—not until I say. Don't you dare.

Ryan: Now... move faster. Get yourself close.

Cooper: I'm so close. I can't hold on much longer.

Ryan: Good. But don't cum yet. Now, imagine my mouth on you, kissing, licking your pussy... tasting you. God, I remember exactly how good you taste, Coop—just drives me crazy. You're trembling under me, wanting me so badly you can't even think straight.

Cooper: Jesus. Ryan. You're killing me.

Ryan: I'd suck your clit now. I can hear the sounds you'd make. And I'm so fucking hard for you, it hurts.

A moan escapes me.

Cooper: Fuck, Ryan. When can I cum?

Ryan: Not yet. I want you to hold it. Feel it build, feel the tension, knowing you can't cum until I tell you to.

Cooper: I can't wait. I want it now.

Ryan: Oh, you can. And you will. Now... stop. Right there.

Cooper: What? Are you serious?

Ryan: Yeah, stop. Don't move. Keep your hand right where it is, but don't you dare finish.

I do exactly what I'm told. And it almost kills me. The pulsing of my desire drumming in my ears as I barely hold on.

Cooper: Ryan, please… don't make me wait. I need this.

Ryan: Oh, I know you do. But you're not going to get it. Not today.

Ryan: Because if you want me to make you cum… you're going to have to leave Brad. No more games, Cooper. No more teasing. You want this? You want me? Then make it happen.

What the actual FUCK?

Cooper: Ryan, don't be an ass.

Ryan: You'll just have to wait, babe. Enjoy the frustration. Maybe next time, we'll finish what we started… but only if you're free. Merry fucking Christmas.

I send him the middle finger emoji, and run inside to find my bullet from my purse. I can't believe him. What a dick… *Ugh—and a dick I still want… in more ways than one.* I settle under my blanket and find my release. Then, feeling content, I snap a picture of my bullet and send it to him.

Cooper: Guess I don't need you after all.

I smile, satisfied.

Chapter 24

COOPER

The afternoon is complete chaos with Mason opening all his presents. It's adorable, and it makes me hope that I'll have kids one day. But then I look at Brad, and an uneasy feeling washes over me. Do I really want to have kids with Brad?

I glance at my dad, and a wave of sadness hits as I think about how different my life might have been if he hadn't cheated on my mom. If he'd been home more, a loving and devoted husband and father. I love him, but it sucked going through that. I'd never want my kids to feel the way I did. A lump forms in my throat, and I excuse myself.

I wander into my bedroom and plop onto the bed. Brad's phone sits on the nightstand, charging. I pick it up, curious. Six text notifications light up the screen. I swipe up but hit the locked screen and need a password. I type in a few guesses, convinced that if I could just get in, I'd find evidence of him cheating again. But nothing works. And the fact that I don't know his password really irritates me.

I set his phone back down and stare at the ceiling. A few minutes later, Brad comes in.

"Hey, baby. What are you doing up here?" He lies down next to me.

"Oh, I just wasn't feeling great," I lie.

He turns on his side and slips a hand under my sweatshirt, his thumb brushing over my skin. "I feel like you're avoiding me. What's going on?" But all I can think about is Ryan's text about his hand under my sweatshirt.

I turn to him, frowning. "What's your password to your phone?"

Brad scrunches his forehead. "What?"

"What's your password?"

"Baby, we have passwords for a reason. I'm not giving you my password."

"Why not? I'm your fiancée."

"Don't we all deserve a little bit of privacy?" he says, his voice softening as if he's trying to diffuse the situation.

"Yeah, I get that you want privacy. But I want to know your password, Brad."

"I'm not giving you my password."

"Why not? Do you have something to hide?"

He sighs, running a hand through his hair. "No, I don't have something to hide. God, where is this coming from?"

"Okay… well, then open your phone and let's go through it together. You can show me. Who's texting you on Christmas Day?"

Brad stands, frustration clear in his voice. "Why are you being crazy, Cooper? Where is this coming from?"

"I'm not crazy, Brad."

"Fuck. Did you talk to Ryan?"

"What?… No." We stare at each other, the tension simmering.

"Then why are you asking to see my phone all of a sudden?"

"Why are you asking if I talked to Ryan?" I'm genuinely confused. Why would he even bring Ryan up? Does he know about my texts with him?

"You didn't talk to Ryan?"

"No…" I say slowly, unsure of what he's getting at.

"Fine." He grabs his phone and lies back down next to me. He enters his password deliberately, making sure I see it, and then opens his phone, holding it out.

I reach for it, but he pulls back just before I can grab it. "Now get yours. We'll trade. You can go through mine, and I'll go through yours."

Shit. I did not see this coming. Panic consumes me.

"My phone's downstairs."

"No problem. I'll get it. Where is it?"

I sit up quickly. "No, I can go get it."

"No. I'll get it. Where is it, Cooper?"

"Um… I'm not sure. Somewhere in the kitchen, probably." My heart pounds wildly in my chest.

Brad turns on his heel and heads downstairs. I take a shaky breath and reach under the pillow for my phone. Swiping up, I quickly open my text messages. I delete the entire text thread with Ryan—I don't have time to be selective. It's all or nothing.

I go to the top of the stairs. "Brad?" I call out. "My phone's up here."

Brad appears at the bottom of the stairs, looking up at me, and then climbs back up, meeting me at the top.

I hand him my phone. "Sorry, I forgot I left it in the bathroom."

He gives a curt nod. "Right."

We sit side by side on the bed, the silence heavy between us. Guilt gnaws at me; I feel like a hypocrite. I wanted to see Brad's phone because I was so sure he had something to hide—that he was cheating on me. But it turns out, I'm the one with secrets, with text messages to hide, feelings for someone else. He handed over his phone, and I had to lie.

I scroll through his texts, emails, social media accounts. I hate this. It feels gross. What kind of relationship is this if I feel like I have to do this? I'm not even sure what to look for. I know there are secret apps people can download that look like normal apps to hide affairs, but I wouldn't even know how to check for something like that.

The first time I found out Brad was cheating, he'd left his computer screen open, and I happened to see his messages. The next time, a friend told me she'd seen him out with another woman. I hated her for telling me and chose not to believe her because I didn't want to. After that, paranoia took over, and I started looking for anything to prove her wrong. I couldn't find anything—until the woman's husband found me and told me Brad was sleeping with his wife. The last time, the girl herself called me, upset that Brad had tried to break things off with her. I guess she wanted to get even.

I let out a loud sigh and set his phone on the bed.

He hands me mine with big apologetic eyes. "You satisfied?"

I nod, my lips smacked together.

"I'm sorry. You can have the password from now on."

I start crying. I hate crying. But the worst part? I think I'm upset that I didn't find anything. I'm upset that Brad's not cheating. I wanted to find proof—something that would give me the courage to leave—the shove that I so desperately need.

"Hey, baby." Brad pulls me into him, his arms warm and secure. "What's wrong? God, it kills me to see you like this." He slides his hands up under my shirt, rubbing my back, his touch familiar and steady. He kisses me gently, murmuring that everything will be okay—that I can trust him, that he loves me. And all I can do is think of Ryan, and how I wish it were him holding me, kissing me, whispering in my ear.

I hate that I'm this person. I hate that I'm weak.

Brad's kisses become more sensual. Pressing them along my jaw now, down my neck. I tip my chin to give him access, but I'm not in the mood. He makes his way to my lips, softly sucking my bottom lip. And I kiss him back. I let him remove my sweatshirt, then my pants. We make out. I let him touch me. I go through the motions because that's what I do. It's what I've always done, and I don't know how to change. I don't know how to say no.

My mind drifts back to freshman year, to Gavin. God, he messed me up in ways I'm still uncovering. After him, it was just one wrong choice after another, each guy a faint echo of the last. One decision, one misplaced trust, and suddenly, you're on a path you can't seem to escape. Here I am, thirteen years later, too afraid to make the choices I know I need to make.

Brad's hands explore, moving over familiar territory, but I feel nothing—no spark, no thrill, just an overwhelming sense of numbness. I'm trapped in my own body, going through motions that used to mean something, but right now, they just… don't. His hand slides between my thighs, and still… nothing.

A tear slips down my cheek, and I choke back a sob.

Brad kisses me, and I kiss him back. His hands roam over me, and I play the part. I move my hands, make the sounds, arch my body into him. And when it's time to feel the way I usually do. I don't.

So, I fake another orgasm.

When we're finished, I lie beside Brad as he starts talking about his next work trip. I'm only half-listening, my mind racing with thoughts of what to do. *Why am I still like this?* I've spent years molding myself to fit into men's lives, meeting their needs. But what about my needs? Where's my self-growth? Something has to change.

I have to change.

January

I roll my luggage into the entryway, stopping to sort through the mail Brad left for me on the console table next to my grandmother's glass bird. A small smile tugs at my lips. We were close—sleepovers on the first Saturday of every month, late-night talks, way too much popcorn and candy.

She kept this bird in her china cabinet, along with a bunch of other glass figurines. For some reason, I was always drawn to it. I couldn't even tell you why. But a few hours before she passed, she placed it in my hands and told me she wanted me to have it. I cherish it more than anything.

My stomach growls, reminding me that it's past dinnertime, and I'm starving. I definitely didn't pack enough snacks for the flight home.

I pull out my phone to text Brad.

Cooper: Hey, I'm home. Where are you?

Brad went straight from Newport to New York two days after Christmas and got back a few days ago. I thoroughly enjoyed the time away—spending time with Casey, warmer weather, and, if I'm being honest, the space from Brad.

My phone dings, and seconds later, Brad's laptop chimes from his office. Curiosity pulls me as I read my text.

Brad: Hey, baby. Went out for drinks with Jared.

I glance toward his desk. His laptop is open. Just sitting there.

Brad never leaves it open when he's not home. I walk into his office and sit down, ready to play detective, praying the password for his phone is the same for his laptop.

I freeze. Wait. Why isn't the screen locked?

Brad isn't careless. He plans everything. Always.

Another ding from my phone, followed by the laptop. But I don't need to check my phone—the text message pops up on the screen.

It's from Ryan.

Ryan: You home yet?

My heart drops to the pit of my stomach, my breath catches, and a wave of nausea washes over me.

Oh my God. Brad's somehow connected my phone to his computer without me knowing.

My brows knit together. *Did he want me to see this?* With shaking hands, I click into the text messages, my fingers trembling as I navigate to the text thread with Ryan's name. I click it.

Shit. Every single message since Christmas Day is there. My pulse pounds in my ears as I scroll through the many flirtatious, explicit texts between Ryan and me this past week—not to mention the ones where Ryan asked when I'm leaving Brad. I feel even sicker wondering when Brad set this up. Was it before Christmas Day? Has he seen the texts where I got off to Ryan's messages while Brad was asleep inside? That would explain his sudden possessiveness and paranoia.

I'm frantic to understand the extension of this invasion. I pull up the settings, trying to figure out exactly what he's connected to—can he see my emails, my socials?

Another ding.

Brad: I'll try to be home by 10. Don't go to bed without me. I'll want you when I get there.

My mind races. How long has he known? And if he knows, why is he acting normal?

Because he's jealous.

A cold sweat breaks out across my skin.

He knows.

He fucking knows.

He *wanted* me to see this.

He wants me to panic.

This isn't just about jealousy. He needs to control the situation. Control me.

A chill creeps over me. Brad isn't overtly aggressive, but he has a temper. A nasty one. And he's capable of being downright calculating and manipulative. The thought makes my stomach tighten.

I can almost feel his anger simmering below the surface, waiting—patiently.

Dammit. What the fuck is he planning?

I make a beeline for the kitchen, grabbing a bottle of wine off the rack. I rummage frantically through the drawers for the opener, pouring myself a full glass. I down it like I've been stranded on a deserted island.

I pour another. I walk numbly into the living room and sink into the sofa, setting the glass on the coffee table. Leaning forward, elbows on my knees, I let my head hang heavy in my hands. A low groan escapes me as I grip my hair. "Oh my God." My voice is barely a whisper. My eyes fill, but I'm too numb to cry—too scared. "Fuck." I sit up, breath shaky, hands unsteady, and take another sip. I slump back, staring into the abyss.

I don't know how long I've been sitting here, but at some point, the wine bottle ended up beside me, nearly empty. I chew on my thumbnail, eyes fixed on the door, waiting for Brad to walk through and... And what? What am I even waiting for? A fight? For him to take me to bed—another round of emotionally detached sex where I'll fake yet another orgasm? What the fuck am I actually waiting for?

I glance at the time—10:15. He should be home any minute now. A sense of dread hovers over me.

Another ding.

Ryan: Can't wait to see your beautiful face on Monday.

A feeling of warmth rushes through me as I read Ryan's text, and despite my heavy buzz, clarity hits, quick and sharp. I don't have to be here, waiting for Brad. I stand, calm and steady, and walk to the kitchen, pouring the last of the wine into a travel mug. I grab my luggage, put on my boots, bundle up, and, with my phone in hand, I walk out the door.

And I don't look back.

Chapter 25

RYAN

I stare at the text I sent an hour ago, willing it to vibrate with a new message.

Ryan: Can't wait to see your beautiful face on Monday.

I just got home from another "date" with a girl named Megan. And by date, I mean I spent an hour at a bar, listening to Megan talk about herself while I nodded, asked questions, and thought about Cooper the entire time.

Now, I sit at the kitchen counter with a beer, with only the lights from under the cabinets on, the rest of the house dark. Leo and Vivian are out of town, still in Utah visiting her family for the holidays, so I have the house to myself. I came home New Year's Day—a rough travel day after partying with friends the night before.

I glance at my phone again and groan. God, what am I doing? Why can't I just go to bed? It's pathetic, sitting here with my beer, waiting up just in case Cooper texts me back. But I opened this beer, so I should finish it. I turn on *The Office* to distract myself.

Twenty minutes later, close to midnight, my phone buzzes.

Cooper: Hey. You up?

Relief floods through me.

Ryan: Hey, yeah, I'm still awake.

I try to play it cool, like I haven't been sitting here waiting for her text.

Cooper: Can I come over?

What? If there was ever a bad idea, it would be Cooper coming over.

Ryan: Are you being serious? Or is this just flirty texting…?

I'm so confused.

Cooper: I'm outside. I think. Wheich honestly is yours isnt due.

Now I'm really confused. I watch the texting bubble pop up again, telling me she's typing.

Cooper: Sorry in a little drunk.

I frown at my phone. She's drunk?

Cooper: Can you come outside?

Cooper: I think I'm on street.

What the hell? I grab my coat and shoes, heading out quickly. I scan the row of townhouses, about to call her when I hear someone shouting.

"Ryan!"

I follow the sound and spot her walking along the trail in front of the townhouses near the river. She's bundled up, and rolling her luggage behind her. A mix of emotions flood through me as I hurry toward her.

I have so many questions.

"Jesus, Cooper, what are you doing out here? It's fucking freezing."

She bulldozes into me, wrapping her arms tightly around my waist. "I just needed to see you," she murmurs, her words slurring.

I pull her close, steadying her. "What happened? Why are you drunk and out here alone?"

The thought of her wandering the streets of downtown Chicago—drunk, in the middle of the night—it kills me. The streets are almost deserted with the brutal cold, and anything could've happened.

"Brad knows," she says with a heavy sigh. "He knows all the things."

I pull back, trying to read her face. "What do you mean, he knows? Knows what?"

"That I like you. And that I want you, and he knows everything about… you and me and all the things."

"Alright. Let's get you inside, okay?" I still have no idea what she's really saying.

"Did you know," she starts, then stops moving, looking at me earnestly. "I NEVER stop thinking about you, Ryan. I never stop. I think about you aaaaallllllll the time."

I take her luggage and put my other arm around her to keep her moving forward, but she keeps talking, her voice loud and unfiltered.

"I think about you at breakfast, and I think about you at lunch, and I think about you at…" She plants her feet suddenly, eyes on the sky, then bursts into laughter. "Oh my God, I can't even remember what the last one is called." She loses her balance, stumbling into me. I catch her, tightening my hold. "Do you know what it's called?"

"Jesus, Coop," I say, half-smiling despite myself. "How much did you drink?"

She scowls, her brows knit together. "I'm not sure," she says, holding out her tumbler like evidence. "But my wine is all gone." She lets it slip from her fingers, watching it hit the cement. "I'm tired. I need to sit."

"No, no, no." I quickly wrap my arms under her armpits, lifting her just as she starts to sink to the ground. "Come on, Cooper. We've gotta keep walking. Let's get you inside, okay?"

"No. I don't want to go inside." Her voice is a shaky whisper, and then it's like she's talking to herself. "I even think about you when I have sex with Brad… God, I'm so fucked up, Ryan. Why am I so fucked up? What's wrong with me?" Tears start slipping down her cheeks, and it wrecks me.

"You're not fucked up, you're just… very drunk. Come on." My anger toward Brad is off the charts, and I don't know exactly what he's done, but I know he's behind this. The fact that she's been out here alone like this is enough to make me wish every terrible thing upon him.

Between Cooper, her luggage, and the tumbler she dropped, it's quite the challenge getting her inside. I finally settle her on the couch, taking off her coat and boots. I'm exhausted, and I haven't dealt with this kind of drunken mess since college. No one likes babysitting a drunk. But with Cooper, it's different—seeing her like this doesn't just suck; it worries me.

I grab a bottle of water from the kitchen, and when I return, Cooper's wrestling with her shirt, trying to yank it off. "Get this fucking"—the fabric twists in her hands until she finally frees herself—"thing off." She throws it to the floor with a sigh and curls up on the couch, leaving me gawking.

I quickly head upstairs for a T-shirt because there's no way I can let her stay shirtless.

Nudging her gently, I say, "Hey, Coop. Can you sit up?" She stirs, swatting at me with a groan. "Come on, sit up. I've got a shirt for you… and water." She really needs to get some water down—and put a shirt on.

"Idontwanit."

With some effort, I manage to sit her up and bring the water to her lips. She takes a few sips before pushing it away and lays her head in my lap.

I close my eyes, taking a deep, steadying breath. Jesus. Cooper's in her bra, drunk, and practically breathing on my dick. Naturally, I feel myself getting hard. *I can do this*. My concern is for her well-being right now, but… I'm still a guy—and, fuck. She looks good.

Forty-five minutes later, I've managed to get her into one of my shirts and into my room. I carried her up the stairs after getting her to drink a full glass of water. She's a little less belligerent now but still very drunk. I wait on the edge of the bed while she's in the bathroom, only for her to come back out… without pants. She drops onto the bed, crawling her way up to the top, flashing her blue thong, and bare ass along the way.

I turn, trying to keep my gaze in check. "Why don't you get under the covers and rest?" I need her to get covered up—now.

She shakes her head. "No. I'm hot."

"Alright… How you doin'? Do you need anything?"

She looks up at me with those deep brown eyes, saying nothing at first—just patting the bed beside her. "Just you."

My stomach twists with how she's looking at me. The shirt I gave her has ridden up, showing her stomach, and even though I know I shouldn't, I can't help noticing how sexy she is. I swallow, doing my best to keep control. She needs me to be here for her, and I need to man up and not act like a typical guy right now.

I prop some pillows behind me and settle into a seated position beside her.

"Ryan." Her voice is barely a whisper, and I meet her gaze. The muted TV glows in the background. "I like you… a lot." A faint smile tugs on her lips.

I smile back. "I like you too, Cooper… a lot."

Her smile widens, but a tear slips down her cheek. She takes a shaky breath. "Why?" she asks, her voice so soft it's almost a breath. "Why do you like me?"

I lie down beside her so we're face to face. "There are a lot of things I like about you. For starters, you're funny. You make me laugh. And you're smart." I brush a loose strand of hair from her face. "I honestly don't know anyone who's as beautiful as you and also smart and funny. You can usually find two out of the three, but all three? That's rare."

She lets out a soft laugh, and I feel a smile tug at my lips as I continue. "You're actually really kind… to everyone but me," I tease. That makes her laugh again, and I join her. "I mean it. You have a huge heart. You just… love to torment me."

"I do love it," she admits.

"And you're an incredible leader." I pause, letting that settle. "I bet you don't even know that I've spoken to everyone on your team about you. They all respect you. They think you're amazing. And that says a lot about the kind of person you are."

"They do?"

"Damn right they do." I brush my thumb along her cheek, watching her search my face for any hint of insincerity. She won't find it—not here. "I have fun with you. That one matters. And let's not forget that you're an insanely good kisser, among other things." I grin.

"And most importantly," I pause, letting the words linger, "I feel something when I'm with you. Something I can't explain." I chuckle, trying to ease the weight of the moment. "Maybe it's vibes, who knows?" She laughs as tears run down her cheeks. I lean in, pressing a gentle kiss to her forehead. "You wanna talk about what happened? Or are you still too drunk?"

"Hmm. Not gonna lie, the room still spins when I close my eyes. But I'm not drunk. I heard everything you said, and I know exactly what I'm doing."

"Yeah?" I smile softly. "You going to be alright?"

"Yeah." She reaches for my hand, interlocking her fingers with mine. "Thanks, Ryan." Her expression shifts, becoming serious as her eyes search mine. "All I've ever wanted is for someone to see me—all of me…

through to my soul and"—her voice drops to a soft whisper—"and to love me… all the way down to my bones." Her fingers lightly toy with mine. She swallows, seeming a bit overwhelmed. "And I don't know… for some reason, I feel like you do."

I let her words sink in, feeling the depth of hurt behind them, even if I don't know the whole story. It guts me—like a knife to the stomach. "I do," I say, my voice low and rough. I reach for her, pulling her close in a hug. "I do see you." I release her and roll onto my back, hands interlocked above my head. She shifts closer, resting her head on my chest, her arm draping across me. My pulse quickens, and as I glance down, the sight of her bare ass, long legs, and blue thong sends a jolt through me. My breathing deepens, a growing ache building. I'm in a terrible situation—one where, no matter what I do, there's no winning. But at the same time—there's nowhere else I'd rather be.

"Good night, Ryan." Cooper's voice cuts through my conflicted thoughts.

"Mmm. Good night." The words come out as a hoarse whisper. I take deep, steadying breaths, trying to manage the storm raging inside me. I don't know what to fucking do. I haven't had sex in ten months, and the last time was with her. Aside from that quick blow-job Beth gave me last month, I haven't been touched by anyone but myself—and Jesus, at my age, that's not normal. The dirtiest images enter my mind: Cooper's mouth wrapped around my cock, my hands on her as I take her from behind. I can practically hear her moaning in my ear.

I grip my hair, tugging hard just to keep my hands off her. She's not even doing anything—just lying here, not even touching me—and it's still too much. "Fuck," I mutter, letting one hand fall to her back, where I trace slow circles over the fabric of my shirt that she's wearing. Just the sight of her in my shirt has me undone. I'll never wash it again.

My fingers drift lower, grazing the hem and the warm skin beneath, drawing me closer, like a moth to a flame. The temptation's too strong. I need to feel more of her—the warmth, the softness.

So I do.

I let my fingers drift farther down, brushing against the soft skin of her stomach, inching ever closer to the edge of her panties, where temptation beckons me. She shifts, pulling herself even closer until our bodies are flush together.

Then her hand starts moving. She slowly rubs it back and forth over my stomach, and I freeze—too turned on to move or think. Her fingers slip beneath my shirt, and Lord Jesus, I'm in deep shit.

Her fingertips trail across my skin, each touch burning into me like a match being dragged across my flesh. I squirm beneath her touch, unable to help myself.

I refocus on my own hand, needing to feel composure. My fingers grip her hip, my thumb brushing slowly over her hip bone, tracing along her panty line. I feel her breath hitch. Grinning, I hook my thumb around the fabric, giving it a gentle tug. She gasps and instinctively grinds against me.

My fingers dip a little lower, slipping just inside the top of her panties, toeing the line I'm so dangerously close to crossing. Her fingers slide under my waistband, teasing, taunting.

I trace my fingers back and forth, stopping just at her pubic bone. The smoothness beneath my fingertips sends a rush through me, knowing she's bare—and that thought alone is almost enough to make me lose it. She stills.

"Ryan." Her voice is a soft, steady breath.

"Hmm." It's all I can manage.

She props herself onto one elbow, her eyes locking onto mine. "We're close to crossing lines I know you don't want to cross."

I swallow hard, my voice rough. "I'm guessing you didn't break up with Brad tonight?" It's barely a question—more like a lifeline.

She shakes her head slowly. "He wasn't home, and… I didn't want to see him."

"Fuck," I mutter under my breath.

"You need to leave," she murmurs. "Unless… watching me touch myself isn't crossing the line, because I'm about to lose all control."

Is she serious? There's nothing I'd want more than to watch her. Maybe even more than touching her myself. Goddamn, I can't think straight. My mind races, my body aching. *Pull yourself together.*

"It's probably crossing the line." It's the hardest sentence I've ever forced out. "But there's nothing I'd want more than to watch you do that." I shake my head, swallowing hard. "Fuck, Cooper."

She holds my gaze. "Then you need to leave."

I drag a hand across my face, groaning. "Alright. You're right." I reluctantly pull myself from her. "You gonna be okay?"

She smiles softly. "I'll be okay… Thanks for taking care of me." She reaches for the water on the nightstand, taking a few slow sips.

"Okay. I'll be on the couch if you need anything." I shut my eyes, forcing myself to stand.

She takes a long breath. "Good night, Ryan."

"Good night, Cooper." I head to the door, dragging a hand through my hair, every part of me resisting the urge to look back.

Chapter 26

COOPER

I wake up in Ryan's room, my face pressed against the pillow, feeling only half-alive. God, I'm a mess. I wander into the bathroom to attempt damage control, my head pounding with each step. I glance in the mirror. Shit. I look like I'm dead. I splash cold water on my face, pinch my cheeks, and find a brush in Ryan's drawer. My hair's so kinked on one side from laying on it, there's no hope of making it look normal. I'm so not ready for Ryan to see me like this, not yet. I rummage through every drawer and cupboard until I find a blow-dryer and do my best with his shitty brush to at least smooth the kinks out and give my hair body and shape. I pat my cheeks once more and settle on the slight improvement.

My pants are on the bathroom floor, but I have no idea where my shirt is. I slip them on, and head downstairs. Ryan's asleep on the couch. His body's stretched out, one arm slung across his chest, the other resting by his side. It reminds me of our first night together. He looks just as good as he did that first morning, and damn. I could watch him sleep all day. I quietly tiptoe to my purse and find my phone. I have over thirty missed calls and messages from Brad.

I sigh, not wanting to read them. I look anyway, despite knowing what they'll say.

Brad: Hey, baby, it's getting late. Are you okay? Where are you?

Brad: Getting a bit worried here. Please text me back and let me know you're safe.

Brad: I don't know what's going on, but please call me back, okay? I just want to
know you're alright.

Brad: Cooper, it's almost midnight. Do you have any idea how worried I am?

Brad: I can't believe you'd just disappear on me like this.

There it is. I suck in a deep breath. This is when the side of Brad he keeps hidden from the rest of the world starts to surface.

Brad: Seriously, Coop. If you cared about me at all, you'd at least have the decency
to text back.

I shake my head in disgust. He always finds a way to turn it on me—every single time.

Brad: Where the hell are you?

Brad: Answer your damn phone. I'm done playing games.

This is where he'll take things from bad to worse.

Brad: Are you with someone else? I swear to God, Cooper, if I find out you're with
Ryan…

I turn my phone off with shaky hands, bile rising in my throat. I can't bring myself to read the rest.

I made sure to turn my location off last night after I left. The last thing I need is Brad showing up at Ryan's looking for me. I apply some lipgloss and gather my things. I don't want to wake Ryan, but I can't leave without saying goodbye, not after all he did for me last night.

I stand in front of him, nudging his shoulder softly. "Hey, Ryan."

He peeks at me with one eye, making a deep throaty sound, a sound that always does something for me. "Oh, hey, you're up." He reaches his arms above his head into a deep stretch and my eyes fall to his abs as his shirt lifts, exposing skin and the deep V carved into his sides. Holy hell, how does that simple thing turn me on so much? I feel Ryan's eyes boring into the side of my face as I gape at him. I jerk my head over to his, meeting his gaze… and a smirk of satisfaction. "What time is it?" he asks, groggily.

"Almost nine."

"Damn. I'm tired… How are you feeling?" He sits up.

"I'm okay… Listen, I'm gonna go. Gonna grab a coffee, check myself into a hotel, but I wanted to thank you for last night, and see if you have a Tylenol. I have a pounding headache and…" He cuts me off.

"What do you mean you're checking into a hotel? Why would you do that? Just stay here."

I hesitate. "I don't think that's a great idea after last night." His gaze is intense and it melts my insides.

"Okay… But at least stay for a bit. Have some breakfast… and I can make you coffee."

I nod. "Alright. If you're sure it's okay?"

"Of course it is. I don't want you to leave yet."

I smile, then with embarrassment, I ask, "Do you know where my shirt is?"

He points to the other side of the room, where my shirt lay crumpled on the floor.

"Did I…?" My face scrunches into a grimace.

"Yep." He nods. "You sure did, Coop. Just took it off right in front of me."

I wince. "Sorry."

He stands. "It's not like I'm mad about seeing you in your bra." He smirks, cocking a brow. "I'm just mad I couldn't do anything about it."

I smother a smile.

Me too.

I follow Ryan into the kitchen, taking a seat at the counter while he makes us lattes with the espresso machine.

He hands me mine. "Thanks. Do you have a Tylenol?" I ask, rubbing my temples.

"Yeah." He grabs the Tylenol and leans across from me, coffee in hand, resting his elbows on the counter. His gaze locks on mine. "So… do you want to tell me what happened last night?" His eyes are warm, full of concern.

I sigh. "Not really… but I will." He waits for me to continue. "When I got home last night, Brad wasn't there, and long story short, through text messages, I found out that he had synced my phone to his laptop." I look down at the counter, blinking rapidly, the invasion of it—damn, it stings. I meet Ryan's eyes again. "Anyway, all of our text messages were right there on his computer."

Ryan takes a deep breath, straightening. "Shit."

"Right?" I say, barely pausing for breath. "And do you know what hit me before the anger? The guilt. Like it's just this habit I can't break." I let out a nervous laugh. "Can you imagine? I felt guilty about the texts you and I exchanged. After everything he's done, somehow I'm the one feeling bad. It's ridiculous." I shake my head, still reeling. "Then the anger hit—*how dare he*, you know?"

Ryan watches me, his gaze steady, grounding me. I can't tell exactly what he's thinking, but he's listening intently, and his presence feels like an anchor.

"So, before I really had time to think, I grabbed a bottle of wine. Started drinking… I just wanted to block it all out… I was too numb to even process it." I take a quick breath, needing to keep going. "And then, this moment of clarity just hit. I was sitting there, thinking, *What the hell am I doing?* Why am I here? Why am I waiting for him to come home, to face… whatever twisted thing he has planned?" I bury my head in my hands for a second, groaning.

Ryan shakes his head in disbelief, his brows furrowed.

"And that's when your text came in… about seeing me on Monday." I look up at him, shrugging, the words tumbling out. "I don't know. I didn't think, I just left, with one thing on my mind." I lock eyes with him. "You."

Ryan walks over to me. "Come here," he murmurs, pulling me from my chair into his embrace. His strong arms wrap around me, and he pulls me close, his chin resting on my head. "I'm glad you came here." He kisses the top of my head, pulling me closer.

I melt into him, relief coursing through my veins.

And I've never felt safer.

But as his hand runs soothing circles across my back, he exhales deeply, breaking the silence. "Coop… I need to say this. I know this—us—whatever this is… it's not exactly innocent. I know I've crossed lines I shouldn't have. And, I'm sorry." He pulls back slightly, just enough to meet my gaze. His eyes are sincere, filled with something raw. "I care about you too much to pretend otherwise. But I also know this isn't fair to you—or even to him. Not until you figure out what you really want."

His words hit me like a soft blow, painful but somehow comforting in their honesty. I nod slowly, the weight of his admission settling deep in my chest. Then, before I can stop myself, I whisper, "I'm not sorry."

His eyes widen slightly, searching mine, but I don't look away. "I should be," I add softly. "But I'm not. Not even a little."

A smile tugs at his lips as he pulls me back into the hug, holding me like he's trying to shield me from the storm raging in my life. "I just want you to be okay."

For the first time, I let myself believe, if only for a moment, that things could be different—that maybe happiness isn't out of reach. Ryan's presence feels real, stable, honest. I know he wants me, but if this were only about sex, he would have taken advantage last night—any other guy I've been with would have.

But Ryan didn't.

I tighten my grip around him. This is twice now. Last night, and that night in Newport, he was careful, respectful—concerned, even. A part of me can barely process it, knowing how many times I've woken up in a stranger's bed, with that sick feeling of regret, wondering why I let it happen. Wishing I'd been stronger. Too many men have used me, preying on my vulnerabilities—whether I'd had too much to drink or was just too worn down to resist. But with Ryan, it's different. Somehow, I know that if I were passed out, he wouldn't just avoid taking advantage—he'd make sure no one else could, either. And I welcome it—that rare and fragile feeling of trust.

Chapter 27

RYAN

"Checkmate," I say, moving my knight strategically, trapping her king.

"What the hell, Ryan? We've been playing for five minutes."

I shrug. "I'm good at chess."

"You're good at chess? No, *I'm* good at chess," she says, pointing to herself. "You're stupid good at chess." She drags a hand through her hair, and I watch as the Chicago Bears sweatshirt slips further off one shoulder, showing skin I'd give anything to kiss right now. She must have cut the neck or something—a football sweatshirt that shows skin? It's sexy as hell. "Were you on the fucking chess club or something?"

I laugh. "Something like that."

Her eyes widen. "Wait. Were you really?"

I shrug again. "Yeah, I really was. In middle school." I can't help but grin. Part of me still wonders if I should be proud or embarrassed by that. "Don't drop your panties yet. I was also on the debate team, as well as the math club."

She raises her eyebrows, giving me a look like she's seeing me for the first time. "Oh my God. You're such a nerd."

I raise one hand in a half shrug, leaning back. "Make fun all you want. But before you do, you should also know—this nerd was captain of the golf team junior year."

She laughs. "Is that supposed to make you cooler?"

"Come on. What if my girlfriend was the head cheerleader?" I ask, amused.

"Was she?"

"No," I say, laughing. "She was on the debate team as well."

"Stop! You're not being serious." She's laughing so hard. "This is just a whole side to you that I can't picture."

I laugh just as hard. "Hey, I was a good student, okay?"

She finally calms down, exhaling slowly. "Well, you're the hottest nerd I've ever met."

I press my hand to my chest, grinning. "I'm flattered. Do you want to play again?"

"No. I want to play something I can win."

"And what would that be?" I ask, raising a brow.

She leans in, eyes full of mischief. "I don't know… I'm really good at strip poker." She raises her brows in a teasing challenge.

"Well, that's a game I'd definitely want you to lose. Nothing more vulnerable than being stripped down, covering your sack with your hands while the girl you like stares you down, fully clothed."

"I wouldn't mind that one bit," she says playfully. "And don't say 'sack.'" She shakes her head. "That's gross… Not sexy."

"No? How about 'nuts'?"

She cringes, shaking her head, barely holding back laughter. "Absolutely not."

"Scrotum?"

She laughs. "God, no."

I laugh with her. Damn, my cheeks hurt from all the laughing today. "Alright then, enlighten me. What should I say?"

"Cock." She says it low and seductive, with a mischievous smile, biting her bottom lip just to drive the point home. "You say cock, Ryan. That's what a woman wants to hear."

Damn.

And just like that, my *cock* twitches. She gets me going way too easily. We've been playing games for over an hour now—starting with Monopoly, then Trouble (a blast from the past), and then, of course, I dominated her in chess. I'm having so much fun, I almost forgot why she's really here. "Well, go get the cards." I say, nodding toward the game closet, daring her.

She cocks a brow. "You're serious?"

I lean back, crossing my arms. "Dead serious. Unless you're scared of losing." I say casually, loving the way this pushes her buttons. I'd never actually take it too far—not yet, anyway.

She narrows her eyes. "Oh, I'm not scared. Just making sure you're ready to be cock out at the dinner table."

I laugh as she eyes me down, and I can't help but watch as she walks to the game closet. Don't even get me started on her ass in those leggings. Every time she stands to get something? Hell, I'm hard just thinking about it.

She returns to the table, sitting down with a confident smile, and hands me the deck of cards. "I look forward to watching you manhandle your cock, Ryan. I'm not going easy on you."

I chuckle. "Oh, we'll see about that, babe. Five-card draw or hold'em?"

"Five-card." We lock eyes, challenging each other, both trying not to burst into laughter.

"So, what's the deal? Do we bet with clothing, or does the loser just take something off?" I ask.

"I think the loser just takes something off." She smirks, giving me a slow once-over. "You'll be naked in about three hands."

I glance down at what I'm wearing and shrug, dealing the cards. I get absolute shit—no face cards, no pairs—just junk. I swap out four cards and end up with basically the same damn thing.

She grins wickedly, as she lays down two of a kind. "Do you seriously only have a shirt, pants, and underwear?"

I grin back, even though I know I'm fucked. "Yep."

She raises an eyebrow. "Alright. Show me what you got, big boy."

I make a face. "Don't say big boy… That's gross. Not sexy."

She giggles. "Really? I was trying it on for size."

I shake my head, chuckling. "Nope. Doesn't work."

"It's not a vibe?"

"Definitely not a vibe."

She presses her lips together, trying to hide the cutest damn smile. "Alright, let's see it, Ryan."

"Prepare to strip, woman, because I have," I pause for dramatic effect. "Absolute shit," I say, tossing my cards down and grabbing the hem of my shirt, pulling it over my head. I roll it up into a ball and toss it at her. "Fuck."

She laughs, her eyes roaming over me, and I feel that familiar heat between us. "Hmm. I think I like this game." Her gaze lingers, and she lets out a low, appreciative whistle. "Goddamn. Who looks like that?"

She loses the next round, and removes…a ring. Then a necklace. And then, an earring.

I lose again. "Dammit, Cooper, if I'd known you'd stacked up with all this jewelry, I'd never have agreed to this," I say, chuckling.

"Woo hoo. Let's see those boxers, big boy." I give her a look, and she grins, unfazed. "I'm keeping 'big boy.' Now, come on, don't be shy." She waves her hands up and down, gesturing for me to stand.

With an exaggerated sigh, I stand proudly and peel off my joggers, crumpling them into a ball with mock frustration before tossing them her way.

She does a little victory dance while I'm left standing here like a jack-ass in my underwear.

I scoff, rolling my eyes. "Whatever, Coop. I'm determined to get that sweatshirt off."

"Dream on, big boy."

"Are you calling me that because of my huge cock?"

Her smile widens. "You bet I am." She leans across the table, her voice dropping to a low, sultry whisper. "I don't forget a cock like that, Ryan."

Jesus. That'll do it. My cock only gets harder, and I let out a chuckle of defeat as I sit there in my boxer briefs. She's barely holding in her laughter, fully aware of what she's doing, and I move a hand to cover my very obvious problem.

I deal the next hand—and lose.

Standing up, I pretend I'm about to strip down completely.

"Ryan. Don't." Cooper puts both hands up, palms out, as if to stop me. "I'm telling you right now, if you take those off, I will be fucking you on the couch."

I raise an eyebrow. "Is that supposed to make me *not* want to remove them?"

My hands slide to my waistband, thumbs slipping inside.

"Fine. Your morals go out the window, not mine. Where's the popcorn?" She leans back, crossing her arms, ready for a show.

Dammit. She's taken the upper hand, and I groan, gripping my hair with both hands. "God, I lose strip poker, and you call my bluff? Give me my fuckin' pants."

She holds them up triumphantly before tossing them over to me.

I step into them, adjusting myself as I pull them up. "My shirt?" I hold out my hand, ready to catch it.

She lifts it, flashing a playful smile. "Nah, I think I'll hang on to this for a while longer." Her eyes light up, a genuine happiness radiating from her, and it hits me right in the chest. My only hope for today was to take her mind off things—to make her laugh, have a little fun.

She grips my shirt with both hands, bringing it to her nose and breathing in deeply. "Mmm. Smells like you."

"And I smell good?"

She nods slowly. "Oh, yeah. Really good."

"What do I smell like?"

She brings the shirt closer, taking another deep breath. "Cedarwood," she murmurs, inhaling again. "Cardamom," another sniff, "and... man."

I chuckle, watching her hold my shirt so close, breathing in my scent. She has no idea what that does to me.

"Careful, I'm blushing," I tease, walking around the table until I'm standing right in front of her, my abs level with her face. I hold out my hand for the shirt.

But she just shakes her head. "No, I'm serious. I'm not giving this back. I'm keeping it." She brings it to her nose again, closing her eyes, almost reverent.

"Fine," I say, my voice low.

I'd give her anything she wanted right now.

A part of me feels guilty, like I'm harboring a fugitive—hiding someone else's fiancée, having fun with her, wanting her. And it makes me think about Beth. Did she hang out at her boss's place, playing games, laughing? I tell myself it's different because I'm not sleeping with Cooper—but is it? Jesus, it eats at me, but not enough to push her away. Not when her boyfriend's a narcissistic fuck, and she's this close to leaving him.

I could tell her. Right now. About Brad. About the cheating. It would make her decision easier, maybe even solidify it. And *God,* part of me wants to. Keeping this secret is eating me alive.

But she's already drowning. She's had to deal with so much, and I don't want to be the one to rip away this tiny moment of fun.

And then there's that other part of me that's genuinely worried about her well-being—and, yeah, a selfish part that wonders how it'll affect my life if she leaves Brad. For me. Will she have trust issues? Will she need ongoing therapy?

I push the thoughts down, bringing myself back to the present—where the beautiful girl I've crushed on for ten months is in the kitchen, pouring more salsa into a bowl to share with me.

* * * * *   * * * * *

I flip through the streaming options, sneaking a glance at Cooper as she tucks herself into a blanket beside me. She looks… relaxed, but there's a hint of worry buried behind the brave front she puts on.

"Got a preference?" I ask, keeping my voice casual. "Or should I just pick something you'll pretend to hate but secretly enjoy?"

She elbows me, rolling her eyes, but a smile sneaks through. "Just nothing intense. I need something light to keep my mind off things."

I keep scrolling, but I can't shake the question sitting at the back of my mind. Part of me doesn't want to bring it up—she's clearly not eager to talk about it. I set the remote down, looking over at her.

"Hey, Coop…" I start slowly, keeping my tone gentle. "Have you talked to Brad at all today? Does he know where you are?"

Her shoulders tense for just a second, her fingers playing with the edge of the blanket. "Nope." Her eyes flick to mine. "I know I should, but…"

I nod, trying to stay open, supportive. "Look, I get it. I can only imagine how heavy it all must feel. I just… you can't avoid him forever, you know? You'll have to face him eventually." I watch her, the once relaxed expression now hardening into a scowl. "Do you have a plan?"

She looks at me. "No. I'd love to avoid him forever… sneak in when he's gone, grab all my stuff, leave a note on the counter saying, "peace out," and be done with it." She forces a laugh, and even though she's joking, I get the feeling she wishes it were that easy.

"Are you really that afraid to face him?" I ask carefully. "You said he doesn't hurt you. What is it that makes you so nervous? Or is it just the confrontation… the fight?"

She stares at the blanket, rubbing it between her thumb and index finger, her gaze fixed downward. "I hate who I become when he's upset. I turn into this… robot, retreating into a shell. I'm a wimp around him. I'll say anything to keep the peace. It's either that, or we end up yelling, and it turns into this toxic, aggressive battle that ends in twisted, fucked-up angry sex." She glances up at me, pain flashing in her eyes. "You don't know what he's like when he's mad. He doesn't just get angry—he turns everything back on me. Makes me feel like I'm some… ungrateful whore who doesn't appreciate all he's supposedly 'done for me.' The last time I tried to break up with him—when I met you—he called me some pretty awful names, said I'd end up alone, that no one else would put up with my 'bullshit' like he does."

She looks away, swallowing hard. "And then he… he went so far as to threaten me. Said if I left, he'd… somehow ruin things for me. I know it sounds crazy, but I just remember how calm he was when he said it." She pauses, rubbing her temples.

"Then he'd soften, you know? Play the wounded act—charm me back. He'd promise he'd change, be better, swear he'd never really looked at another woman—not the way he looks at me. And I… God, I always believe him, every time. Or at least, I want to. I know it sounds stupid, but he makes everything feel like it's my fault, and then somehow, I'm the one apologizing." She pauses, taking a shaky breath, her voice lowering. "And I just fall for it… because maybe, deep down… I think he's right."

"He's not right, Cooper." I shake my head, jaw tight, trying to absorb all that she's said. "God, what a *fucking* bastard." Words don't feel strong enough for what I'm feeling right now; there's no way to describe how much I hate him for putting her through this.

Cooper stands, walking calmly over to her purse. She digs around, pulls out her phone, and tosses it into my lap. "Here. You can see the kind of shit he does."

I hesitate, glancing at her. "You don't want to look at them first?"

She shakes her head. "No. I already looked at some of them this morning."

I glance down at her phone. Twenty missed calls, fifteen unread messages. I open them, scrolling up to find the earlier ones, and start reading.

"Oh, read some of them out loud," she says, her tone casual, but I can see the tension in her eyes.

"Okay," I reply, hesitant but knowing it's what she wants. *"This is really how you want to treat me? After everything we've been through? Unbelievable. Come home. Now. Where the hell are you? Why are you ignoring me? I'm not playing around here. Are you with him? If I find out you're with him…"* I glance up at her, my stomach clenching.

She manages to play it cool, barely blinking. "Keep going… there's more. You haven't even scratched the surface."

I look back down at the messages. *"Answer. Your. Damn. Phone. Cooper, this is pathetic. Stop acting like a child and come home. Are you really this desperate for attention?"*

Then, as I keep scrolling, his tone changes, as if a switch has flipped—a full Jekyll-and-Hyde shift.

I continue reading. *"Coop, I'm just worried about you, that's all. Please just let me know you're okay. You know I care about you. This isn't like you, disappearing like this. I'm sorry if I came off wrong earlier. Let's just talk, okay?"*

I sigh and set the phone beside me. "He's such an asshole," I mutter, shaking my head. "Why have you stayed so long, Cooper? He's a fucking narcissist."

"I don't know." She stands, taking a deep breath, arms wrapping around herself as if warding off the chill of reality. "I better get going. I've got a room booked at the Hyatt until we leave for Austin on Tuesday."

"Don't you want to watch a movie?"

She shakes her head, her gaze dropping to the floor. "Not really. I think I just need some time to be alone."

"Coop. Don't go. Just stay here. There's a bedroom for you… I'd feel better if you weren't alone right now."

"I appreciate it, Ryan, but…" She looks away, clearly struggling with her words. "I think I just need space."

I watch her closely, the way she folds into herself. Damn, she's shutting down, putting up walls I don't know how to break through. What the hell has Brad done to her? It kills me to see her like this—like she's disappearing right in front of me.

* * * * * * * * * *

She gets checked in, and I walk her to her room, pausing outside her door. "Can I pick you up on the way to work tomorrow?"

"Sure. That'd be great. She wraps her arms around me, and I pull her into me. "Thank you… for everything," she says, breathing in deeply. "There's that Ryan smell." She pulls back, offering a soft smile. "Goodnight. I'll see you tomorrow."

"Goodnight. Please text or call me if you need anything, okay?"

She nods, her gaze lingering, her eyes meeting mine in a way that takes my breath away every time.

Finally, she lets go, and I watch, helpless, as she slips inside her room, leaving me standing in the hallway, wishing I could protect her from everything that causes her pain. I rake my hands through my hair, frustrated as hell. I've never felt this fucking powerless before.

Chapter 28

COOPER

I close the door behind me, leaning against it as everything crashes down. My body trembles beneath me, and I feel myself breaking—splintering into pieces. A loud sob escapes my lips, and I clasp a hand over my mouth, terrified that Ryan might still be standing on the other side of the door. I squeeze my eyes shut, stifling a cry as I roll my luggage into the room.

The silence in here is depressing, pressing down on me like a suffocating fog—making me feel lonelier than ever. My phone dings, the sound cutting through the quiet like a blade. I glance at it, dreading what I already know will be there.

Brad: Are you really this desperate? Throwing yourself at someone like Ryan? I deserve better than this bullshit.

Another comes immediately after.

Brad: Go ahead. Keep ignoring me, acting like a whore for him. You'll regret this— I'll make sure of that. I know your deepest, darkest secrets, Cooper. Remember that.

The words hit me like a slap, and a cry rips from my throat—a raw, primal sound I can't control. My hands clutch at my hair as the anguish floods me. It feels like I've been stabbed in the gut, the blade jagged and twisting. The pain isn't new; it's been simmering for years, dull and constant, like a wound I've learned to live with. But now? Now, it's unbearable, the knife plunging deeper, festering and infected, stealing what's left of me.

I crawl onto the bed, curling into myself as I rock back and forth on my knees. My breaths come in short, frantic gasps, each sob tearing through me, threatening to shatter what's left of my heart.

It feels like a blindfold has been ripped away—like a blind person suddenly given the gift of sight. The overwhelming awe at the simple beauty of the world, mixed with the gut-wrenching sorrow for everything they've missed. That's exactly how I feel—but with love. For every breathtaking moment of clarity, there's a sharp ache, the devastation of realizing everything I've been blind to was within my grasp—if only I'd known to reach further.

I've been here all along, surrounded by the possibility of love, of being seen, of being valued—but I couldn't see it. And now? The pain of knowing what I could have had—it's almost too much to bear.

It's not just the five years with Brad—it's everything before him: the childhood dreams of who I wanted to be, crushed by men before him; the wrong lessons about what love was supposed to look like; all the hurt I let shape me. I see it now, the choices I made, the way I kept choosing men who used my weaknesses against me, who whittled away at my confidence.

I wipe at my cheeks, the sting of my tears lingering. God, if only we could go back and redo the things that fucked us up—armed with what we know now. But I guess that's the cruel joke of it all, isn't it? The scars teach us. But they also mark us, forever reminding us of what we've lost.

I clutch the pillow beneath me, resting my hot cheek against the cool pillowcase—desperate to ground myself. For a brief moment, the sensation calms me, like a balm against the cracked, raw surface of my emotions. But the truth doesn't stop—it sweeps through me, wild and unrelenting. I didn't just lose years—I lost myself. And now, I can't help but wonder: did I ever truly know who I was? When I'm with Ryan, someone else emerges—someone I don't recognize. She's unfamiliar, almost foreign. She feels happy. *God, how long has it been since I've felt that?*

The silence presses on me like a weight I can't bear. I fumble with my phone, the smooth glass screen trembling beneath my fingers as I open Spotify. I tap 'Today's Hits,' needing something—anything—to fill the suffocating emptiness around me.

Two songs play as tears streak my cheeks, my mind spinning in endless circles. "Favorite Song" by Toosii comes on next. I've heard it before, but this is the first time I really *hear* it. The lyrics hit me immediately, like they were written for me—for this moment, wrapping around me like a blanket. The song speaks of exhaustion— the hurt, the lies, the cheating— and the relentless thoughts of leaving.

The words seep into me, cutting deep. The chorus begins, and its message is unmistakable: you need someone who doesn't make you question yourself. Someone who doesn't leave you waiting or doubting. Someone who loves you without needing a reason—who can bring peace to your chaos. Someone… like Ryan.

I think about the way he held me earlier, his arms strong and steady, like they were built to shield me from the war inside me. The scent of his shirt lingers faintly in my mind, and I laugh-cry at the memory of him asking for it back. And the way he looked at me—not with pity, but with something deeper. Something safe. Something real.

Tears stream down my cheeks, falling not just for the years I wasted, or the damage Brad inflicted, but for the possibility of something better. For the chance to be with someone who doesn't just see the cracks but wants to help me mend them.

But what if I'm too broken for someone like Ryan? What if he sees my mess and decides I'm not worth it? I've spent so many years being used, being left, being told I'm not enough or that I'm really only good for one thing. What if I'm not enough for him, either?

I push that demon aside, reminding myself: Ryan's seen me at my worst—mean, spiraling, drunk.

He's still here.

He's still waiting.

The final chorus hits me like a challenge, daring me to believe—in me. Nobody but you can make you change the things you don't like about yourself. Change isn't easy, but it's possible. Maybe Ryan isn't here to save me; maybe he's here to remind me that I can save myself.

I loosen my grip on the pillow as the song fades. My tears slow, and I take a deep, shaky breath. For the first time ever, a flicker of hope stirs within me—small, fragile, but real.

Ryan doesn't make me feel weak. With him, I feel steady, strong—capable. And maybe, just maybe, I can believe in that.

Believe in him.

Believe in me.

I exhale slowly, breathing out the doubts, the pain, and the ghosts that have haunted me for too long.

And my next breath feels a little lighter.

* * * * *   * * * * *

"I really liked Jennifer. She was quick and smart, and I think her experience as a leader is crucial," I say as we walk through the hotel lobby, the faint smell of perfume lingering from the woman in front of us. We just interviewed four different people at the new work location in Austin, and with travel this morning—it's been a long day.

"I agree. She was really good. Definitely outshined everyone else today. What should we do for food tonight?"

"I'll eat wherever." I honestly don't care where we eat; my brain feels like it's been running a marathon all day, and I'm too drained to process anything extra. I've been constantly thinking about everything, especially Brad. I still haven't talked to him. And I know when I do, it needs to be in person, and we're both traveling for work this week, so... Plus, I'm avoiding it for obvious reasons.

"Should we just go to that food truck around the corner?" Ryan asks as we step into the elevator.

I press the button for my floor and his. Ryan was upgraded to a suite, so we're on different floors this week. He generously offered it to me, but I declined.

I lean against the wall, glancing at Ryan. He looks good, dressed in his best work clothes—a light blue button-up with navy blue dress pants and a suit jacket. His brown shoes and matching belt give him an extra polished look. I love how his top few buttons are always left undone, giving him a casual yet dressy vibe. Plus, his chest is just sexy.

I glance down at my own outfit. I kept it simple today, wanting to look professional but not distracting—a champagne satin button-up tucked into white dress pants.

Sudden exhaustion hits me, a mental overload from the long day. "What if we just stay in instead? You know, change into something comfortable, order room service, watch a movie?"

He hesitates, shifting from one foot to the other, his lips pressing together like he's thinking. "I don't know, Coop."

The doors open for my floor, and being the gentleman that Ryan is—and because we aren't done talking—he exits with me.

The carpet muffles our steps as we walk down the hallway. My room is the fourth door down, so we're there in mere seconds.

He continues. "Honestly, I don't trust myself in a room alone with you right now."

I turn to face him, leaning my back against the door of my room. I exhale. "I get it. I can respect that. I'm just tired, you know…" I trail off.

"Okay. We'll stay in. But we're hanging out in my room since it's bigger."

"Obviously," I say, a smile tugging at my lips.

"Can you just…" He pauses, rubbing the back of his neck as a smile tugs at his lips. "Can you put something really baggy on? Please?"

"I don't have any baggy pants. But I have a sweatshirt?" I offer, smiling.

"Is it that Chicago Bears one that slides off your shoulder?"

I bite my bottom lip, nodding.

"Jesus. Yeah, we can't have that."

I laugh. "Oh my God, Ryan, it's just a sweatshirt."

"Yeah, and that sweatshirt turns me on." He combs a hand through his hair, shaking his head like he's trying to push the thought away. "Fuck. Everything you wear turns me on."

I smack my lips together. *Damn. He's so cute.* "We can go to that food truck and eat in the lobby instead," I suggest. "But I promise, if we stay in, I'll be good."

"Alright. Go on in and get changed. I'll wait for you out here."

He's so great to me. This isn't a big thing, but it feels like it. "Thanks. I'll be quick."

I change quickly into a heather gray SKIMS jersey set. The tee is fitted and hits just above the waistband of the spandex pants, which hug my ass but flow loosely through the legs.

When I meet him back in the hall, his eyes sweep over me, an eyebrow raised.

"Don't give me that look," I say, pointing a finger at him.

"You can't be serious with that outfit."

"Of course, I'm serious. It was this, or leggings and the sweatshirt… you said not to wear the sweatshirt. It's not like I'm pulling from a closet here. I only brought a few things."

He puts a fist to his chest, squeezing his eyes shut like he's in agony. "You're killing me, Coop. This is torture. Actual torture."

"Oh, come on," I say, shoving him playfully on our way to the elevators. He trails behind, letting out a low, appreciative whistle, and I can't help but smile.

Two hours later, I'm laughing my ass off on the bed with Ryan. A spread of plates and room service dinnerware sits between us. I pick at my fries and pour myself another glass of wine. We rented *Borat*, and I haven't stopped laughing. I think Ryan's laughter is mostly at me, not being able to contain mine.

When the movie ends, I gather our boxes and clean up the bed, setting all the room service items into the hallway. We ordered two bottles of wine—white for me, and red for him.

"Do you want another glass?" I ask picking up the bottle as I pass by.

"Sure," he says, holding out his glass for me.

Tipsy, I give him an extra-large pour. "Oh my God. I can't believe I hadn't seen that movie. I haven't laughed that hard in so long."

"Well don't forget about the time we laughed our asses off in the pool with those edibles."

"Oh, yeah. How could I forget that memorable moment?" I plop down in the middle of the bed, crossing my legs to face him. "The night I went batshit crazy and somehow didn't scare you away forever?"

Ryan chuckles. "I like your batshit ways," he says, his voice softening as he looks at me with a longing that makes my insides warm.

"You like when I go batshit?" I raise a brow, eyeing him down.

"Yeah… I think it's cute when you get all feisty and worked up. It kind of turns me on." He laughs, as if he knows what he's saying is insane.

I tip my head back, laughing. "Oh, you've completely lost it. Isn't Leo a therapist?" I tease, nudging his leg with my foot. "You might want to unpack that—it sounds like a weird mommy issue."

"I don't have mommy issues." He moves faster than I expect, tackling me. In one quick motion, he pulls me down and rolls to his back, wrapping his arms around my waist as I land on his torso. Before I can react, his fingers dig into my sides, tickling me mercilessly.

"I have Cooper issues," he says as I kick my legs, screaming with laughter.

"Are you seriously tickling me? God… You're such a teenager!" I yell through the giggles. He wraps his legs around mine, forcing them to hold still as his hands continue their relentless attack.

I can't stop laughing, kicking and flailing like a kid. It's ridiculous, but I don't feel like I have to hold anything back. And that feels… good.

"If you don't stop, I'm going to shove my finger up your nose." I jab my index finger blindly upward, poking at his face as laughter bubbles out of me.

"Stop!" he shouts, laughing as he grabs my hand. I twist, kicking a leg free, but he moves faster, rolling me onto my back. Suddenly, we're face to face. His breath is warm on my cheek, and the firm grip of his hands on my wrists sends a jolt of electricity through me. His face hovers inches from mine, our lips so close we're sharing breath. My heart pounds, and butterflies flutter all the way to my chest, making my breath come out shaky and uneven.

We lock eyes, but his gaze shifts to my lips briefly before returning to mine. His expression shifts into something I can't quite place. He licks his lips and blinks hard.

"Coop, I need to tell you something… It's been eating me alive, and I can't keep it in anymore." His voice comes out low and rough, tinged with something that makes my pulse quicken.

I look at him, my stomach knotting. The energy in the room has shifted—it's heavy and unsettling. "What is it?"

He sighs, rolling onto his back. "While you were in Newport, before Christmas." He pauses, his jaw tightening as he laces his fingers into his hair and tugs hard. "Fuck, Coop... I went to this private club with Leo and Vivian and some of their friends, and... I saw Brad there. He was making out with some girl, hanging on her all night."

The words hit me like a blow to the chest, knocking the breath out of me. I sit up, turning to him. "What?" My thoughts spiral. "Before Christmas? He wasn't in Chicago... He was on a work trip." The air feels stifling, my mind racing as I rack my brain for where he was supposed to be. "New York. He said he had to be in New York."

Ryan sighs, his voice heavy. "He wasn't. Or if he was, he wasn't gone as long as he said he'd be."

"No." The denial escapes me in a whisper. "He said he flew from New..." My voice quits. My gaze drops to the sheets below me, my fingers clutching them tightly. "Are you sure it was him?" I ask, my voice barely audible.

He nods, sitting up. "He talked to me. Tried to convince me and Leo into thinking it was all good. A one-time thing." He swallows hard, his gaze dropping to his lap before meeting mine again, sorrow heavy in his eyes. "He said there was no need for you to find out... to get hurt. I'm sorry," he says, shaking his head. "I should have told you sooner."

My brows knit together as the tears threaten to spill. "Why didn't you?" My voice is soft, but there's an edge to it now. The hurt is sinking in, morphing into something familiar. "Why the hell would you sit on this for weeks?"

Ryan exhales, rubbing his palms over his face. "I didn't want to be the bearer of bad news. No one likes the fucking messenger, Coop." He drops his hands, his eyes pleading. "And I didn't want you to resent me for it."

I shake my head, my chest tight. "So, what? You thought I'd just be better off living a lie?" My voice wobbles, my emotions tangled between anger and heartbreak. "Jesus, Ryan. You saw him, you knew, and you just—let me go on like nothing happened?"

He sighs, tracing a finger across my hand, the touch gentle but weighted. "No. I wanted to give him the opportunity to do it. To man up, do the right thing." He looks at me, his eyes pleading for understanding. "I told him I'd give him a month to do it himself, and if he didn't, I was going to… I wasn't trying to protect him. I was trying to protect you."

I nod slowly, the words sinking in. *Protect me.* Maybe he really thought that. Maybe he didn't want to be the reason my world crumbled. But it doesn't change the fact that he knew. "By letting me continue to sleep with the cheating bastard?" I let out a shaky breath, staring at the sheets beneath me. "I need to go," I whisper.

Ryan reaches for my hand, his touch warm, but I pull away.

"Coop, don't. Stay here. You can sleep right here, next to me." His voice is soft, almost desperate.

I swallow hard, blinking back the burn in my eyes. "No, that's okay." I swing my legs over the edge of the bed. "I actually think I'd really like to be alone." I try to meet his gaze, but the storm of shock, confusion, and the fight to not cry makes it impossible.

Ryan's shoulders sag, but he nods, watching as I stand. "Alright… if you're sure."

I nod. "I'm sure." He walks me to the door and pulls me into a hug before letting me go.

I head down the long hall toward the elevators, moisture spilling onto my cheeks faster than I can wipe it away. *How could I have been so blind? Brad's cheating again? What a selfish asshole. And why am I even sad? I wanted* this—I wanted proof he was unfaithful so it would be easier to leave. But it still hurts. It hurts so bad. And more than anything, I'm just embarrassed. Embarrassed I didn't see it. *Fuck. Has he been cheating the whole time?* I mean, Jesus, this is who I picked? I chose him. I chose to move in with him, to go back to him. Hell, I even told him I'd marry him.

The worst part is, I really did love him. I'm ashamed of that. And now I wonder if he ever even loved me. God. Ryan probably thinks I'm so weak. How could he not?

I slow my steps, the memory of our playful exchange in the hotel room flashing through my mind. And then that last conversation…. I'm hurt he didn't tell me sooner. Maybe I could have avoided the past few weeks of agony with Brad. But no, it wouldn't have mattered. I've been wanting to leave for three years, yet here I am. The only thing that's given me the strength to believe I can leave is hope—for a future with Ryan.

I stop walking. *Ryan... Ryan.* What the hell am I waiting for? My relationship with Brad has been over for a long time. These text messages, his toying with me—it's all a fucking game to him. A sick, twisted game.

And I'm done playing.

Chapter 29

RYAN

I sink down on the edge of the bed after Cooper leaves, my head falling into my hands. Helpless. Completely fucking helpless. It sucks watching someone you care about suffer. And God, do I care about her. It's like I'm right back there with Beth again, sitting by her side, powerless to stop the cancer from taking her. Now, it's Cooper—different circumstances, same feeling. That aching, gnawing sense of uselessness that tears at me.

I probably should have walked her to her room, made sure she was okay. I wanted her to stay, to hold her, to make her feel better. But she couldn't get out of here fast enough.

Dammit. I screwed up. I should have told her about Brad weeks ago. That night has haunted me, replaying in my head every time I looked at her, knowing I was keeping something from her that she deserved to know. Who knows? It might have pushed her to leave weeks ago. And instead of sitting here worried, we'd still be laughing. Or maybe, we'd finally be doing what we've both been wanting to do for months now.

I let out a frustrated sigh, my knee bouncing with restless energy, the anxious rhythm mirroring the way my body feels. My thoughts are interrupted by an urgent knocking on the door. I glance around the room, thinking maybe Cooper forgot something, but there's nothing.

Confused, I open the door to find Cooper. Her eyes are red and misty. "Ryan," she chokes out, pushing her way in. Before I can say a word, she slams me against the wall, her lips crashing into mine. The door shuts behind her with a thud as she clings to me, her arms sliding up my chest and around my neck. I meet her kiss with equal intensity, gripping her waist and pulling her closer. The things this woman makes me feel.

She draws back just enough to yank her shirt over her head, and God, I've never wanted anything more than I want her, right now. Her lips meet mine over and over, desperate and unwavering. It feels like I'm a well filled with water after days in the desert. She's thirsty, parched—dehydrated—and I'm more than happy to quench her need. *Damn, she feels incredible.*

Her fingers tangle in my hair, pulling just enough to make my senses explode. The craving I have for her grows stronger, deeper. My hands roam her body, exploring every curve, every soft inch of skin. Excitement surges through me as I press her back against the wall.

My dick throbs with need, but my heart longs to explore what's between us. I want to give her something real. Something safe in this hell she's been living in. I'm completely lost in her—in the way she clings to me, in the chemistry that sizzles between us like a live wire.

But I can't get lost in her—not yet. No matter how sad she is or how desperately I want her, it's not right. My body screams at me to keep going, every part of me aching to feel her, to give her whatever she needs from me. I want to. God, I want to. To bury myself inside her. To feel every inch of her.

"Shit," I mutter, pulling back, forcing my hands to obey. My fingers grip her waist, holding her steady as I fight for composure. I press closer into her, my resolve wavering. *This is torture—pure fucking torture.* My grip tightens, my jaw clenched. My desire's evident, pressed against her where I know it feels good—for both of us.

"Ryan," she whispers, her voice a ragged breath. Her eyes meet mine, raw and intense. "I need you."

I squeeze my eyes shut, unable to look at the pain in hers. The last bit of strength I have pulls me back. "Coop," I murmur, my voice thick with restraint. "You know how bad I want you. But not like this. You've got to talk to him first, make it official. We have to wait… just a little longer."

"There's nothing to wait for," she says bitterly, shaking her head. "It's over… God, it's been over for so long."

"I know. But it's still wrong. You still live there…"

Her big brown eyes lock onto mine. "That's never stopped him."

True.

She steps closer. "If it's so wrong, why does it feel like the only thing in my life that's actually right? Why does this feel like the one thing that makes sense when everything else is falling apart?"

She's not wrong. It does feel right. It always has.

Her hands slide down my chest, wrapping around my waist, her touch scorching every vein. "Huh? Why has everything aligned so perfectly for us? Every bad moment, every mistake led to this—us, right here, right now." Her gaze intensifies, her grip tightening. "If this is so wrong, it's **the most perfect wrong** I've ever known."

My eyes meet hers. "I know." I swallow hard. "But two wrongs have never made a right." Gently, I release her grip on me and step back, lowering myself onto the bed. I take a deep, steadying breath, my chest tightening as my eyes drink her in. Jesus, she's something. And I'm half-shocked I'm denying myself the chance to have her.

She tips her head back against the wall, a single tear slipping down her cheek. Fuck. It feels like a kick to the balls seeing her like this—hurt, vulnerable. And now I've just added to her pain with rejection.

"Brad and I are done," she whispers, her voice trembling but sure. She looks at me with a determination in her eyes. "You want to know how done we are?"

She walks to where her purse is on the floor, pulling out her phone with shaky hands. "You want to know how much he doesn't care about me? Listen to this message he sent me last night."

She swipes her screen and starts reading, her voice wavering. *"Maybe this is just who you are, right, baby?"* She glances up at me before continuing. *"The whore who's been passed around by assholes and now can't even be a real partner because she's too busy running from her own shit. Look at yourself. Every time things get tough, you bail. You're too selfish and broken to handle a real relationship, and it's pathetic. You don't even have the decency to respond. You'll be sorry, soon enough."*

I suck in a breath. I cannot fathom calling any woman a whore, let alone threatening her. *I swear to God...*

"We're over, Ryan. He doesn't even deserve to know." She tosses me her phone. "Here. Read the latest one I woke up to this morning."

I hold the phone in my hand, not wanting to read it. "Go on," she urges me.

"Coop, I don't want to."

"Ryan." She meets my gaze, her eyes glassy. "Read it."

I take a deep breath, my stomach knotting as I glance down at the screen. *"Let's be real, Cooper—you're just used up and washed out at this point... Hell, I got bored of you, had to go looking somewhere else. That's what you're good for, right? I mean, you think Ryan wants you for anything other than your—"* I stop, my throat closing up, unable to say the rest out loud. Anger surges through me as I clench the phone in my hand.

Cooper walks over to me, grabbing the phone. Her voice shakes as she continues reading. *"For anything other than your big tits and tight little pussy? He's like every other guy—you're just a good fuck, maybe a halfway decent blow job, if that. Get it through your head, Coop: no one's ever gonna want you for more than that. If you're with him, don't even bother coming home. You're damaged goods at this point."* She tosses her phone to the ground.

I'll kill him.

"You see?" The hurt in her eyes is so deep, it cuts me just looking at her. "I never want to see him again. We're done. We're fucking done."

Her hand flies to her ring, tugging it off her finger with frantic determination. She chucks it across the room, the sharp sound of metal hitting the wall echoes through the room—evidence of its finality. "He doesn't deserve..."

I'm on my feet before she can finish, crossing the space between us in seconds. My mouth crashes into hers, cutting her off, completely submitting myself to her. Fuck Brad. Fuck his bullshit. He's going to tell her not to come home? Yeah, he's dead to me.

I kiss her with a new kind of urgency, a desire that's been building for ten goddamn months. Our mouths meet again and again as my hands explore her body. I slide my palms up her back, fumbling with her bra until the clasp gives way. The straps slip over her shoulders, and I toss it aside. Breaking our kiss, my gaze drops to her bare tits, and I soak in every detail, my heart racing as I take her in.

I glide my hand up, sweeping my thumb across her plush skin, her nipple hardening beneath my touch. I circle it lightly before rolling it between my fingers, pinching just enough to make her gasp as her nails dig into my shoulders. The sound sends a shudder of electricity through me.

I skim my lips across hers, building a heat between us that's sure to explode. Her hand cups the back of my neck, pulling me closer as she presses her lips firmly to mine. Our tongues tangle as I kiss her harder, deeper, with a desperation that fuels us both. She moans into my mouth, the sound whipping through me like wildfire.

Rocking my hips into her, my hard-on slides against the soft fabric of her pants, pressing right against her pussy. "God," she murmurs, frantically lifting the hem of my shirt, yanking it upward. We break away for mere seconds to tear it off, and I pull her closer, her warm skin pressing into mine.

I trail kisses along her jaw, down to her neck, where I scrape my teeth lightly against her skin. I lick past her collarbone and suck hard, marking her with the force of my mouth. A breathy moan escapes her lips as she arches into me, an invitation I can't resist. Her nails drag down my back, sending shivers all the way down my spine to the tip of my dick, triggering everything primal inside me.

I slide my hand between her legs, skimming over her, teasing where I know she's desperate for pressure. I caress her with feather-light strokes, back and forth, just like that night in the elevator. She arches again, but I keep the pressure barely there, watching her come undone. "Damn you, Ryan," she pants, her voice filled with frustration. Her hand moves down, finding my cock through my joggers, and she does the same damn thing to me. Barely grazing her fingers along my length—teasing, taunting—driving me insane.

I lift my hand away, chuckling wickedly against her neck. "You're so evil," I tease, kissing my way down to her tits. I suck a nipple into my mouth, swirling my tongue over it as my hand slips into her pants. My fingers slide over her clit and dip into her warmth. Her gasp rings in my ear, spurring me on.

Fuck, she's dripping.

The way she feels makes my head spin, and somehow my dick gets harder. She arches into me again, her movements anxious, mirroring my own impatience. My hands move to her waist as I pivot, backing her toward the bed. I lower her onto it, hovering over her. For a moment, I pause, tucking her hair behind her ear. I need to slow down, to take this in, to make it last. *God, she's so damn beautiful.*

Leaning back, I tug at her pants and underwear. She lifts her hips, letting me slide them down her legs, and I toss them aside. My eyes rake over her naked body, soaking her in.

"Damn, babe," I murmur, my voice rough with awe. I remember how incredible she looked in Newport, but my memory didn't do her justice. Jesus Christ, I couldn't have prepared myself for this. My cock aches for her, every bit of me strung tight with yearning.

My fingertips trace the edges of her thighs, teasing the smooth skin beneath them. Her eyes stay locked on mine, unflinching and intent, and it sends a rush through me. I slide my fingers up her torso, pleasure sparking with each inch of skin I touch. My hands reach her face, and my thumb brushes her cheek. Lowering my lips to her jaw, I let my breath fan over her skin. "Do you have any idea what you do to me?" I murmur, my voice low and gravelly. I kiss her jawline. "You're so damn beautiful."

Gently, I trail kisses down her body—her neck, her shoulder, making my way down. Her gaze never falters, even as her chest rises and falls with uneven breaths. She arches into me slightly, soft gasps and moans spilling from her lips, her hands gliding over my arms and chest.

I kiss my way through the center of her tits, her grip tightening around my biceps. "Oh, God," she murmurs, her voice shaky and raw. I glance up; her eyes are closed, her head tipped back. I press soft kisses down her torso, savoring every part of her. My lips travel lower, making my way to where I know she wants me.

Gripping her thighs, I spread her legs, opening her up for me. She arches into my touch, and I slide my tongue up the center of her. She presses against me, her fingers weaving into my hair and tugging hard enough to make me groan. "Fuck," she gasps, the sound shooting straight to my dick.

Everything about her drives me wild—the softness, the warmth, the soaking wetness of her. Even the faint, intoxicating scent of her. I flick my tongue against her clit, and she jolts beneath me. "Jesus, Ryan," she breathes, her voice raspy and strained.

I work her with rapid strokes, my tongue circling and teasing as I plunge a finger deep inside her. Her cries echo in my ears like the sweetest fucking music. I pause, drawing it out, loving the way she curses under her breath, filthy words tumbling from her lips. She has such a dirty mouth, and everything she says only turns me on more.

I suck on her swollen clit, releasing it with a wet pop, then dip my finger deeper, curving it upward to hit just the right spot. I lick her again, tasting her, my movements faster, more precise, until she's gasping for air. She's so close I can feel it.

Her pussy clenches around my finger, tight and strong, and Jesus, it's almost too much. She cries out, arching upward, her voice breaking on a breathless "Fuck!"

The satisfaction of feeling her come against my tongue is pure, unfiltered bliss. She tugs on my hair. "Ryan," she whispers, her voice barely audible, coated with exhaustion and desire. "Come up here. I want you... I want you inside me."

God, I want to be inside her too. But the pull to stay down here, tasting her, is strong. I could live down here. "Ryan," she pleads.

I reluctantly press soft kisses to her thighs before making my way back up. Not before touching, kissing, and licking every inch of her incredibly sexy body.

She meets me halfway, her hands frantically tugging at my pants. I help her, quickly freeing myself from the confinement.

Her hands roam over my chest and wrap around my neck, pulling me down in a commanding hurry. She sucks my bottom lip into her mouth, and God, her lips are irresistible. I could kiss her forever—I can't get enough.

She gets a wild look in her eyes, blazing with raw hunger, and something shifts. She pushes me to the side, rolling on top of me—her mouth, possessive over mine. I can't help but grin beneath her lips as she takes control. She's always known exactly how to take what she wants—even at work—and damn, I'm happy to give it to her. Everything about this feels so fucking good.

Her fingers wrap around my length, and a groan tears through me. It's like she knows every inch of me, every spot that drives me crazy. She's toying with me, teasing, and every stroke makes it harder to hold back. My body's begging for more, but I want to make this last—I've waited too damn long for this.

She hovers over me, brushing against me in the slowest, most tormenting way. I try to pull her down, but she restrains, her lips tugging into a sexy smirk that sends me reeling. She loves torturing me—always has.

She leans down, whispering in my ear, "Hold still, Ryan. Don't you dare move until I say you can." Her lips float over mine, just close enough for me to feel her breath but too far to taste her. She grinds against me, slow and deliberate. "You feel that? You're so hard… that's because of me."

I chuckle, low and deep. What a teasing little devil, using my own words against me. She lowers herself just enough to give me a taste of her warmth, and holy shit, it's maddening. I push upward instinctively, desperate for more, but she lifts away, shaking her head. "You want permission to enter, don't you? You want me, huh?" she murmurs, flicking her tongue against my ear. A soft moan escapes her as her hands wander down, leaving a trail of fire in their wake. "You're ready to come, aren't you?" she adds, her tone dripping with seduction.

I groan, a deep, guttural sound that's part frustration and part pure need. My chuckle rumbles through the air as I nod, my hand sliding around to cradle the base of her neck. "Feels so fucking good," I mutter. My gaze locks with hers, and I can't help but add, "You feel so good."

Her lips curl into a playful smile, one brow cocking in challenge. "Good," she whispers, leaning forward. She shifts slightly, and my breath hitches as she rubs her clit up and down my length. "How would you like it if I stopped? Huh?" Her tone is teasing, daring. "If I left you here, ready to fuck me?"

She rolls her hips in the smallest, most agonizing circles, the friction sending shocks through every nerve in my body. Her voice drops to a husky whisper, her breath hot against my neck. "Don't you dare come until I say so."

I grin as she grips my wrists, pinning them to the bed, even though we both know I could break free. God, she's incredible. Everything about her has me mesmerized—the confidence, the playfulness, the way she takes charge. She leans in, her lips brushing mine softly, her teeth grazing my bottom lip before pulling it lightly before releasing it. "Good boys wait their turn."

Jesus. This is so hot. I clench my fists, every muscle in my body tightening as I fight the urge to take over. I can't take this much longer. The throbbing in my dick pulses through me like an electric current. Every soft moan, every flit of her tongue, every roll of her hips sends me closer to the edge. She's toying with me like I'm hers to command.

And maybe I am.

And I'm more than okay with it.

I groan as her fingers trail down my chest, slow and deliberate, her nails dragging just enough to send sparks of heat shooting through me. She stops at my hips, her nails pressing slightly into my skin as she adjusts her position. She leans back, her eyes locked on mine with a mischievous grin.

"Beg me," she whispers in a sultry voice, eyes searching mine. "Beg me to let you have me, Ryan."

My jaw tightens, every muscle in my body trembling with restraint. I force out a chuckle. "I don't beg." But my God, my resolve is slipping—fast. If she keeps this up, I'll be begging in no time.

"Oh, you will," she murmurs as she slides lower, her mouth finding its way to my hips. Her tongue presses against my hip bone, her teeth grazing the sensitive skin, sending a jolt through me that nearly unravels me. I swear to God, I'm seconds away from losing it—from showing her exactly who's in charge.

She tastes her way back up my body—my abs, my chest, my neck—leaving a trail of sizzling heat in her wake until her lips brush mine. Her voice is a whisper, her breath warm against my skin. "Ask for it, Ryan. I want to hear you say it."

I snap. I need her—now.

"Fuck this," I growl, gripping her hips and flipping her beneath me in one swift move. Her gasp turns into a laugh, and I lean in, chuckling low into her ear. "Looks like I don't need to beg after all." My lips claim hers, hungry and commanding. She threads her fingers into my hair, pulling me closer as our tongues play.

Her hips shift beneath me, provoking, and my control is fraying at the edges. I pull back just enough to look at her, my breath uneven. "You win," I mutter, my voice rough with need. "I'll beg, Coop. I'll do whatever the fuck you want. Just tell me you want this as bad as I do."

Her eyes widen slightly before softening with something deeper, more vulnerable. "I want you, Ryan," she whispers. "I've always wanted you."

"Good," I murmur, brushing my lips against hers, the contact sending a shiver through me. "Because I want you so fucking badly I can't think straight." My knees press against her thighs, spreading her wider as I trail my lips down her neck. I pause, my voice dropping to a low whisper. "I'm begging you to let me show you how much."

She grins. "Oh my God," she breathes, her voice soft but demanding. "Fuck me. What are you waiting for? Fuck me already." Her hand wraps around my length, guiding me, swirling the tip at her entrance.

The head of my cock dips inside, and I suck in a breath. "Jesus." I push into her, and holy hell, she's everything. Tight, warm—better than I remember. She gasps, her nails scratching into my back, pulling me closer as I fill her entirely. I pull back and thrust again, finding a rhythm, rocking my hips into hers. Her legs wrap around me, shifting me even deeper, until there's no space between us.

I fuck her, the tension between us unraveling with every thrust. The room fills with the sound of our ragged breaths, the slick rhythm of our bodies. She cries out my name, and that's all it takes. She tightens around me as she comes, her head falling back, and I follow, my hips faltering as a wave of euphoria crashes over me. "Fuck," I groan, my body taut as I spill into her, every nerve sizzling until I'm seeing stars.

I tremble over her as the rush subsides, pressing a deep kiss to her lips before collapsing onto my back. My body quakes as the aftershocks roll through me, and I chuckle softly. "Holy shit, babe."

She grins with satisfaction. I pull her into my arms, holding her close, needing her to feel wanted, appreciated and seen. Not just for her body—but for who she is. "That was…" I pause, catching my breath. "God, that was fun."

She laughs softly. "That was really fun." She kisses me. "I'm going to go clean up. I'll be right back."

I watch her walk away. Damn. I don't think I've ever felt this satisfied in my life. That was incredible. I didn't think it was possible to want her more, but fuck, I'm already thinking about round two.

When she returns, she slides back into bed, her skin warm as her legs tangle with mine. She glances up at me, her lips curving into a teasing smile. "I never wanted to admit this… but you're really good at sex."

I chuckle, pulling her closer. "Well, it's not exactly hard to be good at sex when it's with you." I press my lips to hers, savoring the way she melts into me. I could kiss her forever and never get sick of it.

"Yeah, right," she says, rolling her eyes playfully. "I bet all the ladies you've been with still think about it to this day."

I laugh, shaking my head. "Their sex lives would have to be really sad if that were the case." I pause, meeting her gaze. "Besides you, I haven't been with anyone but Beth in twelve years."

"I'd still be thinking about this in twelve years," she says softly. "Just like I've thought about Newport for the past ten months." Her fingers trace a lazy path up and down my chest and abs. "I've thought of that more times than I can count."

"I've thought about it a lot too… an embarrassing amount of times." My fingertips brush along her shoulders. "I was so frustrated when I found out you were engaged—not just because I thought you cheated—but because it meant you were unavailable."

Her lips twitch into a faint, bitter smile. "Oh, trust me. If anyone was disappointed that I was engaged… it was me."

Her honesty hits me hard, bringing me a mixture of happiness and sadness. Everyone wants to be told they're good in the sack, but hearing her admit she's thought about me as much as I've thought about her… damn, that feels good. But just as strongly, I hate that she wasted years with Brad. He's chipped away at her confidence, at her worth, with every selfish thing he's done. God, my heart breaks for her.

I tighten my grip around her, pulling her closer, as if holding her tighter could protect her from the pain, from the weight of everything waiting for her back home. From him. She deserves so much more. She deserves…

Damn.

She deserves everything.

Chapter 30

COOPER

I lie next to Ryan, the heat of his skin pressed against my cheek, his steady heartbeat beneath my hand as I graze his muscular chest. His fingers brush across my skin in long, smooth strokes, leaving a trail of goosebumps in their path.

"What are you thinking?" I ask, my gaze drifting over the rippling lines of his abs and the sheet barely covering his cock that's still half-erect.

Ryan chuckles, the sound low and vibrating through his chest. "You don't want to know."

I tilt my head to look at him. "Now I definitely want to know. Spill."

He hesitates, then shrugs. "Fine. Honestly? I was wondering how long I need to wait before I can taste your pussy again." A wicked grin spreads across his face, his eyes locking with mine. "You taste so fucking good."

Heat rushes through me as he leans in, his lips brushing against mine. The warmth of his kiss spreads through me, like taking a sip of something hot on a cold winter day.

My stomach flips, and I'm already turned on. Round two comes fast and urgent—like we're ravenous, starved for each other, and there's nothing else in the world that could satisfy us.

His hand moves between my thighs, and God, it's like the first time all over again, except I'm already warmed up—sensitive, aching for more. Every stroke and dip of his fingers sends electricity coursing through me, tightening deep in my stomach. My orgasm coils, ready to spring. It builds hotter, deeper, until it erupts like molten lava, pleasure radiating through my core and spreading, melting everything in its path.

I ride the high, barely coming down before Ryan settles between my legs, his cock already pushing inside me. I open wider, welcoming him in, and he thrusts deep, hitting my G-spot. My second orgasm crashes into me, quick but so damn powerful it steals my breath. "Oh my… God," I moan, my body trembling as the waves ripple through me.

I roll him over, desperate for more, craving a new angle. My hips rock against him as I lean down, capturing his lips. God, his lips are divine. Everything about him is divine—I have yet to find a flaw. His body, his touch, the way his hands roam over me like he can't get enough. But it's not just his body—he's kind, funny, smart, and maddeningly perfect in every way.

Dammit. He's perfect.

He groans, his voice raw and desperate. "Jesus, you feel so fucking good. I love your tight little pussy."

Oh yeah, and he's a freak in the sheets—and ridiculously good in bed. Perfect.

Ryan grips my hips, his hands strong and commanding, quickening the pace. His movements grow urgent, his hips rising to meet mine in perfect rhythm. He pulls me close, his breath hot against my ear, a throaty groan escaping with each ragged breath as I kiss along his jaw.

I whisper into his ear, my voice low and teasing. "Your big cock feels so good, Ryan. Fuck me harder."

"Good God," he moans, his pace becoming relentless, his breath heavy and uneven, like he's racing to the finish.

I'm so close I can feel it building, so I shift slightly, sliding my hand between my legs to rub my clit. His grip tightens, and with one last powerful thrust, he releases, his body trembling beneath me as I follow, my orgasm pulsing through me, squeezing around his cock.

I collapse onto him, too tired and satisfied to even lift myself so he can pull out. I just melt into him.

Ryan's arms wrap around me, holding me tight, our sweaty bodies sticking together. He lets out a deep sound from his chest—a mix between a grunt and a laugh. "I love doing that with you."

I grin, lifting my face to meet his, brushing a sweet kiss against his lips. "I love it too." He kisses me again, slow and deliberate, and I eventually roll off him, my limbs heavy with exhaustion.

I head to the bathroom to clean up, and when I come back, Ryan takes his turn washing up. I settle back into the bed, sinking into the comfort of the sheets. When he returns, he slides in beside me, pulling me close. Snuggling into him feels incredible—like we're intimate in every way, not just physically. Everything about tonight has been incredible.

"*Now* what are you thinking?" I ask, a smile tugging at my lips as I look up at him.

"Hmm." Ryan's fingers trace lazy, soothing patterns on my back. "I'm thinking I want to know everything about you."

"You do?"

"Yeah."

"Well, what do you want to know?"

"I don't know… What's your favorite childhood memory? What's the best thing that ever happened to you? What's something you want more than anything?"

I rest my hand on his chest, feeling the steady rise and fall beneath my touch. "My favorite childhood memory? Hmm, that's tough—there are so many good ones. But… it'd probably have to be the last family vacation we took. You know, before my parents got divorced."

I scoot a little closer, wrapping my leg over his. "We went to Hawaii for the first time when I was nine. We stayed in this beach house, right by the ocean. Literally, you'd step out, and you were on the sand—just like at my dad's place now. There were turtles on the beach every morning. I thought it was the coolest thing in the entire world. We'd wake up early and walk the beach together, all of us."

The memory's bittersweet. I can't help but smile, even though a pang of sadness hits me simultaneously. "It was the last time I really remember us all together… happy, you know?"

Ryan grunts softly. "That's really cool. Did your parents fight a lot?"

"Not a lot… at least not that I heard. But when they did, it was nasty— a full blowout—usually my mom screaming at the top of her lungs. She'd find out about another conquest and freak the fuck out at him. But most of the time, she just pretended everything was fine." I scoff, shaking my head. "She'd even talk about him like he was the best damn husband in the world. That annoyed the shit out of me. I loved my dad—he was a good father—but he was a terrible husband."

I pause as my words settle over me. "Wow. I've been doing the same thing, haven't I?"

"It's understandable," Ryan says softly. "For one, you saw your mom do it… But now, you probably understand why she did it, right?"

I sigh, the realization hitting hard. "Yeah, I guess. She was embarrassed. She knew she should leave and just stayed." I scoff again, a bitter laugh escaping. "God, I'm just like her. But she had kids—that's at least an understandable reason to try to make it work. What was mine?"

"Didn't you say that Brad threatened you?"

"Yeah," I whisper. "Yeah, I guess he did… a few times, actually." I don't expand, and Ryan takes the hint, his silence a comfort rather than pressure.

"What matters is that you're done now, babe." He kisses the top of my head, and I tighten my grip on him.

I tilt my chin up to him, smiling softly. "I like when you call me babe."

"You do? It's not too early?"

I shake my head. "No. Not too early." I lean in, sweeping my lips against his, the kiss soft but full of meaning.

"I could kiss you all day, you know that?" he murmurs, kissing me again before pulling back slightly. "Now, what about the other two questions?"

I push up onto my elbow, meeting his gaze. "Ah. Well, those two are easy." My eyes lock with his, my voice soft but steady. "They both have the same answer."

Ryan's brows lift slightly, curiosity sparking in his expression. "Oh yeah?"

I nod, a slight blush creeping up my cheeks. "You. You're the best damn thing that's ever happened to me. And right now? What I want more than anything is for this to work out—you and me."

He grins, pulling me in for yet another kiss. "You're the best, you know that?" He rolls me onto my back, his upper body hovering over mine as he tugs my bottom lip between his teeth. My hands glide around his bulging biceps, savoring the feel of him as the kiss deepens. "Your turn," he murmurs against my lips, pulling back just enough to speak.

"My turn for what?"

"Ask me a question."

I pause, thinking for a second. "Okay… What's something interesting not very many people know about you?" A mischievous grin spreads across my face. "Aside from the fact that you carry an oversized weapon in your pants every day."

His laugh bursts out of him, loud and unrestrained. "Jesus. Are you serious with that?"

"Oh, I'm dead serious." I smirk. "Come on, Ryan. You know you have a huge dick. There's no way you saw other guys in high school and thought, '*Hmm. Yep, mine's average.*' God, I bet your friends were jealous as hell."

His head drops next to mine as he dissolves into laughter, shaking his head over me. "Oh my God. You're unbelievable."

"They probably gave you shit for it, didn't they? I bet you even had a nickname."

He presses his lips together, trying and failing to stifle his laughter. "Jesus, Coop." He chuckles again, rolling onto his back, his hands running through his hair as he shakes his head. "No way."

"Oh my God, you did! What was it?" I prop myself up on my elbows, needing to see his face while he tries to wiggle his way out of this. I nudge him, grinning. "Come on, what was it?"

His smile stretches wide, reaching his eyes as he looks at me. He puffs out another laugh, clearly mortified—and it's the sexiest damn thing I've ever seen.

"Fine." He sighs dramatically. "They called me BDR—Big Dick Ryan."

This time, I lose it, laughing so hard I clutch my stomach. "Oh my God," I manage between breaths. "BDR? Are you serious?"

His face is red, but he's laughing too, shaking his head in defeat. "You're never going to let me live this down, are you?"

"Not a chance," I say, still grinning. "BDR—this is officially the best conversation I've ever had." My cheeks ache from laughing. "Oh my hell. I knew it."

"How did you know?"

"Look, I've been with my fair share of men. And believe me when I say, your dick is setting records for a white guy."

He laughs, shaking his head. "Should I be proud of that?"

"Hell yeah, you should. It's an accomplishment." I lean back a little. "Might even deserve a trophy."

The laughter lingers between us, the kind that comes with ease. When it finally settles, I shift, my smile softening. "Alright, but seriously, what's something not very many people know?"

He studies my face, his expression turning serious. "That I'm crazy about you."

His voice is deep and husky, each word reverberating through the air like the low strum of a guitar in a quiet room. It vibrates through me, seeping into my core with a warmth that dissolves any lingering fears I had about him.

My hand cups the side of his face, my thumb brushing his jaw. "Who else knows?"

"Just Leo… maybe Vivian… and now you." A quiet laugh slips out as he grins, his eyes locked onto mine. "I'm so fucking crazy about you, babe."

I smile against his lips as they slowly meet, and we lose ourselves in each other—kissing, touching, talking—until the hours stretch into the early morning. Sleep doesn't come for hours, but neither of us cares.

This night, this moment—it's one of the best of my entire life.

Chapter 31

COOPER

Ryan pulls up to my building. "You sure you don't want me to come up with you?"

I shake my head. "I'm sure. I'm just grabbing a few things to throw in my car. I won't be long. I'll meet you back at your place… you said there's guest parking, right?"

"Yeah, but it's not cheap."

"That's okay. It's just for a few days." I lean across the console, pressing a quick kiss over his lips. "See you soon."

"Bye, babe."

I glance over my shoulder as I open the door, unable to hide the giddy smile spreading across my face. "Bye." I blow him a kiss before shutting the door behind me.

Taking a deep breath, I steady myself and head inside, crossing the lobby to the elevators.

Our work trip was short—just two days. But wow, how much can change in such a short time. I smile to myself as I step into the elevator, thoughts of Ryan and last night replaying in my mind. We interviewed more candidates this morning and caught an early evening flight. It's almost nine now. My plan is simple: grab a few more clothes and essentials, load them into my car, and head back to Ryan's until I can talk to Brad.

I finally texted him this morning, telling him I'd be back tonight and would come over Friday—after he got back—to talk. I also asked him to stop texting me until then. He was strangely cordial, replying with nothing more than a simple acknowledgment. No snide remarks. No guilt trips. Just, "Okay."

I open the door to the apartment, and the unease hits me immediately. This is home but… am I even going to miss it?

The thought evaporates the moment I see Brad sitting on the couch, beer in hand. My heart stops dead in my chest. Shit. I am not prepared for this. Panic rises, but I take a deep breath, forcing myself to stay strong.

"Look who finally decided to show up," Brad says, his voice cold. His eyes narrow, gaze piercing as he leans forward, jaw tight.

I force a small smile. "Hey," I say, keeping my voice as neutral as possible. "I thought you were out of town until Friday." God, this is so uncomfortable. I don't want to do this—not right now.

"I was." He tilts his head. "Changed my flight after your text this morning." His stare drills into me, and I can't tell if it's hurt, anger, or frustration—or maybe a mix of all three. "It was nice to finally hear from you. To know you were alive."

My gaze drops to the floor for a moment as I gather my courage. "Yeah, I uh… I'm sorry." I take a deep breath, making eye-contact. "I probably should've let you know I was okay. But you gave me no reason to respond."

"Baby, it's not like I didn't have a reason to be upset." He pauses, his jaw twisting like it always does when he's calculating his next move. I know this look too well—it's the one he wears before flipping the script. "So," he starts, voice deceptively calm. "How was the work trip? Or should I ask, how was Ryan?"

He smirks. I can see the game he's about to play, the one where he doles out just enough to wound me without going for the kill—yet. It's all about the timing with Brad. He's a master at this, dragging it out, making me pay. He knows exactly which cards to play and when to hold back. He always has—he's a lawyer, after all. He makes his living by getting what he wants.

I ignore the question, moving to the chair that sits adjacent to him on the sofa. My nerves are shot, palms damp, hands trembling. I force myself to sit, trying to project calm, even though I feel anything but. "We need to talk, Brad," I say, my voice as steady and confident as I can manage.

He scoffs loudly. "Yeah, no shit."

I close my eyes briefly, taking a deep, calming breath. "Brad, please, I don't want to fight. I just want to—"

He cuts me off, standing abruptly. His movements are sharp and deliberate as he begins to pace the room.

"Oh, now you wanna talk? Where were you four fucking days ago, Cooper? Out with Ryan?" His voice rises, dripping with venom. "Went and got yourself a boyfriend while I've been worried sick about you?"

He paces the living room floor, running a hand through his hair with exasperation. "Well, news flash, baby. You're already taken. You have a fiancé, remember? Or do I not matter at all? You don't even have the decency to let me know where you are for days while you're off fucking Ryan."

I'm too scared to speak, my pulse racing as my breaths grow shorter and sharper. Dammit. I don't want to be wimpy Cooper—apologizing, retreating into my shell, too afraid of what he might say or do if I stand my ground. But I can't lose my temper, either—can't let this devolve into screaming matches that end with our clothes on the floor and us calling it something it's not. Like it's some sick, twisted version of love-making.

It's fucked up.

It's wrong.

After being with Ryan all weekend, especially last night, it's never been clearer. This—whatever this is—that Brad and I have? It's not love.

It never has been.

Not even close.

I picture Ryan, the plan we came up with, his words echoing in my mind: *Don't let his words poison you. Hold your ground, Coop.* I stand, refusing to let Brad cower over me.

"Brad, I understand that you're upset. You have every right to be upset that I didn't respond, and I'm—" I stop myself. No. I will not apologize. Not for this. Not for anything. "I should have let you know I was okay," I say, my gaze fixed on his. "But that does not excuse the things you said to me."

Fuck. I can feel the burn behind my eyes.

Don't cry. Don't let him have this power.

"This hasn't been working for a long time," I add, my voice steady, even as his gaze shifts past me, refusing to meet mine. There was a time when I would have walked over to him, put my arms around him, tried to kiss and fuck the problem away, like that would solve anything.

But not anymore. I cross my arms, my stance firm, every inch of my body screaming *stay the fuck back*.

"Brad..." I try again, but he still won't look at me. Fine. Whatever. I shake my head, frustration bubbling over. "Okay, I don't know an easy way to say this, so I'm just going to say it. I'm not happy. I haven't been for a long time."

Reaching into my pocket, I pull out the engagement ring and set it on the coffee table. "I'm done trying to make this work."

He doesn't say anything. In fact, he looks so calm it scares the shit out of me. Still, I go on, assuming he's hearing me, waiting for me to finish so he can retaliate with whatever plan is brewing behind that cold stare.

"I'm going to grab a few things tonight, and then I'll come get the rest of my stuff this weekend, okay?" My voice is still steady by some miracle, but it takes every ounce of effort to keep it that way.

I exhale in frustration and turn to leave for the bedroom, but his voice cuts through the air, stopping me dead in my tracks.

"So that's it then? You're just going to throw away everything we've built for... for what? For *him*?"

His chuckle is low, menacing—fucking chilling. "God, you're so easy—predictable, too." He starts walking toward me, slow and deliberate.

"Let me guess," he continues. "He says all the right things, tells you that you're not only beautiful, but that you're smart and funny too."

I flinch, and he notices. Of course, he notices. He feeds off reactions like this. And now he knows he's on the right track.

"You think Ryan wants you?" He laughs, bitter and cruel. "He'll drop you as soon as he realizes what a mess you are."

"Stop, Brad." My voice shakes, but I force myself to hold steady. I meet his gaze, and for the first time, I realize something: I fucking hate him.

Not just right now, in this moment—but deeply, truly, in a way that's been building for years. I've spent so long trying to talk myself into loving him, clinging to the idea of us, that I never saw it for what it really was.

He takes another step toward me, and I instinctively back up. "Or maybe he'll realize that you're just an average fuck, and he'll tire of you like I did." He shrugs, his tone dismissive, like what he's saying is no big deal—like I'm no big deal.

That one hits. I can practically hear Ryan's voice in my mind, calling me incredible, telling me I'm everything. But Brad's words claw their way in, dragging me back to all the times he made me feel small, unworthy. My chest tightens, and I squeeze my eyes shut, desperately trying to hold on to the memory of last night—Ryan's gaze. The way he said he was crazy about me. That was real… wasn't it?

I open my eyes, meeting Brad's icy stare, and force the words out. "Fuck you, Brad." I turn and move toward the door, the overwhelming urge to escape drowning out everything else. I don't even care about grabbing my things anymore. I can deal with that later. Right now, I have to get out before his words bury themselves too deep.

Just as I reach the door, Brad's calm, steady voice stops me dead in my tracks.

"I wouldn't do that if I were you… Not if you care about Ryan."

I freeze, my hand hovering over the doorknob.

"And both your jobs."

Goddammit. I turn, frustration boiling over as he once again finds a way to get under my skin. "What are you talking about?"

He holds out a stack of papers, a winning gleam in his eyes. He makes no move to hand them to me, his smugness dripping like poison. I exhale sharply, my patience thin, and step closer. When I reach for the papers, he pulls them back, just out of reach. A smile tugs at his lips and it sickens me.

"You know, Ryan seems like such a stand-up guy. Honest, even. I wonder what people at work would think about him if they knew about your little affair."

It's like the air's been punched from my lungs. Threatening me is one thing. But Ryan? It's a line I never imagined Brad would cross. Panic and fury swell in my chest as my hand balls into a fist at my side. I'll do whatever it takes to keep Ryan out of this.

Anything.

Brad lowers the papers, and the second they're within reach, I snatch them from his hand. My stomach coils as my eyes skim the page. My breath catches in my throat, and I instinctively bring a hand to my mouth.

It's mine and Ryan's text thread from Christmas morning—the one where he asked me to touch myself, and I did. The one where I came to his words while Brad was inside, asleep—or worse, reading this thread as it happened.

I stare at the page, the words blurring together as humiliation and rage wash over me like a tidal wave. This wasn't just manipulation. This was invasive. Predatory. He'd taken something private—something vulnerable and, in its own twisted way, beautiful—and turned it into a weapon.

My knees weaken, and I clutch the edge of the counter to keep myself upright as bile rises in my throat.

"Christmas morning, huh? While I was sleeping in the next room? That's when you decided to finger yourself for him like some desperate porn star? Jesus, Cooper. That's pretty low... even for you."

Tears threaten, but it's too late—they slide down my cheeks as shame hits me. I want to scream at him, throw the papers in his face, tell him he's a monster. But his words slice too deep, and the threat of what he might do freezes me in place.

Brad smirks, leaning casually against the counter. "Do you think he'll still want you once everyone knows what a slut you are? Or should I just send them out now and save you the trouble of pretending to be respectable?" He grins. *God, he's enjoying this. He actually enjoys this.* "What do you think his boss will say when he sees these texts?" He straightens, closing the distance between us, and I instinctively step back, my legs brushing against the wall. "I mean, I'm sure your company has a strict policy about this sort of thing, right? Probably won't sit well that the VP's screwing the new project manager. And on company time, too? Traveling together? It practically writes itself."

He chuckles again. "Yeah, real fairy-tale ending from here."

There's that knife again, tearing through every ounce of strength I have left. He's always known how to find the weakness in my armor and twist the blade.

God, I can't breathe.

My chest tightens, and my heart is pounding so fast I feel like it's going to explode. Am I having an anxiety attack? The room tilts, the walls closing in, and my legs threaten to give out. *Fuck. I can't do this.* He's going to trap me, again. My hope—everything I dreamed of with Ryan— slips further out of reach with every word.

A sob escapes me, raw and uncontrollable. I clutch my stomach, the pain radiating through me like an open wound, my hands trembling as I gasp for air.

Brad tilts his head, his expression softening into something almost kind. Almost.

"Hey, hey," he soothes, his voice suddenly quiet and concerned, the cruel edge vanishing like it was never there. He takes a step closer, lowering his voice. "Baby, don't cry. You don't have to go through this. Look, I get it. You're confused. Things got messy, but it's not too late. We can fix this. You don't need him, Cooper. You've never needed him. You have me."

His hand reaches out, brushing my arm, and I flinch, but he doesn't stop. "Come on, baby. Let me help you." He takes the papers from me, his voice softening further. "If you stay, I'll rip them up. No one ever has to know. I'll keep your little secret safe."

I blink, struggling to process his words through the fog of my panic. His tone is gentle, but his words are dangerous, threading themselves through my thoughts, twisting them until I almost believe him. God, he's good—too good. But this time, things are different. I have Ryan. And he's waiting for me.

I take a slow, steadying breath, pulling myself together.

"You don't want to ruin Ryan's career, do you?" Brad presses, his eyes narrowing just enough to remind me of the power he thinks he holds. His hands grip my waist, and I cringe as he leans closer, his lips moving toward mine.

Think, Cooper. Think.

And then it dawns on me.

Brad wants to threaten mine and Ryan's careers? He wants to play this little game of chess where I've always been the pawn? Well, guess what? Ryan was on the chess club, and his best friend? He's the goddamn king.

I push Brad back, my voice low and calm. "You want to play chess, Brad? Fine. Go ahead and send those texts. I don't care." I cross my arms, standing taller. "But just remember who Ryan's best friend is. Or did you forget? Leo Weston. You saw him last month at that private club—you know, the one where *you* were cheating on me."

His jaw tightens. "What are you getting at?"

I step closer to the door, my confidence rising with every word. "You love to threaten reputations? Then let me remind you that Leo knows everyone who matters in this city. And if you so much as think about sending those texts, he'll make sure you don't land another deal. Ever. You know it, Brad. He's respected."

"Bullshit," he snaps, his composure slipping. "You wouldn't dare."

"Try me, Brad. I'm done playing your games."

I stride toward the door, my pulse racing, but my head held high, proud as hell of myself for standing my ground.

Brad beats me there, his frame blocking my way.

"Wait—don't go! I didn't mean it, baby. I'm sorry!"

"Move, Brad." I keep my voice steady, though inside, a hurricane of anxiety rages, every nerve on edge, my heartbeat pounding in my ears.

I take a step forward, but his hand shoots out, gripping my wrist tightly. The sudden pressure sends a jolt through me, and my breath catches.

"Brad, let go." Panic zips through me.

His grip tightens. "You walk out that door, and you're going to regret it."

"Ow, Brad. You're hurting me. Let go."

My heart races faster than before, fear all consuming. Brad's never crossed this line before—never hurt me physically.

And it scares the shit out of me.

"Brad, if you don't let go, I'm calling the cops."

"You're not going to call the cops, baby. I know you love me."

I reach into my purse with my free hand, taking out my phone, my thumb hovering over the screen.

He hesitates, his grip loosening slightly, though his eyes burn with a mix of panic and anger. "Come on, baby. I love you. Don't do this." His voice softens, pleading now, but I don't trust it for a second.

"Let go of me, Brad. Now."

He just stares, his grip a silent reminder that he thinks he still holds all the power.

I take a deep, calming breath, swiping up on the screen, my hand shaking. My voice is cold, resolute. "Test me. See what happens."

"Fine." He lets go and backs away from the door, arms raised in mock innocence. "But if you leave, everything you care about here is gone." He walks to the console table as my hand grips the door handle. "Like this."

I whip around, alarmed, my stomach dropping as I see him pick up my grandmother's glass bird—the one thing that holds value to me over anything else. It was my favorite thing of hers as a child, and she gave it to me on her deathbed.

"Brad, don't!" My voice breaks as I lunge forward, reaching out as if I can stop what's about to happen.

But it's too late. He fists the delicate bird in his hand, his expression unreadable, and smashes it to the ground.

Everything feels like it's moving in slow motion—the bird shattering, Brad's expression, the sound of my cries blending with the sharp crash of glass scattering across the floor. The fragments spread like shards of my heart, piercing every ounce of strength I have left. He's already taken so much from me, but this—this was deliberate. The one piece of me he hadn't broken yet—he destroyed that too.

He looks at me with satisfaction and pity. "Get the fuck out of here, Cooper. And don't you dare come crawling back when Ryan dumps your ass."

I can't leave like this. Not with him getting the last word. I can't let him have it—can't let him win. But I'm in tears, my breath coming in short, shaky gasps. The hurt cuts so deep, it's like it's hollowing me out from the inside. I square my shoulders, forcing myself to stand taller.

"Oh, I'll be back," I say, my voice laced with bitter cynicism. "Saturday. To get my things. And I'll be bringing Ryan and Leo with me." My gaze hardens, locking with his. "I suggest you not be here if you don't want your ass kicked."

I grip the door handle and swing it open, clinging to the last fragile thread of my dignity as I walk down the hallway toward the elevator, tears streaming down my face. The elevator ride feels excruciatingly long, and when it stops halfway down to let a couple on, humiliation burns through me. I try to hide my face, but it's useless—I know they've noticed. My nose is stuffed, my head pounds, and I stare at my feet, desperate to disappear, as if avoiding eye contact will make me invisible.

When we finally reach the parking garage, I rush out, gasping for breath like I've been held underwater.

I manage to hold it somewhat together until I reach my car. The second I shut the door, everything crashes down on me. Tears pour out, fast and unstoppable, and I completely lose it. I fold my arms over the steering wheel and bury my head in them. My shoulders shake with every sob, each one more painful than the last, until I lose all sense of time and just let myself break.

I sit up, frantically searching for tissues as the snot becomes impossible to manage with sniffles alone. My hands fumble under the passenger seat until I find a crumpled box. I yank one out and blow my nose. Leaning back against the seat, I squeeze my eyes shut, willing myself to calm down.

My hands move to my head, gripping my hair as I rub my temples, my head pounding. Keep breathing. Keep it together.

Eventually, the storm inside me settles into a quiet hum. I grab another tissue and peek into the visor mirror, wiping streaked mascara from my cheeks. God, my face is a disaster—puffy, red, blotchy. I don't even know how long I've been sitting here.

I check my phone. It's almost eleven. A flood of missed calls and texts from Ryan fills the screen. His earlier texts are directions to Leo and Vivian's and a simple request: Let me know when you're on your way.

The newer messages are different, laced with worry.

Ryan: Hey… starting to worry. Everything okay?

Ryan: Coop, Where are you?

Ryan: Call me.

Ryan: You okay?

The last one was sent ten minutes ago, right after his most recent call. He's tried multiple times, and guilt settles heavy in my chest. I'm not ready to talk—I need more time to pull myself together. But I can't leave him in the dark, so I type out a quick response:

Cooper: I'm so sorry. Brad was home… Yes, I'm ok. And no, I'm not ok. I'm leaving now. See you soon.

Chapter 32

RYAN

I'm worried sick until Cooper's text finally comes through. Knowing she had to face Brad unprepared makes my stomach churn.

I head to the parking garage. It's freezing out, but I don't care. Ten minutes later, her car pulls in. Even from here, I can tell she's been crying. I run a hand through my hair, rushing to meet her.

I open her door just as she wipes under her eyes. She steps out, and I pull her into me, practically knocking her off her feet.

She buries her head in my chest, fists clutching my shirt. She doesn't make a sound, but her shoulders shake with silent sobs.

"Jesus, Coop." I stroke her hair, resting my chin on the top of her head. "Hey, it's okay. I got you."

She nods, but the tremble in her body tells me she's far from okay.

"Let's get you inside, alright? Do you want to pop the trunk? I'll grab your things."

"I don't have anything." Her voice is barely above a whisper, raw and defeated.

I rub her back, shutting my eyes for a moment. *What the hell did he do?* "Okay, let's go in." I take her hand, holding it tightly. She needs to know she's safe here—that I'm safe.

We head up the two flights of stairs to my bedroom, where I brought her suitcase up from earlier. Damn. She's been living out of that same bag since before Christmas. It's mid-January now, and I know she was looking forward to grabbing more of her clothes for work.

She immediately starts rummaging through the suitcase, pulling out toiletries. I grip the back of my neck, trying to read her. "You know, I probably should've asked—do you want your own space? I can set you up in one of the guest rooms if you'd prefer."

She stops rummaging, her brows knitting together as her eyes lock on mine. "Wherever you are, is where I want to be." She stands, walking over to me, placing her hands on my chest. "Of course I want to stay with you."

I cradle her face, my thumb brushing softly over her cheek. "What happened?"

She hesitates, her voice flat and distant. "Brad was there. I told him we were done. He said some really nasty things." Her gaze drifts away, and my chest tightens at how detached she seems—like she's left her body, and all that's left is this shell.

"He threatened me, broke some things…" She swallows hard. "And then I left."

My jaw tightens. "Wait, he threatened you? What did he say, Cooper?"

She shrugs. "Does it matter?"

"Yes," I say firmly, my voice rising. "Yes, it fucking matters."

Her eyes meet mine, desperate for escape. "He had our text thread from Christmas Day printed out. You know… when we…"

"I know which one," I say softly, my voice gentle, hoping to ease her tension. "I remember."

She nods, her gaze falling to the floor. "He said he'd send them to our work… to your boss."

"Coop, you know I wouldn't give a shit if he sent those, right? God, you have to know that."

She nods faintly. "I'm really tired," she murmurs, staring into the distance. "Can we talk about this later? I just… I need to rest… to process everything."

"Of course," I say softly, rubbing her shoulders. "You sure?"

"Yeah, I'm sure." She leans in, pressing a soft kiss to my lips. "Thank you, Ry." Her eyes flutter shut for a moment before she adds, "I think I'd like to take a shower. Do you mind? You don't need to wait up. I know it's late."

"Not at all. Take your time, babe." I kiss her forehead, lingering for a moment before letting her go. I watch as she gathers her things and heads into the bathroom, the door clicking softly behind her.

After waiting anxiously on the bed for twenty minutes, the water's still running. There's no way in hell I'm sleeping without her right now. Plus, I need to brush my teeth.

I drag my hands over my face, frustration simmering. I wish Leo were here to give me some damn advice. Do I go in? Wait it out? Try to get her to talk, or let her be? Fuck, I'm not a therapist—I've never dealt with anything like this.

I tap on the door, loud enough for her to hear, then slip inside.

"Hey, just need to brush my teeth," I say, gesturing to the sink. I glance at her briefly but keep my focus on the task, giving her space.

I can feel her gaze on me the entire time. When I finally turn, I'm met with the saddest eyes I've ever seen. She's facing me, her back to the shower head. The tiled wall transitions to glass, framing her upper body.

I can't help but stare. Yes, her glorious tits are bare, but I'm not even looking at them. I notice them—but that's not what grips me. It's her face. Sad, raw, beautiful. Her bloodshot eyes tell me everything: she's been crying this whole time. Even through the shower's steam, I can see the tears streaking her face. She looks hollow, a ghost of herself. A fierce need to hold her—to protect her—takes over me.

I pull my shirt over my head and step out of my pants, leaving only my boxer briefs. I need her to know this isn't about sex. I walk to the shower, open the door, and step inside, never breaking eye contact.

When I reach her, I wrap my arms around her, and she melts into me. I press a kiss to her forehead, then gently tilt her chin up and kiss the tears from her cheeks. More follow, and her lips gravitate toward mine, brushing softly. I let her take the lead, offering only comfort, not pressure.

Her lips press into mine, soft and slow. Her arms slide around my neck, and it's like something awakens in her—as if she's been drowning, and I'm the air she desperately needs. Her kiss deepens, filled with fervor, slow but purposeful.

I match her intensity, cradling her head with one hand, pouring every ounce of care I have into the kiss, as if I could somehow draw out her pain. My lips trail to her jaw, her neck, and when a sob escapes her, I pull her back to me, capturing her mouth again.

We kiss in silence for what feels like an eternity, with only the sound of water hitting our skin and the tiles below.

I'm hard as hell, but that's not why I'm here. I pull back and shut off the shower, grabbing a towel. I dry my face quickly before turning to her. Carefully, I bring the towel to her face, dabbing away the water. Then I move to her hair, wrapping the towel around it and giving it an awkward rub, causing her to smile. That smile—it's like seeing the sun after a storm. I grin back, encouraged, and keep going, ruffling the towel over her head just to make her smile again. She does, so I continue.

Her eyes track me as I work, drying every part of her, my lips following the path of the towel, leaving soft kisses as I go. When I reach her wrist, though, I freeze. A faint bruise marks her skin, an obvious shadow of Brad's grip. My jaw tightens, and I shut my eyes, forcing myself to breathe through the surge of anger.

Slowly, I raise her wrist to my lips, brushing a kiss over the mark as if I can erase it. She closes her eyes and I don't linger. I can't. Not without losing it.

I continue. I don't know what she's thinking—she looks almost lost, confused—but fuck, I don't know what's come over me either. I'm worshiping her, treating her like she's my salvation. And maybe, in a way, she is.

When I left Beth, I couldn't imagine feeling this way about anyone again. But Cooper—she's filled an empty part of me with something pure and real. I kneel, drying each toe and then bringing a foot to my lips, kissing the top of it. A soft, broken laugh escapes her lips. The sound is everything—fragile, hopeful, raw. It feeds something deep inside me.

"Ryan," she says softly, her voice thick with emotion. "You don't have to do this."

I look up at her, my gaze meeting hers. "I want to." My voice is steady, certain. Her hands comb through my hair as I slowly wrap the towel around her calf, dragging it upward, then repeating. When I reach her thighs, my breath catches, her bare pussy is right in front of me. My instincts roar to touch her, to taste her, but I shut them down. As tempting as it is, this isn't about me—it's about her. She's trusting me with her pain, and I won't ruin that by giving in to my urges.

I finish drying her, my hands steady despite the fire raging inside me, and press a kiss to her pubic bone. It's not sexual—it's reverent, a silent promise that I see all of her, and I'm here for more than just the physical.

Standing, I grip her hips and lift her effortlessly. She wraps around me, arms and legs clinging as if I'm her anchor.

I carry her to the bed and lay her down with care.

I'm still wet, my boxer briefs soaked. I let go, intending to dry off, but she clings to me, pulling me closer. Her lips find mine, her bottom lip sucking gently at mine before her tongue strokes in, coaxing me deeper. I collapse into the kiss, giving her all that I have.

She breaks our kiss, locking eyes with mine. "Thank you," she whispers, her voice soft, trembling. "No one has ever done something like this for me." Her eyes search mine in disbelief, her hand gently stroking my cheek. "Ever."

Her lips return to mine, urgent this time, her hips lifting into me. I meet her with the same intensity, my hand drifting to her tits as she tugs at my wet boxers. I peel them off and toss them aside. Our movements are slow, deliberate, each touch filled with unspoken appreciation.

God, I love her.

I've felt it building for days now, and I'm sure of it. I started falling for her a long time ago. She had me in that damn pool… I fell hard that night. The laughter, the connection, the magnetic pull between us—it was undeniable. We were high as kites, but what we shared was more than a physical attraction. Against all the odds—Beth, cancer, Brad, hurt, timing—we found each other.

My hand moves between her thighs, drawing a soft gasp from her lips that ignites something primal in me. God, she's so wet. Her body arches into mine, her breath catching as I stroke her, and I feel the raw, unfiltered desire between us. She grips my shoulders, her nails digging in as if I'm the only thing keeping her grounded.

I push into her, slow and deliberate. As I fill her, a sense of completion washes over me—like she's the missing piece to this fucking puzzle called life. I focus on her, the sounds of her moans, and the way my name falls from her lips as we come together. The moment is pure rapture, leaving me breathless.

A few minutes later, after cleaning up, we're back in bed, her head resting on my chest. I debate whether to push her to talk, unsure if it's the right time. Finally, I decide to try.

"Hey," I say softly, breaking the silence.

She tilts her chin toward me but doesn't speak.

"Tell me what happened. What did Brad say… What'd he do?"

She hesitates, her eyes glistening with fresh tears. Guilt stabs in my chest—I hate that I'm making her relive it, but I have to know.

She finally speaks, her voice barely above a whisper. "He tried to get in my head. Said I was an average fuck, a whore—that you'd get bored of me. That you wouldn't want me if you really knew what a slut I was…" Her voice cracks. "Stuff like that."

"Coop, I would never." The words rush out, my body recoiling, muscles tightening with anger.

She takes a shaky breath. "I started to believe him." Her gaze drops as she rests her cheek on my chest. "It's still there… gnawing at me. Like a voice in the back of my mind, whispering that if you actually knew me, you wouldn't stay."

"What do you mean if I *actually knew you*?"

She doesn't answer, her silence heavy.

"Babe," I coax, keeping my tone gentle.

She sighs, rolling onto her back and pulling the sheet up to her chest. Her hands press together in a prayer, fingers touching her forehead. Eyes shut tight, she shakes her head slowly, like she's trying to will the thoughts away.

"Babe," I say again, softer this time, turning to my side to face her. "It's okay. You can tell me."

Her eyes meet mine, but they're clouded with fear. "I don't want you to know these things."

I pause, choosing my words. "I'm not going to push you, but…" I cup her cheek gently, my thumb grazing her skin. "I want to understand."

She takes a deep, trembling breath, rolling to her side so we're eye-to-eye. Her gaze locks on mine for a moment before she speaks. "I'm afraid," she admits. "I'm afraid that if you know certain things about me… about my past… you won't—" She swallows hard, blinking rapidly as tears threaten. "You won't want to be with me." She closes her eyes tightly, shaking her head. "I don't want to lose you," she whispers, the words breaking on a sob.

"You're not going to lose me."

"No." Her voice catches, and she takes another shaky breath. "You don't understand. I'm not a good person, Ryan. Not like you." A tear escapes, rolling down her cheek. "You're too good for me. I don't deserve someone like you. And when you know how…" She trails off.

My brows pull together as I force a smile, hoping to ease her fears. "Hey," I say, my thumb brushing away the tear on her cheek. "Don't you dare break up with me before I have the chance to make you my girl-friend."

Her hand moves to cover mine on her cheek, and I let my words settle.

"See?" she says, a laugh breaking through her tears. "You're too good. God. Where did you come from?"

I lean in and kiss her fiercely, cupping her face in my hands. "You can tell me anything. I don't care about your past. I care about the person you are now. I don't scare that easily."

She nods, but her eyes still hold doubt. "Are you sure? Because you left Beth after twelve years… and she made one mistake. I've made a hun-dred."

Fuck. That lands hard, straight to the gut, but I push the feeling aside.

I take a steadying breath. "Coop… just tell me."

She hesitates, biting her lip, then whispers, "Fine. But I feel like I should start packing now… for when you ask me to leave after."

I sigh, moving closer. "Come on. Have some faith in me."

"Okay." She hesitates. "I guess I'll start at the beginning. Kind of a funny story, actually. The first time I gave a blow job, I didn't even know what it was." She lets out a hollow laugh, the kind that makes my stomach twist. "I had a crush on this guy, Jared, and his friend Gavin told me if I blew him, he'd get Jared to ask me out. Said Jared liked me but didn't think I was interested. I was fourteen. I didn't even know what he meant. So, he pulled his dick out, and I blew on it."

I smile softly as her laugh fades into an uneasy silence. In a different context, it might be funny, but this? Not in the slightest.

"Of course, Jared didn't ask me out. Not at first. But he did ask for sexual favors—promised he'd make me his girlfriend if I gave him a blow job, or let him go down on me…" She pauses, her voice cracking. "Or if I slept with him."

Tears streak down her cheeks, faster now, and I feel like my chest is caving in. "He eventually made me his girlfriend, you know, because then he could have sex with me whenever he wanted. Not that it stopped him from sleeping with everyone else. I was a freshman, and he was a junior, captain of the JV football team. Girls threw themselves at him, and he didn't turn them down."

This kid was a complete piece of shit. "Why didn't you break up with him?" I ask softly, anger burning beneath my words.

"I tried," she says softly. "We'd fight, and I'd threaten to break up with him. Then he'd talk me into staying—tell me he loved me, that he'd do anything for me, get me anything. God, I was so young, so naive." She pauses, glancing at me like she's bracing for judgment, but I stay silent, letting her continue.

"I realized I had something those other girls didn't—experience. I knew him, knew what he liked, what he didn't. And even though he had power over me, I learned I could use sex to get what I wanted. If he cheated and still wanted sex from me? Fine. Take me shopping first. It was sick, but it worked until he left for college and broke up with me."

She shrugs like it's no big deal. "At that point, I was just known as Jared's girlfriend. Everyone knew who I was and that I put out. The guys who asked me out all expected something, and I had this 'fuck them' attitude. Like, 'You want to use me? Fine, I'll use you.'"

Her laugh is brittle, a sharp edge of self-loathing in it. "Basically, all through high school, I was a bargaining chip for guys. The good ones never asked me out—they weren't the type to date someone like me. And when

I did have a boyfriend, he was never faithful." She scoffs. "I was such a shitty teenager. I'd sneak off to smoke in the parking lot, and I was getting drunk at fifteen. Honestly, drinking made it easier to do what they wanted."

She shifts, meeting my gaze briefly before looking away. "I even stole shit. I was a little thief."

"By senior year, I started to straighten out. My mom was threatening to kick me out, and my dad agreed I couldn't live with him. They both expected me to get into a good college. Somehow, I'd managed to keep my grades up, but high school was hell. The girls were bitches, the guys were predators, and I just wanted to escape. So, I worked my ass off, graduated early, and got into Northwestern by some miracle—and a sorority."

She exhales. "By then, I'd only ever been in toxic relationships. I liked sex—a lot—but the way I used it was anything but healthy. College didn't help. My sorority was full of pretty girls who loved to party, and we had a reputation for it. I had one boyfriend, Damion, who was actually great to me, but that only lasted three months before he moved away."

Her voice tightens as she shifts uncomfortably. "Then there was this math class I was struggling in. My professor was cute. I was nineteen, and he was thirty. I don't know if he knew things about me or just sensed them, but one day after class, he pulled me aside and said there was a way I could bring my grade up." She scoffs. "I bet you can guess what it was. I went along with it. We ended up together for months. He told me he loved me."

She hesitates, her shoulders trembling as she shakes her head. Her voice cracks as she continues. "God, Ryan… I didn't know." Her hands cover her face, and she chokes on a sob.

My heart breaks at the sight of her. "It's okay," I say gently, reaching for her hand. "What didn't you know?"

She looks at me, her eyes red, full of hurt and worry. "That he was married." Her voice gives way. "God, I was the other woman—and I didn't even know."

And suddenly, everything clicks. Her pushing me to forgive Beth, her insistence on redemption, the relentless comments about men being cheaters and assholes. Jesus, she's never known anything else.

"But that's not even the worst part." Her voice breaks, dropping to a whisper. "After I found out, he broke up with me. And then I met Brad. I had no idea he was friends with him. Brad knew about the affair, about how it started. He knew I'd slept with my professor to raise my grade." She exhales shakily. "But he didn't tell me he knew—not at first. Not until about a year in, when things started going south between us. I tried to break up with him, and that's when he played his hand."

Her breath hitches. "God, he was so patient. He held on to that information for over a year, waiting until he could use it to trap me. He told me I didn't even earn my degree. That no one would hire me, knowing I'd just try to sleep my way to the top. That I was worthless, only good for one thing. That if I left, he'd destroy my reputation. He said no one would want me if they knew who I really was."

I grip the sheet in my hand, fighting back the anger surging through my veins.

She looks away, almost ashamed. "And I stayed. I believed him. Then he got me the job with his brother, so he could keep an eye on me, make sure I wouldn't screw around. He even told me his brother wouldn't help me advance without me earning it." She laughs bitterly. "When Genevieve approached me for this position, it felt so fucking good. For the first time, someone believed in me for my skills—not what I could give them. And then you were there. And now…" Her voice cracks again. "Now look at us. God, I really am what Brad says I am."

I shift closer to her, propping myself up on my elbow. My free hand brushes a strand of hair from her cheek, and I let it rest lightly on her jaw. "Are you sleeping with me for a promotion?" I ask, my voice low but teasing.

Her eyes widen, and her lips part in shock. "No. God, no," she whispers, shaking her head like she can't believe I'd even ask.

"Good," I say, my thumb grazing her cheekbone. "Because nothing you've told me makes me think you're a bad person. All I see is someone who's been through hell and met some really shitty people along the way."

Her breathing slows, her gaze locked on mine as I speak. "And honestly? Who didn't do dumb shit as a teenager? I mean, I walked into a Nike store once, put on a pair of shoes, and walked out like I'd just bought them. Still feel bad about it. And I was the nerdy chess club kid."

She laughs—a small, breathy sound—but it's real.

"But seriously, Coop," I murmur, leaning just a little closer. "You were a kid. Your innocence was stolen from you, and it fucked with your head—made you think all that shit was normal—it wasn't. But it's not who you are now. You're kind. You're smart. You're fucking resilient. And you deserve so much better than the crap you've been through."

I let my hand cup her face, my fingers threading gently into her hair as I make her look at me. "You deserve someone who sees all of that, who loves all of that. Like I said, I don't scare that easily. I have two sisters, I'm patient as hell... So you're stuck with me."

Her eyes search mine, looking for lies. "Are you serious, Ryan?"

"Serious." I pause, thinking back. "Remember when I told you being human was sexy?"

"In Newport?" She smiles. "Yeah. I remember... You like all my humanness?"

"I *love* your humanness," I say, kissing her lips. I tilt my forehead to hers, my voice steady and soft. "I'm not perfect, either, babe. But I'm serious about you."

"You're too good to be true." She pauses, her eyes sweeping over mine.

"If that makes me too good to be true, then I'll just have to prove to you that I'm real." I brush my thumb across her cheek. And for the first time tonight, I see a flicker of hope in her eyes. I press my lips to hers in a kiss that says everything I can't put into words—a silent vow to show her, every day, that I'm here. That I'm real. And that I'm hers.

She grins against my lips. "Are you planning to prove it right now, BDR?"

I chuckle, leaning into her ear, my voice low and teasing. "You bet your ass I am."

She laughs softly, her breath warm against my neck. "Guess I'm pretty damn lucky, then. All that giant dick, all to myself." Her lips crash into mine as her hand slides down, wrapping firmly around my length, stroking with deliberate confidence. And just like that, I get lost in her.

Her touch.
Her smell.
Her taste.
Her laugh.
Her body.
Her lips.
Her.

I pull back, my forehead resting against hers as I catch my breath. I wrap her in my arms, holding her tight. Our bodies pressed together, the sound of our breath hanging comfortably in the air, until eventually, we fall asleep.

Chapter 33

COOPER

I pull up to Mom and Steve's sprawling Highland Park mansion—a seven-thousand-square-foot estate on four pristine acres, just minutes from Lake Michigan. It's beautiful, the kind of house that could be in a magazine, but all I feel as I sit idling in the driveway is dread. This conversation is going to suck.

Steve's my stepdad. He's wealthy, treats my mom well, and has been around since I was eighteen. But we're not close. Same with my mom. We don't fight anymore, but I avoid her as much as possible. I'm not a great daughter, no matter what my dad says about me living here to "be close to her." The truth is, Chicago isn't about her—it's about me feeling stuck. Trapped with Brad for the past five years.

I haven't been here since Thanksgiving, and even then, I hardly talked to anyone. My mom calls every week, and I've answered exactly once.

I sigh, gripping the steering wheel. *I'm such an asshole.*

I know I harbor resentment toward my mom, which is messed up when I think about it. I'm closer to my dad—the one who cheated, lied, and broke our family. But my mom? I blame her for putting up with his shit. For not setting the bar higher—for not showing me and my sister what we should want in a relationship. I've held on to that blame for so long, but maybe it's time to let some of it go.

What am I even going to say? *"Hey, mom, sorry I haven't talked to you in over a month. Can I live here for a few weeks?"*

I groan, rubbing my forehead in frustration, then turn off the car and head up the long driveway to the porch.

God, I don't even know if she's home. It's Thursday, and Ryan told me to take the day off or work from home, so here I am.

I knock, my stomach twisting with unease. A few moments later, her smiling face appears in the doorway. "Hey, Coop. What are you doing here?"

"Hi, Mom."

She pulls me into a hug with so much vigor that my instinct is to pull away—it's too much right now.

"Ah, what a pleasant surprise." She steps back, studying me. "Is everything okay? I haven't heard from you in weeks… This is so unlike you."

I force a half-smile. "Yeah, Mom. I'm fine. Just wanted to talk, if that's okay?"

Her brows knit with concern. "Of course, sweetie. Come on in."

I follow her into the kitchen, spacious enough to make my apartment look like a closet—well, what used to be my apartment.

"Is Steve here?" I ask, grasping for anything to fill the silence.

"No, he's in Toronto for work. He'll be back tomorrow. Do you want something to drink? Sparkling water? Wine?" she offers, like I'm some guest from out of town. If we were close, she wouldn't need to ask. I'd have helped myself, walked in without knocking—moved around this kitchen like it was my own. But I honestly don't even know which cupboard holds the glasses; there are dozens of them.

"Sure," I say hesitantly. "I'll take a sparkling water." Because, Jesus, who wants wine at ten in the morning?

She grabs a Pellegrino from the fridge and gestures toward the massive kitchen table—a setup fit for a family of twelve, illuminated by an elaborate chandelier. "Take a seat, honey. Make yourself at home."

We both sit, me on one side, her on the other. I grip the water bottle, the condensation already wetting my hands. My gaze settles on the bubbles as they rise and pop, my mind drifting to last night. Brad's threats. His cruel words. I swallow the lump in my throat and try to refocus.

"What's going on, Cooper? You never visit unless you have to." Her voice is soft, gentle—motherly—full of concern. I truly don't know why she hasn't written me off. I would've a long time ago.

I stare at the table, afraid she'll see right through me. Even though we're distant, she still has that motherly intuition everyone talks about.

My eyes well up.

Shit.

"Coop, honey." Her hand reaches across the table, covering mine. "What is it?"

I force myself to meet her gaze, and the dam breaks. Tears spill over before I can stop them, and a sob rips from my chest. My hands fly to my face, but it's too late. My mom rushes to my side.

Dammit.

She pulls me into her arms, rocking gently like I'm a child again. "Shh," she soothes, her voice a soft echo in the dining room.

Guttural sobs wrack my body as she rubs my back.

She's a saint.

She holds me for what feels like forever until the storm inside me finally starts to settle. I take a deep breath, sitting up and wiping at my face.

"Sorry," I mumble.

"Don't apologize, sweetie. I'm your mom. As much as I hate seeing you like this, I love being able to comfort you… I wish you'd let me more often." She pauses, her eyes full of concern. "Tell me what's going on."

I focus on my fingers, pushing at my cuticles. "I broke up with Brad," I whisper, unable to make eye contact.

"Oh, honey. I'm so sorry… Did something happen?"

I glance at her briefly, a scoff slipping out before I can stop it. "Yeah, something happened. He's an asshole."

Her gaze burns into the side of my face. I don't know what she's thinking—I've never known what my mom thinks of Brad. She's never said anything, just quietly supported whatever I decided.

"Is it for good this time? You've broken up a few times before…" Her voice trails off.

"It's for good this time," I say firmly, finally meeting her gaze. "I need somewhere to live until I find my own place. And I was hoping…"

She cuts me off before I can finish. "You don't even have to ask. You know you can stay here anytime you want."

I force a smile. "Thanks. I won't be here much, but I need a place to keep my things."

Her brows furrow again, concern etched on her face. "Where will you be?"

I exhale. "I'm… sort of seeing someone."

Her expression shifts from confusion to doubt. "So soon?"

I sigh, annoyed. "It's not like that, Mom. We work together. I've known him a long time."

"Did you have an affair?"

"Ugh!" I groan, throwing my hands up. "Are you really going to lecture me about affairs?" My tone comes out sharper than I intended, but I can't help it.

She looks taken aback, clearly offended. "You know what I went through with your father. I'd hate to think you'd ever do something like that."

I laugh bitterly, the frustration spilling over. "Are you serious, Mom? What about me? What about Brad cheating on me for five fucking years?"

She flinches, and I can't tell if it's from the information or the delivery—probably both.

"Cooper, please don't use that word in my house—it's not necessary." She rubs her temples, her tone weary. "I don't want to fight with you. And I don't want to make you feel guilty." She takes a sip of her water, calm and collected, as I gape at her. "All I've ever wanted is for you to be happy."

"Then why don't you ask me if I'm happy instead of judging me and assuming the worst, like you always do?"

She exhales, her frustration mirroring mine. "Are you happy, honey?"

"No." My voice trembles. "No, I'm not happy. I haven't been happy since I was fourteen." The words hang heavy in the air, and my chest tightens. "But when I'm with Ryan? I feel… glimpses of happiness. It's the first time in my life that I think maybe I could be happy. He's like nothing I've ever had and everything I could ever hope for." My voice cracks, tears threatening again. I soften, willing her to understand. "I didn't cheat on Brad… but I… crossed some lines. But only because I felt so trapped."

My mom's silent for a moment, and I brave her gaze, expecting judgment. But all I see is concern.

"I never liked Brad," she says softly, her voice tinged with regret. "I didn't want to push you away by saying it, but I saw through his crap from the beginning. I'm just worried this Ryan guy might be the same. You know, getting involved with you while you were engaged—it's not a good sign. That worries me." She frowns. "Your picker's broken, Cooper. Always has been. And I blame myself for that—for not showing you what a healthy relationship looks like." She pauses, sipping her water. "I'm sorry. And I'm sorry I haven't been here for you."

Her words hit me in waves, stirring up a tangle of emotions: anger, relief, understanding, compassion, love. Maybe Mom's right to worry. My "picker" *has* always been broken, and a part of me still can't shake the nagging doubt that Ryan's too good to be true. But I don't want to ruin this by letting my doubts take over me.

"If you knew about Brad," I say bitterly, "why didn't you ever talk to me about it? Why would you just sit there and let me suffer in silence?"

My mom sighs, her shoulders slumping in defeat. "Oh, Coop. I mentioned something a long time ago, when you were first dating." She shakes her head. "You haven't listened to me since you were twelve, and you weren't exactly receptive to it. And hey, I get it—I've been there. But instead of destroying our relationship trying to get you to see what was in front of you, like many of my friends did to me, I chose to support you from a distance."

"Destroy our relationship? What relationship? We've never had one, Mom," I snap, frustration spilling over. And shit, I vaguely remember her making a comment about Brad in the beginning, but hell, that was five years ago—I was barely twenty-three. She's right. I didn't listen. I never have.

"Not because I haven't wanted one," she says softly, her voice cracking just enough to make my heart ache.

A fresh flood of tears streams down my face. "I'm sorry, Mom. God, I'm the worst. I've been so mad at you, all this time. I blamed you for everything." My voice falters, and I shake my head as the weight of my own stupidity crashes down on me.

She hugs me fiercely. "It's alright. All I've ever wanted is this. For you to come back to me, to forgive me."

I nod, pulling back. "Why did you stay with dad all those years?"

She shrugs. "I was scared. I didn't want to be a single mom, raising two girls on my own. I didn't want to get a job or worry about how we'd pay the bills."

"Was Dad mean to you?" I ask, even though part of me doesn't want to know.

"Not in the way you mean. He lied and cheated. That's not exactly nice, but no, he wasn't cruel. Your father's a decent man, all in all—he's just a terrible husband." She laughs softly, a hint of sadness in her eyes. "But he loves you girls. He always paid child support and alimony, and he never gave me a hard time after the divorce."

She pauses, concern softening her features. "Was Brad mean to you?"

I nod, swallowing hard. The words stuck in my throat, but I force them out. "Yeah. He was pretty fucking mean."

Her eyes widen, and I wince. "Sorry," I mumble. I really need to learn to filter better.

But then it all hits me again, and the emotion bursts out of me, loud and ugly. "He broke Grandma's bird," I sob, burying my face in my hands. My shoulders shake, and the tears flow uncontrollably.

My mom scoots closer, rubbing my back gently, murmuring softly, "Shh, sweetheart. It's okay. Let it out." She takes a deep breath, her voice steady but full of anger. "I'm so sorry. He had to know what that bird meant to you."

"He did," I choke out, my voice breaking with emotion. "He knew."

"Then he's an asshole," she says, the venom in her words startling but oddly comforting. She holds me until the sobs taper off, the ache in my chest easing just a little.

"Mom?" I ask softly, breaking the silence.

"Hmm?"

"Can we be friends?" My voice wavers, barely above a whisper.

Her arms tighten around me. "I would like that very much."

I sit up, wiping my face with the back of my hand, feeling lighter—like some invisible barrier between us has finally been lifted.

"Why don't you tell me about Ryan?"

"He's nothing like Brad. He's the opposite of anyone I've ever been with—one of the good ones. He's smart, kind, and actually invested in me." I can't help the small grin that creeps onto my face. "And he's so hot. Just wait until you see him. I have to pinch myself sometimes to believe he's real."

She laughs softly. "He sounds wonderful. Why don't you bring him over for dinner sometime?"

I smile, a gooey warmth spreading through me. "Yeah, I think that'd be great. Not too soon though—I don't want to scare him off."

My mom chuckles. "Do you think Steve and I would scare him off?"

"No. I just… I want to take things slow. I know I'll spend a lot of time with him, but I'm also looking for my own place. I need to do this on my own for a bit—figure my life out. I've relied so much on Brad for every-thing, I feel like I've lost my independence. And I know Ryan will want me to succeed on my own."

"Well, he really does sound great. I'm excited to meet him."

"Thanks," I say with a soft smile. "I think you'll like him."

We spend the next hour catching up—talking about Steve, Ryan, work, Casey—and it feels good. Really good. The anger and resentment dissipate, like we're finally starting to bridge the gap between us.

I leave my mom's house feeling lighter—hopeful, even. I promised to call more and let her know when I'll be staying with them. Sliding into the car, I pull out my phone to check for any missed calls or texts.

A slew of notifications awaits me: one from Casey, two from Ryan, and, of course, several from Brad.

"Fuck," I mutter under my breath, exasperated.

Casey: Tried to call you. Need over the phone details about Ryan. No more of this text BS. Need to hear your voice.

I laugh to myself, shaking my head. I'd texted Casey yesterday about the sex with Ryan, but the day had been so hectic I hadn't had a chance to call her back.

Ryan: Hope you still like me—just emailed HR. We're officially dating at work.

Relief floods through me. Thank God we don't have to worry about that anymore.

Ryan: Got us dinner reservations for tomorrow night. Dress code: whatever you feel sexy in. Underwear optional (smirk emoji)

A smile tugs at my lips. Why is he so damn cute? He's taking me out tomorrow night. Our first official date.

Cooper: Oh, panties will definitely be left behind. Just hope you save room for dessert… I bought whipped cream. (winky face emoji)

My gaze shifts to Brad's messages, and I'm tempted to delete them without reading. But I need to text him anyway—to let him know what time I'll be over on Saturday to get my things. Leo and Vivian don't come home until next weekend, so my threat to bring Leo won't pan out. Not that Brad needs to know that. And I'll be bringing Ryan with me.

Brad: Coop, I'm sorry. I was out of line last night. I don't even know what came over me.

Brad: You know I'd never hurt you on purpose.

Brad: I'll fix the bird, Coop. I saved all the pieces.

I scoff, shaking my head. Disbelief doesn't even cover it—not with Brad. His behavior is exactly what I expect.

Does he really think trying to salvage my grandmother's bird will erase what he did?

Brad: I hope you won't start telling people lies about me.

Brad: I still love you, you know. I don't want to fight. Just call me, please.

I stare at the screen, incredulous. He doesn't want to fight? Is he delusional? I start typing.

Cooper: There's nothing to fight about. We're done. I'll be by Saturday at noon with Ryan and Leo to get my things. If you don't want things getting messy or the cops called, be gone from 12-5.

I grip the phone tight, anger erupting through me like a poison. A scream tears from my throat, raw and loud, releasing it into the empty air around me.

My nostrils flare as I take a deep breath, forcing myself to exhale slowly. My eyes drift back to my phone, catching another text from Ryan. Instantly, the tension in my body eases, replaced by a flood of relief and a small smile.

Ryan: God, I hope you're serious. I'll lick the entire can off your delicious body.

I grin, my mood officially salvaged. I guess my next stop is the grocery store.

I need whipped cream.

Chapter 34

RYAN

Last night was incredible. I took Cooper to dinner, and then we went for dessert—in my bedroom. Images of licking whipped cream off her body flash in my mind. Jesus, that was hot. But when she took over, licking it off me, her tongue swirling, her lips tight around me... Goddamn. We made a mess, and it was worth every second.

I'm getting hard just thinking about it. *Not the time, Ryan. Get it together.* I glance at Cooper beside me, gripping my hand like it's her lifeline. Her anxiety practically vibrating off her.

I give her hand a reassuring squeeze as the elevator climbs to the eleventh floor. She looks pale, her breaths shallow.

"You okay?" I ask.

"No. I feel like I'm going to be sick. What if he's here?"

"Then things will get ugly," I admit. God, I hope he's not here. I've only ever been in one fight in my life, but if Brad's here? I don't know if I could hold back. I wouldn't want to.

The elevator dings, and we step into the hallway. Cooper's grip on my hand tightens.

Inside the apartment, her voice trembles as she calls out. "Brad?"

Please don't be here. Please don't be here. Not just because I don't want to end up in jail, but mostly because I don't want Cooper to have to see him—deal with him. Not today.

She lets out a sigh of relief. "I don't think he's here."

I stay close as she moves to the entryway table, where a pile of broken glass sits next to a folded piece of paper. My chest tightens as I step behind her, reading over her shoulder.

Coop,

I'm sorry about the bird. Here are the pieces. I hope you're able to put it back together. I've always loved you, baby.

She crumples the note into a tiny ball, her knuckles white as she grips it. "God, that makes me want to puke."

She marches through the living room without another word, and I follow her into the bedroom. A knot twists in the pit of my stomach as I take in the scene: everything from her nightstand—pictures, books, her jewelry box—scattered across the floor in a chaotic mess.

Fucking dick. My jaw tightens. *Real mature, Brad.*

She shakes her head, exhaling sharply. Without a word, we move to the bathroom, where the chaos continues. Drawers hang open, her belongings scattered across the floor in a deliberate mess. Watching her take it all in, the fury inside me rises like a furnace about to explode.

She mutters something under her breath and strides through the bathroom into the closet.

"Motherfucker!" she yells, her voice shaking with rage. I rush to her side. "Goddamn him."

The knot in my stomach twists tighter as I take in the sight. Most of her clothes are heaped in a pile on the floor, shredded, slashed, completely ruined. The few pieces still hanging have been defaced with thick black Sharpie—'whore,' 'bitch,' 'slut,' and other sick words scrawled across the fabric.

My teeth clench, fists tightening at my sides, and I have to fight the urge to punch the wall. "Jesus Christ." I mutter under my breath.

Her eyes well with tears, her breathing quick and erratic as she presses a trembling palm to her forehead. "Ryan," she chokes out, her voice raw. "I need you to go on the balcony for five minutes so I can flip the fuck out."

Her hands lace behind her head as she starts pacing the closet. Each inhale is deep and slow, but the exhales are loud, shaky, like she's barely holding it together.

"Ryan," she snaps, her eyes wild. "Please. I don't want you to see me this way."

She grabs my hand, tugging me out of the closet toward the hallway.

"Coop, I'm not going anywhere."

"No, Ryan, please. I'm going to lose it." She tugs harder, but I plant my feet firm, pulling her into me.

I cradle her face in my hands. "Then lose it. Scream. Cry. Throw shit. Do whatever you've got to do. But I'm not leaving. I'll be right here, no matter what." I look her straight in the eye. "I'm not going anywhere. And I'll still be here when you're done."

Her bottom lip trembles as tears streak her face. I press a kiss to her forehead, lingering for a second. "How about I wait on the couch?"

She nods faintly, and I let go, giving her space.

As I head to the living room, her cries erupt from the closet, raw and guttural. I force myself to keep moving.

The living room's a disaster. Pillows scattered across the room, torn photos of the two of them litter the floor like shrapnel. An empty whiskey bottle and crushed beer cans sit on the counter like some pathetic monument to his rage. I take it all in, anger simmering just below the surface.

He ruined her clothes.

What a fucking prick.

I step into his office, and it takes everything in me not to pick up his shit and chuck it all against the wall.

From the bedroom, I hear a loud crash followed by Cooper's string of obscenities. A small smile tugs at my lips. Good. She's getting it out. Not that it makes them even—not even close. There isn't enough damage in the world to balance what he's done. But if smashing his crap helps her, even a little, I'm all for it.

I walk back into the bathroom to find her frantic, yanking open drawers and slamming them shut.

"You fucking motherfucker," she mutters, her voice sharp with anger. "Where did you put them? Goddamn son of a bitch." She keeps searching, her hands tearing through everything. "Where the fuck did you put them?"

I follow her as she strides to the office and opens the safe. She pulls out a note, and as she skims the page, a gut-wrenching sound escapes her lips—something caught between a bitter laugh and a defeated cry.

"What is it, babe? What are you looking for?"

She doesn't say a word, just hands me the note before walking past me, her body rigid with tension. My hands tremble with the fury as I unfold the paper.

Baby,

Did you really think you could walk out on me and still keep those things? The toys, the lingerie? Those were for me, and now you think you're going to take them to use with him? Think again.

I knew you'd come crawling to the safe, desperate to get your little stash. Guess what? You're not taking anything from this house that I bought to keep us satisfied. You don't get to use those things when he isn't cutting it for you.

I didn't buy those things to spoil you. I needed something to make you remotely exciting. Good luck keeping Ryan interested without them. Let's hope he doesn't get bored with you as quickly as I did. I hope he's up to the challenge.

Well, as a matter of fact, Brad, I am more than up to the challenge.

I find Cooper in the bathroom picking through the remnants of her belongings, filling up a duffle bag.

I step behind her, wrapping my arms around her waist and pressing a kiss to her neck. "Hey, babe," I murmur. "I'm more than happy to refill your bin with new toys." I kiss her jaw, trying to coax out a smile. "And I'll buy you the sexiest lingerie. Whatever you want."

She huffs out a bitter laugh. "He took all my bras and underwear, too. Just my daily fucking essentials."

"It's okay," I whisper against her skin. "We'll get you new ones."

Her voice wavers as she turns to face me, resting her arms on my chest. "And all my…" She chokes up, her throat working as she swallows hard. "All my clothes are gone. I know they're just clothes, but this is going to drain all my savings to replace them."

Tears well in her eyes, and I pull her closer, my arms tightening around her.

"He took me off all the accounts, Ryan," she whispers, the panic creeping into her voice. "I can't get to any of our money. All I have is what's left from my last two paychecks in my new account." Her brows knit together, worry written all over her face. "God," she cries out, her voice breaking as she sinks into me.

I hold her close, letting her lean into me as her tears fall. Her body trembles, and I rub slow circles on her back until her breathing steadies, her body softening slightly in my arms.

I tilt her chin to meet my gaze and kiss her with everything I have to give. "Take your clothes off, Cooper."

Her eyes widen. "What?"

My voice drops, a growl laced with determination. "I want to fuck you."

"Now? Here?"

"Yeah." My lips brush against her cheek. "Right here… in his bed." I nibble her ear. "I'm not letting this be your last memory. I want you to leave here smiling, remembering us—what we have. Not him. Not his shit. Just you and me."

Her breath hitches, uncertainty in her eyes—but then it melts into something different—something wild, determined.

Her lips crash into mine, and I walk her backward toward the bedroom, our kisses growing more desperate with every step. "I want to make you feel so damn good that when you think about this place, all you'll see is fucking stars," I murmur, my hand slipping between her legs. She gasps, her body arching into my touch.

Her fingers fumble with the button and zipper of my pants, frantic and needy.

I chuckle low in my throat. "That's it, babe. Let it all out. Take it out on me." I yank her shirt over her head, pressing her back against the wall, her bare skin hot against mine. Her hands move to my waistband, tugging roughly at my pants and boxer briefs until they hit the floor. I step out of them, and her fingers are already pulling at my shirt, her urgency matching my own.

Her eyes blaze with fury and hunger as she shoves me toward the bed. "Get on the bed, Ryan," she demands, her voice shaking with emotion. "I want you to fuck me right where he sleeps."

I grin, loving the way she takes charge. There's something so damn sexy about her when she's demanding. I do as I'm told, settling onto the bed.

She straddles me, unhooking her bra and tossing it across the room. "He can have that too," she mutters, her lips crushing into mine as she grinds against me. Jesus Christ, she's irresistible. The way her mouth moves over mine, the way her body fits so perfectly against me—I never stood a chance. She walked into my life and took me by the balls back in Newport, and I've been hers ever since.

I grin against her mouth, unable to help myself. "You're the sexiest fucking woman in the world."

"Shut up," she whispers, her breath hot against my lips. "More touching, less talking."

Her hands slide down, shoving her pants and underwear off. She positions herself over me, sinking down onto my dick, and we both groan at the connection. She moves with purpose, her hips rolling in perfect rhythm as I match her pace.

"Make me forget about him, Ryan," she murmurs, her lips brushing my jaw, her voice trembling with emotion.

My grip tightens on her ass as I sit up slightly, flipping her onto her back with one swift motion. I hover over her, my eyes locked on hers.

"Challenge accepted." I lean into her ear. "I'm going to make you come so hard, babe, you won't even remember his name when I'm through with you."

I trail kisses down her torso, savoring every inch of her soft skin until I'm between her legs. My tongue flicks over her clit, teasing her, licking and tasting her like she's the most exquisite thing I've ever had. I stay there, relentless, until she's trembling beneath me, her cries filling the room as I make her come not once, not twice, but three times.

When I'm finished, I flip her onto her stomach, wrapping an arm around her waist to pull her ass to me. The sight of her, the erotic curve of her back, has me harder than ever. I grip her hips, sliding into her from behind.

She cries out, her voice ragged and desperate. "Jesus... Fuck me, Ryan. Fuck me hard."

She doesn't need to ask me twice. I thrust into her, deep and hard, losing myself in her. She meets me with every movement, backing her ass into me, burying me deeper inside her.

I pull her up so we're both kneeling, my chest pressed to her back. One hand grips her boob, kneading, while the other snakes around to her clit, stroking her in time with my thrusts.

"Fuck, Coop."

This is so fucking hot.

The angle. The way one of her hands wraps up and around the back of my neck. Her loud moans and gasps. The view I have of her body. Her other hand trails over herself, teasing, touching, driving me crazy. I move her hair, damp with sweat, out of the way and press my lips to her neck. I nip at her shoulder, working my way up to her ear.

"It's just you and me, babe," I whisper, stroking her clit, my voice deep and steady.

"God, Ryan," she moans, her voice desperate. "I'm so close." Her hand brushes over mine, her hips moving urgently. "I'm going to come."

She arches her back, her head pressing into my chest, and I feel her squeezing my dick as she comes undone. The sensation is too much, and I let go, pleasure tearing through me as I release into her. "Fuck," I groan, my grip tightening on her as my body tenses with the intensity.

We ride the high together, her body soft and pliant against mine. She shifts, slipping off me and turning, meeting me with a passionate, unrestrained kiss. Our skin slides together, slick with sweat, as she pulls me down onto the bed with her, her legs wrapping around my hips. I prop myself on my forearms, hovering above her.

She laughs unexpectedly, her fingers combing through my hair. The sound is light, carefree, and it makes me smile.

"You're the best, Ry. Seriously. The best," she says, nipping at my bottom lip before cupping my cheek, her voice dropping to a whisper. "Thank you."

"Don't thank me for that. There was something in it for me too." I brush a strand of hair from her face. "And for the record—you'll never need lingerie or toys with me. You're fucking perfect just the way you are. But if you want them, I'm all for it."

"Says the man with a six-pack and a giant penis," she quips, grinning mischievously. "Wouldn't it be amazing if what's his name walked in right now? I kind of wish that would happen."

I laugh, shaking my head. "Jesus, no. I wasn't planning on dying today."

Her eyes narrow. "But don't you wish he could see this? Just a teensy, tiny bit?"

I grin, her smile making my chest tighten in the best way. "You've lost it." I press my lips to hers. "Now let's get cleaned up, so that *doesn't* happen."

"Okay, fine," she relents, pulling me closer and stroking my cheek with her thumb. Her voice softens. "But seriously… thank you for taking a painful moment and sprinkling some good into it."

"I just want you to be happy," I say, giving her one more lingering kiss before we get up. I glance at the bed, my eyebrows raising. "Uh… shit, we might have a bit of a situation here. There's… uh… remnants of sex on the sheets."

"Good," she says, grabbing her underwear and tossing it onto the bed. "He can have these too if he thinks they belong to him. Plus, I just want him to know we fucked here." She pulls her pants up over her bare ass.

"You going commando?"

"Yep."

"Damn. That's hot."

She laughs softly. "Let's get the hell out of here, Ryan. I don't want anything from this place except what's in this bag."

I gesture toward the hall. "After you."

I follow her through the apartment, carrying her duffle. She stops at the entryway table, eyeing the shards of glass. Her hand hovers over them before cradling the largest piece. Her expression somber. Her thumb strokes over the jagged edge as her other hand dabs at an eye. Without a word, she clutches the fragment and turns toward the door, leaving the rest behind.

Chapter 35

RYAN

I'm on the couch watching ESPN in the dark, waiting for Cooper to get here for our date. It's been a long damn work week, and I'm excited to spend time with her this weekend. She told me she had errands to run after work and would be here at seven. She planned the date, since I took her out last week, but she wouldn't tell me what we're doing—just to dress casual.

At seven, she texts me that she's on her way. Ten minutes later, there's a knock at the door.

When I open it, my jaw practically hits the floor. Cooper stands there bundled in a coat that stops mid-thigh and a hat with a police badge perched on her head. Her legs are bare from the knees down, with high, strappy heels that make her legs look impossibly long—and sexy as hell.

I'm stunned.

"Good evening, Sir," she says, her voice sweet as she slowly unbuttons her coat, revealing a tiny cop uniform—if you can call it a uniform. The dress barely covers her ass, and it's zipped low in the front, giving me an unapologetic view of her cleavage. She raises her brows. "There was a noise complaint for this address… Said they heard screaming." Her lips quirk into a smirk. "Were you making someone scream?"

Holy shit. She's role-playing.

I can't help the slow grin that spreads across my face as I realize what she's doing. "Not yet," I say, my voice thick with intent. "But I hope to be soon."

She bites her lip, trying to hold back a grin but failing slightly. "Hmm… I'm going to need to take a look around. You know… investigate."

"By all means, Officer." I wave her in, my grin widening as her coat falls to the floor. My gaze locks onto her—bare legs, smooth skin, tits I can't stop staring at. My jeans tighten instantly, my cock hardening at the sight of her. *Jesus, she's so sexy.*

"So, tell me—have you been a bad boy?" Her tone is a perfect mix of authority and seduction.

I play along. "Do you *want* me to be a bad boy?" My pulse quickens, excitement building. Whatever she has planned, I'm all in. I love date night so far.

Her lips curve into a sly smile. "Maybe." Her hand presses against my chest, as she walks me back toward the wall. "Now, answer the question. Were you making someone scream?"

I let out a low chuckle, my eyes dropping to the cleavage peeking from her dress, my cock pressing hard against my jeans. "That depends," I murmur. My hands slide around her waist as I lean in close, whispering against her ear. "Are you a screamer, Officer?"

She looks down, her shoulders shaking as she laughs quietly. Her gaze flicks to my hands as she pulls out a pair of handcuffs, twirling them slowly around her finger. "You know," she says as seriously as she can. "I could arrest you for touching me."

I hold my hands up in mock surrender. "What can I say? I'm a bad boy. And I've got a thing for hot cops."

Her laughter slips out again as she presses closer. "Is that so?" She hooks a finger into the waistband of my jeans, pulling me closer until her lips are just a breath away. "Bad boys like you need to be… punished."

"I can't imagine anything feeling like a punishment while you're in that dress."

She laughs, shaking her head. "Dammit," she says softly. "Stop making me laugh."

I chuckle, meeting her gaze.

She takes a steadying breath, her expression turning serious—almost. "Well, since you can't keep your hands to yourself, I think a little restraint is in order." She slips my hands off her hips and steps back. "Take your shirt off first, though."

I arch a brow. "Why does it feel like I'm about to be rewarded?"

She presses her lips together. "Now! Or I'll add resisting arrest to your charges."

Laughing softly, I grab the hem of my shirt and pull it over my head, tossing it aside. "Satisfied, Officer?"

Her eyes roam over me, and damn, the way she's looking at me could make a saint sin, and I'm about two seconds away from begging her to skip the games.

"Almost," she murmurs, stepping closer.

She grabs my wrist and snaps a cuff around it, her smirk never faltering as she leads me to the staircase, threading the cuffs through the railing. "Hands here," she says as she guides my free hand behind my back, the cold metal snapping shut with finality.

I test the cuffs, tugging lightly. "This doesn't seem very fair. How am I supposed to make you scream if I can't touch you?"

She leans in, her lips brushing against my ear, her breath warm. "I guess we'll have to get creative, won't we?" Her tone is playful, teasing, and it shoots straight to my dick.

"Jesus, babe," I mutter.

"I'll need you to stay quiet while I finish my investigation," she says, tapping her finger against my chest as she circles back in front of me, inspecting me like I'm her prey. "Now, as for your punishment…" Her nail drags down my abdomen, sending chills racing through me.

My eyes follow her every movement. "I can't wait." A grin tugs at my lips. "You're really taking this seriously, huh?"

Her fingers hook into the waistband of my jeans, tugging lightly as her eyes lock with mine. "You have no idea," she purrs, as her hand brushes over my length, sending a jolt through me.

"Fuck," I chuckle, shaking my head. She completely owns me right now. As much as I want to touch her, being handcuffed adds a level of submission I didn't know I'd like. I'm so turned on I can barely think straight.

Her hands move to the button on my jeans, popping it open and dragging the zipper down—slow, deliberate, teasing. Then she pauses, her eyes darting up to meet mine. "Let's see if you can really make me scream."

She's killing me.

"Oh, you'll scream. But I'm going to need my hands."

"I recall you being quite good at getting a woman off without touching her."

"But I want to touch you, babe."

She pauses, cocking a brow. "Yeah? What would you do if you could?"

I swallow hard, my gaze flicking to the zipper of her tiny dress, teasingly low but nowhere near low enough. "I'd start with your zipper. I'd pull it down so I can see your tits."

Her fingers trace over the zipper. "Like this?" she whispers, dragging it down to her sternum, the material barely covering her nipples. My dick throbs in response.

"Yeah… Then I'd pull you close, so you'd feel how hard I am for you."

She steps closer, pressing herself against my hard-on, as her hands glide up my chest. "Go on," she says, her voice soft and breathy.

"Show me your tits, babe," I say, my tone edged with desperation.

She grips the neckline of her dress, slowly pulling it open, flashing me her perfect boobs. Her nipples are hard and pink, practically begging to be touched.

"Jesus," I groan, my head falling back against the railing before snapping my gaze back to her. "I'd grope your tits, pinch your nipples."

She slips a hand into her dress, cupping one of her boobs, and rolling a nipple between her thumb and forefinger. Her lips part, and a soft moan escapes, making my cock pulse even harder. "And then?"

"Then I'd push your dress up," I say, my voice rough and strained, "I'd run my fingers over your panties to tease you, feel how wet you are for me."

Her eyes lock on mine, daring me to look away as her fingers drift down, hiking her dress up just enough to make me lose my damn mind. Her fingers brush over her white lacy underwear, and I can't fucking breathe.

"Like this?" she whispers.

"Exactly like that," I rasp. Holy shit. This is the hottest thing I've ever done. Heat courses through every vein in my body, and I feel carnal—like a wild animal trapped inside me—hungry, raging, desperate to break free.

Her jaw drops as she lets out a gasp.

"Coop, you're driving me fucking crazy." I groan.

"Good," she says with confidence. "Now, what's next?"

I bite back a curse, my eyes glued to her hand, aching to touch her. "I'd dip my fingers into your panties," I say desperately. "Feel how soaked you are."

Her fingers slide down, disappearing beneath the fabric. "Like this?" Her head falls back as a moan escapes her lips, loud and unrestrained.

Jesus Christ, I'm barely holding on here. "Tell me how wet you are, babe."

Her eyes lock with mine. "Oh, I'm drenched, babe. I'm fucking drenched." She hooks her fingers into the waistband of her G-string, dragging it down an inch before stopping, waiting for me to beg.

I chuckle. "Stop torturing me, and show me your pussy."

She grins, her brow arching as she slides them a little farther.

"Fuck," I hiss, the word drawn out like a plea as she finally lets the fabric slide down her thighs. She steps out of them, kicking them to the side, her eyes never leaving mine. Every movement deliberate, killing me in the best way.

"Keep going," she urges.

"I'd sink to my knees," I growl, my voice thick with need. "I'd kiss my way up your thighs. Slow. Torturously slow. I want you begging for me before I finally taste you."

Her teeth graze her bottom lip, and a soft gasp escapes as her hand begins to move, brushing against herself in light, teasing circles. My restraint shatters. "Coop," I plead.

She ignores me, her hand moving in slow, deliberate circles. "Like this, Ryan?" she pants, her voice shaking with the same desire that's consuming me.

"Just like that," I grind out. "But I'd go deeper. Harder. I wouldn't stop until you were begging me to let you come—until you're screaming my name."

Her pace quickens, her breathing growing faster and more uneven, and she leans against the railing for support, her free hand gripping a rod tightly. My cock strains painfully against my jeans, screaming for release.

"Coop. Let me touch you. Let me take care of you."

She shakes her head. "You are taking care of me." Her body trembles, her gaze locking with mine, desperation in her voice as she whispers, "Can I come, Ry?" Her words are breathless, pleading—like she's handing me the power.

"Yeah, babe," I murmur, my voice rough. "Show me how you come for me."

Her lips part, her head falling back as a breathy moan escapes her, her body arching as the tension breaks. The way she comes—completely undone—has me gripping the cuffs tighter. I can't do a damn thing except watch, helpless and so turned on it hurts.

Her movements slow as she rides out the waves, her cheeks flushed, chest rising and falling with each ragged breath. She steps closer, her tits press against my stomach, her pussy grazing my aching cock, and I swear I'm seconds from coming.

"That was sexy as hell, babe. Now, uncuff me so I can fuck you."

Her arms slide around my neck, and her voice drops to a seductive whisper. "Patience, Ry. I'm not done with you yet."

She lowers herself slowly, her hands trailing down my chest, her eyes never leaving mine. Her knees hit the floor, and she looks up at me with a wicked smile. My heart pounds as I realize she's about to suck me off. Fuck, I can't touch her, can't run my hands through her hair or hold her head the way I want to. But the lack of control only heightens everything. It's unbearable—but so fucking good.

Her fingers hook into the waistband of my boxer briefs, tugging them down along with my jeans in one smooth motion.

"Jesus…" I groan, the cool air hitting my skin as my cock springs free, hard and pulsing. I shudder under her touch. "You're killing me, babe. Fuck me already. Wrap your lips around my cock and fuck me with your mouth."

"Relax, babe," she whispers, her warm breath ghosting over me as she leans in. Her lips brush against me, featherlight, teasing, and I groan, my hands clenching into fists behind me.

Her tongue flicks over the tip, and my hips buck instinctively. "God…"

Her fingers trace slow circles over my hips and thighs, her touch maddeningly light. "Stay still," she commands, her hand wrapping firmly around the base of me as she takes me into her mouth. The heat of her lips, the way her tongue swirls around me—it's heaven and hell all at once.

I'm completely at her mercy, my body taut with desire as she moves, slow and deliberate. She takes her time, her movements measured, her eyes never leaving mine. The sight of her on her knees, her lips wrapped around me—it's too much. I'm not going to last long.

"Fuck," I groan, my voice hoarse and trembling. "God, you're incredible."

She hums in response, the vibration sending shocks of pleasure through me. Her pace quickens, her hand stroking in time with her mouth, and my breaths come faster, ragged. I'm on the edge, teetering, completely undone.

"Cooper, I'm—" I can't even finish the sentence before I'm coming, my release hitting me like a freight train. She doesn't stop, taking everything I give her, her hand and mouth moving until I'm completely spent.

She sits back on her heels, wiping the corner of her mouth with a satisfied smile.

I chuckle, still catching my breath. "Now get these damn cuffs off me so I can touch you."

Cooper laughs. "Hmm. I don't know." She pulls a key from her pocket. "You've been pretty naughty."

I grin. "Well, you're making it damn near impossible to behave."

"I think I'll need at least one hand for this next part of the investigation." She unlocks one cuff and swiftly snaps it around the railing. I don't even care because I'm too excited to touch her.

She tosses the key over her shoulder. "Let's see if you can earn your second hand back, Ryan."

I waste no time. My free hand slides up her thigh as she leans into me, her hands gliding up my chest. She gasps softly as I trace circles along her skin, moving higher until—

A distant sound freezes us both.

The door slams shut downstairs, followed by voices. Vivian's laughter carries through the air, unmistakable.

"Shit," Cooper whispers, scrambling away from me. "Shit. Shit. Shit." She drops to her knees, frantically searching under the couch. "Where is it? Where's the damn key?"

"Forget the key!" I hiss, glancing at the staircase. "Just grab my fucking pants! Hurry!"

She flings my underwear at me instead, her whisper frantic. "Oh my God, why didn't you tell me they'd be home?"

"We were supposed to be on a date!" I whisper-yell, fumbling to tug the fabric over my hips with one hand. "I forgot everything the moment Officer Sexy showed up at my door!"

Footsteps echo up the stairs, and my heart races. "Cooper, find the key!"

"I'm trying!" she whispers harshly, crawling around on the floor like a cat burglar.

"Just put my pants on me!"

She throws her hands up, glaring at me. "Do I look like I have time for that?" She frantically pushes her dress down, yanking the zipper up as high as it goes.

"Ryan?" Vivian's voice carries up the stairs.

Cooper pops up from behind the couch, holding the key like it's the Holy Grail. "I found it!" she whisper-shouts, rushing to me, fumbling to unlock the cuff from the railing.

"Uh… don't come up!" I yell, panic in my voice, but it's too late. The lights flip on, and Vivian steps into the room.

Cooper freezes mid-motion, the key in one hand, her other hand gripping my wrist. My boxer briefs are barely hanging on, my pants nowhere to be seen.

I sigh, slumping back against the railing. "Christ," I mutter.

Vivian's mouth falls open. "Oh. My. God." Her eyes shut tightly, but not before an amused grin tugs at the corners of her lips.

Leo's right behind her, Isla in his arms, his expression shifting from surprise to barely contained laughter. "Holy shit." He arches a brow, his grin widening. "Seriously, mate?" His voice cracks as he smothers the laughter threatening to burst free.

I drag my hand down my face in agonizing embarrassment, my other wrist still cuffed to the railing, while Cooper attempts to shrink behind me.

"Oh my God, we're so sorry!" Vivian sputters out.

Leo stands there, clearly reveling in the chaos, arms crossed over Isla, his grin smug. "Well, don't let us interrupt," he says, his voice thick with amusement. His gaze shifts between the two of us—me, shirtless and cuffed to the railing, pants nowhere in sight, and Cooper, trying to disappear in her barely-there cop dress. He chuckles. "Honestly, this is the best thing I've ever seen. I can't wait to give you shit about this for the next year."

Vivian nudges Leo.

"Jesus Christ," I groan, yanking my underwear higher as best I can with one hand. "Cooper, for the love of God, uncuff me."

Cooper's face turns beet red as she fumbles with the key. "I was… uh, we were just—"

Vivian waves her off, her lips twitching as she struggles to stifle a laugh. "No need to explain. I mean, I'm curious, but…"

Leo grins as he turns to Vivian, his tone serious. "I feel like we've been doing date night all wrong, love."

"Totally," she agrees without missing a beat. Her gaze shifts to me. "You're leaving those handcuffs behind when you move out, right?"

Cooper finally manages to unlock the cuff, and I yank my arm free, rubbing my wrist. "Fuck." I shake my head, a reluctant chuckle escaping despite the mortification. "You've got to be kidding me."

Leo grins, handing Isla to Vivian. "I'll grab the luggage, babe. You put her to bed."

Vivian whispers something to Leo, kissing him softly before turning to us with a wide grin. "Just pretend I'm not here," she says breezily, scurrying past us to the stairs.

"Right. Don't stop on our account," Leo says, smirking as he heads toward the stairs. "Carry on. Just try to keep it down." He pauses mid-step, his smirk growing wider. "Oh, and Cooper? I think you're missing a vital piece of your outfit."

I follow his gaze to the edge of the wall, where her underwear lies in a crumpled heap.

Cooper buries her face in my shoulder, groaning. "Oh my God. I'm mortified. I can never look at him again."

I shake my head, chuckling despite the embarrassment as I step into my pants. "At least you weren't the one handcuffed to the railing in your underwear."

"But I don't know them. This is so much worse for me."

I pull her into a hug, pressing a kiss to the top of her head. "You have nothing to worry about. They won't make it weird. They're cool, I promise."

She peers up at me, a mortified laugh escaping her lips. "You're never going to let me live this down, are you?"

"Not a chance."

She smacks my arm playfully, and I pull her closer, pressing a kiss to her lips. "Let's keep the handcuffs in the bedroom from now on, okay?"

Chapter 36

COOPER

I slide back into bed, curling up next to Ryan. Is there anything more annoying than having to pee in the middle of the night? As I settle under the covers, the memories of last night come rushing back, vivid and mortifying.

Easily one of the most humiliating moments of my life. Even after exhausting ourselves in the sheets, it took forever to fall asleep. I just kept replaying it over and over.

Ryan's already over it. We couldn't stop laughing as we went to bed, because—let's face it—it *is* funny. Hilarious, even. But for me? Mortifying. I barely know Leo and Vivian. I've met them once, and they walk in while I have Ryan handcuffed to their railing.

Now, I'm the kinky, sad girl with the shitty ex, semi-living in their house like an awkward, unwanted houseguest. Exactly the kind of impression I was hoping to make. *Perfect.*

I roll over, sleep nowhere in sight. Tapping my phone screen, I squint against the brightness. Almost five. Ugh. A sigh escapes me as I drop the phone back onto the nightstand.

Ryan's been keeping Leo in the loop, reassuring me they're more than happy to have me here, but still… God. I press my palms to my forehead, trying to quiet my restless thoughts.

Fifteen minutes of tossing and turning pass like an eternity.

Fuck this.

I slip out of bed, grabbing leggings and a sweatshirt. If I'm going to be awake, I might as well make it worth it—with coffee.

Tiptoeing downstairs to the second floor, I make my way to the kitchen. The bedrooms are all on the third and fourth floors, so I don't really have to worry about waking anyone. Working quickly and quietly, I pull out the espresso machine, froth my milk, and pour it over the steaming shot.

"Good morning." Leo's voice startles me, his British accent carrying through the quiet kitchen. I whirl around just as he pulls a shirt over his head, his skin still glistening from a workout.

My brain stalls. Jesus Christ. It's not like I'm ogling him, but damn—those abs could give Ryan's a run for their money. Trying not to stare, I force my eyes anywhere but on him.

"Um…" I scramble for something—anything—to focus on. The wall. Perfect. "Good morning," I mumble, sipping my coffee like it's a lifeline.

The discomfort is overwhelming, an awkward cocktail of mortification and uncertainty. I don't know this man, not really, but here I am, standing in his kitchen after last night's debacle.

"I'm just going to take this upstairs," I add quickly, clutching my mug. "I'll get out of your hair."

"You're not in my hair at all." He gestures to the stools at the counter. "In fact, I'd love the company."

"Really?" I grimace.

He nods.

Oh, my hell. I've got to get over this. Sliding onto a stool, I grip my coffee cup and blurt, "I'm just going to rip the bandaid off. I'm so sorry about last night. I'm mortified. I'm just some random girl who's all but moved into your home, then handcuffed your friend to the railing. Compromising positions doesn't even begin to cover it. Seriously, I'm so sorry."

Leo's lips twitch, his expression softening as he steps away from the counter. "You've nothing to apologize for, love," he says, his tone easy and warm. "Honestly, I was more amused than anything. And as for the compromising positions—let's just say I'm glad to see my friend being so well taken care of." The smile he flashes is both teasing and disarming. "I'm happy for you both. Really."

I let out a breath, the weight of my embarrassment lifting—slightly.

"Gah!" I bury my head in my hands, laughing despite myself. When I look back up at him, I shake my head. "Thank you. You don't even know how stupid I felt. I barely slept."

"I can only imagine what was going through your head," he says with a soft laugh, moving to the espresso machine.

"What are you doing up this early?" I ask, cradling my coffee.

He glances over while pulling a shot. "I always wake up this early. I like to work out and have some quiet before the girls wake up."

"I get that," I say, nodding. "Ryan mentioned you guys were in Utah. How was that?"

Leo leans back against the counter, folding his arms, his mug cradled in one hand. "It was good. We bought a place there a couple years ago. Vivian's family lives nearby, so we spend the holidays there—skiing, catching up with friends. It's a nice change of pace."

I nod, Leo's casual demeanor makes it surprisingly easy to talk to him. But then I remember he's a therapist—this is what he does, talks to people—and I can't help wondering what he must be thinking about the whole reason I'm here.

"Listen, Cooper..." His tone is gentle. "I hope you don't mind—Ryan's filled me in on some of the things you've been going through." He grins, the corners of his mouth lifting in a way that feels reassuring rather than prying. "Actually, he's been filling me in on you for months now. He's got a bit of a thing for you, in case you hadn't noticed."

I laugh softly, the tension easing as I smile into my cup. "Yeah... I've noticed."

"Well, I just want you to know that you're welcome here. Anytime. Vivian and I are happy to have you—even after Ryan moves out next week, if you need a place to land."

"Thank you. That means lot."

"Of course." He pauses, then hesitates, a flicker of caution crossing his face. "How are you doing... with everything?" He gestures vaguely, as if trying to encompass all of it. "And no pressure to talk to me—you can tell me to fuck off if you'd prefer."

"I'm okay." I manage a soft smile, even as my voice wavers. "Just trying to process it all…" Dammit. Tears prick the corners of my eyes, and I struggle to get the words out. "You know?"

Leo nods, his expression warm and understanding. He steps closer to the island, leaning forward on his elbows. "I can only imagine how hard all of this is for you. Look, I've met with a lot of couples over the years. Many, unfortunately, in situations like yours. I know leaving wasn't easy—took a lot of courage. And damn, I hope you're proud of yourself."

I nod, choked up, and afraid I'll cry if I try to speak.

He continues. "If you ever need someone to talk to, I have a friend, Meredith. She specializes in this kind of therapy. I really think she could be great for you."

I give him a small smile, just enough to acknowledge the gesture. I don't want therapy—not now, anyway—but I appreciate his thoughtfulness.

"Plus," he adds with a grin. "She's kick-ass, and I think you'd get along brilliantly with her."

I swallow hard, forcing back the tears threatening to spill. "Thanks, Leo. I'll think about it."

Before he can say anything else, we're interrupted.

"Jesus, will you two keep it down?" Ryan's teasing voice cuts through the air as he strides into the kitchen. He pulls Leo into a brotherly hug, clapping him on the back. "Welcome back, man. Did you guys have a good time?"

Yeah, it was great," Leo says, surveying Ryan with a grin. "It's good to see you with your clothes on, mate."

Ryan smirks, leaning casually against the counter. "Well, don't get too comfortable—I can't promise they'll stay on for long… If I'm lucky." He waggles his brows in my direction, earning an eye roll from me and a chuckle from Leo.

"Maybe just keep the handcuffs upstairs next time, yeah?" Leo says.

Ryan laughs, not missing a beat. "Oh, don't worry—they'll stay upstairs. Vivian's already called dibs. Pretty sure she's got big plans for them."

Leo raises an eyebrow, his grin widening. "You really don't think we already have our own?"

"Can we not talk about the handcuffs while I'm in the room?" I teasingly interject. "I just managed to get over the embarrassment."

Ryan steps behind me, planting a kiss on my cheek. I turn to meet him, giving him a proper kiss on the mouth.

"What are you doing up this early?" he asks, settling a hand on my shoulder. "You hate waking up early."

"Oh, I couldn't sleep," I reply pointedly, raising an eyebrow. "Kept reliving a nightmare involving you, handcuffs, and certain people walking in."

Ryan laughs, sliding into the stool next to me. "Sounds like a good time to me."

I laugh as the three of us settle into a comfortable rhythm. Mostly, I listen while Ryan and Leo talk, but it's nice—watching Ryan in his element with his best friend, and getting to know Leo better.

By seven, the sound of footsteps catches our attention, and Vivian appears, Isla in her arms.

"Morning, my Loves," Leo says, crossing the room to greet them both with a kiss.

Vivian smiles, setting Isla in her highchair. "Morning, everyone." She gets Isla settled while Leo moves to the espresso machine to make her a coffee.

As soon as Isla is happily munching on her breakfast, Vivian walks over, slipping her arms around Ryan and me for quick hugs. "Good morning, you two. Cooper, I need the link to that cop uniform. That's going to be my birthday gift for Leo this year." She winks, earning a laugh from Ryan and a groan from me as I shake my head.

"Oh my God," I say laughing. "Are we ever going to stop talking about this?"

Vivian grins, not missing a beat. "Oh, honey, we walked in on Ryan in his underwear, handcuffed to the railing. This story's going to have legs."

Ryan laughs again, nudging my shoulder. "She's right. It's a classic. You should be proud."

"Proud?" I shake my head, though I can't help laughing.

Vivian stands next to Leo, nudging him playfully as their gazes lock. "Should we tell them?"

"Now's as good a time as ever, babe," Leo says.

I glance at Ryan, who's grinning at the two of them. "Are you two finally getting married?" Ryan guesses, his tone teasing.

Vivian shoots him a pointed look, shaking her head with a grin. "I'm pregnant."

"Ah, congratulations!" Ryan and I say in unison, our voices overlapping.

"And..." Vivian continues, looking at Leo expectantly.

"And..." Leo says, grinning as he reaches for Vivian's hand. "We're getting married."

Ryan jumps out of his chair. "Yes!" he shouts, his excitement filling the room. He pulls Vivian into a hug, then Leo. I follow suit, wrapping them both in warm congratulations.

"Ah, Viv, now when I call you Leo's wife, it'll actually be true," Ryan says, running a hand through his hair and laughing. "Seriously. I'm so happy for you both."

"And..." Vivian says again, her tone teasing.

Ryan glances at me. "Oh, there's more?"

Vivian grins. "We're getting married in six weeks. We want to be married before the baby comes, and I don't want to look pregnant at the wedding."

"Six weeks?" Ryan whistles, shaking his head. "You two don't mess around."

Leo steps in. "It'll be a destination wedding—nothing too big. Just family and close friends. We'd love for you both to be there if it works with your schedules. We know it's short notice."

"Where?" Ryan asks, a grin plastered to his face.

"Turks and Caicos," Leo says. "We booked a resort on a private beach a few days ago. It was tricky finding something last minute, so I had to buy out the resort. The wedding will be on a Wednesday, but we made it work."

Ryan lets out a low whistle. "You bought out a resort? Casual," he jokes, shaking his head. "That's incredible."

Holy shit. A fancy resort with a private beach—and with Ryan? Somebody pinch me. My life just went from miserable with Brad to private beaches and Turks and Caicos with Ryan. I can't stop smiling, though part of that is for Vivian and Leo. I'm genuinely thrilled for them.

The rest of the morning is filled with excited chatter and wedding plans. Vivian and I dive into details as she shows me her dress—a stunning piece that's simple, elegant, and just the right amount of sexy. Meanwhile, Leo effortlessly whips up brunch.

Vivian is incredible. One of the most genuine people I've ever met, and by the end of the morning, she's already insisting we go shopping this week to get me some essentials for the trip. I didn't even hesitate before saying yes because, let's be honest, I need a whole new wardrobe, and shopping with Vivian sounds like just the kind of fun I need.

Chapter 37

COOPER

I poke my head into Ryan's office. He's on the phone but waves me in.

I sink into the chair across from him, letting my gaze wander around the space before landing on him. My heart swells just from looking at him. I've never felt anything close to what I feel for Ryan—not even remotely. I'm afraid to say that I love him. My past hasn't exactly given me a clear picture of what love is. But this? Whatever this is, it feels different. It feels big.

Our eyes meet, and he winks at me, his lips curving into that sexy grin that never fails to make my pulse quicken. Damn. He's effortlessly handsome. And mine. How did I get so lucky?

"Alright, thanks, Jon. Talk to you next week." His voice snaps me out of my thoughts as he ends the call, still not taking his eyes off me. "Hey, babe. You ready to go?"

"Yep."

Ryan gathers his things, standing with a stretch that pulls his shirt taut against his chest. As he moves around the desk, his eyes sweeps over me, smoldering with intent. "Then let's get out of here," he says, his tone dropping slightly. "I'm getting hard just thinking about what I want to do to you when we get home."

A flood of warmth zips through me, but I can't help the laugh that escapes me. "Oh my hell. Can you keep it in your pants for one minute?"

He steps closer, leaning down so his mouth is just inches from mine. "You love it," he murmurs, his voice low and teasing.

And dammit, I do.

I love how he says *when we get home*. Technically, it's not my home, and I don't live there, but I love the sentiment. Ryan moves tomorrow, so tonight is our last night at Vivian and Leo's.

I laugh, nudging his arm. "Who says I'm putting out?"

He smirks, his confidence practically oozing. "Last I checked, you were pretty into my giant cock."

"Oh, I dig it, BDR," I tease, narrowing my eyes. "But don't forget, I'm going shopping with Vivian tonight."

He swings the door open, ushering me toward the elevator. "I haven't forgotten. I'm talking about later—when you get back."

The elevator doors slide open, and we step in together. As soon as they close, I wrap my arms around his waist, pressing into him. "You know," I say, my voice dropping seductively. "We have a lot of history in elevators."

He chuckles. "Yes, we do." His lips meet mine, his tongue sweeping over my bottom lip. "Shit. You're getting me hard."

"I love making you hard… Boss," I say, biting my bottom lip to suppress a grin.

"Damn. I like it when you call me boss," he says, his eyes darkening. "Can we incorporate this into the bedroom?"

I cock a brow. "Oh? You're into role-playing now, are you?"

The elevator doors slide open, and Ryan slides his hand into mine as we walk toward the parking garage.

"I never said I wasn't."

"I mean, it seemed like you weren't into it."

He shakes his head, grinning. "Babe, I told you what to do, watched you touch yourself, and then you sucked me off while my hands were cuffed to the railing. What's not to like?"

The way he says sucked me off—Jesus, it shouldn't turn me on like this, but it does. I can't help the small smile that tugs at my lips as I glance at him. "Well, you didn't like not being able to use your hands. And then there was the whole Leo and Vivian situation…"

We reach the car, and Ryan opens my door, chuckling. "Well, that's the thing, babe. This time, you're the one getting handcuffed, and I'm the one in charge."

He shuts the door as I slide into my seat, the cold leather seeping through my pants, sending a chill up my spine. When he opens his door, I raise a brow at him. "Why do you get to be in charge? Did you buy a uniform?"

He slides into the driver's seat. "No, I just get to be the boss… You can be my secretary."

I look at him, trying not to laugh. "So… you're going to be a boss who handcuffs his secretary? Sounds a little creepy to me, Ry."

"That's not what I—" He stops mid-sentence, shaking his head, clearly flustered. "I just want to be the one torturing you while you're handcuffed."

"Oh, now you want to handcuff the secretary and torture her?" I say, making a concerned face as he pulls onto the road. "Sounds like we need a different storyline. Maybe you're a criminal who kidnaps me. And to make you less creepy—for whatever reason—I consent to you handcuffing me and having your way with me."

Ryan drags a hand through his hair, shaking his head. "Never mind," he mutters.

I laugh, leaning over the middle console. "I'm not mad at the idea, Ryan," I whisper in his ear. "Maybe I've been a bad girl who needs to be… punished." My lips graze his jaw, and I feel his muscles tense as he tries to focus on the road. My hand trails lightly over his thigh. "Are you going to punish me? Show me who's boss?"

He exhales sharply, gripping the wheel tighter. "Jesus, babe. You're making me want to pull over and fuck you in the back seat."

"Don't threaten me with a good time." My hand slides over the hard length straining against his pants. I let my fingers glide teasingly over him. "Have I been bad?" I murmur with just enough seduction to make him look at me.

Ryan chuckles darkly, his voice low and wicked. "Oh, you've been so bad. You're gonna get it."

I love when he plays along. His words send a thrill through me, making me want to push him further.

I slip my hand into his pants, finding his cock, and give it a hard stroke.

He sucks in a sharp breath through his teeth. "Jesus."

I exhale slowly, the heat of my breath brushing against his neck. "What am I going to get?" I whisper, nibbling on his earlobe and trailing kisses down to his collarbone.

He swallows hard, his Adam's apple bobbing. "I'm going to bend you over and give you my hard cock the second I park this car."

I grin. "Promise?"

The light turns green, and moments later he pulls into the parking garage. Before he can even put the car in park, I'm climbing on top of him.

"We have to hurry," I say between hot, breathless kisses. "I told Vivian I'd be ready to leave five minutes ago."

"Dammit," Ryan mutters, sliding his seat back as far as it will go. "There's no room in here." His hands fumble with my pants, and I reach down to help, quickly shimmying out of them. "Aren't you worried we're going to get caught?"

"Yes. That's half the fun." I grin against his mouth before he captures my lips in a deep, heated kiss.

* * * * *   * * * * *

"What do you think about this for the night of the dinner?" Vivian holds up a gorgeous mini dress that Robert brought to the dressing room.

"It's beautiful. You'll look stunning in it," I say.

"No, not for me." She holds it up to me. "For you. Oh my God. You have to try this on. This color on you is to die for."

I glance at the price tag—nearly five hundred dollars. Normally, I'd splurge on something like this for a special occasion, but with having to buy an entirely new wardrobe, it's just not an option right now.

The look in her eyes makes it hard to say no, though. "Alright. I'll try it on."

"Yes," she says excitedly. "Robert?" She calls out. "Can you bring some shoes for Cooper to try on with this dress? Size…?" she looks to me.

"Six," I say, glancing around. Shopping with someone rich is an experience I've never had. Brad made really good money, but nothing like Leo—and it's not like he let me spend it freely. Watching Robert respond to Vivian's every request, bringing her item after item, feels almost surreal.

He knows her, too—they've been chatting and laughing like old friends. But it's clear it's just because she shops with him often. We've been here a little over an hour, and thirty minutes ago, Robert had someone else pick up food for us.

Now, we have an entire spread of food and clothes in a massive dressing room together. I'm not going to lie—it's been a lot of fun.

Vivian has a stack of clothing piled up for the wedding trip—for her, Leo, and Isla. She's even thrown in a new suit for Leo.

I glance down at my modest keep pile. I've found a lot of things I want, but I've been picky, only choosing what I love and know I'll wear often. Essentials for work, a few casual weekend items, and a handful of pieces for the trip.

Stepping into the dress, I pull the straps over my shoulders and zip up the back. Crap. It's gorgeous—and it looks great on me.

Vivian gasps the moment I turn around. "You look incredible in that. You have to get it."

I grimace, genuinely bummed. "I can't. It's too much."

"Oh no, hun. I'm getting it for you," she says without hesitation.

"No, no," I say quickly, shaking my head. "I don't feel right about that."

"Cooper," she says, her tone soft but firm. "It's for my wedding. I'm buying this dress for you. Please, let me. You wouldn't need this dress normally. And, in fact, I want to cover everything you're buying for the trip."

Damn. She knows. She knows what Brad did to my clothes.

"Vivian," I say, swallowing hard. "I can't let you buy me a bunch of clothes… Did Ryan tell you what happened?"

She makes a face. "Am I that transparent? I'm sorry. It just makes me sick for you." Running a hand through her hair, she sighs. "Look, I know it's weird and uncomfortable to take help or have someone else buy you things, but… Leo insisted that I get you to accept."

"God, that's so sweet of you guys," I say. "But also a little embarrassing. As much as I appreciate it—and even need it—it just feels weird."

"I get that," she says, nodding. She glances down for a moment, her hands fidgeting in her lap. When her eyes meet mine again, they're filled with tears.

"Cooper," she begins, her voice trembling, "I know what it's like to be in a situation where you need to lean on the people around you." She swallows hard, blinking quickly. "I don't know if you know why I moved to Chicago, but I lost my husband—and my unborn daughter."

Her voice cracks, and a lump forms in my throat, tears stinging my eyes as I watch her choke back emotion.

"God, sorry," she says, laughing awkwardly as she wipes at her eyes. "Anyway, I just remember people always asking what they could do to help, or saying the stupidest shit, not knowing what to say. And it was so annoying. Sometimes, it made things worse." She pauses, taking a shaky breath. "But I needed them, Cooper. I needed their help. I had people coming to clean my house and bring me groceries because often times, I couldn't even get out of bed. And it was so embarrassing. God, I wanted to die sometimes."

Tears stream down my cheeks as Vivian bares her soul to me. This gorgeous woman, who seems to have it all, lost everything she loved. I appreciate her so much in this moment—her honesty, her vulnerability. No one but Ryan has shared something this personal with me before. It means more than I can put into words.

"So, please. Let us help you in the way we know how." She laughs again, wiping at her cheeks. "If it makes you feel any better, this is like a dollar for Leo."

"Oh my God," I laugh, shaking my head. "It does. A little."

"I know you'll feel weird about it for a while, but then you'll put this dress on, look in the mirror, and say, 'Damn, I look good,' and you'll forget all about it." She clasps her hands together in a prayer. "Please?"

I scoff, rolling my eyes. "Fine. I'll let you. But just know that I feel very weird about this."

"I know," she says, her grin widening.

"But," I add, meeting her gaze, my voice softening, "I'm also truly grateful. Beyond words. Thank you."

Vivian pulls me into a hug. "You're welcome… Can we also please get you some sexy lingerie for this trip? To wear for Ryan—because I'm also just so happy for him."

I laugh. "I guess if it's for Ryan, then… okay."

"Yay!" She claps her hands together, practically bouncing with excitement. "Robert?" she calls out again, her voice ringing through the dressing room.

I smile as Vivian starts explaining to Robert all the things I'm going to quote-unquote *'need'*. Her enthusiasm is contagious, and I can't help but laugh softly to myself.

Wiping another tear from my cheek, I feel a deep wave of gratitude—for Vivian, for this moment, and especially for Ryan. Not only do I get to be with this incredible guy, but he's brought wonderful people into my life. Generous, kind, beautiful friends who make me feel seen and cared for in a way I never expected.

Chapter 38

RYAN

"Oh my God, look what I found."

I glance over at Cooper. She's holding up an old journal with a mischievous grin, ready to dive in.

"Don't read that!" I call out from across the room, quickly making my way over to her.

We're in my new condo, surrounded by boxes stacked against the walls. It's been an all-day affair. Leo, Michael, and Adam just left after helping with the heavy lifting. Now everything's here—we just have to unpack. The new place is a high-rise close to work, a short ten-minute walk.

"Oh, come on," she teases, flipping the journal open. "Where's the fun in that?"

She lands on a random page and starts reading aloud, her voice exaggerated with a dramatic flare. "*March 3, 2008. Went to a party tonight with Jeremy. Amanda was there. She didn't talk to me, but we made eye contact.*" She pauses to shimmy her shoulders, grinning. "*Ooh, eye contact…*"

I laugh as she looks for another page to read.

"God, I was so pussy-whipped over Amanda," I admit. "I bet I beat off to her when I got home." I pause, then correct myself. "No, I definitely did. I remember beating off to her a lot."

She raises an eyebrow, grinning. "Did you ever get to touch Amanda?"

"No. Not in the way I wanted to, anyway. We became friends later, but she friend-zoned me."

"Ouch." Cooper's eyes skim over the pages, a sly smile creeping across her face as she stops. "Oh, I found one."

I lean over to see what she's looking at. "Shit, don't read that one. This is possibly the most embarrassing entry in the whole book."

She glances up at me, grinning. "Well, now I have to read it."

"God, here we go." I mutter, chuckling under my breath.

"Come on, it's fun! This is who you were. It's endearing." She clears her throat dramatically before reading aloud. "*June 8, 2008. Tonight, I touched a boob.*" She rolls her bottom lip between her teeth, waggling her brows at me. "Earmuffs, kids—it's about to get PG-13."

I laugh, nudging her as I reach for the journal, but she steps back, keeping it just out of my reach.

"*Julie Morrison's boob,*" she continues, pausing for maximum effect, "*and it was... awesome.*"

I laugh again, standing in front of her now, arms crossed. "It was awesome," I reiterate.

"*It was even better than I thought it would be. I took her out to Applebee's.*" Cooper bursts out laughing, her head falling back as she does. "I mean, I'm definitely putting out if someone takes me to Applebee's."

"Shut up. That was the cool place to go back then."

She keeps reading. "*When I was driving her home, she put her hand on my leg and started to rub it.*" She pauses, looking up at me. "Wait— 'it,' as in your dick? Or 'it,' as in your leg?"

"Oh, just my leg," I admit with a puff of laughter. "Yeah, and I almost came in my pants right then."

Her grin widens, and I can't stop smiling. This is why I love her. She can always find a way to make me laugh, even when she's roasting me.

"*Then she started kissing my neck, and I thought I was going to crash the car, so I pulled over at a park.*" She looks up at me, feigning shock. "Oh my God, is this girl stealing my moves?"

I shrug, letting her continue.

"We started making out, and sweet Jesus, it was awesome." She pauses again, grinning. "Wow, you really loved the word awesome... *She started rubbing me over my pants, and then climbed onto my lap, so I grabbed her boob. She made a sound like she liked it, so I grabbed the other one. Her boobs were so awesome. I love boobs."*

Cooper doubles over laughing. Her laughter is infectious, and I'm right there with her, the sound of it filling the room.

She cocks a brow at me, still grinning. "No wonder you're such a sucker for a car fuck. Your first boob grab? You weren't messing around last night."

"The car fuck last night was hot as hell," I say, grinning. "But that was just because it was you. Now, please stop because it's about to get real embarrassing."

"Oh, we aren't at the embarrassing part yet?" she teases. "No way I'm stopping... not after that teaser."

She clears her throat again, diving back into the journal. *"I kept rubbing her awesome boobs, and then she started grinding on me over my jeans. It felt so good. It was so awesome. I could feel myself getting ready to blow, like when I jerk off, but I couldn't stop it. I blew my load in my pants, and it was so awesome."*

Her laughter becomes uncontrollable. "Ew. Blew my load?" She pauses, trying to catch her breath as she wipes at the tears forming in her eyes. "I can't... I can't stop laughing." She takes a deep breath and continues. *"I don't think she knew, though, because she just kept grinding against me and kissing me."* She gasps for air, clutching her stomach. "Oh, Ry. She knew... I promise you, she knew."

I can't hold it in. My shoulders start to shake, and I bury my head in my hands.

"Then she took her shirt off, and holy shit, it was so... awesome." She barely manages to get the words out between fits of laughter.

"Oh my God," I cry out, laughter pouring out of me. "This is fucking... *awesome.*"

Our laughter consumes us, the kind that leaves you breathless, your stomach aching. It reminds me of the night we were in the pool, except that night we were high. Right now, though? It's just us being us.

She meets my gaze, tears still shining in her eyes from laughing. She closes the journal, her expression shifting, turning serious in an instant.

Before I can process it, she closes the gap between us, her lips crashing into mine with a force that leaves me reeling. Her arms wrap tightly around my neck, pulling me in, and I kiss her back just as deeply, matching her vigor with my own.

She pulls back, her grin lighting up her face. "You're so fucking awesome, Ryan. Will you please grab my boob like you did Julie's?"

I chuckle against her mouth, unable to stop smiling. Her beautiful, perfect mouth. "You're the awesomest. And hell yeah, I'll grab your boob," I say, gliding a hand to her tits, letting the soft fullness fill my hand.

She runs her tongue across my bottom lip, her mouth exploring mine like it's the first time. Jesus Christ, her lips—they're incredible. Full, soft, and completely consuming.

My hand slides down to her ass, her leggings barely a barrier between her firm roundness and my palm. The feel of her under the thin fabric makes me instantly hard. Things escalate fast—tension building between us like a storm.

Her hands fist the hem of my shirt, pulling it over my head, her gaze dropping to my chest before her lips follow. She presses soft kisses along my shoulder, then drags her tongue down my pecs. When her teeth tease my nipple, a sharp jolt of heat shoots through me as her thumbs brush the muscles at my hips. The sensation slices deep, setting every nerve on fire, my dick aching for her touch.

She kisses her way back to my mouth, her breath hot against my lips. "Your body turns me on. Makes me so wet…" Her voice is low, seductive, as she kisses along my jaw.

I groan, her words turning me on all the more, desire surging through me, needing more of her in every way.

My hands scramble to pull her shirt and bra off, desperate to feel her skin on mine. My grip on her hips tightens, pulling her firmly against me, eliciting a sharp gasp that she releases right into my ear.

I back her up against the wall, my hand gliding up her stomach, over her tits, until I reach her throat. I hesitate for just a second, then slide my hand lightly around it, my fingers wrapping around her gorgeous neck.

She gasps, biting her lip, her eyes darkening with that dangerous, irresistible look.

I lean in, my lips brushing her ear. "You like this, don't you?"

She nods, her hand reaching down for me, but I don't let her. I grab her wrist, pinning it behind her back.

"No, no," I murmur, my voice low and commanding. "You don't get to touch. I'm in charge. I'm the boss." My thumb strokes the side of her neck, slow and deliberate. Her lips curve into a grin.

"I want you begging for me," I whisper against her mouth.

"Anything you want... just don't stop." Her hips arch toward me, already begging for more.

My free hand brushes against her waist, sliding lower, teasing the edge of her leggings. I skim her thighs, fingers light as a feather as she shifts beneath me, trying to guide herself toward my touch.

I grin wickedly, capturing her plump bottom lip between mine and sucking gently. Her breath catches, her need radiating off her in waves.

"What do you want, Coop?"

"Touch me."

I move my hand up to her tits, circling her nipple with my finger, feeling it harden beneath my touch. "Your nipples are so fucking sexy," I murmur before leaning down to take one into my mouth, flicking it with my tongue before sucking gently.

She moans loudly, her hips rolling into me again.

"Ryan, touch me," she pleads, her voice thick with need.

I trail kisses up her neck. "I am touching you."

"I know," she whispers. "I want more."

My eyes flick to hers. "What do you want exactly?" A smile tugs at my lips. "You'll have to be more specific, babe."

She meets my gaze with a challenge in her eyes. Her lips part, her voice a sultry demand. "I want you inside me." She tries to move forward, but my hand holds her back, pinning her in place.

I pause for a beat, considering her, then lean in, brushing my lips over hers, slow and teasing, my finger skimming the curve of her cheek. "What else?" I whisper.

"I want to come against your fingers… your tongue… and your hard cock."

"God," I groan, pressing into her. "You're so hot. I love when you talk dirty."

My hand slides beneath the waistband of her joggers, but I stop just short, holding back.

"You're driving me crazy, Ry," she groans, her voice trembling. "I'll do anything… just fuck me already."

I break our kiss, needing to see her face as I slide my fingers into her panties. She's drenched, moisture coating my fingers instantly. I grin, pulling my hand back and bringing my fingers to her mouth. Slowly, I run a wet finger along her bottom lip.

Her tongue glides across her bottom lip before her eyes lock with mine. She parts her lips, and I slip my fingers inside. Her mouth closes around them, warm and soft, her slow, deliberate suction spreading a wave of arousal that drives me to want more as I draw them back out.

"Fuck, babe," I breathe, my voice shaking. "That's the hottest thing I've ever seen."

Her voice drops. "Now kiss me so you can taste me."

Christ. It's like she knows every dirty fantasy I've ever had. I crush my mouth against hers, and the second her tongue sweeps inside, the faint taste of her unleashes a need so primal it makes my head spin.

Before I can react, she slips her hand free from behind her and presses against my chest, gently pushing me back just enough to give herself space. My pulse races as I watch her dip her fingers into her waistband, pulling them back up to my lips.

She drags her wet fingers along my bottom lip, her eyes daring me. I move to taste her, to pull her fingers into my mouth, but she pulls back at the last second with a wicked grin.

Her lips wrap around her own fingers, and she makes a sound—a low, soft hum like it's the most delicious thing she's ever tasted.

Jesus fucking Christ.

The ache of my cock takes over, and I lose all sense of control. She must see the carnal hunger blazing in my eyes because she grins, hooks her fingers into the waistband of my pants, and pulls me closer, pressing her hips against mine.

I tug her leggings down, peeling them off with a sense of urgency I've never known. She's doing the same, yanking at my pants, and I step out of them quickly.

"How do you want it?" I rasp.

"I don't care," she gasps. "Just give it to me."

I spin her around, bending her over. Her hands press against the wall to steady herself as my hands grip her ass, pulling her to me. I slide into her from behind, deep and deliberate.

Her moan is loud and raw, spurring me on as I press deeper, my hips snapping into hers. I thrust into her, long and slow at first, before quickening to a rapid pace. The sight of her tits bouncing with every movement, the sound of her ass slapping against me—it drives me wild, pleasure shooting straight through me.

"Oh my…" she trails off, her words dissolving into a moan as I feel her tighten around me, coming hard. The sensation is electric, pulling me over the edge with her, and the combination of her soft moans, her smooth skin beneath my hands, and the warmth of her body consumes me entirely.

"God," I groan, gripping her hips tighter as I push into her one last time, the euphoria ripping through me. "You feel so fucking good."

I pull out of her slowly, the aftershocks still rippling, my dick sensitive as hell. I take a moment to catch my breath before meeting her in the bathroom moments later. She's washing her hands, her hair slightly mussed, and the sight of her makes my chest ache. I step behind her, pressing gentle kisses to her shoulders.

"I like having you here… at my house," I murmur, my lips brushing against her skin.

She meets my gaze in the mirror, her smile soft and genuine. "I like being here."

"No." I wrap my arms around her stomach, resting my chin on the top of her head. "I don't think you get it. I really like having you here. I don't think this move would feel the same without you."

Her brows furrow. "What do you mean?"

"I don't know," I say, kissing the top of her head. "It would just feel… empty. Knowing I was starting over, without you here?" I sigh, the weight of it pressing on my chest. "It would suck."

She turns around, her hands sliding up my chest, grounding me. "Trust me, I get it." Her eyes wander over my face. "And I wouldn't want to be anywhere else."

I lift her onto the counter, her legs wrapping around me instinctively. "Will you spend the night?" My hand cups her cheek, and she nods.

"Of course," she whispers, leaning forward to press a kiss to my chin.

My heart pounds as I pull her closer, wrapping her in my arms, her naked body pressed against mine. She rests her ear against my chest, and I know she can hear my heartbeat—loud, fast, unsteady.

The words I want to say are right there, teetering on the edge of my tongue. *I love you.* But I chicken out, fear gripping me. What if she doesn't feel the same way? What if it's too soon?

So, I don't say it.

Instead, I kiss her.

I hold her.

I bring her to my bed.

I make love to her, slow and deep, pouring every unspoken word into the way I touch her, the way I move with her.

But I don't tell her.

We fall asleep, her body wrapped around mine, sinking into me like she's a part of me. I pull her closer, my arm tight around her waist, never wanting to let go.

For the past year, I've felt disconnected, like nothing could feel like home. I dreaded the thought of getting my own place, of confronting that void—until now.

Because being here with her fills it. She doesn't just feel like home— she is home.

Chapter 39

COOPER

March

I squeal as I walk into the elaborate villa. "Are you kidding me? Look at this place!"

Before Ryan can respond, I'm already in the next room, exploring every nook and cranny of the massive suite. Marble tile stretches across the floors, gleaming under modern luxury lighting. The space is filled with sleek, tasteful furniture and carefully curated art pieces. Floor-to-ceiling windows and doors line the outer walls, letting the light flood in.

The kitchen is a dream, decked out with everything you could ever need. The ceilings are impossibly high, making the whole place feel even more expansive. It's absolutely stunning.

We arrived in Turks and Caicos less than an hour ago, and as soon as we stepped foot on the island, we were whisked away to this resort. Vivian and Leo had already checked us in, arriving a few days earlier with her parents. The rest of the friends and family are trickling in over the next few days before the wedding on Wednesday.

"Babe?" Ryan's voice carries from somewhere in the villa. "Come outside."

I walk through the living room toward the oversized patio, my breath catching at the sight of lush greenery, elegant outdoor furniture, and a large pool that sits between us and the villa next door.

"Where are you?" I call out, scanning the premises.

"Through the master suite," he answers.

I make my way back inside, find the master bedroom, and step out onto the private outdoor patio. My eyes widen at the sight of the secluded space—a hot tub, a mini pool, loungers, a dining table, and massage tables.

"Oh my God," I murmur, taking it all in. "How wild is it going to get out here?"

Ryan's laugh is low, drawing my attention to him. His gaze lingers on me, slowly tracing over every inch of my body, making my pulse quicken. He licks his lips, and a mischievous grin tugs at the corner of his mouth.

"Oh, it's going to get really wild," he says, stepping closer until his hand grips my waist, pulling me into him. His voice drops, rough and full of promise. "I can't stop thinking about all the different ways I could fuck you out here."

"Ooh. Tell me more," I murmur, sliding closer and bringing my lips to hover just over his.

"You'll have to wait and see," he says, kissing me deeply before giving my ass a firm smack. "Now, go get dressed so we can go."

I whine dramatically. "Nooooo. Don't we have time for a quickie? I'll be fast—pop on, pop off."

He chuckles, shaking his head. "As much as I love a pop on, pop off, we don't have time. Vivian said six o'clock for dinner, and we only have ten minutes."

I quirk a brow, smirking. "Are you underestimating what can be done in ten minutes?"

"Are you overestimating?" He laughs, grabbing my hand and pulling me inside. "We have to get dressed."

"Ugh. Fine," I grumble, letting him drag me along. "But you better be ready for this build-up. Between the torturously long flight of you teasing me and now?" I point at him, grinning as I peel off my shirt. "You better just be ready for me."

His eyes immediately drop to my chest, and I can't help but smile. I love that it still gets him—every single time.

"I'm always ready for you," he says, his voice low and full of heat as he opens his suitcase and starts undressing. "I could literally fuck you anytime, anywhere. Over and over."

"Good," I say, sliding my panties down around my ankles.

"I can't see you like this right now, or we're going to be late."

Ryan turns away, quickly changing into nicer clothes, while I slip a dress over my head. Five minutes later, I've done the best I can to freshen up with the time I had.

We're ten minutes late to the on-site restaurant to meet Leo and Vivian. But when we arrive, they aren't there. Ryan sends a quick text, and three minutes later, they appear, looking guilty as hell.

"Oh my God, they totally just did it," I whisper to Ryan.

"Sorry, mate," Leo says, gripping the back of his neck with a sheepish grin. "We, uh, got a little preoccupied."

"Goddammit!" I exclaim, throwing my hands up. "Do you see this?" I ask, pointing at the two of them. "They're late because they were doing it!"

Vivian throws her hands up in mock surrender. "We're sorry, but have you seen the outdoor patios?"

"Oh, I've seen them!" I say, pointing at Ryan with a playful glare. "And this one here said we didn't have time."

Leo grins. "Well, I highly recommend being late next time, mate. Totally worth it."

I shove Ryan lightly. "I think you forgot we were meeting the king and queen of sexcapades for dinner."

Ryan chuckles, his arm sliding around my waist as he kisses my cheek. "I'm sorry, babe. I'll make it up to you."

"Yeah, you will," I say before turning to Vivian. "Geez. He says we don't have time for a quickie." I shake my head dramatically. "Priorities, babe... Where's Isla?"

"Oh, my parents took her for the evening," Vivian says, her grin widening. "Wanted to let us have some alone time."

We follow the hostess to our table, settling into the cozy yet elegant atmosphere of the restaurant.

"So, when does everyone else get here?" Ryan asks, glancing at Leo as he picks up the menu.

"Everyone else gets here tomorrow," Leo replies, setting the menu aside. "Except for Michael and Stella. They're flying in on Tuesday. It's tough for him to take time away from the restaurant."

We all place our drink orders, Vivian sticking to water.

"Does it suck knowing you can't drink when everyone else will be shit-faced after the ceremony?" I ask.

She laughs. "Yeah, it definitely sucks. Mostly because I'll have to deal with his drunken ass." She points to Leo, a teasing smile tugging at the corner of her lips.

Leo sets his drink down with a scoff. "Come on, you love a drunk shag more than anyone I know."

"Yeah. When I'm drunk, too," she fires back, her grin widening.

"You don't want me to drink?" he asks.

"Oh, no, I want you drunk. I love a drunk Leo." She pauses, her eyes narrowing playfully. "Just don't get plastered."

He blows out a puff of air. "Can't make any promises there, babe."

Vivian laughs again, leaning in to kiss him. "Guess I'll take whatever you give me."

God, they're so cute. Over the past month, we've spent so much time with them—double dates on the weekends, more shopping with Vivian. They've become good friends.

Ryan's hand squeezes my thigh, his touch lingering. His thumb brushes back and forth, slipping just under the hem of my dress. The light, teasing strokes send tingles straight to my core, heating me from the inside out.

I glance at him, catching his smug smile. Of course. Goddamn him. He's toying with me. He raises his brows, daring me to react, and I smother a laugh, my heart so full it could burst.

My grin matches his, and for a moment, it's just us—wrapped up in our own bubble. Leo and Vivian are ridiculously cute, but so are we. We've got our own thing, our own connection, and I hope we're building something as deep and lasting as theirs.

I rest my hand over his, giving it a squeeze. He squeezes back, his thumb brushing against my skin one last time before I pull my focus back to the table, where Vivian is looking at me expectantly.

"What are you ordering?" she asks, her voice breaking through my thoughts.

* * * * *   * * * * *

We barely made it to the room before tearing into each other like starving animals. My dress was halfway down before we even walked through the door. Afterward, I slip into the bathroom to freshen up, pulling on a little number Vivian convinced me to buy—a silky slip in a soft pink champagne shade with ivory lace across the top. My cleavage peeks through the delicate trim, the lace barely covering my nipples. The matching G-string leaves just enough to the imagination.

I glance over my shoulder in the mirror, twisting slightly to catch the way the fabric grazes my hips, how my ass peeks out from the hem. A grin spreads across my face. Yeah, Ryan's going to lose it.

When I step into the master suite, the sliding doors are open.

"Ry?" I call out.

"I'm out here," his voice comes from the patio.

I follow the sound and find him stretched out on the sofa lounger, joggers riding low on his hips, shirtless, beer in hand. There's a glass of wine waiting for me on the side table, condensation trailing down the stem.

"Saved you a seat." He pats the space beside him.

I snuggle up next to him, his arm immediately wrapping around me, anchoring me in place. His hand finds my skin, his palm resting on my bare ass like it belongs there.

"Whatever this is," he murmurs, his thumb lazily skimming the edge of my slip. "I like it."

His fingers brush lightly over my skin, sending tiny sparks through me as we take in the lush scenery. Everything feels perfect—this place, this moment, him. And it's impossible not to compare it to where I was just two months ago. The difference is staggering. The difference in men. In happiness. In me.

Being with Ryan has unearthed a version of myself I didn't even know existed—a better version. People always say to find someone who makes you the best version of yourself, but I never truly believed it was possible. No one had ever done that for me before. If anything, I liked myself more when I wasn't with Brad.

I smile to myself, letting my finger trace the contours of Ryan's rippling muscles, appreciating every groove—a testament to the man he is. Ryan doesn't half-ass anything. He pours himself fully into what matters to him, and his body is no exception.

I happen to be one of those things.

And damn, I'm lucky.

My hand flattens against his stomach, fingers moving with intent as the thought settles in. He doesn't just show up—he cares. About me. About us. About making this work.

His fingers dip beneath the edge of my panties, and I grin, biting softly on my bottom lip as excitement flutters in my stomach. I shift, straddling him. My hands roam over his chest, savoring every inch of this beautiful, impossibly perfect man who somehow chose me. He shifts beneath me, his abs flexing as he scoots up on the lounger, half lying, half sitting, his gaze locked on mine.

Smiling softly, I brush a piece of hair off his forehead, letting my fingers linger for a moment.

"What are you smiling at?" he asks, a smirk tugging at his lips.

"Just... you."

There's something in his eyes that holds me captive as my focus shifts to the sensation of his touch. Ryan's hands glide up my legs, slow and deliberate, leaving a trail of goosebumps in their wake. His fingers linger just above my knees, sending chills through me as they move higher. When he reaches the inside of my thighs, his grip tightens slightly, making my breath hitch.

He holds my gaze as his thumbs brush back and forth in maddening strokes, hovering just shy of where I crave him most. Each movement is agonizingly slow, every pass stoking the fire until it's nearly unbearable.

I keep my eyes on his as I lower my lips, inch by inch. It's torturously slow, the anticipation crackling between us like electricity. When my lips finally brush against his, he moves to kiss me, but I pull back just enough to keep him out of reach. His grunt of frustration makes me grin, and I lower to his ear, flicking my tongue along the edge before taking his lobe into my mouth, sucking gently. He groans, his fingers digging into my thighs.

I trail kisses down his neck, grinding my pelvis against him in a slow, deliberate rhythm. The hard press of him beneath me sends a rush of heat coursing through me, and I gasp. His hands slide to my waist, gripping me firmly, guiding me, pressing me downward and shifting me back and forth.

"God," I moan, tipping my head back as the sensation builds, the friction intoxicating. When I meet his gaze again, his eyes are blazing, and one hand slides up my body, rough and urgent, until it grips the back of my neck. He pulls me down to him, capturing my lips in a kiss that's raw and all-consuming.

My hips move faster, the movement so perfect I can't hold back the sounds spilling from my lips as shivers ripple through me. I never thought I could come from something so simple—not since high school, when the world was simpler, and pleasure felt new. But this is different. It's deeper. It's him. It's us. And it feels so damn good that I don't care.

He toys with my tongue, teasing and tasting, then captures my bottom lip with just enough pressure to leave me trembling. My hips move faster, desperate and instinctive, as if my body knows what it needs and refuses to stop until it gets it. The pressure swells inside me, relentless and consuming, building to an unbearable peak that has me teetering on the edge of control.

My hands slide over his chest, desperate to feel him, to ground myself in the solid reality of him. I'm tempted to pull back, to just look at him—admire the strength in his arms, the sharp definition of his abs—but this feels too good. And I don't need to see him when feeling him is enough.

I close my eyes, surrendering to the moment as Ryan's touch fills every part of me, pushing out the lingering shadows of my past. My heart swells with gratitude as the weight of the pain loosens—Brad's lies, the manipulation, the hollow intimacy, the loneliness even when I wasn't alone. And not just Brad—the others too. The men who used me, who left me feeling small and powerless, as if I needed them to matter. As if I were worthless.

I shut the door on them—on all of it.

For the first time, I don't feel like I'm trying to measure up to some impossible standard. With Ryan, there's no shame, no fear of not being enough. There's only this—a man who sees me, touches me, and cares for me exactly as I am.

Tears prick at the corners of my eyes, and I bite my lip, overwhelmed by the enormity of what I'm feeling. Because this man beneath me—holding me like I'm something precious—has changed me. His words echo in my mind, telling me I'm beautiful, that I'm strong, that I'm more than enough. I cling to those words, holding them close, and in that moment, I let go—of the guilt, the shame, and the blame I've carried for so long.

And for the first time, I let myself believe I am enough. That I deserve this. That I can be happy.

A tear slips down my cheek, and Ryan stills beneath me. I feel his eyes on me, his quiet concern.

But I keep my eyes closed.

"I'm okay," I whisper, my voice shaky but certain, as I pick up my pace. His grip tightens around my waist, his breath uneven. The distant crash of waves blends with the pounding of my heartbeat. I feel his steady pulse beneath my fingertips, the warmth of his skin—the connection between us so vivid it blurs the line between where I end and he begins.

The rise of my climax sweeps through me, lifting me higher and higher until it explodes. I fall—hard. My body arches, my head whipping back toward the sky as a guttural moan tears from my throat. It's more than just pleasure. It's a release. Years of hurt, doubt, and the weight of everything I was never meant to carry burst free all at once.

The intensity consumes me, my body trembling as tears stream freely down my cheeks, unbidden and unstoppable. It feels so good—so raw and overwhelming—that a cry escapes my lips, equal parts ecstasy and catharsis. It's almost too much—so powerful it leaves me slightly embarrassed by the sheer effect it has on me.

Slowly, the overwhelming sensation ebbs, and I come back down to earth, breathless, my chest rising and falling in time with the lingering waves of pleasure and relief.

I exhale and open my eyes, meeting Ryan's gaze. His understanding and quiet devotion dissolve the last remnants of my vulnerability.

His lips curve into a devastatingly sexy smirk, his eyebrow cocking as his hand traces soft circles on my thigh. "That good, huh?" His voice is low, teasing, but his eyes search mine with sincerity. "Are you okay?"

A laugh escapes me, blended with the last remnants of my tears. I nod, smiling through the lingering emotion. "Yes. I'm more than okay. I'm great."

He grins, his thumb stroking my cheek. "I don't know what that was, babe, but it was sexy as hell to watch." He pulls me into a kiss. "You want to tell me what that was about?"

My fingers thread through his hair, searching for the right words. "Self-discovery," I murmur finally, my lips ghosting over his as I speak.

His eyebrow arches. "Care to elaborate?"

"Just me, figuring stuff out… realizing things."

His grip on me tightens, his cock still hard as hell, but his focus doesn't waver. "Like what?"

I lean down, capturing his lips in a fervent kiss, pouring everything into him. When I pull away, I rest my forehead against his, our breaths mingling in the heavy air between us. "That I love you," I whisper, my voice trembling with emotion. I pull back just enough to meet his eyes, needing him to see the truth in mine. "I'm so in love with you, Ryan."

His eyes search mine, glassy with unshed tears. The rawness in his expression nearly undoes me. "Fuck, babe," he chokes out, his voice breaking as a tear escapes down his cheek. He cradles my head in his hands and crashes his lips against mine, and it's everything.

He breaks the kiss, his hands framing my face as if he's afraid to let go. "I love you too. I love you so fucking much," he says, his voice thick with emotion. And then he's kissing me again—deeper, harder. It's overwhelming in the most beautiful way.

He loves me.

Seeing him like this—so emotional, so vulnerable—is the sexiest, most heart-stopping thing I've ever experienced, and it makes me love him even more.

Ryan lifts me off him effortlessly, swinging his legs to the side as he stands. He peels off his joggers with a grin before reaching for me. He pulls my slip over my head, leaving me bare except for my G-string.

He lifts me like I weigh nothing, and I wrap my arms and legs around him, laughing softly as he carries me toward the dipping pool.

I kiss him again, slower this time, savoring the taste of his love. His hand moves to my breast, his thumb brushing over my nipple, and the combination of his touch and the gentle splash of the water sends a tingling current spiraling through me. My arms tighten around him, holding him close, letting myself soak in every piece of this moment:

The water.

The scenery.

His hands.

His lips.

His body.

And the hard, unrelenting press of his cock, a reminder of how much he wants me, how much he needs me.

This is everything. He's everything.

"You're so beautiful," he murmurs, his voice low and full of reverence. His eyes find mine, holding me in place. "Coop?"

"Yeah?" I whisper, my heart thundering in my chest.

"I see you. And I love you… all the way to your bones."

The words hit me like a tidal wave, and my lips break into a grin that I can feel through every part of me. I laugh, the sound choked with emotion, tears threatening to spill again.

It's all I've ever wanted.

"You remember that?" I ask, my voice barely above a whisper.

"Of course I remember. I pay attention to the things I'm interested in."

I shake my head, my throat tightening with emotion. "You have no idea how much that means to me."

He chuckles, leaning in to plant a kiss on my lips, gentle and unhurried.

I kiss him back like it's the last kiss I'll ever have.

And I let myself soak in all of him—the way he loves me, sees me, cherishes me. Every part of him, every word, every touch.

Sometimes, someone comes into your life when you least expect it, and they become your light in the darkness. For me, that someone was Ryan—my saving grace, exactly who I needed, even before I knew it myself.

Chapter 40

RYAN

One year ago I was at my lowest. Desperate, lonely, and looking for something—anything—to be a distraction, to fill the emptiness inside. That's when I met her. Taking her back to my hotel room felt like a way to forget—a quick fix for the lonely desire raging inside me. But little did I know, she would change my life in the best possible way.

I deepen our kiss, pouring everything I have into her. My fingers slip under the thin fabric clinging to her hips, the memory of the pool months ago flashing through my mind. How hard it had been not to untie that bikini string, to resist the temptation of pulling her closer, kissing her deeper. But now? Now there's nothing holding me back.

Being here, in the pool with Cooper, is a goddamn dream. The feel of her wet skin under my hands, the soft gasps she makes when I tease her like this, my fingers inching closer to where I know she wants me—it's exhilarating. Her hand slips into my boxer briefs, wrapping around my cock, still throbbing from the way she dry-humped me earlier. Jesus, that was the sexiest thing I've ever witnessed. Watching her move like that, so lost in emotion, and then erupting on top of me.

And then she told me she loved me.

She strokes me harder, and it feels like the building force in my cock might actually knock me out.

Her hands push at my waistband, her voice breathless. "Ry, take these off."

I peel my boxer briefs off, then slide her panties down to her thighs, my hand immediately finding its place between her legs. She bites down on my shoulder, a soft moan slipping past her teeth, and it drives me wild. I love how easy it is to pull pleasure from her. I plunge a finger into her, watching as her head tilts back, her eyes rolling.

"Oh, God."

A primal hunger courses through me—I need to see all of her. My hands move to her hips, lifting her to the edge of the pool with ease.

Leaning in, I grip the waistband of her panties with my teeth and pull them off.

Her eyes widen. "Okay. That was hot."

"Spread your legs," I say with desperation. "I need to see you."

She leans back on her hands, slowly opening her legs, and motherfuck. I've died and gone to heaven.

"Scoot closer. I want to taste you."

She moves without hesitation, her body arching slightly in invitation. My hands grip her hips, spreading her open with my fingers as I lean in, my tongue running along her pussy, relishing every inch of her.

"How do I taste?"

"Like pure fucking sin," I groan against her.

I spread her open wider, my mouth finding her clit. Her body reacts instantly, her back arching as a loud gasp falls from her lips. The sound resonates through me, driving me crazy as her taste and the way she writhes has me teetering close to the edge.

I move my tongue rapidly, flicking and teasing, devouring her like I can't get enough. Her legs begin to tremble, her gasps turning into cries as she grips the edge of the pool. She lets out a sharp, breathless moan as she comes against my tongue, her body shaking beneath me.

Damn. She's incredible.

"Fuck. Get in here." I pull her into the water, wasting no time before I push up into her. Her legs wrap tightly around me as I thrust into her, the water lapping around us with every movement. My hips rock back and forth, driving into her with a desperation that matches my need for her. She takes my tongue into her mouth, tasting herself, and that's it—that's all I can take.

"God," I groan, giving one last forceful push as I release into her. Her hand moves between us, fingers finding her clit. She rubs herself with a fervor that sends her spiraling over the edge, her cries mixing with my heavy breaths as she comes with me.

"Babe," I say afterward, still catching my breath. "When you kiss me after I've gone down on you… It's so sexy."

She grins, her voice a soft purr. "I know… and it turns me on to turn you on."

I look at her, completely mesmerized. Her chocolate-brown eyes stare back at me, shining with happiness, and the realization hits me like a freight train—I'm totally fucked. She has me wrapped around her little finger, by the balls, by the heart. She has me. I'm hers, completely and utterly hers.

I chuckle, shaking my head. "You own me, Cooper Bradley… Jesus." I press a kiss to her forehead, and she tightens her hold on me, her arms encircling me like she never wants to let go.

* * * * * * * * * *

"Babe, we have to leave in ten minutes," I call out, shifting on the sofa lounger. My cream pants and white linen dress shirt already making me warmer than I'd like.

"Okay, give me five. I'm almost ready."

A few minutes later, Cooper appears, and she's absolutely stunning.

"Whoa." I stand quickly, needing to touch her. I steal a kiss, then step back to take her in from head to toe. Her dress is sexy as hell—low-cut, thin straps, tits out. "Jesus, babe. You look beautiful."

"Why thank you," she says, grinning. "Don't get too excited in those pants. You won't be able to hide the AK47 you're carrying. That color won't be forgiving."

"Ha. Ha. Very funny," I say, pulling her close. My hands slide down her back, and I groan. "Oh, shit. An open back?" My fingers trail over warm, soft skin, and all I can think about is dragging my mouth over every inch. "Do we have time for a quickie?"

"No." Her hand finds mine, guiding it down to her inner thigh. "And also…" She leans in, her voice a sultry whisper. "There's a high slit."

My fingers brush against her panties. "Babe… That wasn't very nice of you," I tease, my cock straining hard against my pants.

She glances down, smirking. "Better get that boner in check, Ry. Come on, we've gotta go, or we'll be late."

"Jesus." I reluctantly follow, adjusting myself as I walk to the door.

These past few days with Cooper have been some of the best of my life. This vacation—being here with her—I'll remember it forever. This place is beautiful, romantic as hell, and we've had so much fun. Not only have we had an insane amount of mind-blowing sex, but we've also connected in ways that make me love her even more. The laughter never stops. It feels like a crime to be this happy, almost surreal.

Thirty minutes later, we're seated on white folding chairs lined up along the sand, Stella, Michael and Adam next to us. The ocean stretches out in front of us.

Vivian's mother walks arm-in-arm with Leo down the aisle, hugging him briefly before he turns to face the crowd. A string quartet begins to play, and cute little Isla makes her way down the aisle, tossing flowers with the utmost concentration. Cooper squeezes my hand, and I glance at her, catching the soft smile on her lips.

Then Vivian appears, her arm linked with her father's, and the entire crowd rises as she walks down the aisle.

"Oh my God, Vivian looks so beautiful," Cooper whispers.

And she does. She looks absolutely gorgeous—every bit the bride she deserves to be.

Leo and Vivian face each other, hand in hand, grinning at each other. The officiator welcomes everyone and gives a short speech, thank God. I hate when these things drag on. Finally, he hands the microphone to Leo for his vows. They agreed to keep them short and simple, but knowing Leo, I'm sure they'll still pack a punch.

Leo takes a deep breath, his eyes locked on Vivian's. "Vivian… I thought I knew what life was all about, that I had it all figured out before I met you." He chuckles softly, his voice steady but thick with emotion. "I thought I couldn't get any happier."

He pauses, glancing down for a moment as if to gather himself. Vivian's gaze doesn't waver, her soft smile encouraging him on.

"But then you showed up, practically on my doorstep, and flipped my world upside down. Every day since, I wake up thinking, '*This is it. This is the happiest I'll ever be. The best it can get...*' Somehow, you keep proving me wrong. Every day with you just gets better."

Leo crouches down to Isla's level, his voice softening as he meets his daughter's eyes. "And Isla… your mum and dad love you so much. You've made us happier than we ever thought possible." He presses a kiss to her forehead before standing again, his gaze returning to Vivian.

"Babe, you complete me. You've made me whole. I promise to love you, to live for you, and to cherish the beautiful family we've built together—for as long as I live."

Vivian dabs at her eyes with a handkerchief, her lips trembling with a smile.

"Damn," Cooper whispers beside me, wiping her own eyes. "That was beautiful."

I glance at Cooper, her eyes shining as she smiles at the couple. "You're beautiful," I whisper, squeezing her thigh. She places her hand on top of mine, and our fingers weave together.

Leo passes Vivian the mic, his eyes never leaving hers.

"Great. I have to go after that," she says with a watery laugh, dabbing at her tears. She's already crying. She probably should have gone first.

"Leo," she begins, her voice trembling slightly. "There was a time when I didn't know if I would ever truly be happy again." She pauses, letting the emotion settle. "Until I landed on your doorstep. And oh my God, you put me through hell."

The crowd chuckles, and Leo grins sheepishly.

"But it was worth it," she continues. "Because with you, every day feels like a gift—a beautiful, unexpected gift." She shakes her head, her voice softening. "I didn't just find love when I found you—I found my best friend. And I'll choose you, every single day, for the rest of my life. I love you to the moon and back. And I promise to love you, and our children, always. Forever."

She holds out the mic for the officiator, but Leo steps forward, cupping Vivian's face, and kisses her softly.

"Not yet, not yet!" the officiator scolds, his tone light. "Sheesh."

Leo steps back, grinning unapologetically. "Sorry," he mutters.

They exchange rings, and finally, the officiator announces that Leo can kiss the bride. I watch as my best friend pulls Vivian into his arms, kissing her like he never wants to stop. She wraps her arms around his neck, and they kiss again and again, in a way that makes everyone watching believe in forever.

"Woot!" Cooper cheers beside me. I glance at her and grin, my chest tightening as I take her in. She's incredible. The thought hits me like a wrecking ball: I want this. I want her. Not just now, not just for tonight, but for always.

The ceremony ends with applause and cheers, guests scattering to mingle as the sun begins to dip below the horizon. By the time night falls, the reception is in full swing. A dance floor has been set up on the sand beneath strings of lights. Music fills the air, and the rhythmic crash of waves nearby is a soothing contrast to the storm of emotions swirling inside me—my love for Cooper.

I tighten my hold around Cooper's waist, pulling her closer, never wanting to let go. Our footsteps slow, barely moving as we sway together, lost in each other. Her gaze holds mine, and everything else fades into the background. The crowd, the music, the chatter—it's all just noise. It's just us.

A smile creeps onto her lips. "Is that a gun in your pocket, or are you just happy to see me?"

Her laugh bubbles out, and I can't help but grin. "Are you seriously recycling BDR jokes?" I tease, raising an eyebrow.

"Sorry." She shrugs, still laughing. "Are you getting sick of them?"

"Men don't get sick of hearing their girlfriends tell them how big their dick is."

"Good. Because I feel like I'm walking around with my own personal 007."

I suck a breath in through my teeth. "Well, unfortunately, I don't think my skills using a weapon quite measure up to James Bond's."

"That's okay, babe. That weapon's only meant for me… and so far, you're nothing but a straight shooter." She grins, standing on her tiptoes to press a kiss to my lips.

I laugh against her mouth. "Well, it took months of me chasing after you before I perfected my aim."

She grins. "Well, you got me. Right in the bullseye."

I cock a brow, letting a teasing grin tug at my lips. "The vagina?"

Her jaw drops as she playfully shoves my chest. "God, no!" She shakes her head, though she can't quite hide her smile. "I was thinking more like my heart."

"Oh… Yeah, that would've been the better answer."

A beat of silence passes, her expression softening, her fingers tracing along my neckline. "I can't believe I didn't want to get to know you," she says, her voice quieter now, almost wistful. "Thought I'd only want one night with you… God, I've made a lot of stupid decisions in my life." Her thumb strokes my neck, and her eyes meet mine, filled with regret. "But that might've been the dumbest one of all."

My eyes wander over her face, taking in every detail like I'm memorizing it. "When you told me not to ask you anything personal." I scoff, grinning. "Damn. That almost killed me."

"Do you think if I'd agreed to go on a date with you, we'd be here right now? That things would've worked out?"

I pause, considering her question, my thumb grazing the bare skin on her back. I've been fighting back a hard-on all damn night, but right now, it's the furthest thing from my mind. "I don't know," I admit. "But I wouldn't change a thing if it meant there was even the slightest chance we wouldn't be here right now."

She smiles softly as she leans into me, resting her head on my chest. "Me neither."

The moment stretches, quiet and comfortable, before her voice seeps through. "Ry?"

"Hmm?"

She tilts her head up, her eyes searching mine. "Will you take me to Rome?"

I pull back slightly, my brows lifting in surprise. "Yeah… Hell yeah, I will. Let's go this summer."

"Really?"

"Really." I lean down, kissing her like it's a promise.

She pulls back just enough to grin, biting her bottom lip. "Do you have a special permit to travel?"

I raise an eyebrow, confused. "What?"

Her expression turns serious. "You know, to be able to take a gun on an airplane."

A laugh bursts out of me, louder than I expected.

"Too much?" she asks, her grin widening.

I shake my head, still laughing. "Never."

The song fades, the DJ seamlessly blending it into something more upbeat. "I'm going to grab a drink. You want anything?"

"Will you get me another Chardonnay, please?"

"Yep. Be back soon."

"I'll just be out here dancing my little heart out."

I make my way to the bar, glancing over my shoulder to catch Cooper finding Vivian and her friend, Sarah, on the dance floor before they let loose, dancing wildly.

When I return, drinks in hand, I take a seat at a nearby table, setting her glass down and sipping mine. My gaze is immediately drawn back to her. "The Time" by Black Eyed Peas blares from the speakers, and I can't look away. She's stunning—so alive and unapologetically her. Her laughter carries over the music, her dance moves full of carefree energy as she, Vivian, and Sarah, jump up and down, completely lost in the moment.

I smile, my heart full of love and gratitude. Seeing her like this— happy and free—fills me in a way I never thought possible. It's impossible not to reflect on how far we've come. All the shitty things we went through, the pain, the uncertainty. Somehow, it all feels like part of the journey, the cracks that let the light in, necessary steps to reach this point. To come out the other side smarter, stronger—happier.

She catches me staring. Her eyes sparkling, her lips curving into that smile that never fails to knock the air from my lungs. She's so perfectly right for me.

Cooper makes her way over to me, and I rise to meet her, unable to stop the grin spreading across my face.

"What are you staring at?" she asks amused.

"You."

"Well, come dance." She grabs my hands, tugging me toward the dance floor, but I plant my feet firm. I can't resist her. I never could. Instead, I pull her into me. "I love you," I murmur.

Her hands slide up my chest and around my neck, sending a shiver through me. "I love you too, Ry." She kisses me, and the world around us disappears. It's just her—her touch, her love—anchoring me to the purpose I didn't know I was missing.

I brush my thumb along her cheek, my brows knitting together with concentration. "One day, I'm going to marry you, Coop. And it'll be the best damn day of my life," I whisper.

Her grip tightens, taking a deep breath as she takes it in, her eyes glistening with unshed tears. "You'd better," she whispers back. Then her lips find mine, and the love in that kiss is unlike anything I've ever known.

She's it.

She's the one.

She's my everything.

And I love her—all the way down to her bones.

Epilogue

COOPER

March 15

One Year Later

I sip my coffee, letting the sounds of the waves and the warmth of the heat lamp wash over me. I sink into the sofa chaise, pulling my cozy blanket closer, savoring the moment. God, I really do love it here.

Ryan and I decided to escape the Chicago cold for a long weekend with my dad. And while it hasn't been exactly warm, it feels like summer compared to home. I sit in my favorite spot on my dad's patio, facing the ocean, a smile plastered to my face. Life is good.

My phone buzzes.

Ryan: What are you wearing?

I laugh, shaking my head.

Cooper: Nothing.

Ryan: Damn, I better hurry. You alone?

My grin widens, stretching across my face.

Cooper: Yep. Just waiting for the hot guy to run by so I can flash him my boobs.

Ryan: Damn. He's a lucky guy. If I run by, will you flash me?

Cooper: We'll see. Have you been a good boy?

Ryan: Depends. Define good…

I roll my bottom lip between my teeth, grinning. It never gets old playing with Ryan.

Cooper: Are you running with a shirt on? Because that would definitely be bad behavior. Rude, really.

Ryan: Why don't you turn around and see for yourself.

I spin around to see Ryan heading toward the patio door—from inside my dad's house—pulling a shirt over his head.

"Hey, that's not very nice!" I exclaim as he walks over to me, grinning. "Take that back off."

He smirks, clicking his tongue. "Maybe I need to make sure you've been a good girl before I show you the goods. Scoot up," he says, motioning me forward so he can slide in behind me.

He settles onto the sofa, his joggers soft against my legs as my back presses into his chest. His arms wrap around my waist, pulling me closer, and he kisses the top of my head. And it's just like he said it would be all those months ago, back when everything was a mess, and we blurred the lines of right and wrong through text messages.

"I remember the first time I saw you here," he murmurs, trailing kisses down my neck. "You were beautiful… but you looked so sad."

"I was sad… until I saw you running down the coast." I fold my arms over his, squeezing his hand. "God, you gave me butterflies. I remember it like it was yesterday, thinking how pathetic it was that a random guy— a stranger—could make me feel things I hadn't felt in so long."

I shift, trying to get comfortable, my hands brushing against his thighs. "What's in your pocket?" I ask, startled by the hard bulge.

He laughs, the sound vibrating against my back. "It's nothing. Just my phone."

"That is not your phone." I reach for his pocket, but he's faster, pulling out his phone with a triumphant grin.

"See? Just my phone. I'm surprised you're not making a dick joke."

"Well, I can feel that too," I tease, narrowing my eyes. "But there's something else in your pocket."

He chuckles, reaching over the back of the couch to grab a small, gift-wrapped box. Settling back behind me, he places it gently in front of me, his breath warm against my ear as he whispers, "Got you something."

I turn my head to look at him, my brow lifting. "What's this?"

"Open it and see."

I scoot forward, twist to face him, and fold my legs beneath me. His knee bends against the couch, the other stretching out long on the opposite side. His expression softens, a serious edge to his smile as he gestures toward the box. "Go on, babe. Open it."

I scrunch my brows together, curiosity flickering as a smile tugs at my lips. "Okay."

Slowly, I unwrap the gift to reveal a used Amazon box, taped shut. My fingers work at the tape, and when I finally open it, my heart stutters. I gasp, my hand flying to my mouth as tears spring to my eyes, my throat tightening with emotion.

"My grandmother's bird," I whisper. "How did you—?" My voice falters as I lift the delicate glass figure from the box, holding it as if it might shatter in my hands.

"I found it on eBay," Ryan says softly. "I know it's not the one she had, but your mom helped me track down the exact same one."

My fingers trace the intricate glasswork, awe filling me.

"Ry, I…" I blink away a tear and meet his gaze, overwhelmed. No words feel big enough to express my gratitude for this—for him. My voice is barely a whisper. "Thank you." I lean forward, and he meets me with a kiss.

"It's from the 1930s, apparently," he says, brushing a hand along my thigh. "Do you like it?"

I nod vigorously, laughing through the tears. "Yes. Yes, I love it." My voice cracks, and I shake my head. "God, I don't even know what to say…" I lean in and kiss him again because this man never ceases to amaze me.

"My grandma got hers when she was a little girl," I say softly, bringing the bird to my chest. Memories flood back as I think about the last time I saw mine whole. It's bittersweet, holding this bird now, tracing its delicate wings.

When I walked out that door a little over a year ago, I was shattered. But slowly, with time—and with Ryan's love—I've pieced myself back together. Now, I feel whole. Strong. And looking at this bird, its wings spread wide, I realize I've finally learned how to fly.

"Thank you," I say again, my voice thick with emotion as I rub his thigh. "You're the best."

"You're welcome." He presses a tender kiss to my lips before standing and pulling me to my feet. "But I'm not done yet. There's something else I want to show you."

"Okaaaay," I say, narrowing my eyes, though I can't keep the smile off my face.

He takes my hand, and I follow him onto the sand, the cool grains shifting beneath our feet.

"Where are we going?" I ask, glancing at him curiously.

He glances at me. "Just over here."

I don't know what he's up to, but my heart races with anticipation. We walk about fifty feet along the sand before he stops, his hand tightening around mine.

"Do you know what this place is?" he asks.

"Umm… Newport Beach?"

He chuckles. "Well, yeah, it's Newport Beach, but it's more than that."

I glance around, my brows furrowing as I try to figure it out. "Okay… I give up."

He steps behind me, his arms circling my waist, pulling me close. "This," he murmurs against my ear, "is where I was the first time I saw you."

A smile tugs at my lips, and I tilt my head back to look at him. "It is?"

"Yep," he says, kissing the curve of my neck. "Turn around and see for yourself."

I turn, following his gaze toward my dad's house. My stomach flutters as I glance back at Ryan, and my breath catches. He's grinning, and before I can ask what he's up to, he reaches into his pocket and pulls out a small velvet box.

"Oh my God!" Laughter bubbles out of me as my hand flies to my mouth. "I knew something was in your pocket!"

Ryan drops to one knee, placing the box gently on the sand before taking my hands in his. His eyes lock with mine, steady and full of emotion.

"Cooper," he begins, his voice low and trembling with sincerity. "Two years ago, I'd never felt more uncertain about what my future held. My life was a mess—unexpected and full of hurt. I wasn't looking forward to what was next. But then I saw you, sitting on that patio." He glances toward the house and back at me. "You were this quiet force that I couldn't ignore. I didn't know why, but I felt this pull to you. I was actually excited to go running the next morning, just for the chance to see you again. And then the next morning, and the one after that."

He laughs softly, his grip tightening on my hands. "And then I saw you at Tipsy. God, I remember this magnetic pull, like fate was shoving me toward you. I had no idea what it was, but I knew I had to follow it. So I asked you out." He shakes his head, smiling. "And you said no. You told me you only wanted a fun night, nothing else. And I thought, if I could just spend one night with her, maybe she'd change her mind. But you didn't. I woke up the next morning, and you were gone."

Tears stream down my face, and I don't bother wiping them away. My cheeks ache from smiling, but I'm sobbing all the same.

"Life got worse after that," Ryan continues, his voice heavy with emotion. "For me... and for you." He exhales, shaking his head as if to steady himself. "But when you walked into that office in Chicago, I knew—I knew—there was a reason why. And when I found out you were engaged..." His voice breaks, and he presses a hand to his forehead. "I thought I'd lost any chance. All hope."

He swallows hard, his Adam's apple bobbing as he fights back the tears welling in his eyes. "But then, in Austin, when I found out how unhappy you were... I told myself right then and there, I'll fight for her. I'll wait. I won't give up."

I laugh through my tears. "Of course you did."

"But then something incredible happened." His smile softens, his gaze steady as he searches my face, waiting.

I blink. "What?" I whisper, barely audible.

"You didn't give up either," he says, his thumb brushing over my knuckles. "Not on yourself. Not on me. Not on us."

"God," I cry out, my voice cracking as I swipe at the tears streaming down my face.

He chuckles softly. "I love you, Cooper Bradley," he says, pausing before adding with a grin, "Not to be confused with Bradley Cooper."

I tip my head back, laugh-crying. "Shut up. You're so… *awesome*," I choke out, my laughter mixing with sobs.

Ryan picks up the ring box, flipping it open with care. The sparkle of the diamond catches in the light as his eyes lock on mine, his smile growing. "Will you marry me?"

I nod, frantically, the lump in my throat too big to speak.

His grin grows. "Is that a yes?"

"Yes," I cry out. "Yes."

He takes the ring out of the box and slides it onto my trembling finger. It's gorgeous—perfect—just like him.

He kisses my hand, and I tug him to his feet. Before he can fully stand, I smash my lips against his, nearly knocking him off balance. "I love you," I whisper between kisses, my arms wrapping tightly around his neck.

He laughs softly, lifting me and spinning us in a circle. "I love you too, babe," he murmurs. His lips find mine again, this time slower, deeper. His hands cradle my face, his thumbs brushing away tears I didn't realize were still falling.

I pull back, breathless, needing to see him, to memorize every detail of this moment. Pure, unapologetic joy courses through me, lighting me up from the inside out. I cup his cheek, my thumb gliding over the damp trail of his tears. "Thank you for loving me when no one else did… when I couldn't even love myself."

His eyes glisten, and instead of answering, he kisses me again—fierce, devoted, endless. Then he lifts me, my legs wrapping around his waist as he carries me toward my dad's house. The ocean waves crash behind us, and all I can think is that nothing about this has ever felt wrong.

With Ryan, it's always felt right—like this was exactly where I was meant to be.

Perfect.

Acknowledgments:

As always, I owe everything to my husband–my real-life book boyfriend and best friend. He is, without a doubt, my biggest cheerleader. Babe, thank you for always believing in me and my crazy dreams, for picking up the slack around the house when I get too caught up in writing to pull away, and for just being you.

To my amazing kids–thank you for letting me get away with some questionable mom moments, for manifesting in Target and airport bookstores with me, and for loving me unconditionally. I love you both more than you could ever know.

To my beta readers–thank you for your support, excitement, and friendship, and for always being willing to read just one more chapter. This book wouldn't be what it is without your feedback. The text messages, FaceTimes, endless GIFs, and inside jokes have been some of my favorite parts of this whole process. In no particular order: Nikole Allred, Bree Dodge, V.L. Williams, Shauna Haddock, Lauren Andrew, Reese Stockman, and Danielle Knox.

A special thank you to my editor, Celia Killen, who once again worked her magic in perfecting this book. You have a gift, and I'm so grateful for your patience, insight, and the suggestions that helped shape Cooper and Ryan's story.

To my friends who have stood by my side from the very beginning–I love and appreciate you.

Thank you to my Bookstagram community. Damn, you ladies are the best. Thank you for taking a chance on me, for reading and reviewing my books, for supporting me, posting, sharing–the list goes on and on. I will never forget you and the role you've played in this journey.

To the overwhelming number of people in my inner circle who opened up to me while reading–sharing your own stories of emotional abuse–the numbers are staggering. Your vulnerability and honesty mean more than I can express. As much as I hated hearing how many of you saw yourselves in Cooper, nothing could have prepared me for the honor of hearing your truths and the validation this story brought you. I'm truly grateful.

Music is a huge inspiration when I write, and this section wouldn't be complete without thanking the incredible artists whose songs helped shape this book. To every artist who contributed to The Most Perfect Wrong playlist–thank you.

A shoutout and thank you to some of my favorite authors who have inspired me in one way or another: Meghan Quinn, Sarah J. Maas, Colleen Hoover, and Elle Kennedy.

And last, but surely not least, to you, the reader. Thank you for picking up my book.

About The Author

Erin Cornia lives in Austin with her husband, two children, and two mini golden doodles. She rediscovered her passion for reading after a long break when *It Ends With Us* by Colleen Hoover fell into her hands. Now, she has a deep love for romance novels—contemporary, fantasy, and historical alike.

Some of her favorite authors include Sarah J. Maas, Colleen Hoover, Meghan Quinn, Tessa Bailey, Elle Kennedy, Judith McNaught, and Rebecca Yarros with *Throne of Glass* by Sarah J. Maas holding the spot as her favorite series of all time.

When she's not reading or writing, she enjoys playing pickleball, working out, traveling, and spending time outdoors. You can often find her watching *Schitt's Creek*, *Sex and the City*, *Friends*, or *Emily in Paris*—with a bowl of homemade popcorn, of course.

Instagram: @erincornia_author

Facebook Reader Group: Erin Cornia: Romance, Heartbreak, Healing & Hard Earned HEAs

TikTok: @erincornia_author

Don't miss the next book in the Chicago Series from ERIN CORNIA

A Love That Broke Us

Releasing 9/20/2025

Alley Evans has never met anyone like Jensen Adams. He's confident, funny, and makes her feel like a million bucks. She falls fast—and hard. In no time, he becomes her favorite person. Her safe place. The man she wants forever with.

Jensen Adams never expected to meet the girl of his dreams while coming out of anesthesia—but life's weird like that. He can't stop thinking about her. So when he runs into her again at a coffee shop, he knows he won't make the mistake of letting her go twice.

Their love story is easy. Effortless.

Until one day—it's not.

Now, five years later, they're fighting for the love that once held them together—and now threatens to break them apart.

A Love That Broke Us is a raw, emotional story about addiction, resilience, and what it means to fight for a love that once came easy—and what it takes to let go. Because sometimes, you have to lose the thing you love most to save yourself.

This is book one of a Duet that ends on a cliffhanger. The conclusion of the duet releases November 2025.